RUNNING AWAY

'Children!' she echoed. 'Deborah, Willie! Come out here!'

They arrived with an alacrity that suggested they had been waiting. In their nightclothes they stood on the top step, looking down.

'Children,' intoned Sarah with deep drama. 'Say goodbye to your father. He is running away.'

'Where will you go, Daddy?' called Deborah who had an interest in geography.

As Nicholas went towards the door Willie shouted: 'Can we have our pocket money?'

Leslie Thomas was born in Newport, Monmouthshire in 1931, the son of a sailor who was lost at sea. His boyhood in a Barnardo's orphanage is described in his hugely successful autobiography *This Time Next Week*, and he is the author of numerous other bestsellers including *The Virgin Soldiers*, *Tropic of Ruislip* and *Revolving Jones*. He lives in Salisbury with his wife Diana.

LESLIE THOMAS

Running Away

Mandarin

A Mandarin Paperback
RUNNING AWAY

First published in Great Britain 1994
by Methuen London
This edition published 1995
by Mandarin Paperbacks
an imprint of Reed International Books Ltd
Michelin House, 81 Fulham Road, London SW3 6RB
and Auckland, Melbourne, Singapore and Toronto

Reprinted 1995 (twice) 1996 (twice)

Copyright © 1994 by Leslie Thomas
The author has asserted his moral rights

A CIP catalogue record for this title
is available from the British Library
ISBN 0 7493 1888 0

Printed and bound in Germany by
Elsnerdruck, Berlin

For Diana

BOOK ONE

One

He should, of course, have realised that running in the cemetery would make him unpopular. People appeared frowning from behind vaults and straightened up tetchily from memorial tablets. One woman shook her fist and shouted after him, her condemnation echoing over the tombstones. The alerted cemetery keeper waylaid him as he loped for the gates.

'Running's not allowed,' he said whirling his finger. His cheeks were red from the graveyard sun and wind. On his cap was a grubby badge which Nicholas fancied might be crossed bones but was more probably crossed keys. The keeper took in the suit and tie. 'It's not as though you're even a jogger,' he said. 'And joggers are not allowed either.' His face creased into a plea for decency. 'This,' he waved his arm, 'is sacred ground.'

'I apologise,' said Nicholas. 'I wasn't thinking. It's only to get some fresh air.'

'In the cemetery?' the man sniffed as though to test it.

'Yes. It gets you so pent up being in London all day. And there's nowhere else on my way home. Here it's easy to park and a couple of laps around the outside is all I need.'

'Pressure,' the man sympathised. 'I know all about pressure.' As if offering a deal, he said: 'There's nothing to stop you *walking*, no regulations. You can come in here any time, free.'

'I'll walk,' Nicholas promised.

'But not *fast*,' the keeper warned. 'And stop now and again and look at a few graves. There's some interesting stones.'

He thrust out a hand as though they had·struck a bargain. Nicholas shook it; it was unexpectedly warm. 'For myself,' the man confided, 'I like to see an individualist.'

They parted and unthinkingly Nicholas almost fell into another trot. The custodial cough caused him to turn and smile an apology. So he walked, gravely at the beginning, taking in the epitaphs, but it was no way to summon a decent August sweat and that was the reason he was there. A touch of perspiration on the body and the shirt, a little dust on the shoes. Unfortunately he had not noticed the soap in his ears.

Tilting a gin and tonic, he was watching the early evening news when Deborah, his fifteen-year-old, put her index finger in his ear and said: 'Soap.' She brought out the particle. Willie, younger by two years, squinted into the other side and said: 'There's some in here too.'

On the screen the world was going about its daily mayhem; people were being blown up in several countries. 'I couldn't have wiped them out this morning,' Nicholas said casually pushing his own finger in his right ear.

'That *was* careless,' said Sarah, his wife, taking the white morsel from her daughter's fingertip and passing it below her nose. 'Hmm, nice,' she murmured. 'Expensive.'

'I' wouldn't know one soap from another.' His mumble became a grumble. 'And I'm trying to watch the news.'

Briskly she turned and went into the kitchen. Her parents were coming to dinner and Sarah did not want an atmosphere. Nicholas was watching more explosions and mentally kicking himself. Imagine not wiping his ears out. He knew what Caroline would do when she heard. Laugh.

He went upstairs as the children switched channels and took his second shower in two hours. Furiously, as if they were to blame, he gouged his ears with the towel. From the kitchen below he could hear Sarah giving instructions to the girl who was helping. There would only be the four of them but Sarah enjoyed having someone to serve.

He went downstairs into the warm garden and walked moodily along the yews of the path. The seven o'clock sunlight caught the arriving red roof of his in-laws' car. He sighed and wandered towards the gate.

There was no hurry. They always took ten minutes, minimum, to get out of the car. Herbert checked the controls like a captain having safely landed a Boeing. He inspected the empty ashtray. Doreen had to tidy up. First the interior, wiping the dashboard and the steering wheel with a special duster, and making another check of the ashtray. 'There's a dead fly on the windscreen, Herbert,' she called like someone spotting a bargain. Ponderous and panting, Herbert manoeuvred himself around to the front of the car and she again targeted the fly. It had crashed fatally into the centre of the screen and Herbert had to hitch up his trousers and heave himself across the bonnet. Doreen passed a tissue. Herbert climbed down and, with his handkerchief, wiped the bonnet.

Doreen bent back into the car and pursed her stringy lips in the driving mirror. The pair walked to the garden gate; Nicholas opened it.

'I can never get over you and Sarah living in a *vicarage*,' Doreen said surveying the house. She had said it before but she rarely said anything for the first time. 'Not after writing a book like that.'

'We should get it done you mean – purified,' suggested Nicholas. 'Bell, book and candle. Burn incense.'

'Sanctified,' said Herbert as if he had been thinking about it for a long time. 'Like they do with churches where there's been devil worship.'

'Exorcised,' suggested Nicholas. 'But I don't think it counts with vicarages. They're only houses.'

'It *does* seem funny, that's all,' insisted Doreen. She hobbled between the yews. He was pleased to see that her ankles were bad again.

'*You* should have written a book,' she said when they were eating. Her fork ranged towards her chewing husband.

'Could have,' he nodded. 'Easily. The things that went on in our office. But then . . . ,' he glanced at Nicholas, 'there was never any time.'

'The whole trouble with the book,' put in Sarah firmly and as if he were not there, 'was the title.'

'It was the title that sold it,' pointed out Nicholas patiently. He waved his fork. 'And goes on selling it.'

He studied Doreen and Herbert revolving their jaws in tandem. 'That's all very well,' Sarah said. 'But it's misleading. *Lying in Your Arms* sounds so romantic. . . .'

'Like dear Barbara Cartland,' smiled her mother sweetly, as if she knew her.

'Lots of my friends thought it *was* a romance,' pursued Sarah. 'Which it certainly *isn't.*'

'It's still selling,' sighed Nicholas. 'After three years.'

'Unfortunately he hasn't been able to repeat it,' said Sarah.

'I'm still working on it,' said Nicholas.

Her mother became chillingly chummy. Her ringed hand tapped for attention against the side of his plate. 'Why don't you write a nice book about Cornwall?' she suggested. 'All this nonsense about lying.'

Sarah said deliberately: 'Ah but Nicholas doesn't know anything about Cornwall.'

Sarah lay in their bed, her face pink and puffy, her eyes sardonic. 'Let's do it, darling,' she suggested like a challenge. Her eyes closed as though to shut off him and any excuses. She pushed her dark hair from her forehead. For Nicholas it was the third time that day.

He kept his shirt on and walked to her side of their bed, gingerly, as though crossing a frontier. She opened her eyes, as if to check that he was there, closed them again and lifted up the hem of her nightdress.

How many times over their sixteen years had they done this? Once he had roughly worked it out. He laid himself next to her, and kissed her neck. She scarcely paused in her breathing as he joined her and they were not together long. 'You must be tired,' she muttered. 'You've had a hard day.'

Nicholas did not trust himself to answer. How did it get like this? She seemed to read the question. They were lying apart, distant now. 'I wish you had never written that bloody book,' she muttered.

6

'That poor bloody book gets the blame for everything,' he breathed. He turned on to his back and ground his teeth looking at the ceiling, diffuse in the diminished light as though covered with cobwebs. 'We've got a new house, new cars. It's given us . . . well, freedom.'

'Freedom,' she almost managed to laugh. Neither added to the argument until she said: 'We're different people now.'

He caught her sadness and joined it to his guilt. Leaning over he attempted to kiss her but she moved her face away. Her voice began to harden. 'Anyway, you've dried up, haven't you. You've written your one book, Nicholas.'

'How do you know?'

'In three years you haven't done another.'

It was true. 'It will come,' he said.

Her eyes were wet and she snivelled: '*Who* was it today?' She dropped her eyelids tightly as if to dam the angry tears.

'Who was *what* today?'

'Whose soap did you have in your ears?'

'For God's sake. Not that sodding soap again! It was from this morning, I suppose.'

'Nicholas, it was still wet.' She had reined in her voice but her tears were now coursing down her face. 'Soap doesn't stay wet all day.'

'Soap is soap! Christ, everyone in this house is Sherlock Holmes.'

'You've *been* with someone this afternoon,' she said, her flooded eyes now pinning him. 'One of your fans, perhaps. And after you'd had her you showered and you used her soap.'

He was tempted to tell her he had been to a gymnasium. She might pretend to believe him. But he pushed the temptation aside. 'I'm going,' he grunted. 'I'm getting out of this bed and I'm going.'

'She'll take you in,' she snarled pulling the sheets over her breasts. 'Whoever she is, you can read to her in bed.'

'There is no "she" to take me in,' he snapped. 'I'm just *going*. I'm tired of it all. Everything. I'm clearing out of this house.'

'Running away,' she sneered. 'Your father always said you were good at running away.'

'If *he*'d run away he might not be so dullally now,' he retorted.

'Everyone *wants* to run away at some time,' she said lowering her tone once more. 'I feel like it myself.'

'Well, I don't just *feel* like it, I'm going.'

Swiftly she became angry again, angrier than before. She searched for insults but in the end only said: 'Good. Go.'

He strode in his shirt into the adjoining dressing room where he furiously used the wash-basin. He picked up clothes at random, the jacket of one suit and the trousers of another. For some reason he selected a tie. He looked into the bedroom. Her sobs were inflating the sheet over her head. He went out of the room and down the stairs. His briefcase was in the hall where he had left it when he had come in that evening. As he picked it up Sarah appeared on the landing above. She was holding the lapels of her dressing gown together across her breasts like some repertory actress. 'For God's sake – go!' she howled down at him.

'You'll be looked after,' he told her with a touch of fair play. 'I'll see everything is paid. You and the children won't go short.'

'Children!' she echoed. 'Deborah, Willie! Come out here!'

They arrived with an alacrity which suggested that they had been waiting. In their nightclothes they stood on the top step, looking down.

'Children,' intoned Sarah with deep drama. 'Say goodbye to your father. He is running away.'

'Where will you go, Daddy?' called Deborah, who had an interest in geography.

As Nicholas went towards the door Willie shouted: 'Can we have our pocket money?'

He had left his watch and his car keys on his bedside table and there was no going back now. After he had closed the front door behind him, Sarah had come down, opened it, called him something appalling, and slammed it so hard the frame shuddered. Through the pebbled glass he could see, as though under water, her pale fists raised above her head in wrath, or perhaps triumph, for there came the sound of a woman's manic laughter.

If he needed to know the time the church clock thoughtfully provided it, sounding eleven as if it were short of breath. There were always longer pauses between the ninth and the tenth and the tenth and the eleventh strokes which left the listener in a void of uncertainty, wondering if the clock could ever manage twelve. Feeble as it was, it remained the only active thing about the church which was no longer used for worship, the parish having been reconstituted. The building was for sale, but there had so far been no takers. The spire, which rattled in so much as a zephyr, rose next to his former vicarage, in the heart of what had once been a village.

Boxley had been named after the boxwood trees that once grew there and the aptness remained since the cottages of its original street and tight lanes had been interpolated with boxy modern houses and finally linked to a fifties high street, some old places clinging on with diminishing hope. A short block of deadpan flats had gone up where the village hall had once stood.

Carrying his briefcase Nicholas walked through what existed of the original Boxley, his steps paced out by the clock as long as it chimed; he went towards the high street, his spirits down, his collar up. He turned the corner where the shops began, allowing himself one last glance back at his home before it vanished from his sight, perhaps forever. Downstairs lights were showing and it irked him to picture his family enjoying emergency cocoa and busily discussing the novelty of their future. Along the shut display windows he shuffled, the landscape of that suburbia as familiar to him as a home harbour to a sailor. The August night was hung with clammy clouds, thick over Sainsbury's, W. H. Smith, Dolcis, Good Sports Ltd and the Rio del Monde Coffee Shoppe. Outside Boots two tom-cats baited each other.

There was no one about, a lone car appeared and went

quickly, as though eager to be gone. The sodium-lit road was called Meadowfield, a half-hearted harking back to agrarian times now buried below asphalt.

Outside the newsagent's was a billboard announcing next Saturday's 'Olde Village Fête'. Nicholas projected his tongue at it. At least he would be spared the fathers' race, the tug-of-war team and the annual jealousies over the choice of a simpering carnival queen.

Low security lights frowned from within the Himalaya Restaurant, reflecting sombrely on the maroon flock walls. A camera with a red eye guarded the Oxfam shop. A scrap of litter wandered about the pavement. It was a downcast journey but at the top of the rising street, like a lighthouse, was the Metropolitan Line station, its aura of late yellow light encouraging, suggestive and beckoning. He began to walk up the incline. The glow became, it seemed, more lambent, more enticing. He straightened up and began to stride. As he approached he heard the stiff sound of a broom and a whistled dirge. He arrived in the station booking area like an actor making an entrance on the wrong cue. A man wearing a peaked cap was beating the base of the ticket machines with a long-handled brush.

'Last train gone?' enquired Nicholas. It was his only escape route.

'Standing at the platform now,' responded the man wafting the broom in that direction. Dust fell from the brush-head. He began striking the ticket machines again, like someone working out an old grudge. 'Unless you're going towards Watford and that's gone. Five thirty in the morning, the next one.'

'No, this one will do.' Nicholas felt in his pocket and cursed; his money was on the bedside table with his watch and his car keys. His credit cards were in his briefcase. 'Don't say you're wanting a ticket,' the station man enquired in a pained way. The aperture of the booking office was gagged with a shutter. 'These,' the man said again banging the standing ticket machine with the broom-head. 'They're switched off, bloody things, always packing up. I don't want to open up again. Not just for one.'

'I'll get it the other end,' said Nicholas gratefully.

'I want to get 'ome,' said the man. 'I've got a wife and family.' He rammed the broom-head into a corner and grunted. 'That's why I'm working late.'

Nicholas wished him goodnight and hurried down the stairs. The Metropolitan Line train like an empty corridor was humming at the platform. The guard was conversing with the driver and they seemed both surprised and oddly gratified to see him for they waved as he entered the train. At once he saw that he would have a companion, a coated lump huddled at the front of the long compartment, the top of a head emerging from a scarf wound around like that of a Bedouin. Nicholas crept to the opposite end.

He was puzzled by the way he felt. Over his guilt and uncertainty, there was now a skein of elation, like an airy tune played over a dirge. Sarah had been right as she so often claimed to be; he was running away again. His life had been punctuated by abrupt departures. He had run away half a dozen times from school, once from the boxing ring. Even now he could hear the headmaster's assembly boom: 'You are well-named, Boulting!'

The guard wished a goodnight to someone unseen, and the doors emphatically closed. The train jolted, an apparent signal to the crouched figure at the far end of the carriage who, with a flying scarf and coat, stumped up the aisle and, like some uninvited Fate, sat opposite. His eyes were like oysters, his face broken, his sparse hair smacked damply across his forehead.

'Where you off to then?' A morsel of light glimmered in the damaged eyes but the enquiry was friendly. 'This time o' night?'

'London,' Nicholas told him. 'I'm going to all-night wrestling.'

No surprise appeared on the questioner's face. 'That's why I'm going,' he nodded. 'Not for all-night wrestling but for *life*. I been up in the North, doing things up there, but I can't stand it, being away from London too long. It's the lights, the excitement.'

To Nicholas's relief, he did not intend to stay. As he rose he pointed to an advertisement for a West End musical. 'See,' he said. 'That's what I miss.'

Stiffly the man returned to his distant seat. He rewound his scarf and his head submerged into it again. Nicholas watched the endless belt of London suburbs rolling by the window; squared lights upstairs, people going to bed, getting ready for their ordinary tomorrows.

His muted elation had now given way to an uncertainty that grew as the train travelled. He was forty years old and he was running away. Whatever was to become of him?

The train scuttled through the retiring suburbs and then nosed underground to Baker Street where Nicholas, dozing against his chest, was abruptly roused by the hollow call of the platform porter. 'All change! All change!' The words rang like a prophecy.

The unkempt man at the other end of the carriage stood and stretched, and whirled his scarf. He began to sing in a high, soft voice: 'Here we go, here we go, here we go.' With a wave towards Nicholas he marched blithely away.

There was no one collecting tickets or unpaid fares. Outside were late lines of westerly traffic in the Marylebone Road; people going home to bed. His sense of isolation grew. Almost furtively he crossed onto the south side of the road and turned into one of the side streets. A tramp, his ashen face nesting in a massive black beard, was sleeping in a cardboard box in a doorway, an alarm clock placed on the step beside him. Further along the street were some lights illuminating a porch and the neon name of a hotel. He went in that direction.

There were columns, white and fluted, each side of the hotel door, making it appear more imposing than, on closer inspection, it merited. A night porter, his coat green as a snooker table, was reading a newspaper behind a polished desk. Yes, they had a room. As Nicholas was signing the registration form, the man, detecting no sign of luggage apart from his briefcase, enquired: 'Been travelling long, sir?'

'About forty-five minutes,' answered Nicholas. He looked firmly at the porter as if it were important to convince him. 'I've run away from home.'

'Very fashionable right now, sir,' responded the porter affably. 'All sorts of people at it. My own family, we've got a tradition of running away. The male line.'

'I don't know whether I've done right,' admitted Nicholas. 'I may go back tomorrow.'

'It's one of those matters,' agreed the man looking wise, 'that's better reviewed in daylight.' He spread his arms. 'Look where it's got me.' For a second time he peered over his counter to the floor. 'No luggage then, sir?' He paused: 'Except your personal briefcase.'

Nicholas nodded: 'It was a rush job.'

'Spur of the moment,' nodded the porter. 'Would you like a drink before going to the room? It might help you see things in a more optimistic light.' He picked up some keys. 'It's no trouble to open the bar.'

Nicholas thanked him. 'I will. A double scotch. I could do with some bravado.'

The man led the way and switched on the lights in a small chintzy lounge. He unlocked the grille around the bar and poured the whisky. 'Have one yourself,' suggested Nicholas.

'I will. Thank you, sir. It might help me to face the terrors of the night.'

Nicholas drank the whisky swiftly and put down the glass for another. 'Oh well,' he said wiping his mouth with his hand. 'I've gone and done it now.'

'I expect you'll be able to go back,' reassured the porter as if he knew Sarah personally. 'Women are amazingly accommodating in these circumstances. They may say "good riddance" or words to that effect, but they don't want another woman to get hold of you.' He winked genially. 'They know only too well that there are a thousand bereft females on the prowl.'

'That's a thought,' agreed Nicholas brightening. He finished his second drink and the porter showed him to a room on the first floor. There were lace curtains inside the main drapes and the lights of occasional cars fluttered across them. The porter made to pull the heavier curtains but Nicholas told him not to bother. 'I may want to just sort of gaze out of the window,' he said. He had drunk the two double scotches quickly.

'Don't jump, sir, if that's what you're thinking,' requested the porter lowering his eyes. 'It's my job to clean up the pavement.'

After he had gone Nicholas sat on the bed and looked around the close chamber. His gloom returned and increased. He glanced at the telephone and looked at his watchless wrist. It must be somewhere after midnight. He rang Caroline's number. Her response was muffled by bedclothes.

'It's me, Nick,' he said. 'I've run away.'

'How far have you got?' Her voice lacked enthusiasm.

'To Baker Street at the moment.'

'That's not very far.'

'It's a start,' he responded a little petulantly. 'Sarah found your soap in my ears.'

'Christ,' said Caroline waking up at that. 'She doesn't look in your ears, does she?'

'The children spotted it.'

'Nice to have observant kids. You're right in it then?'

'I didn't admit to anything but I'd say that's a fair summing up. We had a sort of final row and I cleared out. I got the feeling she had been waiting for it. I may go to America.'

'That means you're running away from me as well,' she observed.

'Oh come on . . .'

'You sound a bit drunk.'

'I've had a couple of scotches, that's all. Don't *you* start nagging.'

'I see. Only wives are permitted to nag, not mistresses,' she responded tartly. 'Anyway I was sleeping, dreaming about Richard Gere, so I'm going back to see if he's waited for me. Call me tomorrow. Have lots of fun.'

She put down the phone and, with a grimace, he did likewise.

She had written to him admiringly after the publication in paperback of *Lying in Your Arms*, one of a number of responses from women who claimed to recognise themselves in it. When they had first become lovers she had enjoyed reading the sexual passages aloud to him as a prelude to re-enacting them, but he had thought for some time that they were reaching the end, if not the climax, of the story.

He surveyed the room again as though it might provide either some solace or some answers. It remained aloof. During the manoeuvre he came face to face with himself in the dressing table mirror. That was him – Nicholas Andrew Boulting, author, forty, five feet ten, a bit on the thick side, dark hair needing cutting, black ringed eyes needing sleep; a fugitive.

He did not want to stay in the room. It was too enclosing even with the curtains open. There was a street-lamp outside the shape and colour of an egg. There was only the occasional car now. Nocturnal anti-climax had set in. He wondered what other runaways did, felt.

There had to be somewhere to go. He made for the door, locking it behind him. His briefcase and contents, his entire available possessions, were in the room. There must be a place to go, to be. After all, this was London and it was only – he stared challengingly at the clock in the hall as he went downstairs – ten to one.

The porter was sitting moodily, nibbling at a glass of whisky.

'You've made me wonder, sir,' he said when he saw, unsurprised, Nicholas on the stairs. He brought out a bottle of Johnny Walker from below the polished counter, and another glass.

'About what?' asked Nicholas in the tone of one anxious to help. He poured himself a drink and raised it.

'About running away,' said the porter. 'The trouble with me, I wouldn't have a clue where I could run to. It's not easy, is it? The life you know might well be better than the life you don't.'

'Very profound,' acknowledged Nicholas.

'I thought so, sir,' responded the man replenishing Nicholas's glass. 'But then, I *am* a bit of a philosopher. A lot of people in this job are. You have to fill the solitary hours.'

'That's what I need to do,' said Nicholas. 'Fill in time. Now I've bunked off I can't simply go to bed can I? I could have stayed in bed at home. In the spare room.' He leaned towards the porter and lifted an eye. 'Is there anywhere I can go at this time of the night?'

'A walk,' suggested the man disappointingly.

'A walk?'

'If you're thinking of something more exotic, wicked women, dancing, and so forth, then there are places in the West End. But I never recommend anything I haven't sampled myself, so I can't give an opinion. I can't afford them.'

'I'll go for a walk,' decided Nicholas. 'Something may happen to me.' He finished the whisky raising the glass once more, then went towards the exit. It was no longer wide open. The porter had converted it into a revolving door and, although he felt only mildly unsteady, Nicholas had difficulty with it.

'Other way, sir,' advised the porter remaining behind the desk and making arm movements. 'Clockwise. At the moment you're trying to go widdershins.'

Nicholas reversed and pushed the other way. The door flew around and he was almost projected into the warm night. Recovering himself, he looked each way. There was no movement in the street, although he could see passing lights on the Marylebone Road at the junction.

Walking in the other direction, he experienced surprising difficulty in keeping a straight line on the pavement. He regarded his hunched reflection in successive shop windows. Two cats, like the pair he had seen outside Boots in Boxley High Street a few hours before, were taunting each other, one arched on a wall, the other snarling on the street. Cats never seemed to be short of insults. He reached the corner and was about to turn back, surrender, and go to bed, when he heard the muffled beat of music. With excessive caution he peeped around the window of the end shop. Sounds were drifting up the barren street towards him. He sniffed the damp air, as if that might give some pointer, and began to move in that direction.

Around another corner he came upon the party. There were lights in all the windows of the tall, shabby-faced, Victorian house and there were people sitting out in the mild night in a front garden bounded by a crumbling wall. The bump-bump-bump of the music was coming through the front entrance and an open window. When he reached the gate one of the people sitting in the garden, a black man, called to him: 'Hey, Moley, it's you!'

'It's me,' acknowledged Nicholas wafting his hand. He wondered who Moley was. He strolled, staggering mildly towards the front steps. 'Go in and have a drink, Moley,' called the man. Nicholas waved acknowledgement.

There were three girls in sagging dresses and ringlets on the top step. Two were trying to keep the other one sitting up. They were shaking her and as they did so, her breasts toppled like dumplings from the yawning top of the dress. Her friends put them away for her. Nicholas went into the house.

The place was stuffed with people; the thick air loaded with voices and bumping music. There were revolving lights and faces of shades and colours. Every room was full. He picked up a bottle from a table, took a long swig and began dancing with a nearby woman.

'What's widdershins?' he shouted at her over the thudding music. He could not see her properly although she was close. 'What does it mean?'

'Widdershins?' she answered, her face moving like the moon. Her black dress went from her armpits to the floor. 'I don't know.'

Decisively she clasped his hand and tugged him through the crowd. There seemed to be a lot of enjoyable-looking women. This was more like it. It just showed what you could find; what was waiting out here.

17

His companion pushed into the crush, trawling him behind. She seemed to know where things were for she thrust open a door and led him into a darkened room where there were several people on the floor. Drunkenly Nicholas excused himself as he stepped over them. His partner was heading for a wall of books. 'Stand there,' she instructed firmly. 'Don't fall over them. I'll find it.'

How long she took Nicholas did not know. He was trying to keep himself upright. He swayed involuntarily and held onto a standard lamp which fell away as though avoiding him. Nobody seemed to mind. It remained shining on the carpet. His companion called from the bookshelves. 'I've found it. The dictionary.' Although the room was revolving her voice was succinct.

She reached out, he made a few steps and she gently caught his hair and pulled him toward her. 'What was it . . . widd . . .' She began to turn the pages of the dictionary.

'Widder . . . widdershins,' he repeated vaguely wondering why she was doing it.

'Here,' she said sounding oddly excited. 'Widdershins. It means . . . wait. It says "See withershins".'

'Widdershins,' muttered the swaying Nicholas. 'Withershins.' Where would all this end?

Awkwardly she turned the pages. 'Right. Withershins, also widdershins. Direction contrary to the course of the sun. Considered unlucky. Also anti-clockwise.'

Nicholas heard himself say: 'Oh good. Unlucky.'

When next he attempted to focus on her she was regarding him fiercely. He could see the brightness in her eyes even though the rest of her face was soft darkness. 'Upstairs,' she told him firmly. 'It's too crowded here.'

It was all so simple, so easily done, that in his mazed state he thought she wanted to go somewhere to dance. But they went upstairs, stepping their way through people sitting, lounging or sprawling on the treads. He accepted another drink from a proffered bottle.

On the landing she took a key from deep in her dress and

unlocked a door. 'You live here, do you?' Nicholas endeavoured to say.

'No. I stole the key. I know the people. They're away.'

She led him, kept him upright, manoeuvring him around the door. The room was dark but the window was uncurtained, an oblong of grey. 'Lie down there,' she said edging him towards the double bed. 'But don't drop off. I don't do this for everyone.'

'No,' mumbled Nicholas. 'I don't expect you do.'

'And keep your eyes open or you'll miss everything.'

Desperately he tried to watch her as she undressed. She did it slowly as though doing so gave her pleasure, and with deliberate movements as if to test his concentration. His eyelids kept falling. He cursed the whiskies of the hall porter. Who would want to drop off to sleep at a time like this?

He watched her easing her dress over her shoulders. She wore nothing underneath and her breasts projected like eyes through the gloom. He forced his own eyes to remain open but he could not focus. There seemed to be four nipples. 'Wake up,' he heard her saying from an immense distance. 'Wake up, you dolt.'

But sleep he did. Deeply and for several hours. He awoke wearing only his shirt, and his first view was of the remainder of his clothes in an unkempt pile by the bedside. There was a warm someone at his back. Slowly, and with some expectation, he turned and came face to face and breath to breath with a round Chinese man who lifted his heavy lids at the same moment.

The man registered only a mild squint of surprise, as if this sort of thing was bound to happen now and then. His face seemed to unroll, and he said: 'Must go away' before sliding ponderously from the bed. He was wearing a purple suit with a green shirt and bow-tie. He stretched a little, like a token exercise, left the room and Nicholas never saw him again.

Nicholas found he was incapable of following. He tried and failed to rise from the mattress. Something seemed to be pinning him there. He tried to ascertain if he were injured by starting at his fingertips, moving them, then the whole fingers, the hand, up his arms and through his body. His head sounded full of drums, his mouth felt like a clogged chimney. God, he felt dire. Oh, where was his wife? Where were his children?

It took him twenty minutes to get clear of the house into the daylight air. He failed to find a lavatory that was not occupied by a recumbent figure, or figures, and eventually eased an unconscious man from the pan in a bathroom and hung him across the bath, before relieving himself. It required care to negotiate the stairs, for on them people were slumped in sleep. Giddiness overtook him and he had to sit by two embraced and sleeping men until he had recovered sufficiently to negotiate the next tread.

Downstairs played-out music was still playing. Two people kept each other upright while they danced. Nicholas tried to recall what his friend of the night looked like but failed. Only her four nipples came to mind. Someone was shouting and sobbing down a telephone from the back of the house. He decided to leave. Outside the front door was a thin, everyday woman in a bright pinafore, briskly sweeping broken glass and other debris from the step.

'Morning,' she said as if providing information. Her dull eyes took in his shattered appearance. 'Off for a jog?'

'Later,' Nicholas smiled grittily. He thought he was only two corners away from the hotel but he was far from certain which two corners. He did not know the time, although the streets were well into their daily business. Passing a newsagent's shop he saw that there was a clock inside and peered in at the door. 'You want something?' enquired the Indian.

'Time,' muttered Nicholas. 'Just checking the time.'

'Eleven thirty London. Five thirty Calcutta,' replied the man. 'Teatime.'

He continued along the pavement until, to his relief, he recognised and reached the hotel. Nausea overtook him as he neared the door and he had to sit on the front step. An unknown woman crossed the road and handed him a packet of sandwiches.

'Mr Boulting?' enquired the daytime porter appearing and helping him upright. 'It is; isn't it?'

Dumbly Nicholas acknowledged that it was and passed over the sandwiches. 'We wondered where you had got to, sir. Harry the Night said to look out for you. Will you be all right?' He assisted him like a casualty.

'In a day or so,' Nicholas managed to say as they reached the lobby.

'Here's your key, sir,' said the porter helpfully retrieving it from the reception desk. The clerk regarded him dubiously. 'You *are* Mr Boulting?' he asked.

'I think so,' said the porter studying Nicholas unsurely.

'I'm almost sure,' Nicholas told them. He began to make for the stairs. The porter once more stepped to his assistance and took his key. 'You'll be all right, sir,' he said. 'Had a bit of a cheery night, have we?'

'Quite cheery,' groaned Nicholas.

He did not wake until late afternoon. There was rush-hour traffic sounding outside the window. He looked, once again, at his vacant wrist. He must buy a watch. It was bad enough being homeless without being timeless.

Even lying on the bed hurt. He groaned. His clothes felt like dirty cardboard. He must get clothes; he must get money. With a moan he eased himself from the bed and went towards the small bathroom. While he was sitting on the lavatory he glanced speculatively into the mirrored wall beside the bath. It could have been a haggard and scowling stranger sitting there. 'Runaway,' he muttered at the reflection. 'Wreck.'

This had to stop now. There was no arguing with it. He was hopeless on his own. 'Home,' he told his mirror image. 'Home, humble pie and happiness.' He looked away and then flung another glance at himself. 'And I mean it.'

There was a telephone in the bathroom and, still sitting on the pan, he dialled his home number. Willie answered and adopted a Dalek voice as soon as he realised who it was. 'All enquiries have to be referred to Mrs Boulting's solicitor, Mr David Fawkes of . . .'

'Wille! This is your father. And he's *my* solicitor as well. . . .'

Willie returned to normal. 'Not now. Mum says she's going to have him.' The automaton took over again. 'All enquiries have to be referred . . .'

Nicholas groaned. 'Don't say that again, not like that, there's a good chap. Your mother is not in, I take it.'

'No,' answered Willie in his own voice. 'That's why I'm answering. She's gone to see her solicitor, Mr David Fawkes of . . .'

'All right, all right . . . *I'll call her tonight. Later.*'

'How far did you get, Dad?' The tone was conspiratorial.

Nicholas heard his own voice falter: 'Baker Street.'

'That's not far.'

'I had not intended to go further. It was only a tiff.'

'Mum doesn't reckon it was. She's been down the bank and now she's gone to see her solicitor, Mr David . . .'

'The bank? Oh, I see. Listen David . . . I mean Willie . . . Tell her I'll call back.'

He put the receiver down and flushed the toilet, almost confusing the actions. The bank? That had to be serious. He rang the bank. Yes, said the manager in a concerned manner, Mrs Boulting had been in and had withdrawn everything from their current joint account. 'She left one pound in to keep it open,' he said diffidently. 'So all may not be lost.' He made an attempt at being jaunty. 'I hope you're not running away from us.'

Nicholas then rang Paul Garrett, his literary agent. 'Done a bunk, I hear,' said Garrett genially. Nothing a writer did ever surprised him. 'Well, yes. Sarah's been on. And *on*, and *on*, actually. She's very fed up with you. She wanted to know how much money you had coming in. I told her I couldn't tell her that.'

'Thanks.' Nicholas sighed bitterly. 'It's always down to dosh, isn't it.'

'Their revenge, their reassurance,' mumured Garrett. 'I *do* have the American book money for you, by the way. Fifty thousand dollars' signature advance on a hundred thousand. You want me to hold onto it, I take it.'

'Please. I've got to live on something.'

'Escapes are expensive,' agreed Garrett. 'It might make a novel some time. It's time you produced something else apart from false starts.' He brightened professionally. 'Incidentally *Lying in Your Arms* has just sold in Denmark.'

'Oh good. *Denmark.*'

'That's the eighth foreign publication.'

'Yes, I know. Sorry Paul. You do a good job.'

'You'll need to do a good job soon. Mallinder's are getting restive. They want their novel.'

Replacing the phone Nicholas took off his stiff and grubby clothes. He wondered if there were all-night outfitters in London. He ran the bath. As he turned he saw in the mirror that something was written in ink on his buttocks. It was her telephone number.

He went into the bedroom and returned to the mirror with the notepad from the bedside table. Manoeuvring in front of the reflection and reading backwards he wrote down the number. He got in the bath, first checking that he had transferred the figures correctly. When he stood up he turned his behind to the mirror again. The message had gone. Wrapped in two towels, he returned to the bedroom and dialled the number.

'Oh, hello . . . Is . . . Is . . . Miss Widdershins at home please?'

There was a wait. 'Widdershins? There is no one here of that name. Where did you get this number?'

'Miss Widdershins left it behind.'

He heard her involuntary giggle. '*That's* funny,' she said. 'I'm glad you were able to decipher it.'

'It wasn't easy. The eight was difficult because of where it was written. It could have been a three.'

Again she laughed. He ventured: 'We didn't actually do . . . ?

23

'No, actually we didn't do. You were too far gone.'

'I woke up with a Chinese chap.'

She sighed: 'Those parties.'

'You go to a lot of parties like that?'

'Not at all. Only when I feel the need. Last night will get me through for weeks. I won't be able to see you again.'

'Oh. Why not? You left me the number.'

'I wasn't myself at the time.'

'Who were you then?'

'Another me. I'm married.'

'Oh, I see. So am I. I've just run away.' Now it came out like a mild boast.

She said: 'Perhaps I'll do that one day. But not yet. Why don't you call me in a couple of years. What are we? August. Try the August after next.'

She put the telephone down decisively and he grunted and lay back on the bed and returned to aching sleep. It was almost dark when he awoke. He showered once more and tried to brush down his clothes. Then he went downstairs. Harry the Night was behind his porter's desk like a soldier manning a bunker.

'Where did you get widdershins from, Harry?' he asked.

'Oh, that. An old chap used to come to the hotel. Scotsman. A professor of something. He always tried to go out of the revolving door the wrong way and he always said: "Och, widdershins." One day I decided to look it up and find out what it meant.'

'Anti-clockwise,' said Nicholas. 'I found that out last night.'

'Oh, that's what you were up to. Looking up words. It also means going against the sun.'

'Yes, I found that out too.'

'What are you going to do now, sir?'

'Harry, I'm going out to have a quiet meal. I'm starving. And after that I'm just going somewhere. I don't know where.' He regarded the porter hopefully. 'Go on, you suggest somewhere.'

Harry appeared pleased with the responsibility. 'Egypt,' he

said. 'Egypt's nice, so I understand.' He frowned at Nicholas.
'But, you'll be going east, against the sun.'

'Widdershins,' said Nicholas.

'Exactly, sir. Widdershins.'

Two

Nicholas had never been one for blaming his life on his childhood. His faults and frailties, he knew and honestly admitted, had more immediate causes, shallower roots. On the other hand, ever since he could remember the sudden, and often inconvenient, urge to run away had been lurking within him, a part of him.

As a toddling infant he had been found miraculously in the highly fenced gardens of neighbours once, during a snowstorm, his frantic parents following the tiny prints. At another time he had journeyed to a town ten miles distant in the rear of a removals van. A family from next door, transferring to a new life, were provided with an immediate reminder of the old by the unloading of the sleeping Nicholas in an armchair.

His own earliest memory of the untimely urge was at the seaside, at Boscombe, where, refused a second ice-cream, he had set out to agitate his father and mother by edging off through sunbathers and sandcastles. There had been a wicked pleasure in witnessing the anguish of his parents, observing their fraught search while he was mounted on an adjacent donkey. A woman with a grizzling child had paid for Nicholas to ride tandem, supporting the grizzler on the donkey's back. Astride the saddle he had cruised the beach, passing within a yard of his weeping mother, his eyes fixed like Lawrence of Arabia on the sandy horizon, the smaller child held between his elbows.

But such escapes and escapades were minor compared with his flight at the age of eleven from Athelburn School, Hertfordshire, and the pugilistic Mr Piffer who had oddly picked him out as world-championship material and had instructed him to visit his room for early training. Keen though he was to make his mark in boxing, or in anything, Nicholas had been disturbed by the realisation that from the first donning of the gloves, it was intended that he boxed with the pink-cheeked, puffing Piffer himself.

'He'll give you a big pair of shorts,' forecast those boys who had been that way before. 'And they'll fall down. And he'll try to pull them up.' Nicholas, a stainless eleven, had puzzled why they dwelt on such details. 'But what do I do about the boxing?' he demanded. 'I can't fight a man.'

They told him not to worry because that part was easy. And so it proved, since much of Mr Piffer's instruction involved getting the boy to hit him as hard and as often as possible. The part about the big shorts was also true. They would have fitted a heavyweight, and when they had fallen down about his ankles Mr Piffer, eager-eyed had darted forward to pull them up. Nicholas had acted first and delivered a cross-right to the side of Mr Piffer's pink head which had the master sinking happily to his knees hanging on to the boy's legs and going into a slow dreamy count. 'One . . . two . . . three . . .' Nicholas pushed him away but he was up at eight, dodging and ducking but plainly offering the other side of his head as a target. Instead Nicholas got in a foul below the belt, and Mr Piffer doubled up in ecstasy.

The next day Mr Piffer told him that he had been entered for the county schoolboy championships and Nicholas, knowing no better, had been proud. On the night, thin and shivering, he had climbed into the ring, in front of hordes of crowing boys standing on chairs and stamping their feet. He looked towards the other corner where a giant youth was climbing under the ropes. 'He seems a lot bigger than me, sir,' he suggested to Mr Piffer who, as one of his seconds, was whispering advice in his ear. The flushed master acknowledged that his opponent appeared huge, and shuffling through the programme and the entry forms had muttered: 'Ah yes. I'm afraid, Boulting, there has been a clerical error.'

27

His instruction to Nicholas was to get into the middle and do his level best. The bell went and Nicholas had gone timorously towards his looming opponent who swished at him with a large glove. He ducked and felt the wind move his hair as it passed over. The other boxer observed his puny opponent in a puzzled way as though he might be booby-trapped. The big boy threw another exploratory punch and, in ducking again, Nicholas fell to his knees. Wildly he looked back towards his corner. Mr Piffer was vaguely urging him to get up and fight. His other second, a cringing maths master, was hiding his eyes. Nicholas regained his feet and ran. He ran around the ring, back-pedalling at first and then unashamedly the right way around, with his lumbering opponent in close and frustrated pursuit. Derisive howls and catcalls flew from the spectators. As he passed by Mr Piffer, on his fourth lap, his mentor called some unrealistic instruction, distracting him briefly. It was long enough for his opponent to catch him on the side of the head with a big, uncouth blow. He fell to the canvas. 'Lie there you stupid boy,' he heard Mr Piffer calling through the roaring ocean that engulfed his mind. 'Lie there or he'll kill you!'

The count got to eight and Nicholas almost burst into tears when he was saved by the bell for the end of the round. He slithered, half on his stomach, half on his hip, towards his corner. Mr Piffer and the now openly sobbing maths master got his thin body onto the stool. Eyes bright with the excitement of the evening, Mr Piffer began rubbing Nicholas's stomach. It restored his breath. Nicholas let his lungs heave a couple of times and then produced his only punch of the night, a haymaker containing every bit of strength he had left, which caught Mr Piffer on the chin and sent him toppling backwards over the ropes and out of the ring. Enormous yells of delight and encouragment came from the audience. They had never seen anything like it. They shouted and stamped their feet for more. Nicholas straightened from his stool, clasped his huge gloves on his skinny arms above his head like a champ, and leapt from the ring. He ran. He ran and ran, through the auditorium, out of the door and into the blessed dark and drizzling night. Nobody tried to delay him or catch him. He kept running, the rain washing his tears. He ended up almost five miles away outside a fish-and-chip shop at Tring and there he breathlessly gave himself up to the proprietor.

There was an attitude of triumphant finality about Sarah on the telephone. 'The best sight I've ever seen is you going out of that door,' she informed him briskly. 'And you are *not* coming back.'

'You've changed the locks,' he guessed. Locksmiths must earn a fortune. Sarah said: 'I've changed the door.'

He mumbled that he was considering heading east. 'Go,' she enthused. 'Go, for God's sake. As far as you can.'

'If you do that you come back again,' he pointed out. 'The world being round.' If he hoped she would see the forlorn joke, she did not.

'Just stay as far away as possible.'

'You've been to the bank, I gather. And the solicitor.'

'Both. I've been busy, Nicholas.'

'I wouldn't let you down over money,' he insisted miserably. 'Nor the kids.'

'I'm not taking chances. David Fawkes has told me not to. Not on any account.'

'David Fawkes is *my* solicitor,' he almost howled. 'For God's sake, I've played golf with him.'

'He's acting for me now,' she responded. 'Anyway, I can't keep exchanging small talk with you. I was just on my way out. Keep going east.'

The telephone went dumb. He regarded the receiver accusingly. Out? Where was she going *out*? And what of the children? What had she done with their children?

He might as well start that night. Right away. The quicker he went the better. He thought of Caroline but then shrugged and glared at the bed. He would not be able to sleep. Without being drunk he would be alone and sleepless. There was nothing to get ready, no clothes to pack. He should have bought a razor and a toothbrush. He had no money. He should have got some money. Now the only preparation he could make was to go to the lavatory, wash his hands and haggard face, and straighten his hair. 'Right, let's go,' he almost snarled at his reflection. 'This minute. Before she changes her mind.'

He went downstairs. Harry the Night was gazing out at the second part of his nickname. 'You off, sir?' he guessed quietly. 'Egypt?'

'Egypt it is, Harry.' He stood square and looked through the brightly lit entrance to the dimness of the world beyond. 'How do I get there, d'you think?'

'Turn right at the door, sir. Taxi from the end of the street. Out to the airport.' He glanced suspiciously at the clock on the staircase. 'There may be nothing to Egypt tonight, sir, it's getting late.'

Nicholas nodded glumly. 'I know, mate. But if I don't go now, I never will. She could be desperate for me to go back tomorrow.'

'It's always a mistake,' said Harry knowingly. 'Going back too early. Before you've even tried. That was my mistake. One of them.'

'It *is* Heathrow, I suppose. For Egypt.'

Harry brightened. 'I can ask,' he said, glad to be positive. 'I've got a number.' He opened a frayed book. 'Let's see. Airport Information. Arrivals and Departures. Well, you're a departure if ever there was one. I'll ring them.'

Nicholas thanked him. Despite his bravado, the fall-out from the night before was still on him. His spirit was on its knees. Imagine her stealing his solicitor. What else would she purloin? What else would *they* – she and David Fawkes – purloin? He had always thought Fawkes had fancied her. Could solicitors be struck off for that sort of thing, like doctors? Perhaps he should go home. Now. Kneel on the doorstep and beg her to take him back.

Harry was nodding into the phone. 'Right, thank you. Heathrow for Cairo. Gatwick for Luxor. I've got it.'

He put the receiver down. 'There it is,' he said. 'I'd go to Luxor, if I were you, sir. Cairo is not much of a place. My dad was there in the war. He said he would rather have been home and he hated home.'

Nicholas tightly folded his resolve. 'Right. Luxor it is. Gatwick, here I come.' He signed his credit card chit for the bill.

'Can you cash a cheque for me, Harry? Say fifty? I didn't get to a bank.'

The porter said: 'I can manage fifty myself, sir.' He took the notes from his wallet.

'Give me fifty and I'll give you a cheque for sixty,' suggested Nicholas. 'There'll be a bank open at Gatwick, I hope.'

'Very kind, sir. Very businesslike.'

The porter produced his secret scotch and they had a farewell drink. There was no one else in the small lobby and they rested the glasses on Harry's counter before raising a final toast. 'Here's to you, wherever you might end up, sir,' said Harry.

'Here's to you, mate,' responded Nicholas. He was grateful. Harry had been a friend.

'Look where *I've* ended up.' Harry reflected. 'Here behind this desk. Still, I'd rather not be going to Luxor. There's a time for running away. And mine's gone.'

'Mr Walburton?'

'Hello. Yes. Walburton here.'

'Mr Walburton, this is Nicholas Boulting. I wonder if you could do me a favour.'

'And what would that be, Mr Boulting?'

'I've left my passport in my office. I'd be grateful if you could let yourself in there and send it on to me.'

'Gladly. But I wonder if it's still there. Your wife came in yesterday and went up there and left with a case full of stuff.'

'She did!'

'She did, Mr Boulting. I went up afterwards, since I'm supposed to be responsible for the rooms here, and it was all neat and tidy but it looked like everything in the way of papers had gone.'

Nicholas said: 'Jesus. Women.'

'Exactly. That's why Jesus wasn't married, I fancy. I wasn't here when she arrived but she had a key so that was that.'

With a worried sigh Nicholas slowly replaced the telephone. He was in his bedroom at the Leafy Lane Motel, Gatwick. He had not discovered that his passport was absent from its usual niche in his briefcase until he had arrived at the airport. He rang Sarah.

'Where's my passport?' he said uncompromisingly.

'Fancy leaving it behind,' she replied airily. 'You can't run away, not properly anyway, without it.'

'How dare you clear out my office.'

'Dare? There was nothing daring about it, darling. I just went in and tidied up for you. If you're in some distant, exotic place you won't be needing an office, will you. It's just a waste of money and we don't want to waste money, do we? Not now. I've written on your behalf terminating your rental agreement. You'll still have to pay a month's rent, but . . .'

'Sarah,' he said with fierce patience. 'There may come a time when you'll regret all this . . . this aggravation.'

'Possibly. But I'm enjoying it immensely now. Your children are well, incidentally, just to save you asking. Willie came second in the sack race at the village fête on Saturday. Dougie Mathews won the fathers' egg and spoon race.'

'Oh, good old bloody Dougie Mathews.'

'They had a *running* race for fathers too. Right up your street. Nobody can run like you.'

Nicholas said determinedly: 'Sarah, thanks for all the news. I need my passport. You *are* aware that it is a criminal offence to steal or detain someone's passport.'

'Darling, you can have it. After all if you haven't got it you can't go anywhere. And the sooner you go the better. I'll send it off registered post within the next hour. I'm going to the hairdresser's and the post office is right next door.'

'I know that,' he retorted. 'I lived there too remember.'

'I thought you might have forgotten. What's the address?'

'Nicholas Boulting.' He spelled it out sarcastically. 'B–O–U–L...'

'I know,' she responded sweetly. 'I have the same name myself. At the moment.'

He paused and pulled himself together. 'Leafy Lane Motel.'

'That sounds pretty.'

'It was recommended. Leafy Lane, Crawley, Sussex.'

'Postcode?'

'I'll get it. One moment . . . please.' He got the postcode from a notepad at the side of the bed and read it out to her.

'Got it,' she said with mock triumph. 'Have a lovely time.'

His dinner was solitary and unappetising, eaten at a table with a burn-holed tablecloth and a tumescent plastic tomato sauce holder. He went into the bar where a group of vague and elderly men, wearing clothes they appeared to have had for a long time, were seated around a table confronted by pints of beer and trying to sing 'There'll be Bluebirds over the White Cliffs of Dover'. They had forgotten the second line; then one, after thoughtfully stirring his beer with his finger, recited with a growing smile of achievement: 'Tomorrow just you wait and see.' There were nodding mumbles of memory and they falteringly sang it.

'They come here every year,' said the taxi-driver who had recommended the motel which, it transpired, belonged to his brother. 'There used to be more of them but now they've started to die off.'

The men gave up trying to recall the rest of the verse. 'Remember when old Dusty Miller copped it,' said one whom Nicholas came to know as Marshall. It was as though he were starting a familiar and well-loved game. 'Just after Anzio. Got all through Anzio and then copped it.'

'*Not* Dusty Miller,' argued the smallest and oldest-looking of the men. 'It was Tredger. Mortar got him. His 'ead landed right next to my kitbag. I can see 'im staring up at me now.'

'What did he look like?' asked a third member of the party.

'Sort of . . . surprised.'

Marshall, a hunched and heavy man with short grey hair cropped around his head like a balaclava, intoned: 'The Jerries was all right. Good fighters. Hard but fair. Never knew when they was beaten.'

'Not like the Eyties,' said a man at the end of the table who had not previously spoken. He wore an overcoat and a riven look. 'They always knew. Beaten afore they started.'

'Their women was good though,' conceded Marshall, his voice slowing with the reminiscence. 'What was that one called at that place we used to go?' He made a motion before his chest with both hands. 'Her with all the frontage?'

'Maria,' guessed the overcoated man. 'They was all called Maria.' His face became deep with regret and remembrance. 'Them was the days.'

The taxi-driver said to Nicholas: 'Every year, they come here. They go off to Italy to the battlefields and the graveyards. They have a rare old time.'

Nicholas went to bed miserably. He had been into Crawley and bought some clothes and got money. Now he took off the unfamiliar jacket and unfriendly trousers and hung them in the bare wardrobe. He would have given anything, given *up* anything, simply to go home. The room was cheap. The catch of the window was rusty and a spider was living in the plug-hole of the wash-basin. He lifted it out before cleaning his teeth. This was all wrong. If you were going to run away it ought to be done with style. This was not style. Perhaps he wanted to be downcast.

He sat in bed like a boy, staring at the wall decorated with a faded photograph of Gatwick years before when it was a racecourse. Not everyone could run away, very few in fact. If you were a plumber with a lover the best you could probably hope for was to visit her on the way home from a day's plumbing. Only the richest of plumber-lovers could down tools and up and go to Luxor. Not that he had a lover now. He had discounted Caroline. He was running away alone.

Perhaps it *was* the fault of the damned book. Nobody had

expected it to be published, let alone sell. Sarah had forecast that he was wasting his time. Nicholas had been a sub-editor on *Commercial Television World*, a daily desk drudge but with a middle-distance view of a shiny world. Often when there was a spare invitation in the office, and at times when there was not, he would go unofficially to launchings and screenings and cocktail parties and came to know and study producers, directors, advertising executives and others involved in television commercials. It was an outsider's insight into an array of bright and anxious characters, hatreds and gangs, loves and loyalties, cynicisms and betrayals, raw ambition, good money and greedy sex, that had paved the ground for the outstanding success of *Lying in Your Arms*.

Some of the real participants in this circus had professed hurt and surprise that a mere onlooker had profited so largely from what they did. 'I could easily have written this novel,' announced Jack Birk, director of the famous bra-in-a-car commercial, in a *Sunday Times* review. There were those who complained that they were too close to the real thing or too busy to write about it. Provided with the time and financial motivation any one of several hundred could have hashed up the novel next week or even after the next drink. But not one had done so and it was left to Nicholas Boulting, a fringe man, recognised by few, to go home from the office and write it all down. Damn him.

When the novel was finished nobody wanted to publish it. He entrusted the manuscript to journalistic colleagues who said they knew someone but it was always returned, usually in silence. He sent it to various publishers but it came back so promptly he marvelled at the speed of the post. One kept it for weeks and he was torn between ending his uncertainty by asking for their decision and not wanting to break the spell, his fantasy that it was being seriously considered. In the event it turned out that they had lost the manuscript and, after denying they had ever received it at all, they eventually returned it to Nicholas smeared with either blood or jam.

At that time his novel had a variety of titles which he often altered between rejections. Then in the deepest hour of a winter's night, he had sat abruptly up in bed and almost bellowed into Sarah's sleeping ear: 'Lying in Your Arms!'

Sarah had grunted: 'It's one o'clock.' But the next morning he wrote the title in outsize type on a new cover sheet and dropped the manuscript in at the Kensington office of Mallinder and Co., on his way to work. They telephoned him at his sub-editor's desk before lunchtime. That afternoon he made an appointment with Paul Garrett who at once became his agent.

When it was published *Lying in Your Arms* was dismissed by many critics but praised by others. The *Daily Mail* heralded it as an authentic hard-bitten novel of the nineties. Nicholas found himself in demand; he was on radio and television and spoke at literary lunches. It sold fifty thousand copies in the hardcover edition and a year later sold six hundred thousand in paperback. It was sold in France, Italy, Germany and in Scandinavia and, most importantly at last, to the American publishers Brent Burbach Inc. of New York.

There were offers from other publishers for his next book but Mallinder's were eager to keep him on their list. He signed a contract with them for two further novels with an advance of half a million pounds, eighty thousand on signature. He had begun the first, *Falling from Grace*, and had failed to complete it. The story ran dry after thirty thousand words. Desperately he turned to *Dancing with Delilah* and, shocked, soon found himself at another abrupt impasse. The dance with Delilah slowed and then stopped.

After a year of struggle and frustration with *Falling from Grace* he had taken an office in London, off Regent Street. He had told Sarah that writing from domestic Boxley was not working; he needed the impetus, animation, stimulation, of the West End. Sarah had shrugged and said that if it was that important then he had better have an office. Two rooms were rented and he, more or less dutifully, drove there most days. The result was a diminishing rate of work and ideas; lunch took up the middle two hours of the day after a late morning arrival. He spent many afternoons with Caroline. 'I'm inspiration for you,' she claimed. If she were it was never translated to the page. Uncomfortably Nicholas began to think that he was a one-novel novelist. So did his anxious publishers.

Planes for Luxor left only on Thursdays and Saturdays and that week they were full anyway. 'You ought to have booked in March,' advised the crinkly blonde information girl, unaccustomed to travellers who had no firm destination. She gave him the half-hopeful look of a shop assistant. 'Anything else?'

'Where can I go?' he sighed.

'Lots of places,' she said brightening up. 'Florida.' She smiled confidingly. 'I'm going myself next week, Disney World. My boyfriend's one of the stand-ins for Goofy.'

Easing herself from her seat she surveyed the Arrivals and Departures indicator hanging like an uncertain menu over the concourse. 'The Gambia,' she hummed. 'They say that's very nice.' His resolve was faltering. 'Somewhere not too far,' he asked lamely. 'I may want to come back.'

She regarded him oddly but then became decisive and announced: 'Malaga.' As if to anticipate any negative reaction, she added even more firmly: 'Very nice and warm there now and there's lots of places along the Costa you can go to. Go over . . .' She swung her naked arm like a lighthouse beam. '. . . And ask the airline. They can arrange a hotel for you as well.' She checked the clock and clicked at the keyboard on her desk. Her eyes went to the screen. 'They've got a flight in two hours and there's one seat left.' She smiled as though she honestly knew best. 'Go on. Go for it!'

Nicholas was aware that she was watching him as he walked through the criss-crossing people on the concourse. No one seemed certain but few seemed to be alone. Families in aching day-glo clothing huddled together, pointing and arguing, and trudging to and fro with their luggage. Two young people, the girl with a brief skirt and legs like spaghetti, hung onto each other over a shared coke at the refreshment buffet. Above it all

Nicholas heard Del Shannon singing: 'My little runaway . . . my run-run-run-run-runaway. . . .'

He gave up and got the last seat to Malaga and went disconsolately through passport control. As he opened his passport a snapshot taken the previous year at Bournemouth of Sarah, Deborah, Willie and himself fell onto the immigration officer's desk. 'Very nice too,' said the man.

There was a distraught blonde, large, smudge-eyed and perspiring, trying to get four unruly children through Security. Nicholas had already passed through the prop door and been busily frisked by the man the other side. He was waiting for his briefcase to travel through the X-ray when the blonde thrust a brown paper carrier bag into his hands and, without an accompanying word, went stark-faced towards the disgorging X-ray conveyor belt. A small boy, lying stiffly on his back, came through among the hand baggage. The woman pulled him from the belt and smacked his ear. There were exclamations among the security staff. A man of senior appearance strode over and said to the tearless child, wriggling in his mother's grip: 'Don't ever do that again.'

Nicholas blinked. The boy was half of twins. The second half was being held like a prisoner by a pale and deep-eyed teenage girl, who pinioned him with thin arms. Another, smaller girl, with chocolate over her mouth and dress front, watched dispassionately.

When the family were fully reunited, further warnings issued, and the conveyor restarted, the flustered blonde ushered them away, turning with a haunted smile and taking the carrier bag from Nicholas. Her eyes were wild with worry. 'They haven't got a father,' she explained haplessly. 'Not since yesterday.'

As she drove her squabbling band forward Nicholas moved tactically to the far end of the departure lounge. He kept them in view over the headlines of a newspaper swiftly purchased as a barrier. The first boarding call was for passengers with children and Nicholas watched warily. He saw them only as a group but then realised that the younger girl had become locked in the toilet. While she was being noisily extricated, the other passengers were summoned to board.

Nicholas found his aisle seat at the front of the aircraft. He heard them clamouring down the central gangway and peered nervously over his shoulder. They were heading his way. Swiftly he turned his head to the front and stared, almost praying, at the bulkhead before him. A small, hot, sticky hand touched his shoulder and he turned to see the smeared twin boys eyeing him speculatively. Even the blodges of chocolate seemed identical. ' 'Ello mister,' they said together.

'They're in there,' pointed the mother as she arrived behind them. Her hair was damp, her face pink, her eyes everywhere. The two girls were following, the younger still tearfully describing her lavatory confinement. The woman made no sign of recognising Nicholas. She seemed like someone who met many strangers but only briefly.

Awkwardly Nicholas stood and made room as the twins fought each other for the window seat. The mother leaned heavily across, her bulky bosom nudging Nicholas aside so that He could hear the desperate bounding of her heart. He crouched to give her more space and her stiff blonde hair swept across his face. 'Tupper,' she demanded. 'Sit by the window.' Her reddened nail threatened the boy. 'And *don't* you dare do it.'

The child, pond-eyed, chocolate-mouthed, shook his head unconvincingly. His twin brother threw a mocking fist at him and the boy pushed it away. Nicholas looked from one face to another and then at the mother. 'He shits,' she confided in a whisper to Nicholas. Then, as though she had gone too far: 'Sometimes.'

The twin nodded and then shook his head in acknowledgement of the dual revelations. His brother hit him with his seat-belt. Their mother had retreated and Nicholas could hear her comforting the recently incarcerated girl. He leaned across and after adjusting them clipped the seat-belts around the two boys. 'You don't, do you?' he said darkly to the twin at the window. The boy's brother said: 'He do.' The other muttered: 'Only sometimes.'

As the plane took off, and as though they had rehearsed, both boys began to scream: 'We're crashing! We're crashing!'

'Stop it! Stop it!' the mother shouted from the seat behind. 'I'll clout you if you don't.'

The small girl began to cry again and he heard the woman desperately crooning to her. The twins continued to howl as the aircraft climbed. When it flattened out an annoyed Spanish stewardess appeared and thrust a pile of comics onto the laps of the boys. She gave Nicholas a withering look. He shrugged: 'Not mine.'

It was a two-and-a-half-hour nightmare. Over the Bay of Biscay the twin at the window took on a quiet, almost dreamy, look. From behind the seat-back his mother rose. 'He's done it,' she announced knowingly. Her blonde head poked over. 'You have, haven't you? Done it?'

He had. Nicholas drew back as she fumbled around the seat. The boy was ready. He came out meekly and his brother, and his sisters, leaning over, honked and held their noses.

There was a queue for the toilet but the mother propelled the boy to the front repeating: 'Emergency . . . emergency.' She banged on the door and a shock-faced woman emerged to be hustled aside as the blonde thrust her son into the cubicle. Nicholas pushed his face further into the Spanish airline magazine. The twin at his side was adventurously exploring his nose. From behind came the wail of the small girl complaining that she was frightened. Eventually the mother emerged from the toilet pushing the first twin before her. He wore a grimace of relief. 'Don't go in there yet,' she advised the man at the head of the queue. She manoeuvred the boy past Nicholas and fixed him in his seat. 'It's only this one,' she confided loudly. 'The other one doesn't do it.'

Hovering over him, she paused as if she felt she owed him something. 'I'm Mrs Ware, by the way,' she announced. 'From London.' The smaller girl in the seat behind her began to chant: 'Ware, Ware, brush your lousy hair!'

Nicholas could sense the older girl hushing her. 'Bonnie Ware,' persisted the mother indomitably. She pointed out the twins individually, the boy by the window first. 'And these are the twins, Brian and Bruce. Brian is called Tupper.' She giggled apologetically. 'Because our name is Ware.'

'We've got lice,' confided Tupper.

' 'Undreds,' confirmed his brother clawing his own head.

'No, you haven't. Not now,' said the mother primly.

She whirled her bosom and pointed back at the girls. 'And these two are Penny and Trixie. Penny is my helpmate, aren't you Penny?'

Nicholas heard the teenage girl hum as if she fervently wished it were otherwise. He had contributed nothing but nods during the introductions but now the mother hung herself more ponderously over him, like a waiting avalanche. 'Oh yes, of course,' he said in a lost way. 'Very nice.' The nearest twin, earnest-eyed, pushed a grown-up but sticky hand towards him and he shook it. The other followed suit, his hand ominously clean from the lavatory.

'And you are . . . ?' insisted the mother bowing her big red lips.

'Oh yes. Nicholas Boulting.'

There was a squeal of delight from the seat behind, hushed by the second girl. Two faces appeared above his head. 'That's a funny name!' exclaimed Trixie. There were track-marks of tears down her laughing cheeks.

'Boulting, Boulting, I can see you're moulting!' chanted the younger girl, sending her brothers and her mother all into rolling laughter. The older girl said: 'Stop it Trixie.'

'Oh I *am* sorry,' spluttered the mother. She gasped for breath, putting her hands to her heaving dress. 'They're terrible in some ways.'

'I imagine so,' answered Nicholas defeatedly. He wondered if he could ask to sit with the pilot. A stewardess bearing books and comics appeared like an emergency aid-worker. The children immediately sat and began colouring and clumsily reading aloud. Mrs Ware settled back with the in-flight magazine. Resignedly Nicholas helped the twins to join up various dots to reveal a magic castle and then to assist in colouring a giraffe. They became industriously quiet.

The cabin staff spoiled it by bringing the meal trays. Tupper immediately dropped his on the floor and his brother punched him. They began fighting and Nicholas called hopelessly over his shoulder. 'Mrs Ware . . . ! Bonnie . . . !'

'Stop it twins,' she responded without rising. 'At once.'

'They'll settle down,' she assured him around the edge of the seat. Wearily Nicholas closed his eyes. Another tray was procured for Tupper and the boys tore off the plastic wrapping and covers hungrily and ate everything in sight. The twin nearest Nicholas swallowed the salt, choked, and screeched until enough orange juice was forced down his throat to quench the taste. Tupper pushed a plastic fork in his own eye.

After the longest two and a half hours Nicholas could ever recall, his lap loaded with scraps of food, his own wine spilt down the front of his shirt, the plane descended into Malaga. The two boys and, not one to miss an opportunity, the younger girl, all began screaming with earache. Nicholas sat solidly upright, his eyes tight.

There was a rush to get off the plane. Nicholas, glared at and muttered about by the other passengers, was forced to wait with the family until everyone else had disembarked. Tutting like castanets the stewardesses glowered as the group left the plane and the Spanish pilot came from the flight deck to view them and to stare accusingly at Nicholas. 'You have too many children,' he said.

Nicholas made for the extreme end of the arrivals hall, as far from the family as possible, hoping to get out first. But the older girl spotted him and waylaid him. 'Mum says can you give her a hand,' she asked bluntly. She half-lowered her eyes. 'I reckon she fancies you.'

The mother had two luggage trolleys. She was trying to push both as the twins were swept around the curve on the baggage carousel and disappeared through the aperture in the wall. She watched their vanishing with dulled eyes. 'I hope they don't come back,' she said to Nicholas but then looked ashamed. 'I don't mean that.' She widened her extravagant smile at Nicholas. 'You've been ever so good,' she said. The twins reappeared riding among the luggage, waving. Nicholas took two determined steps and pulled both from the carousel.

'They need a father,' said Mrs Ware. 'I've just walked out on him. Him and his women.' She regarded Nicholas bleakly. 'I've run away,' she said.

At Bob and Beryl's Tango, Rumba and Cha-Cha-Cha Bar, in the middle of Torremolinos that evening, Nicholas sat in an interior recess, dim and cool, away from street noise, thumping music, baked bodies and jolly inebriation, and studied the rising bubbles in his San Miguel beer. Two women came to the door wearing sombreros and carrying toy donkeys under ample armpits. They convulsed with mirth as the stuffed donkeys became jammed in the entrance. 'Leave it! Leave it, Trish!' gurgled one. 'There's only one bloke in here.'

'I'll 'ave 'im!' hooted Trish but to the profound relief of Nicholas they pulled themselves from the aperture and disappeared.

'Don't talk to me about the sun,' said the sullen man behind the bar to Nicholas who had not been talking about it. 'Came down here for sun and now I never see it. I miss Braintree, I can tell you. Worst thing I ever done was come here. At least the wife's gone back home so I don't have her moaning as well.'

Nicholas was in no mood for the troubles of others. Finishing the beer he went out into the early hot evening. Sitting around a table outside were Mrs Ware and her children. He made an attempt to duck back into the dim bar before they spotted him but their eyes were swift and predatory. 'There's that bloke, Mum,' pointed the elder girl.

'Him!' exclaimed one of the twins.

' 'Ello mister,' shouted the other. 'We're starving.'

The smaller girl began to cry. The mother turned weightily. Her big face was incised with lines like a shrivelled balloon. As she smiled her creases moved. 'So it is,' she sighed like someone who has just been rescued. 'It's lovely to see you,' she said with an exaggerated attempt at elegance. She pulled out a chair. 'Do join us.'

There was nothing for it but to sit down. He looked around at the five pairs of eyes pinning him. The table was bare. 'Who would like a drink?' he asked.

The girl Penny returned his look unwaveringly. 'We haven't had anything to eat,' she said plainly. Her mother made the pretence of hushing her but then turned hopelessly to Nicholas and said: 'They haven't. We got thrown out of the hotel.' She surveyed her chastened family. 'They don't like children there and I didn't have any money left anyway.' Puffs began to appear on her face and he thought she was going to cry. She tried to say something but the teenage girl had to say it for her. 'We're in dead trouble,' she said.

Bob from behind the bar appeared and stood framed lugubriously in the door. He appeared to have come across the group before and was about to say something sharp when Nicholas said: 'Can we have something to drink, please. And have you got any food?'

'Food,' repeated the twins together as though to ensure the priorities.

'Got some pizzas,' answered Bob as if he had been awaiting the opportunity. 'I could get them out.'

Exclamations of approval came from the whole family. The smaller girl stopped crying and the twins banged on the empty table with their miniature fists. Their mother leaned closer to Nicholas. There was sweat on her face. 'Thanks,' she said. 'I didn't know what to do.'

'What *are* you going to do?' he asked.

'Go back to *him*, I suppose. There's nothing else for it. I thought if I just cleared off with the kids we could manage. But we didn't really have enough money.'

'We haven't got anywhere to sleep,' supplemented the girl called Penny as though it were time to get it all out. 'Nowhere.'

'I'm tired,' said the smaller girl beginning to wail again. Her mother and her sister fixed her with fierce glares. 'Just stop that,' said the former. 'When we've eaten we'll find somewhere . . .'

'. . . To lay our heads,' finished Penny reciting the words like a waif and looking challengingly at Nicholas.

'I'm sure we can do something,' he muttered desperately.

'You're a Samaritan,' sighed the mother in her soft Cockney. 'A real treasure.'

The pizzas arrived and the drinks and the family became silent except for the sound of their munching. Nicholas had eaten already but he had a slice of pizza to keep them company. His eyes went around the table. Every face was down, every mouth was full.

Then they had a big dish of chips, greeted with cheers, followed by cake and ice-cream. Then the mother said ominously: 'He's going to do it.'

'What?' enquired Nicholas although now he knew the answer before he had glanced around.

'A packet,' said the woman with a soft desperation. 'I can tell by his eyes. Look at them.' Everyone now concentrated on Tupper.

'They sort of swivel from side to side,' pointed out the helpful Penny.

Nicholas stared at the boy and saw his expression change, almost collapse. 'Too late,' shrugged Penny. 'He's done it.'

The boy was shaking his head lyingly. His mother half rose but then looked once again towards Nicholas. 'Will you take him?' she said. 'Please. I can't. Not in a posh place like this.'

Nicholas attempted a protest but he could not frame it. Tupper was already pushing his chair away and held out a trusting hand towards him. Deepily unhappy, Nicholas accepted it and led the boy towards the interior. 'Take a bag with you!' the mother called after him.

He returned grey-faced after ten minutes, Tupper visibly relieved and cheerful. 'I managed to get a bag,' Nicholas said realising that he was falling into their ways, entering their family. He had to escape.

'It's *such* a scream,' giggled the mother flapping her hand at him. 'I always take a supermarket bag with me when I go shopping. An extra one in case it happens, and it usually does, and one day . . .'

Every child's eye had turned expectantly to her laughter-crammed face. Penny continued the story for her: '. . . Somebody took the bag by mistake. . . .' Bonnie was convulsed, her flowered body quivering. '. . . Must have thought it was her own shopping. . . .'

Everyone around the table howled at the familiar tale. Nicholas could do nothing but join in. They had all finished eating and now every hopeful face was fixed on him again. He sighed. 'I suppose we'd better find you some accommodation,' he said. They broke into a round of applause.

He slept little that night. They were six in a bed, clinging like wrecked sailors to a raft. It was a king-sized bed but it was still crowded. The air conditioning laboured. The family's reputation had swiftly preceded them around the resort and reception-desk heads were shaken firmly. There was no room for them anywhere. His own hotel hesitated but by this stage Nicholas was as weary and fractious as the children. Bonnie was dispirited. 'I don't know what the world's got against us,' she complained. She looked around her small group as if counting them. The younger girl was sitting, legs wide, on the floor and weeping; the twins pulled a potted palm to the ground with the crash of a great tree falling in the jungle.

The late-night manager suggested the compromise. The family could share Nicholas's room for one night. It was big and so was the bed. Someone could sleep on the floor. It was only until tomorrow. Defeated, Nicholas agreed and they all trooped into the lift. Bonnie smacked the fingers of the twins as they reached together for the emergency button. Nicholas found himself herding them out on to the landing adding his own threats. The boys began to peep in at keyholes. Hurriedly he unlocked his door.

After exclamations about the luxury and size of the room

and after Tupper had been rushed narrowly to the bathroom, everyone was allocated a space in the bed. Nicholas found himself with the twins snoring crossways at his feet, and the two girls slept on the other side of their mother from whom he tried to preserve a decent space. Everybody slept except Nicholas. The twins kept clutching his feet. Bonnie snored luxuriously, the little girl sniffled as she dreamed. Only Penny was silent.

In the morning they were all subdued, as if they had taken part in a miracle. Someone had shown them kindness. It was not until breakfast that their spirits were restored. The twins went below the cloth and crawled under the neighbouring table occupied by an elderly English couple. The old lady squeaked and Nicholas had to retrieve the boys and apologise. 'Don't bring your wretched offspring here if they can't behave,' grunted the man.

Bonnie said: 'I'll telephone him this morning, Dickie, my husband, if I can use your phone.'

He said he would be glad for her to do so and he meant it.

'You're been ever so good,' she said turning her crumpled face to him. 'We won't bother you any more. I shouldn't have done it. I should have just got on with it like others do. Running away's not as easy as you think. Not for a woman.'

Three

When he said goodbye to them they engulfed him with their hugs and sticky kisses. Bonnie embraced him with huge softness, tears running down what appeared to be set courses in her cheeks. Big-eyed, Penny shook hands gravely before putting her arms out to him and the little girl, Trixie, sobbed inconsolably. Tupper and his brother were, for once, silent and inactive, simply looking at him.

Nicholas walked along the Torremolinos sea front in the morning heat, knowing a mixture of relief and loss. Looking back he saw they were stuck together in a clutch on the pavement, their faces towards him. Penny waved but the others just watched him go. He waved once.

The further he went the more assured he felt. Her summoned husband, reportedly as tear-stricken as the remainder of the family, was already on his way outward for what would no doubt be an emotionally wet reunion. Nicholas sighed and shook his head. He pushed on through the heated crowds; people in bright ugly clothing with bare and blistered flesh. It was only ten in the morning but some were drinking beer at tables overlooking the gritty beach and the harshly reflecting sea. The sun was pouring down and he was sweating. Never, he vowed, would he get involved, entangled, trapped, like that again. A man on the run had to keep free.

Scarcely had he made the resolve than he was halted by a shout from four men hunched around a table topped with beer glasses: ' 'Ere! 'Ello!' He stared in the direction of the call. 'It's our mate from Gatwick!' shouted the man who had recognised him. 'Just the bloke!'

Guardedly Nicholas allowed himself to walk towards them. 'I thought you were all off to Italy,' he suggested attempting a grin. Then, even more cautiously: 'To the battlefields.'

The old men exchanged grimaces and the man who had shouted, the one called Marshall, grunted: 'We was. So we *thought*.'

'We ended up here,' supplemented the one named Chalky White. His hair was the colour of his name. 'Big balls-up.' Fiercely he nodded towards Marshall. ' 'Is bloody fault.'

Marshall glowered. 'It weren't,' he complained. 'My stupid girl, my daughter. Reckoned she'd be clever so she booked us all here instead of Italy like usual.'

'Silly cow,' muttered one of the other men, his cheeks raw with the sun.

'All right, all right,' conceded Marshall edgily. 'I know what she is. And I told her when I phoned. Silly cow, right enough.' He returned his attention to Nicholas. 'Took it into her silly girl's head that we needed what she calls a *proper* holiday, not going looking at graves in Italy and that. I left her to do the booking. And this is where we end up.' He waved a large gnarled hand almost doubled to a fist. 'Look at it. Spanish Blackpool.'

'In an 'eatwave,' grumbled Chalky.

The one called Nobby Clark, more reflective, muttered: 'Trouble was, we thought we *was* in Italy.'

'Not for all that long,' argued Marshall shamefaced. He regarded Nicholas hopefully. 'Anybody would. The lingo sounds the same. All the signs on the shops and everything. . . . How were we to know?'

'We're stuck 'ere now,' said Nobby Clark peering into his glass. He manoeuvred a chair. 'Sit down. We happen to have a spare beer.' He nodded at a full tankard set, as though with a purpose, in the middle of the table.

Slowly Nicholas sat down and took a sip from the glass with a touch of suspicion. He surveyed the oddly expectant faces; it was as though he had by drinking committed himself to something. 'Where's your other mate?' he asked. 'There were five of you at Gatwick.'

'He's dead,' said Marshall bluntly but then lowering his veined eyelids.

'He went and died,' nodded Chalky White guiltily. Nobby said: 'Snuffed it.'

Carefully Nicholas lowered his glass. 'Oh, my goodness. That's terrible.'

Marshall said: 'We haven't told anybody yet.' He glanced at Nicholas and then at his friends. 'You're the first we've let know.'

The fourth of the quartet had said nothing and the others now joined him in his silence. A thin, cold hand knocked on Nicholas's heart. 'You haven't . . . reported . . . ? How long . . . when did it happen?'

'Not long,' said Chalky vaguely.

'This morning,' added Marshall as though deciding to come clean. 'Back at the lodgings. He's still there. Stiff as cardboard.'

'The trouble is we don't even know his *name*,' confessed Chalky. Nicholas felt his own eyebrows rise.

'We forget at our age,' explained Nobby. 'I forget my own name sometimes. We thought he was called Brownjer, but Chalky here reckons Brownjer died a couple of years ago.'

'I'm sure we went to his funeral,' pointed out Chalky. 'I *know* this bloke isn't Brownjer.'

'It's hard remembering funerals,' asserted Marshall and Nobby nodded. 'There's too many.'

Marshall lived up to his name by summarising: 'Anyway, the long and the short of it is, he's snuffed it. Gone, dead, whatever you like. He's in his room. And we don't know what to do next. That's why we're glad we saw you coming along.'

'You'll help us, won't you,' pleaded Nobby. He looked lost, weary, like a man who had walked a long way. He composed a brittle smile. Panic jabbed at Nicholas. He was the one who needed help. He turned his head both ways up and down the street. They were engulfed by people on holiday, people laughing in the hot daylight and drinking and shouting to each other in the various fractured accents of the British. His apprehensive eyes returned to the forlorn men at the table. 'Help us out,' said Marshall in his gruff voice. 'Be a pal.'

Nicholas put his head into his hands. How, why, did these things, these bits of madness seek him out? Bonnie and her brood were only somewhere up the street. 'I've only just . . .' he said looking up with a sort of entreaty. 'I've only . . .' It was no use. Mrs Ware and her offspring would be of no concern to them. It was a different crisis. 'All right,' he surrendered, surveying the anxious faces again. 'Where is he?'

'You're a good mate!' exclaimed Marshall rising and banging him on the shoulder. 'Ain't he?' he said to his friends.

'A good mate,' echoed Chalky.

Nobby said: 'A real friend in need.'

The silent man nodded.

Marshall got to his feet in stages and said: 'We'll show you 'im.' After a moment's consideration, and then apparently deciding it was well worth it, he paid the arriving waiter for the drinks.

'You're quite sure he's dead?' said Nicholas.

They paused and Marshall confirmed: 'Dead as dead.' He studied the old expressions of his comrades. 'We know it when we see it.' They nodded sombrely.

He led the way through the cafés and a street market and then, at the back of the town, up a dusty hill where dogs barked at them. Nobby kicked one of them. A hag squatting in a poor doorway guffawed toothlessly. The dog ran towards the doorway and then the woman kicked at it with ragged slippered feet. The Englishmen trudged to a battered and flaking door a few yards on, above which was a faintly visible sign: 'Hotel.' Marshall said: 'It's worse inside.'

There was a tight marble vestibule with a single chair, empty as though awaiting someone, a small, round table and a plant lolling in the heat. Light coming through a small window at the side made the scene, the chair, the plant, the table, like a still-life painting. 'He's upstairs,' whispered Marshall peering down the corridor and into the adjoining room with the expression of one who fears the worst. 'That's if they haven't found him.'

Heavy-hearted, Nicholas followed him up the narrow stairs to a landing with a single door, the others trooping behind, their feet trudging like a patrol. With a glance at Nicholas the bulky Marshall tapped gently, reverently. 'Just in case,' he explained. 'Mistakes 'ave been known.'

He need not have worried. Only silence was returned. 'We'd better go in,' said Nicholas eventually.

'You go,' amended Marshall. 'We'll be right behind you.'

Nicholas put his hand on the handle and turned it. He sensed the old soldiers shuffling back. The door opened and almost on tiptoe he stepped into the tight room. There was only space for a one-door wardrobe, a bedside cabinet and a bed beside which was a single chair like the one in the lobby. Clothes were haphazardly hung over this, a pair of grey trousers with the braces looping down to the floor. Eventually he brought his eyes up to look at the bed.

The occupant was undoubtedly dead. His face was set resolutely as if he had known where he was going, and the eyes stared out as if trying to see the place. 'That's him,' said Marshall from the doorway, removing the slightest doubt. The others remained behind him, their inquisitive and fearful faces protruding around the door-frame.

'He's certainly gone,' said Nicholas. He had never seen anybody dead before. His father had retained the privilege of a single peep into his mother's coffin before closing the lid with a bang of finality, leaving Nicholas, who was then seventeen, admiring the wasted workmanship of the casket.

'Poor old Brownjer,' said Chalky like a prayer.

'If that's *him*,' argued Nobby. 'I still reckon Brownjer went years ago.'

'Who *is* it then?' enquired Nicholas testily. 'If *you* don't know who does?'

'I don't remember his face from before,' admitted Marshall moving closer and, now more assured, examining it. 'Even at Gatwick I couldn't place him.'

Decisively Nicholas pulled the creased sheet over the defunct stare. This was a signal for Marshall to order gruffly:

'Attention!' Marshall himself straightened and his heels banged together. The others did the same. Nicholas opened the drawer in the shabby bedside table. 'Here's his passport,' he said taking it out. 'At least we'll know who he is.' He opened the document. 'Henry George Brownjer,' he recited. He looked around at Marshall. Marshall's eyes went back to the corpse and unconsciously summing up the situation, he muttered: 'At ease.' The old comrades stood at ease.

'There, I told you,' said Marshall to the other men.

'We must have buried somebody else two years ago,' ruminated Chalky. 'Poor old Brownjer.'

'What do we do?' asked Nobby. The fourth man had still said nothing.

Nicholas sighed. 'Well, the first thing is to tell the people here. The landlady or whatever.'

'She won't like that,' forecast Marshall firmly. 'Someone dying.'

'He paid in advance,' pointed out Chalky.

'She won't have any choice,' said Nicholas. Then firmly: '*You'll* have to get a doctor to certify him dead and get him away to wherever they take him. Then *you'll* have to notify his relatives.'

He turned to confront them, determined that this was as far as he was going, but their lined and baffled faces reduced him to sigh. 'Let's go and tell the landlady,' he muttered.

Obediently they stood back to let him pass. There was nothing for it. Perhaps people who journeyed alone were picked out by fate like this, running from trouble only to run into it again at full tilt. He puffed out his cheeks and descended the stairs. Soberly the others followed. Marshall closed the door with deference. 'Good bloke Brownjer,' he claimed loudly. 'I remember him now. He was at Anzio with us.'

They found a businesslike woman, pale and straight with severe black hair, adding up some figures in the confined room off the lobby. She looked up challengingly as they entered like a deputation and did not seem pleased to see them. She looked at Nicholas twice as if wondering how he had materialised.

'*Señora*,' he began.

'*Si?*'

'*Señora*. A person has died.'

'*No hablo ingles*,' she said shaking her head. Her hair came loose and she gathered it roughly and stuck it behind a pin. '*Paco!*' she bawled so violently she made them jump. '*Paco!*'

In his own time Paco appeared, a flabby, mournfully moustached man. His liquid eyes took in the scene. 'What is problem?' he enquired. 'This place not good?' He waved a sallow hand around the room.

'No, no,' Nicholas assured him. 'Place is fine.'

'It's all right,' confirmed Chalky White from the rear.

The Spanish woman's eyes, shot with suspicion, were going from one face to the next. Nicholas said to Paco: '*Señor*, I am sorry to tell you that one of these gentlemen is dead.'

Paco stared at the party, doubting his English. 'Which one?' he asked.

'No, I'm sorry. One of *their* party. Mr Brownjer. He is upstairs. And dead.'

Alarm flooded the man's face. '*Muerto?*' he said. The woman repeated '*Muerto?*' and crossed herself. She grasped Paco's hand as he was crossing himself too.

'*Muerto*,' agreed Marshall. 'Stone, cold, *muerto*.' He crossed himself solidly and all the old soldiers did too.

With an angry snap the woman stood and glowered at the men as if they had broken a window or set fire to their beds. '*Ingléses!*' she spat. They backed off. She pushed the hapless Paco in the direction of the stairs and strutted after him. Nicholas led the file of old soldiers into the lobby. The señora turned halfway up the stairs and curtly indicated that they should follow. They began to do so timidly.

With an attitude which suggested that she was going to settle this matter in an instant she threw open the door and stepped in. Then she stopped and briskly crossed herself again. Her eyes black, she turned and ordered Paco to go in before her. He did so, crossing himself as he went. The others, now crossing themselves too, followed carefully up the staircase. Having seen the truth, Paco turned pasty-faced and indicated that Nicholas should go into the room also. When he arrived the woman had shaken herself from her shock and, having produced a duster from her pocket, proceeded to wipe savagely around the poor furniture, pausing to pick up the late Brownjer's trousers and hang them in the narrow wardrobe by their braces. The legs sagged onto the floor of the cabinet giving the macabre impression of a hanging man. She then lifted the rest of the clothing, the shirt and pants and shrivelled socks and flung them in after the trousers before slamming the door.

Paco had remained as inactive as the clutch of Englishmen but the woman snapped another instruction and he obediently stepped forward and after a brief hesitation, lowered the sheet from the dead man's face. The Spanish pair confronted it with expressions of almost equal blankness before further crossing themselves. With a jerk of his mother's head Paco replaced the sheet, quite carefully.

'Your friend is dead,' said Paco as one wanting to clear up the matter. He pointed at Nicholas. 'You must call doctor, tell consul, and take him away. We need the room.'

Miserably Nicholas nodded: 'All right, all right.' He stepped aside as the woman inserted herself past him on her way out. She nudged the others with her elbows and Chalky White fell onto the stairs. She did not even glance at him sprawled on the treads but continued down to the lobby and turned into the room where they had first seen her. Paco regarded them with some sympathy once she had gone and even joined in helping Chalky to his feet. The Spaniard seemed to feel that some explanation was in order. 'In this house,' he said, 'my mother not like man to be dead.'

Gloomily Nicholas sat in his hotel room, the old soldiers sitting in attitudes of weary defeat about him. Outside the sun was brilliant and the street noisy. He picked up the telephone and dialled. It was answered promptly. Nicholas said: 'Hello. Good afternoon. Is that the British Consul? It's the office? Oh, right of course. I want to report the death of a British subject. He was on holiday.'

'Oh, bad luck, where did this occur?'

'Torremolinos,' Nicholas told him.

'The black spot. Three this month. What was the name?'

'Brownjer,' said Nicholas thinking of how inconvenient the dead were in so many ways. 'Henry George Brownjer.' He felt required to say something in mitigation. 'An old soldier.'

For a moment the man sounded faintly interested. 'Oh? Which regiment?' he asked.

'No idea,' answered Nicholas. 'I did not even know him. I'm just doing this as a favour. His friends are on the elderly side.'

'They should really stay at home,' confided the man. His tone remained confidential. 'We deal with their lost passports, lost money, lost memories.'

'This one's lost his life,' said Nicholas. The man hummed and said: 'Yes, well, you'll have to get a local undertaker to deal with it all. We can notify the family if necessary but generally people can do that themselves, the deceased's relatives or friends on holiday with them. There's quite a bit of paperwork needless to say.'

Nicholas replaced the telephone. The veteran soldiers were sitting on the bed which the night before had been crammed with Bonnie and her children. Their expressions, their expectancy, were themselves childlike. 'We've got to find out where his relatives are,' said Nicholas. 'Everything else can be taken care of apparently.'

'Even getting him home to Blighty?' queried Marshall with patriotic piety. 'I wouldn't want to leave anybody's bones here.' A difficulty occurred to him. 'I hope he was insured.'

The man who rarely said anything shifted uncomfortably. 'If these gentlemen would leave the room,' he intoned in a northern accent. 'I have something to say to this gentleman.' He pointed at Nicholas.

They all regarded him as if astonished that he could speak, and then looked at each other and at Nicholas. Marshall seemed about to comment but changed his mind. 'Retire,' he ordered instead and the rest of the party stood to ragged attention and left the room. Nicholas carefully went to the door and opened it a brief interval after they had closed it behind them. He discovered them crouched like a gunnery team with Marshall's ear to the keyhole. 'Why don't you go down to the bar,' he suggested to the apprehended stares. 'Have a beer each. I'll sign for them. We'll be down in a minute.'

They retreated, their initial shamefaced steps shuffling backward before they turned and went towards the lift. After pressing the button they stood in silence and Nicholas waited until the cage had arrived and the doors had closed on them before, with a loaded sigh, he returned to the room. The remaining man was short and spare and, despite his conversational reticence, wore vividly striped purple shirt and heavy English brown trousers held up by a snake-buckle belt.

'What did you want to tell me?' asked Nicholas. He sat heavily on the bed.

'He's my brother,' the man said bluntly. 'I'm John Brownjer and he is . . . was . . . Henry Brownjer. He was fully insured. I'll tell his missus.'

Nicholas had thought he was past surprise. 'But . . . why didn't you say so?' he said. 'All this time . . .' He spread his hands. 'Why . . . ?'

'Nobody asked me,' said the man. 'And you seemed to be managing. I sort of panicked inside.' He pointed to his chest. 'And when you turned up and was doing it all I thought I'd not say anything.' He hung his head. 'But I can tell Rose.' He looked up and there were red tears in his eyes. 'I don't know what she'll say, I'm sure but she's not going to be all that happy about it. She didn't want him to come. She'll probably blame me.'

They stood, a small uncertain group, in the great, all but empty, concourse of Pablo Picasso Airport, Malaga, their shapes vaguely reflected in Picasso-like shapes in the marble floor. Nicholas returned with their amended tickets. 'Everything all right?' asked Marshall doubtfully when he was still some yards distant. 'Are we off to Blighty?'

57

'You are,' said Nicholas gratefully.

'It's been the worst week of my life, including the war,' put in Nobby Clark. He picked up his doleful suitcase and sports bag with 'España' written on it.

Chalky White picked up his. 'That goes for all of us. Even including Anzio.'

'Anzio was bad,' pointed out Marshall.

John Brownjer, who had retired to his almost utter silence, broke it. 'It's been the worst week of my brother's life too,' he pointed out sadly.

Marshall patted his back like a comrade in danger of falling behind. 'Come on, mate,' he encouraged. 'At least we're taking him back with us.'

'In a box,' grumbled Brownjer looking around as if wondering where it was. 'I hope they don't forget to load him on.'

'It's on,' Marshall told him with a hint of grim satisfaction. 'I saw them carrying it.'

Brownjer said: 'He's only light.' He turned to Nicholas and said: 'Will you come too? I don't know how I can face Rose. Anything could go wrong.'

The reddened eyes fixed Nicholas beseechingly. Nicholas was about to protest when he realised that he wanted to go home. If not home, then back. He grinned and tapped the old man on the bony shoulder. 'All right,' he said firmly. 'Why not?' He turned and went back towards the ticket desk. He had only his briefcase with him but anything else he could leave at the hotel. Why not go back? Why not? He might even be able to go home.

'Funny bloke that,' decided Marshall as they watched him at the distant desk. 'He can do what he likes. Anything.'

'No obligations,' agreed Chalky.

'Plenty of money,' added Nobby.

Brownjer said: 'He's been good to me.' He surveyed them. 'To all of us.'

Nicholas returned with an animated step. 'Right, that's fixed,' he said. 'I'll ring the hotel. Then let's go and have a beer.'

They bought an extra beer for the deceased Brownjer, a sort of superstition left over, they claimed, from the days of battle. 'If anybody was missing, presumed killed, we always ordered a drink for him in case he turned up,' intoned Marshall who eventually drained the glass.

Nicholas drank his beer introspectively. He had turned so many corners in a few days that one more change of direction made little difference. He resolved to go home to see his children and allowed himself to imagine embracing Sarah in a joyously compulsive moment of reunion. Everything might be miraculously fine and forgiven. They would make a fresh start. A suspicion of happiness came over him.

It was quickly dispersed by the arrival in the refreshment area of Bonnie Ware and her family. He heard them coming; the tumult was unique. Tactically he shifted his chair behind the bulk of Marshall, the biggest of the men. It was too late to run. The family, piled with stuffed toys, garishly hatted, invaded the tables, the twins immediately crawling beneath one of them and pulling the chairs resoundingly to the floor. Bonnie, red as a plum, was smiling and sweating in her bulging dress. Penny, the teenager, tried to extract the twins, kneeling and attempting to pull them by their ankles. The smaller girl was sobbing and being carried in the tattooed arms of a tanned and sinewy man wearing jeans held up by a belt of dummy bullets. His hair was scant at the front and pig-tailed at the back, and he had rings in both ears. Bonnie bundled large, soft toys on the floor. The twins mounted stuffed donkeys and began prancing around the tables. Nicholas knew they would see him and they did. They bounced around the corner of the next table, shouting and urging the coloured donkeys on. Then they were face to face. They looked at him, directly into his eyes; he began a crooked smile. Then, with no further recognition they continued their race.

'Noisy little bastards,' complained Nobby.

' 'Orsewhipping they want,' grunted Marshall.

'Out of control,' said Chalky.

Nicholas kept his face close to his tankard but his eyes were

59

drawn towards the frantic family group. He saw the twins report his presence to Penny who glanced quickly, apprehensively, towards him. Watching her father, she sidled to her mother and whispered. Bonnie's flick of the eyes towards him was so momentary that he was hardly sure that she had looked at all. But her red face stiffened and she turned and put her fat arms around her husband who was wrestling with the bellowing twins. She had a black eye.

Laughing like a cavalier, the father embraced all of them around the table. He counted out some coins and Bonnie went to the bar counter. A moment later Penny followed her. While they stood waiting for their drinks, the girl turned and looked secretly and without expression towards Nicholas. Then she turned her face away. He felt a brief emptiness.

When the flight was called and the family's table was devastated with spilt orange juice, crisp crumbs and packets, the Wares rallied, got up and, hugging each other, went in formation towards the gate.

'That's ours, isn't it?' said Marshall finishing off the beer that had been reserved for a resurrected Brownjer.

'That's right,' confirmed Nicholas. 'But there's no hurry. Let those kids get aboard.' He had a knot of regret; seeing them like that hugging their earringed, tattooed, black-eye-giving father, returning to whatever hell they had fled, gave him a pang; he thought of filling in the dots and colouring the giraffes for the twins, the patience of Penny, the sobs of her sister, the fated hopelessness of Bonnie. But, for all of it, they were a family. They held each other up. He swallowed his beer and determined again to go back to his own.

Throughout the journey he could hear their commotion at the distant front of the plane. Once a stewardess came from there, distraught, with jam on her face and mayonnaise streaked down her dress. The father's rough shouts could be heard. Nicholas closed his eyes. He sat next to John Brownjer, the man unspeaking as his late brother travelling in the hold.

At Gatwick, Marshall, Nobby and Chalky left them abruptly with scarcely a backward glance. Nicholas, standing with the hangdog Brownjer, scarcely had time to shake their hands. 'Talk about deserters,' grumbled Brownjer. They had to wait until the coffin was unloaded from the plane and taken, almost smuggled, into a shuttered side room. Eventually a clerky looking man in a tight collar approached and ushered them in. 'It comes under freight,' he said rustling a sheaf of forms. The coffin was resting on trestles, with a label stuck on it which said: 'Priority.' Brownjer took the forms and was asking where to sign when the clerky man said: 'You'd better have a gander. He might not be in there. Funnier things have happened.'

With no change of expression, Brownjer stepped forward and the man opened the lid of the coffin with a touch of ceremony like a waiter raising a tureen. 'That's him,' said Brownjer decisively. 'I'd know him anywhere.'

As he said it the door opened and an airline official brought in a tear-stained woman. Brownjer just said: 'Rose.' She advanced on her brother-in-law as he let the coffin lid slam resoundingly closed. They half-embraced and both began to sob jerkily. The clerky man looked at Nicholas and shrugged. 'I was waiting outside, where they come out with their luggage,' complained Rose. 'I thought you'd be coming through.'

'You can't just come out like *that*,' said Brownjer. 'Not with a coffin.' He disentangled himself from his sister-in-law and turned to Nicholas. 'We'll be all right now,' he said gratefully. For the benefit of Rose he said: 'He's been helping.'

'We'll manage now,' confirmed the woman. Then without asking who he was she said: 'Would you like to come to the funeral? It's Thursday. You can if you like.'

'You'd make up the numbers,' Brownjer nodded. 'He didn't have many friends.'

Rose regarded him sharply but Nicholas intervened. 'I can't. It's very kind of you, but I can't. I'm . . . I'm off to America tomorrow.'

Rose eyed him speculatively. 'America? I wouldn't mind going there.'

'I'll be on my way then,' said Nicholas hurriedly. He shook hands with them and then, after some confusion, with the clerky man, and made for the door. There he turned and said: 'My deepest sympathy, of course.' Once outside he hurried, almost ran, towards the Customs, went swiftly through the Green Channel and then made for the train exit. There was the shuttle waiting to leave for Victoria. He got in and thankfully sat, alone at last and relieved. As the train travelled towards London through the deep greens of English summer fields he wondered over the events of the past few days; Bonnie and her family; Marshall, and his old misguided soldiers.

Through all the vicissitudes, the crises, the involvement, no one had asked him what he was doing alone in that Spanish town. No one had asked him where he lived or how he lived, how old he was, or if he had a wife. The old soldiers had never even asked his name.

Four

Harry the Night, arrived for duty at the hotel, polished his counter, frowning into it until he could clearly discern his frown, patted the pile of *Evening Standard*s, and opened his private niche to ascertain that his secret whisky bottle remained undisturbed. These routines accomplished he looked out into the darkened street in time to see the arrival of Nicholas.

'Ah sir, hello. And how was Luxor?'

'Never got near it,' sighed Nicholas prepared for the enquiry. 'Landed up in Spain.'

'A faulty compass perhaps,' suggested Harry. 'Or the natural deviation of the casual traveller.'

'Circumstances,' nodded Nicholas. 'Have you got a room?'

'We've got *your* room, I expect,' answered the porter glancing towards the reception desk. 'We do not appear to have been deluged with guests. We'll be down to playing patience on cards night.' He peered over the pulpit of his counter to the floor. 'And you do not seem to have added to your luggage.'

'It's less if anything,' admitted Nicholas. 'I seem to have lost a few bits and pieces on the way.'

They had his room. As he signed the register he wondered how many more times he would return to the hotel; a doleful thought occurred that this might now be his home. He trudged up the stairs, accompanied by Harry, who insisted on carrying his briefcase, and sighed as the porter opened the door. 'Just as I remember it,' he said wryly.

'Probably hasn't been slept in since,' suggested Harry. 'Will you be dining, sir?'

'Somewhere,' said Nicholas.

'Not here,' advised Harry lowering his tone, raising his eyebrows, and adding mysteriously: 'Enough is enough.'

He left and Nicholas sat on the bed facing the same mirror as he had viewed only a week before. The scene was unchanged. If anything he looked more pale and tired than ever. What was he to do? Where was he to go? His reflection provided no answer. Groaning he turned to lie on the bed. His eyes swivelled to the telephone. It had to be done some time.

'Hello, Sarah,' he said hopefully when she picked it up.

She waited and said: 'Hello, who's that?'

Nicholas gritted his teeth. 'This is me. You know who it is.'

'Who?'

'Oh for Christ's sake. It's Nicholas. You remember me.'

'Nicholas?' she repeated as though she did not. 'Oh, *that* Nicholas. Of course. I thought you were abroad. Luxor, wasn't it?'

'Well it was. But I didn't get there.'

'But I thought you'd be gone for ages, months, years. It's only been a couple of days.'

'It's more than that,' he said in a hurt way. 'Almost a week.'

'You can't have gone very far.'

'Spain. I went to Spain. No, I did not enjoy it, to save you asking.' His voice dropped. 'I want to come home.'

'Home?' she sounded shocked. 'Home? Here? But I'm sorry that can't be done. We're finished Nicholas. Done, finished, ended.'

He breathed deeply. 'I'm like a nomad.'

'You wanted to be one. Now you are. You can come and get your belongings if you wish, and your car. They're all ready for you.'

'I'd like to see my children. How are they?'

'Debbie's had a filling in her tooth. But otherwise they're thriving. If you'd like to visit them . . .'

'Oh, I would. When can I . . .'

'Access can be arranged through my solicitor,' she told him icily. 'You know who he is.'

'I know all right.' His tone hardened. 'I'll do that. And I'll come and get my belongings tomorrow. If it's not putting you out at all.'

'You won't be putting me out. In fact, I'll *be* out. Make it early afternoon. The children will be at school. Everything is loaded in your car, which is in the garage. The key's in the door. Help yourself. Please.'

He put the phone down several seconds after she had done so and muttered: 'Shit.' Then he picked it up again and dialled his agent. Paul Garrett did not like being called at home but that was too bad. 'It's me,' he said.

'Who?' asked Garrett.

'Don't you start. It's Nicholas Boulting. Surely *you* remember?'

'You've been speaking to Sarah.'

'How do you know?'

'You're still breathing flames.'

'I can't help it. She was so shitty.'

'I gather it's mutual.'

'You've spoken to her.'

'She's been bending my ear this past week. Where have you been?'

'It doesn't matter. Oh, well, Spain. Torremolinos. Go on, split your sides.'

'It doesn't sound like somewhere you could run away to.'

'It wasn't, believe me. Listen Paul, she's put all my stuff, all my belongings in my car and she says I can take it away.'

'Yes, I got the impression it might be a long-term separation. So you'll be domiciled elsewhere?'

'God knows where. I need to talk things over with you. My whole life.'

'What about lunch tomorrow?'

'I'm going to retrieve my knick-knacks tomorrow. She'll probably dump them otherwise. Lunch on Wednesday?'

'Fine. You can tell me then what you plan to do for the rest of your life. You've got to start writing soon. You have signed a contract. I've had Henry Newby of Mallinder's on. I could hear him tapping his foot.'

'Perhaps I should write a horror story.'

He went back to Boxley from Baker Street, the familiar stations along the line reversing themselves from the night he had left home. It was early on a summer afternoon, close and quiet. There were cricket matches in fields and children playing in urban parks. Disgruntled, he looked out of the opposite window but the train was passing a cemetery.

Boxley was in a suburban stupor, sun reflecting on roofs and roads, moping trees, shop awnings yawning, shiftless dust on the pavements, sweating men delivering crates at Sainsbury's. Nicholas felt oddly affronted that it was so the same, exactly the same, not a noticeable change in an entire week. Unchanging everydayness: the boredom of Boxley.

Moodily he walked from the station. A man he did not recognise waved to him with a newspaper from the other pavement and loped across through the sparse traffic, brandishing an empty straw shopping bag. The man, who wore a Royal Signals blazer and a white open-necked shirt, thrust out his hand effusively and for a moment Nicholas thought he was going to congratulate him on running away. The man's Adam's apple ran up and down his exposed neck. He said: 'Mr Boulting, just the chap! Doug Berry. I wanted to come and see you about forming a Neighbourhood Watch in your area. You remember I mentioned it at the meeting. I take it you'd still like to be involved.'

'Absolutely,' said Nicholas stunned by the enquiry. 'I'm right with you.'

'Good. You're just the fellow for it. You know, we need *responsible* people, people with a sense of *home*, if you understand me, with their feet firmly on the ground, with the welfare of their family at heart. There have been a further three break-ins this week. We don't want Boxley becoming like Chicago.'

'We certainly don't,' agreed Nicholas trying not to look the man in the eye. 'One Chicago is quite enough.'

Doug Berry hooked the straw bag over his elbow and rubbed his limp hands together. He wore a huge watch on a thin wrist. A posy of grey hair appeared from his open shirt-top. 'Excellent,' he enthused. 'When shall I call around?' He took a tiny diary from an inner pocket and squeezed his eyes at it. 'How about Tuesday? Would that suit? Monday's the council and Wednesday the Help for Africa Committee, and . . .'

'Tuesday's fine,' put in Nicholas quickly. Sarah might as well tell him the truth. 'Five thirty all right?' A touch of revenge; Sarah would be watching *Neighbours*.

The man giggled nervously. 'Well, my wife and I generally watch *Neighbours* at five thirty . . . but . . .'

'It will have to be then,' said Nicholas piously. 'I have to be at Watford for a charity meeting at seven. Replacement toes.'

'Good for you,' babbled the man. 'Yes of course. One episode of *Neighbours* is much like another, I suppose.'

'Tuesday, then,' said Nicholas firmly shaking hands again. 'Five thirty sharp. Watching *Neighbours* gives way to Neighbourhood Watch.'

Doug Berry laughed heartily and said: 'Very good, that.' Apparently pleased at the transmission of his keenness, he put his straw shopping bag on his other arm and strutted away. Nicholas felt a streak of mean satisfaction. But he progressed more gingerly now, spying into shop doorways. He wanted to avoid any further encounters but he missed the window cleaner fifteen rungs up a ladder outside the doctor's surgery. 'Hello, Mr Boulting,' called the man. 'Will you tell Mrs Boulting that it will be Wednesday before I can get around.'

'I will,' said Nicholas attempting breeziness. He quickened his stride. Had *nobody* noticed his absence? Running away to Luxor would have been wasted on Boxley.

He turned from the High Street into the road that had once been a lane, the way to his house. The still trees were loaded with leaves and dust, the houses kept their afternoon silence; there were a few parked cars and a dog which he recognised but which did not return the recognition, sitting staring at a cat it was too lazy to chase. His heart sank. What a place.

He knew the house would be empty. Sarah had said she intended to be out and she certainly would be. The children did not get back from school until four thirty. He walked towards the shut front gate of the Old Vicarage.

No house had ever looked so vacant, so indifferent. The lace curtains at the windows were like blind eyes, a new door knocker like a protruding tongue supplemented the chimes. It struck him as odd that the drive had been neatly and newly swept, not a leaf nor a petal on its surface. Someone had trimmed the yews. Who could have done that? Not Willie. He suffered an inward wriggle of concern.

The front door was concealed by yews so no one could witness his cautious approach. They certainly needed a Neighbourhood Watch. He frowned at the lock on the front door. It had been changed but the door, despite her boast, was the same. The new knocker and letter-box gleamed brassily, there was the same dull light behind the button of the chimes.

He lifted the knocker and let it drop. To his astonishment the door was opened almost at once and a long-haired youth in a striped apron stood there. He was holding a knife.

'She's not in,' said the big young man before Nicholas could recover. 'Who shall I say called?'

'Who are you?' asked Nicholas weakly.

'Me?' returned the youth as though no one had ever before wanted to know. 'I'm Dean. I work here.'

'Since when?' Nicholas tried to peer around the broad shoulders. The hall seemed unchanged.

'Last Thursday,' said the youth. Then doggedly: 'Who shall I say called?'

'Mr Boulting,' said Nicholas conscious of the ridiculousness of the situation. 'This is my house.'

Dean seemed disposed to argue. 'Well, I only do the garden bits and clean up a bit. I'm polishing the silver.' He held up the knife. 'I didn't even know there *was* a Mr Boulting. Mrs Boulting told my mother that she was a widow.'

'What!' Nicholas exploded. The youth blinked at his

ferocity. 'Well, that's what she said. How am I to know? Anyway she told me not to let anyone in.'

Nicholas controlled himself. 'I don't require to come in, thank you, sonny,' he said tersely. 'I'm just going to collect my car and my belongings from the garage.'

Dean brightened with comprehension. 'Ah, she did say some bloke would come for the car,' he said.

'Tell her the bloke took it,' retorted Nicholas.

He turned his back and strode towards the garage. He heard the door close behind him. As he had done so many times before he turned the handle on the garage door and listened to the remembered metallic sigh as he lifted it up and over. His car stood there under a thick covering of dust. It looked as if the contents of a week's Hoover bags had been emptied over it. He ran his finger down the coated back window and cursed.

Then he realised that the car was full, stuffed solid and to the roof, with his clothes and other belongings. He could see his golf clubs, their turtle heads projecting clearly over the driving seat, his skis were pointing to the roof. The ignition key was in the door and he hurriedly unlocked and opened it. A cascade of books and papers fell out. With a sick heart he viewed her ongoing revenge.

His suits were screwed into unimaginable bundles, arms in knots, his shoes piled on top, creased and filthy shirts projected from below the seats, there was a bouquet of ties. The rear window was stuffed with old garments, his weekend knocking-about stuff, even a pair of old rugby boots. Sarah had rummaged to the very attic and every remnant of everything personal he had ever owned was jammed in that car. He lifted some of the almost unrecognisable clothes from the front passenger seat. His old typewriter was revealed and a forgotten box of carpentry tools that he had once unrealistically bought at a bring-and-buy. With the deepest foreboding, he went around to the back of the car and opened the boot. It was packed with his books, his own book mostly, in several languages, all covered, as though with a tablecloth, with a big grinning publicity poster of himself—his nose now coloured red

– holding aloft his book with its title *Lying in Your Arms* outstanding. One copy, torn into pages, was on top of the pile. He almost cried as he surveyed the labour of hate. With a sob of disgust he closed the boot.

Attempting to make room in the driver's seat he uncovered a debris of framed photographs, each one with the glass splintered as though trodden by a sharp heel. Slowly he lifted one. Their wedding picture.

His eyes tightened as he tried to see through the perfect cobweb pattern of the glass. There they were close together, happily, idiotically, beaming towards their future. He lifted the rest of the photographs from the car. There were some with the children, one with Sir Handley Mallinder, the chairman of his publishers, and another taken at a fancy dress ball with Sarah as a pregnant princess and himself as a knight in tinny armour.

Suddenly furious, he flung the pictures into the corner of the garage. The glass splintered further and the frames broke. Then he went and carefully retrieved one of the photographs of the children from its askew frame and put it back in the car.

He had to make more room or he would not have been able to drive. He took out the gardening clothes, plus the bulky old typewriter, and put them against the garage wall, cursing as he did so. He burrowed a cavity in the rest of the jammed and jumbled contents and pushed into it the clothes and other items occupying the driver's seat. Then he climbed in among the rest of the stuff, and like a hedgehog in a hole peered out through the grimy windscreen. He turned the key in the ignition. The engine reacted at once; she would not have wanted to delay his departure. He had to be gone when she returned home. That was fine by him.

Like a man navigating a midget submarine through murky waters, he edged the car from the garage. Dean lumbered from the house and called: 'Want any help?' Nicholas muttered: 'Piss off.'

He knew he would not be able to drive like that for long, hunched and squinting through the windscreen. He just wanted to get clear of Boxley.

Somehow he crawled along the High Street and on to the main London road. He stopped at the first garage. The car was almost out of petrol. He pulled into the forecourt and at once evoked the interest of another driver filling up at the pumps. The man bent to examine the solidly packed interior and said: 'Gives a new meaning to the words "car boot sale" don't it?'

Nicholas responded through gritted teeth. He went to get a watering can. He washed and wiped the window as far as he could then again attempted to rearrange the debris within the car. It made little difference; there was still only a constricted driving hole. He filled up with petrol and oil and indignantly set out on the journey again.

Within a tentative mile a policeman he had no means of seeing came alongside him on a motor cycle and waved him down. Nicholas cursed again and pulled into the side of the road. The policeman parked his bike, removed his crash helmet and walked back with an expression of intense curiosity. Nicholas remained crouched and silent in his aperture while the officer peered into the crammed interior. His face was reddened by wearing the helmet. Stepping back as though he feared an avalanche, he said: 'Is this your car, sir?'

'It is,' replied Nicholas unable to alter his hunched posture. 'Unfortunately.'

'Not all that comfortable in there are we, sir?' the officer suggested.

'It's a bit crowded,' muttered Nicholas.

'You can't honestly see to drive, can you, sir?' said the man as though doing his utmost to be fair. He lowered his head and as far as was possible peered further into the car. 'You can't see out of the rear window through the mirror, you can't see the wing mirrors. In fact all you can see is ahead – just.'

'I was only going ahead,' smiled Nicholas lamely. There was no reaction to the joke. He tried to turn in the confined space. 'I've been kicked out,' he said miserably. 'Of my home.'

'I'd already worked out you were going *away* from somewhere and not *towards* somewhere, if you get my drift.' He seemed pleased at the deduction and Nicholas in climbing

71

from the car encouraged him with another weak smile. 'Everything but the kitchen sink,' quoted the officer with a big slow shake of the head.

'You could say that,' said Nicholas.

'How far were you going? Intending to, that is?'

'Baker Street area,' confessed Nicholas.

The policeman's face clouded with additional doubt. He opened the collar of his motor-cycle jacket and breathed more easily. 'I'll be glad when this weather changes,' he said. 'Baker Street you say.'

'That vicinity,' said Nicholas. 'You don't think I'll get there?'

The policeman tutted and moved his protruding head like a big, slow-motion puppet. 'Oh, dear sir,' he intoned. 'I can't see you getting there. If I don't nick you some other copper will. You're a sitting target. Asking for it. You don't have to be Sherlock Holmes to see that this vehicle is a danger to yourself and other road-users.'

'What do you suggest, officer?' asked Nicholas as though he imagined he might harbour special wisdom.

'I don't rightly know,' said the officer. 'All you can do is unload it. Otherwise you'll be nicked. By me for a start.'

He re-zipped his collar and with a salute that was half a warning went back towards his motor cycle. He had left his helmet on the seat and now donned it like a knight setting out to combat evil. With a final half-wave he drove off.

'Shit,' said Nicholas. 'Shit and shit again.'

He remained crouched without hope in the vehicle for another five minutes watching the uncaring traffic of outer London going and grunting along the road. Then he got out and stood by the car, leaning on its roof. He had stopped in a nondescript place. The afternoon remained warm and there was a cloud of flies sniffing around some rubbish on a ragged piece of wasteland by the road. The temptation grew on him to unload the cargo of his car onto the weed-choked ground and just abandon it there. What did he care anyway? Why not drive away and let someone else ponder the mystery of how a man's wardrobe, his golf clubs and his skis came to be piled in north-west London.

On the other hand it would be like tossing away yet another part of his life. His eyes hung in the heat. Like a crushed adventurer he saw, about a hundred yards ahead, the sun glinting on the glass of the open door of a public house, a projecting sign creaking in the dusty wind of passing traffic. It might have been beckoning. Nicholas stretched and went steadily towards it.

The bar was dim and grim. There was hard, dirty linoleum on the floor; the chairs, tables and bar stools were scratched. Sitting on a chair facing the open door was a solitary customer, a man as thin, threadbare and inert as the furniture. His face was like a wedge and his clothes stiff, although from the top pocket of his jacket hung a floppy handkerchief. 'Marmy!' he called.

A barman, who appeared to have been snoozing behind a curtain, appeared scratching his stomach. 'What'll it be?'

'Oh . . . a beer. Yes, bitter. Pint with a handle please,' said Nicholas.

'What did the rozzer want?' asked the narrow man speculatively lifting his glass and emptying it. '. . . 'Im wiv the bike.' The shaft of light from the door caught the side of his face, revealing a glinting squint.

'Thought I was overloaded,' said Nicholas sampling the unappetising surface of the beer. He took a warm mouthful. 'He's right, unfortunately. I can't see out of the car, except to the front and that's difficult.'

'What you got in there then?' asked the barman. He leaned forward over the bar to peer up the road.

'Clothes, personal stuff. Golf clubs. Skis. All sorts.'

'Movin'?' guessed the man with the handkerchief.

'Moving out for good,' confirmed Nicholas.

'Matrimonial,' guessed the barman like someone familiar with suffering. 'I went around to get my pigeons and she'd gone and let them out. They came back like they always will. But I was never there when they came back and she'd let them out again. Bloody spite.'

The seated man had heard it before. 'So what you goin' to do?' he asked Nicholas.

'God knows. I was thinking of dumping the bloody lot on that bit of ground over there and just driving away.'

'Somebody would 'ave it,' said the barman thoughtfully.

The glinting eye of the other man was fixed on the distant car. He said: ' 'Ow much do you want for it?' His attitude suggested that he liked to do quick, direct business. 'Buying and selling, me.' He glanced at the barman. 'Ain't I, Marmy?'

'Buys and sells,' attested Marmy. 'That's 'is line.'

The thin man rose looking even more sparse than he did sitting down. He tugged at his decorative handkerchief. 'Let's 'ave a butcher's,' he suggested.

Nicholas fumbled and mumbled like a misunderstood foreigner, 'Sell it? . . . But I never thought of *selling* it . . .'

'Just now you was thinkin' of chuckin' it away,' pointed out the prospective buyer. He seemed to make a decision to put things on a more intimate but formal basis: 'I'm Mr Kirkpatrick, by the way.' He projected a hand which came like a rod from his coat sleeve.

Nicholas shook the hand. It was oily. 'Oh, yes. How do you do. I'm Nick Boulting.' He shook the barman's hand too. 'Marmaduke,' said the man. 'Known as Marmy.'

'Let's 'ave a gander anyway,' said Kirkpatrick. He became even more businesslike to the extent of taking some greasy steel-framed spectacles from his pocket and fixing them on his straight nose. They went together out of the bar.

'Like the Sahara,' observed Mr Kirkpatrick hunching his shoulders. 'Don't suit London, this 'eat.'

Nicholas agreed vaguely. How could you just sell your clothes? They were approaching the parked vehicle. Mr Kirkpatrick leaned forward as he advanced so that he could see through the window. 'It *is* bunged up,' he said in the concerned voice of a doctor examining a windpipe.

'I'm not sure I want to sell,' ventured Nicholas. 'I may just park it and come back with a taxi.'

'Do you really *want* this stuff?' asked Mr Kirkpatrick

suddenly and shrewdly. 'Why not get shot of it now? I'll give you a fair price. You can start again, all over.'

Nicholas crumpled. Why the hell not? He opened the car door. The other man's thin hand probed quickly, feeling the fabric of the nearest overhanging jacket. He grunted and pulled the garment away from the entangled bundle. He then held it out by the arms. 'Oh dear,' he grumbled like a fashion expert. 'Nobody wears this sort of gear nowadays.'

'There's newer stuff in there,' said Nicholas aggrievedly. 'Quite new anyway. Suits and sports jackets. I always keep things a long time.'

'That's what I mean. Who wears them? I don't for a start.'

Nicholas took in the man's miserable attire and Mr Kirkpatrick noticed. 'My working gear this,' he said. He peered into the car again. 'Three hundred quid for the lot,' he said.

'Three hundred!' echoed Nicholas. 'Each of these suits cost . . . !'

'Listen, that was *buying*. This is *selling*. You want to start your life again or not?'

'What about the skis and the golf clubs?' argued Nicholas.

'All right, keep them if you want. I've just given up golf and ski-ing. Three 'undred and fifty for the clobber.'

'How much for the lot?' said Nicholas. 'Five hundred?'

The man shrugged. 'Four 'undred. That's final. I'll take the chance. Drive over in the pub yard. We'll dump off your previous existence in there.'

Paul Garrett was sitting in his habitual corner of the restaurant. Nicholas knew which way to turn when he entered. Garrett had lunch in there every day, often gazpacho and sausage and mash with two glasses of wine and one of mineral water, although in cold weather he had been known to order oxtail soup. He was tall and lean, almost languid, with greying hair and moustache. He dressed elegantly, but with clothes he appeared to have owned for a long time. He picked his way through life with a casual care.

'You don't *look* any different,' he said studying Nicholas wryly and moving up on the banquette seat.

Nicholas took the seat opposite. 'It's only been a week,' he responded. 'It just *seems* like years.'

The waiter came and Garrett ordered a bottle of wine. He said: 'But I've got a meeting right after lunch.'

It was early and only two other tables were occupied. 'Guess what she did? Guess what?' began Nicholas.

'Put a match to your best suit,' guessed Garrett in his unemphatic way. 'After dousing it with petrol.'

'You're not far wrong, Paul.'

'Attack the clothes, attack the man,' murmured Garrett. He looked pained. 'It's as if they can imagine the husband wearing them. Molly chopped up all my shoes. Every pair I possessed. Fishing waders, dancing pumps, everything. Even my bedroom slippers. I had damn all to put on my feet.'

Nicholas added: 'Mine put everything I had, clothes, golf clubs, the lot, skis even, and jammed it all in the bloody car,' he said. 'Screwed up to hell, tied in bundles. The arms of the jackets in knots, I tell you.' He gritted his teeth. 'Bastard.'

Garrett tutted as the waiter brought the wine. 'Never call a woman a bastard,' he admonished. 'It shows you up in a bad light. Only men are bastards.'

'I meant the situation,' amended Nicholas. 'It was a bastard. There was I stuck on Hendon Way with a copper telling me the car wasn't fit to drive.'

'What did you do?'

'Sold the whole damned lot to a rag-and-bone man.'

Garrett smiled approvingly: 'Hmm, I like that. You should put that in a book some time. All this adversity might be very useful for fiction. Don't just write it off. Write it.'

Nicholas grunted. 'I'm not likely to forget it.' They toasted each other. Garrett with a smile, Nicholas forlornly. 'Bastard,' he repeated. 'That's what it is.'

They ordered lunch. Garrett asked for gazpacho and sausage and mash. 'I like to come in early,' he said. It was as if some explanation were needed. Nicholas ordered smoked salmon and liver and bacon. 'How was . . . wherever it was you ran away to?' asked Garrett.

'I intended going to Luxor but I ended up in Spain, Torremolinos,' muttered Nicholas doggedly.

'Anyone can make a mistake.'

'Mistakes,' corrected his client. 'A whole catalogue of them. Jesus, I somehow became attached to a big blowsy woman with a ready-made horror family. One of the twins kept crapping. It was hideous. When I escaped from them I found myself landed with the corpse of an old soldier and the worries of all his mates.'

'These things happen,' said Garrett examining him calmly.

'They certainly did to me.'

'What are you going to do now? Get to Luxor?'

The waiter came with their dishes. Garrett tested the cold soup as if it were of a certain vintage. He did it every day and the waiter hovered until he had approved it with a raising of the eyes. 'Is it cold enough?' asked Nicholas. He was unsure whether the Luxor remark was a joke.

'Luxor is *out*,' he confirmed. 'For the time being anyway. I'm going to have to stick it out here. I'll need to find somewhere to live.' His voice dropped. 'I won't ever be able to go home again.'

The self-pity was not lost on Garrett who glanced up with a touch of sympathy, holding a pale pond of soup in the bowl of his spoon. He returned it carefully reuniting it with the soup in his dish. 'Don't fret Nick,' he comforted. 'She'll have you back. They nearly always do.' He gyrated his soup and took another spoonful which he held halfway to his mouth. 'Do you love Sarah?' he asked.

'She's my wife.'

'That's no answer.'

Nicholas found himself watching the spoonful of gazpacho as it rose to Garrett's lips. 'I can't understand what you see in that stuff,' he said.

Garrett glanced at the soup with some surprise. 'Water,' he said. 'And small bits of veg.' He took a further mouthful. 'Well?' he persisted.

'Sarah? Oh, well, I do. She's my wife and that *is* an answer, whatever you like to think. And there's Deborah and Willie.'

'And the cat and dog, and the table lamps, the new telephone table, the pictures on the wall, and the rest of it.'

'We don't have a cat and we don't have a dog,' Nicholas told him firmly.

'Maybe you ought to get one of each,' suggested Garrett. 'Animals make good cement for marriage. Very often they're harder to leave than wives or children. There's many an absconding husband been stopped in his tracks by the soulful look of a mongrel. My only regret in leaving Molly was that I couldn't take my St Bernard with me.' He had finished the soup at last. Nicholas had barely started his smoked salmon. He began to slice it.

'All you want,' summed up Garrett, 'is your wife, your children, your home . . . and your mistresses.'

Nicholas sighed. 'I suppose that's it.'

'It doesn't seem an unreasonable list,' said Garrett. 'But it's difficult. Ask any man who's tried it.' He glanced over the restaurant. It was filling now. 'Over there,' he said, 'is Gordon Phipps. He was once a client of mine. Every time he comes in here he's got a different woman with him. He feeds half the female population of London. I don't know how many seductions he achieves by these lunches, but he works hard at them. And he has to make his move at lunchtime. In the evening he has to go home to his wife Stella.'

Glancing carefully Nicholas said: 'Today's is no raving beauty.'

'That's Stella,' shrugged Garrett.

Their main dishes arrived and Nicholas watched as Garrett sliced up his sausages and arranged the pieces like battlements around the mound of mashed potatoes. Garrett observed his attention. 'You tend to play these games when you eat alone,' he confessed with an unsure touch of embarrassment. 'I still play soldiers with my bread and butter and boiled eggs.' He firmly changed the subject. 'So what are you going to do? When you walk out of here today, Nick, you've got to start *doing* something. Begin a new life. A temporary new life, anyway.'

'I don't know how,' said Nicholas.

'Well, you could start by writing another book. Mallinder's would be pleased and I would be relieved. At least write another title. Forget *Falling from Grace*. Forget *Dancing with Delilah*. Start on something new.'

'I know you're right,' nodded Nicholas. 'I got distracted.'

'You got yourself an office where you never did a stroke. Or not any strokes to do with earning a living. You've spent your time mucking about. So far, all right, you've been living off one book. But *Lying* won't keep you forever. Fortunately I think I've sold it for a film.'

Stunned, Nicholas looked up from his plate. 'A film?' he repeated. 'A real one?'

'As far as any of them are real,' said Garrett. 'And it's only an option. Herald International. They're a *real* company. They've actually *made* a couple of films. *Green River* was one. With Will Thingy. And that dopey-looking girl. . . .'

'How much?' asked Nicholas leaning forward.

'I asked for twenty-five thousand for the option. Dollars. We might get twenty. Maybe only fifteen. But at least that means they're serious. When it's made, if it's ever made and most of them aren't, they'll cough up two hundred thousand and five points . . . five per cent of the producer's profits, which because film companies have unique ways of accounting, you'll never see.'

'But . . . this is marvellous,' breathed Nicholas. 'Why didn't you tell me before?'

'I wanted to enjoy your troubles,' said Garrett. He demolished one of the sausage battlements. 'It still may not come off. They're very ephemeral, these people. Don't believe it until you see it on the screen.'

'I won't,' beamed Nicholas. 'But . . . by God, that's given me a fillip, I can tell you.' Then he said: 'Perhaps I ought to ring Sarah.'

Garrett regarded him grimly. 'The less Sarah knows about

your finances, the better, at the moment. This is not taking sides. You've been a shit, Nick. But now it's *done* and that's all there is to it. You've got to do the right thing by Sarah but I should put her on the back burner. Let her simmer for a while.'

'You're quite right,' acknowledged Nicholas slowly. 'You'd have been able to handle the whole thing better than I did.'

Garrett sniffed over the last outpost of sausage. 'I'm the man who had his fishing boots decimated, remember.' He consigned it to his mouth and said while chewing it: 'I've got an idea where you can go for a while. You can't stay in that hotel forever.'

'Oh? Where's that?'

'There's an American, a writer, although I've never heard of anything he's written. Sol Solomon. It can't be his real name unless he had cruel parents. Anyway he's renting, or been lent, or something, a sort of duplex, at Little Venice, just alongside the canal. He told me that he would like to sub-let half of it and I thought of you. Otherwise you are going to have to take on one of those service flats, and they're soulless. I know, I tried it once. It was like living in an empty box.'

'I certainly wouldn't want that.'

'The only way you could move into an apartment, a proper apartment, would be to take on a lease and that's six months at the least.'

'And I may be safe back home by then.' Nicholas looked for encouragement.

Garrett regarded him sagely. 'You got found out. You ran away. Next time wipe your ears.'

Sol Solomon had an extensive bay window in his borrowed place and he saw Nicholas coming. 'I was just looking down on those people in the boats,' he said. 'Take a look.' Nicholas peered down over the late afternoon street and on to the decorated roofs and decks of the barges moored to the side of the canal. The high Victorian street had trees leading up to the traffic of Edgware Road. The severed tops of red buses moved over the canal bridge. It was a heavy day with an excellent

80

chance of rain. A sluggish worker in a yellow plastic breast-plate swept summer leaves and rubbish in the street below.

'They got flowers on the decks,' pointed out Sol. 'Whoever heard of flowers on a boat?' Despite his earlier remark there were no people to be seen. 'Listen, I don't know about boats but I *do* know you can't grow flowers on them.'

'Those barges never go anywhere,' said Nicholas.

'They stay right there? I should have noticed.'

'Yes. They never move.'

'Jeez. Why live on a boat, a barge, if it never sails any place? It's like . . . like . . .' His struggle was ended by abrupt inspiration. 'Taking a nun to the Ritz. You get nowhere.'

He turned hurriedly from the window and went to the word processor, a neat laptop, on the desk beside the window. He touched the keys for a few seconds. 'Never waste a crumb, that's the name of the game.' He looked sharply at Nicholas. 'You don't say much. You're not gay, are you?'

Nicholas blinked at the directness. 'I haven't had much chance to speak,' he said. 'I'm not gay. I'm a closet womaniser. And my wife has just opened the closet. Anyway I don't know what one thing's got to do with the other.'

Sol grimaced. 'One with what other?'

'Being gay and not saying much.'

The American laughed. He had a circle of greying hair surrounding a brown baldness. His eyes were bright but shored up by heavy bags. A cowboy moustache hung over his mouth so that when he smiled only his bottom teeth showed. 'I like you,' he said decisively. 'We're going to get on fine. I've no objection to gays but I need my sleep. A writer needs his sleep.'

Nicholas was about to ask what he was writing when the American picked up a sheaf of paper and thrust it at him. 'You've never read a script like that, nor will you ever. *When Elephants Love* it's called. Greatest thing I've ever done. And that's saying something. It just needs a little work.'

'Who is it for?'

Sol eyed him and said: 'That's confidential, even to you. Now, you want to see the apartment. You have the lower floor.'

There was an open central staircase and Sol went down it briskly. 'There's a door, see?' he said opening it. 'So we can have separate parties. Get me? Even if you have company I still have to come through your place to get to mine. Okay? But if I get some girl up here then you don't have to horn in on it.'

Nicholas followed him through the door. The London daylight filled the window and splashed areas of pale yellow around the walls. 'Nice hey?' said Sol. 'Real nice. Did you ever see furniture, chairs and stuff, this nice?'

'Why are you splitting it up?' asked Nicholas.

Sol looked sorry he had asked. 'Okay, I'll level with you. I need the dough. Several of my projects have been stalled. You know how it is. One day the boss is the boss and the next he's the ex-boss, out on his ass. That's films all over. I'm working on a novel, two in fact, as well as the scripts and I write music too. I write great music.'

'So we go halves with the rent.'

'Not quite halves. We got to start by being honest, Nick. I don't pay rent. The company I'm writing one new script for, it's a great story about a guy who's headless. They got faith in me, I showed them my credits, and they let me have the apartment for free. I only just moved in, so you're lucky. It's a hundred a week, special deal.'

'I'll have it,' said Nicholas.

Sol twirled the spaghetti around his fork with the deftness of a practised harvester. 'Now this is nice,' he said looking around. He took in the faded red-and-white checked curtains of the Carla Rosa Restaurant. 'It's great the way the drapes match the cloths on the tables.' He ate a bale of spaghetti appreciatively.

'It's cheerful,' conceded Nicholas.

'So I should care if it's not? Any time I get taken to dinner, or lunch, or breakfast even, though I've never been to breakfast, it being too early in the day, any time is nice.' He looked up warningly. 'We'll make a deal, okay. You buy the groceries, I do the cooking. I'm a great cook. Just a natural. The Michelangelo of the Microwave.'

82

'How,' asked Nicholas, 'have you been living?'

'Until one of my projects comes good?' It was a question and an answer. 'Or until they stop firing the executives who love my work . . . ? Well, I have a system. Projects. That's the word. You have to have enough *projects*, even if you don't have the scripts, in fact it's better without the scripts because then you don't have to write them. Say you've got twenty, all right fifteen, *projects*, maybe they're just titles. I'm great at titles. I wrote a play once called *The Deer and the Antelope Play*. How about that?'

He rewound his fork and drank some more red wine. 'Love the vino,' he said. He waved the loaded fork. 'So you have, say fifteen, okay twenty, projects, all in different parts of the world, L.A., New York, London, Alássio . . .' He attacked the spaghetti then continued. 'That's Italy, Alássio. I had a project there once. A play. And it was *done*. Produced, staged. Great project. *The Duck and the Devil*, it was called. Sensational. Okay, so each of these places you have something cookin' and when something's cookin',' he grinned coyly at the looming joke, 'you can eat. You *call* people, producers, people who *think* they're producers, directors, people who *think* they're directors, but they got no sense of direction. All of them, writers too, co-writers especially. Actresses. You just keep them warm. Sometimes you get accommodation, like I have currently. And every place you go you can *eat*. Sometimes . . .,' he looked doubtfully around the tatty room, '. . . sometimes real good.'

He had disposed of another load of spaghetti and now he patted Nicholas's wrist with his empty fork. 'I don't count you, in this situation, because we're buddies. But that's how it's done.' He lifted the fork as if it were a telephone. 'Hi Tom. Hi there! Have I got news on the movie! We're ready to go! Two months at the most. Sure, two months. They're building Sodom right now, this minute. Okay, let's have lunch and I'll give you the news.' He studied Nicholas seriously. 'You get a hell of a lot of food that way.'

Nicholas grinned at him. 'And accommodation.'

'That's different, something else. Serious. This current

project is *good*. I feel it's good and so do they. They want it, they even need it. So they give me the apartment so I can work. And have I been working . . . ? Well, you saw. You saw me, didn't you?' He paused and his voice quietened. 'How come you need somewhere? So your marriage broke up, but that happens, all the time to everybody. There's nothing new there. So she caught you playing around. End of the week, so you go back. Everything's okay again.'

'Not with my wife,' sighed Nicholas. 'It's all gone, finished.'

'It's tough, I never have a lot to leave behind but I can understand.' He began to survey the dessert menu. 'Apple pie,' he murmured. 'My mother used to make apple pie.' A thought struck him. 'And you've got kids. You're going to have to see them, take them out to waxworks and things. That's hell for everybody.'

'I don't see it like that,' pointed out Nicholas. 'I miss my kids.'

'I bet. I guess you miss your backyard too. Things like that. Your shrubs. But the name of the game is that you can't have everything, man. *Nearly* everything, but not everything.' He ordered the apple pie with ice-cream. 'You're not having a dessert?' he enquired.

'I think I'm getting my deserts,' said Nicholas sombrely.

Sol regarded him with a little admiration. 'Good, very good. Write it down. I can tell you're a writer. Deserts. Shit, that's good. That's so good.'

He spooned the apple pie into his mouth while Nicholas watched. 'How about the chicks, the girls?' Sol wiped the ice-cream from his chin. 'The ones she caught you out about. They still around?'

'There was only one at a time,' Nicholas answered primly. 'And they were well spaced-out. I didn't make a huge habit of it.'

'Just a little light relief,' nodded Sol.

'You could say that. There's nobody now.'

'Women move on,' observed Sol. 'Like life itself.' He became thoughtful, asked the passing waiter for a pen and wrote the

84

thought on the back of the menu which he tore in two, putting half in the pocket of his jeans. He picked up the other half and put it back on the table.

They had coffee, Sol three cups because he said they made outstanding coffee, and then two scotches each before Nicholas settled the bill and they went out into the indifferent summer night. 'I need to buy you a drink,' said Sol as though the decision had been long-brewing. 'You're a good guy, Nick. We're going to get along. And we're going to find some women, some *additional*, *new* women.'

He changed direction unerringly into the doorway of a pub at the corner. 'Here be women,' he said as an aside as he paused at the step. 'That's another title,' he reflected approvingly. '*Here Be Women*! I don't know how I think of them.'

He pushed the door. The bar was thick and full. A woman shouted at him: 'You promised you'd marry me!'

'A misunderstanding,' Sol called back. She was shaped like a box, pallid, with crimson lips. There was another woman with her, thin and with an equally ashen face slashed with red. A heavy man in a Salvation Army teeshirt and mass of tangled hair was lolling against her. Sol appeared to have forgotten Nicholas. Edging towards the distant end of the bar Nicholas found a vacant stool next to an elderly man who was studying the last vestige of a cigarette. Behind the bar there were mirrors and shelves, on them the various brewery ornaments and display bottles and a toby jug. Nicholas ordered a scotch. He could hear the woman Sol had promised to marry laughing coarsely. He asked the elderly man if he would like a drink and, after a moment of surprise, the man agreed to accept a double Grand Marnier. The barman blinked. Nicholas paid.

His new drinking partner raised the glass, pushing his half-pint tankard disdainfully to one side, and stubbing out the shred of cigarette. 'First bloke that's spoke to me all night,' he said. 'Very decent. Cheers.'

It was some time before they spoke again. 'It must be lonely being a toby jug,' said the man eventually indicating the shelf behind the bar. 'And I know how it feels. I've got a talent for loneliness. I can be lonely at a football match.'

Nicholas saw Sol approaching. The American slid through the crowd. 'I was going to buy you a drink, remember,' he said. He glanced at the lonely man and the glasses on the bar. 'But somebody got there first.'

'Would you like one?' asked the stranger. 'He'll buy you one.' He nodded at Nicholas. 'He's a decent man.'

'I know that,' said Sol accepting the invitation. The stranger agreed to have another. 'Now you do have your key?' asked the American solicitously. 'I don't want to wake you.'

Nicholas had his key. 'You'll be late then,' he said.

'I'll walk her home. I know her from before.'

'You said you'd marry her,' pointed out Nicholas.

'That's a mistake for a start,' put in the ancient stranger. 'I always bang them but don't marry 'em.'

Sol glanced at him. Then he turned to Nicholas again. 'It was a joke. She knows it was a joke. I said I'd go to her place because she wants to be a writer.'

'The lady by the door?' enquired Nicholas flatly.

'That's her.' He slapped Nicholas firmly on the shoulder. 'Aw, come on. She'll never look like Jackie Collins, but who cares? I don't. It makes no odds.' He tapped Nicholas more gently. 'Don't wait up,' he advised.

When he was gone, burrowing through the crowd again, Nicholas said goodnight to his drinking companion, who appeared a trifle disappointed, and went out into the damp air. The canal glowed spectrally but there were orange lights in the windows of one of the moored barges. He went close to the railings and peeped through. A man and a woman, her solid arm around his solid shoulder, were watching television. He walked away and let himself into the main door of the empty apartment.

His bed felt like a dead body. There was a telephone but he could think of no one to ring. The curtain did not close properly and a stream of light tipped into the room. He cursed and lay back and after lying unhappily thinking for half an hour, drifted into sleep.

Forty minutes later he was abruptly roused by Sol crashing through the room accompanied by the square dark woman who giggled every time he stumbled. 'Look at that, you got a spotlight,' pointed out Sol as Nicholas sat up tiredly.

'The curtains don't pull,' grunted Nicholas.

'He does!' howled the woman hideously. '*He* pulls.' Sol was towing her behind him up the stairs.

'G'night partner,' he called back. 'Tomorrow we start our epic. The greatest story ever written.'

'Knackers!' shouted the woman.

The door slammed and Nicholas lay back again with a deep, sad sigh. The light was now across his face and he realised that it must be a moon which had not been in the sky when he left the pub. Either that or the street lights. He closed his eyes and muttered miserably: 'I want to go home.'

Five

He had begun to fear the telephone; both answering it and making a call. Now his hand hovered over it, and he had to push his finger out to tap the number. They took a long time to reply. Outside it was a dumb day and then he noticed that the trees along the canal were a deepening gold. It was amazing, when life was so much trouble, how easy it was to overlook the passing of the seasons. It was not long to Christmas. Where would he be at Christmas?

'David Fawkes and Company.'

'Ah yes. There you are.'

'Here we are. To whom did you wish to speak?'

'David Fawkes please.'

'He's due in court but I may catch him. Who's calling please?'

He gave his name and the girl who was not up-to-date, giggled and said: 'Sneaking off to play golf again you two?'

'No. Not this time, dear. Will you put me through.'

Fawkes kept him waiting. Nicholas had to be careful what he said. Things went wrong on the telephone; there was so much scope for them to go wrong. He had even begun to feel that his crisis with Sarah, his parting from his home and family, was the fault of the telephone. The telephone can endanger your happiness. People said things they did not mean, or only half-meant, or they heard things differently. Matters became mangled across the wires. Face to face was better, even if it were more of a physical trial, or letters. Yes, letters were the answer. Before the telephone people always wrote to each other and had time to consider their words. Not now. Bloody telephones. . . .

'Hello, David Fawkes speaking.' The voice was artificially strong. 'It's Nicholas Boulting, I understand.'

'That's me,' Nicholas responded his heart already grim. 'I used to be Nick, remember? And you were called Guy. Guy Fawkes.'

There was an unpleasant pause. Then Fawkes said: 'I'm afraid that's in the past. I am acting for your wife in her divorce proceedings.'

'Why didn't you act for me? You played golf with me, not her.'

'That, as I have just said, is in the past. Now what can I do for you? I'm due in court at ten.'

The silence now came from Nicholas. He thought he was going to choke. They had won the Fothrington Cup together. 'I'm ringing to find out if I can see my own children,' he muttered eventually.

'You are entitled to access,' said Fawkes in the same tone. 'Reasonable access. When would you like it to be? Sunday is the usual day.'

'All right, Sunday. If it's all right with you.'

Fawkes took the sarcasm seriously. 'It's your wife who has to say whether it's all right. She must agree and, indeed, so must the children. I only give advice.' Nicholas recalled how he had sunk the last putt in the Fothrington and how they had hooted and embraced. Fawkes said: 'I'll call you back this afternoon. Can you give me your telephone number, please.'

Nicholas gave it to him. 'Have a nice time in court,' he said.

His children were already standing outside the door of the house when he walked between the yew trees. Sarah had closed it behind them and they stood in their new clothes, watching him with apprehensive eyes. He wondered if they felt like he did. Deborah was wearing a short skirt and her hair was different. She seemed to have grown up in a couple of weeks. Willie smirked nervously over the rim of his camel polo-neck sweater.

Deborah was taut when he kissed her but he felt her soften

when he held her a moment longer. Willie said: 'Where are we going to lunch?' Somewhere, from one of the windows, Nicholas sensed Sarah was watching.

'Have you still got the same car?' asked Willie as Nicholas ushered them down the vicarage path.

'Of course he has,' admonished Deborah. She looked at her father, her eyes wet. 'You have, haven't you.'

Nicholas turned from her face and said: 'Same car. Same me.'

They climbed in with him. 'Mum said to sit in the back together,' announced Willie.

'If that's what she says,' said Nicholas dispiritedly. He could imagine her telling them the rules of this new game, as set out by David Fawkes. Starting the car he drove up the old road and into Boxley High Street dead with Sunday.

'I got better marks for maths,' ventured Deborah. 'And I did some sketches of St Albans. We had a school trip.' She said it as though she wanted to get it over.

'Billy Proctor fell out of the window at school,' put in Willie more convincingly. 'They reckon he was lucky to live.'

Nicholas, peering at his son in the mirror and attempting to prolong the conversation: 'What happened? Was he hurt much?'

'Broke his ankle,' said Willie.

'He was lucky,' agreed Nicholas.

'That's what everybody said.'

He had chosen the place for lunch carefully. It was only halfway into London because he had foreseen the sudden lack of conversation. Sol had warned: 'They won't have a single thing to say to you. And you won't know what to say either.'

Nicholas had argued: 'But it's not that long since I saw them.'

'It's long enough when you've walked out on them. Left them with a mother to tell them what she likes. I know. When I quit my first wife she told the kids I was in jail. Armed hold-up.'

'That's terrible.'

'Hell hath no fury like a left wife,' Sol soliloquised. 'But it didn't work. They *really* wanted to know all about the robbery and prison. Once they'd got over seeing me again. I got a new status with them. I told them I was out on parole. But . . . *I'd* been gone two years not a few weeks. I ran away a long way.'

Nicholas turned into the car park of the roadhouse pub, the Bedford Arms. Deborah said: 'Mum said you'd want to take us somewhere posh, just to show off.'

Nicholas bit back a remark. 'I don't need to show off to you do I?' he said.

'No,' they answered together. 'We know you,' said Willie.

'I thought we could have a good chat here. And they do hamburgers and chips and things like that. It's not posh. Then we could go to the Natural History Museum. It's years since I've been.'

'The dinosaur will be even older,' said Willie.

They went into the big restaurant of the pub. It was early, barely noon, and it was empty although there was a bar in the next room and busy voices carried through the door. Nicholas surveyed the vast eating area with a sinking heart, the acres of tables, the shining formations of cutlery, glasses each containing a paper napkin standing like imitation trees.

'First in today,' said the plump, black-dressed waitress cheerily. She had already taken in the situation. 'How about a nice table in the corner?' She indicated the remote distance. 'We usually put the fathers and children in that bit, close together. We find the children can chat with children at the next table and so on. Better than sitting saying nothing to their dads.' She glanced at him. 'It's difficult to know what to do with them, isn't it.'

'We're going to the Natural History Museum in Kensington,' said Nicholas stoutly.

'Yes, those museums come in useful,' she said.

Disconsolately he led the children to the corner table. He should have realised that he would not have been the first father to spot the strategic advantages of the pub. The main road outside led directly from the middle-class suburbs to the centre of London. They sat awkwardly until the waitress came with the individual menus and they chose. Nicholas felt ashamed of himself; for the first time he realised fully what he had done. He wanted to apologise for leaving them but he could not bring out the words. Abruptly Willie said: 'Where have you been?'

He stared at his son. The question was like an accusation. 'Tell us,' prompted Deborah but softly. 'Where did you go?'

He drew a breath and tried to smile. 'I went to Spain,' he shrugged.

'Mum reckoned you'd gone to Luxembourg,' said Willie.

'Luxor,' corrected Deborah. 'In Egypt. I looked it up in the atlas at school. But you didn't go there?'

In a strange way the thought came to Nicholas that by not going to Luxor he had let them down again. 'It was difficult to get there,' he said. 'So I went to Spain.'

'Are you going to write a book about it?' asked Deborah.

'I could,' he said all at once relieved because he could see a way out. 'The things that happened in Spain. I somehow got mixed up with these old soldiers from the war who thought they were in Italy.'

'Like you meaning to go to that other place, Luxor,' suggested Willie.

'Yes . . . well that was different.'

'What about the old soldiers?' said the girl anxious as he was to sustain the discussion.

Nicholas patted her neat hand and began to relate the story. They listened politely at first but then with growing interest. Willie brightened when the dead Henry Brownjer was first mentioned. 'Really dead?' he asked eagerly. 'Properly?'

'Dead as anyone will ever be,' his father nodded.

Deborah closed her eyes. 'That's terrible,' she said.

Willie said: 'I've never seen anybody dead. Was he all stiff?'

The conversation got them through the meal. Then another silence fell among them. Eventually Deborah said tentatively, almost whispered: 'Where do you live now?'

Nicholas almost choked, swallowed, and said: 'In London.'

'Near Spurs?' asked the boy. 'I wouldn't mind living near Spurs.'

'It's a place they call Little Venice,' he said. 'Not near Spurs. There's a canal, a bit like the real Venice in Italy, but not all that much, with barges and boats. . . .'

'Do you live on a barge or a boat?' enquired Willie his interest quickening again. His father laughed. 'No, I live in a flat overlooking the canal. I share a flat.'

Deborah blushed vividly: 'With your girlfriend?' she asked directly. She yelped and glared at Willie. 'No need to kick me,' she said.

Nicholas felt himself pale. 'No, I share the flat with an American called Sol Solomon. He's a writer.' He looked directly at her. 'I don't have a girlfriend,' he said firmly.

He could see she was going to cry. He kissed her on the cheek and felt her first tears running against his mouth. 'Come home,' she sobbed quietly.

'I can't, not yet,' he said.

'Mum won't have you back,' agreed Willie confidently. 'She wants a divorce.'

Nicholas wiped the girl's cheeks with his napkin and led them from the restaurant. Three sets of miserable fathers with nonplussed children watched them go.

Deborah had recovered her composure by the time they reached the car park. It was a bland afternoon, the sky opal. The children again sat in the back seat and he drove into London and to South Kensington.

They wandered around the Science Museum first, looking at the clocks and the gadgets and machines. Then they went into the Natural History Museum and marvelled at the skeletons of ancient creatures, monsters, fossilised fish and outlandish birds. There were other lonely men with sad satellite children, treading the same course. After an hour they went towards the exit. He wondered what he was going to do with them now. He had access to them until six o'clock. He could not take them back early. 'What would you like to do now?' he asked hopelessly.

Deborah put her hand in his. 'Show us where you live, Daddy,' she said quietly.

Wearing a black track suit with an eagle balder even than he was on the breast, Sol was crouched in front of the television set when they arrived. 'Have you come at the right time!' he exclaimed his eyes alight. 'You're here for the start of the show!'

Sol was immediately acceptable to young people. Nicholas watched with admiration as Deborah and Willie sat on the floor in front of the television. 'It's *my* script,' Sol told them. 'I'm the guy who wrote it.' He pressed buttons. 'Most of . . . some of it.'

The video film was just beginning. He had that knack too. Timing. All he lacked was talent. The children watched entranced as the opening credits appeared. The story was called: *Long Way to Go Home*.

'I don't go for the title,' shrugged Sol. 'I wanted to call it *The Secret Owls*. I like animals in titles.'

'You must be proud to have your name on the television, Mr Harrison,' said Deborah. She pointed it out to Willie. 'I can read,' her brother protested. 'Script by William Harrison.'

Sol pushed his eyes closer to the screen. 'No, don't go getting the wrong idea. That guy did the original script, see, Harrison. They brought me in to make it work.' He faced them with a raised finger. 'But he had a contract . . . and in the contract it said that *his* name *had* to be credited with the screenplay.'

'That not fair,' said Willie. 'Not if you wrote it.'

'Nothing's fair in films and war,' said Sol. Nicholas thought he was going to write it down but for once it did not occur to him, and he kept his attention on the screen. 'Now this first scene,' he said. 'Watch out for when the guy walks into his office. . . . Here, see this is all my script.'

'He's not saying anything,' pointed out Willie.

'It still needs to be written,' corrected his father.

Sol glanced gratefully towards him. 'Sure, it does. You have to tell the actor what to do. Or he just stands there like a

94

dummy. Some of them do even when they're acting. Now watch, this is where his secretary comes in . . . Sherrie Barnet this was . . . was she a great . . . A nice lady.' He glanced again at Nicholas, this time with guilt. 'Really nice,' he mumbled.

The children said they were hungry again and Sol said he would fix some spaghetti and meatballs. 'Just keep watching the movie,' he said. 'See if you can pick out the good lines.'

He went into the kitchen and Nicholas sat on the chair with one child against each side, Deborah's hair across his knee. The touch of them like that filled him with sadness for the foolishness of life and particularly his own.

No one spoke except to make a comment about the old film. Eventually Sol reappeared just in time for another of his lines. 'See that! Hear that! What a dialogue!' he exclaimed pointing as if it were actually written on the screen. He recited the words: ' "How come you can see your way in the dark?" Jeez, that splits the whole goddam . . . the whole plot upside-down.' His eyes glistened in the light of the television. 'And this one, this next scene, is all mine. Except for a couple of lines at the end.'

They watched the actors going wordlessly about their business. 'There's so much feeling in this scene,' claimed Sol. 'More than words can say.'

He obligingly fast-forwarded the video so that the middle forty-five minutes of the drama was bypassed. 'You're missing nothing,' he promised. 'They really screw . . . fouled it up.' He slowed the video. 'But now, here this is real good. This is where I have all the best lines. After this the president of the company . . . the big guy himself . . . wanted to have me write an epic for them.'

'What was it called?' asked Deborah, her face bright.

'I bet we saw it,' said Willie looking towards him as well. 'We watch films.'

Sol looked crestfallen. 'Well,' he admitted. 'We never got so far as giving it a title, although I had one. *Lions in the Night*. The company went bust. Big financial scandal. So that was that.'

He looked soulful. Nicholas saw the eyes of the children drop

95

also. But they brightened as Sol grinned. 'But it don't matter now. Let's get to the meatballs.'

The girl and the boy had only picked at their lunch but now they ate heartily and were all at once full of conversation. Nicholas watched them, amazed. Willie gave the inside story of Billy Proctor's fall from the school window. Billy was always trying to show off and this time he had gone too far. Deborah waited and then described how secretly she had always written stories. She would bring some of her stories to show Sol.

Full of doubts, sadness and relief, Nicholas drove the children home. It was almost seven. There were lights on in the house and they kissed him in the car and went hurrying through the gate and disappeared between the yews. He heard the front door open and Sarah's voice. Then it was closed again and he was alone in the car and in the darkness.

'Great kids,' said Sol when Nicholas returned.

'Thanks. Perhaps I didn't appreciate them enough.'

'You never do,' said Sol easily. He was re-running the film with the sound off. 'Absence makes your kids grow fonder.'

'They thought you were wonderful.'

'Observant children,' replied Sol still easily. 'I wish I could have done the same with mine.'

Nicholas sat down heavily. There was a bottle of beer by the television and Sol offered it to him. He drank it straight from the neck. 'But they *talked* to you. . . . I didn't know Deborah wrote stories. She never told me.'

'You'd be the last guy she'd tell,' Sol said. He stood and turned off the video. 'Did you ever see such crap?' he grunted. 'Ruined every line I wrote. And they left out the rest.' He glared and sighed at the blank screen. ' "Script by William Asshole Harrison",' he said.

The expletive served to dissipate his mood. He went towards the kitchen. 'Great spaghetti and meatballs,' he said over his shoulder.

Nicholas followed him. 'They certainly were. You can cook, Sol. Almost as well as you write.'

'I didn't,' confessed Sol. 'Last night, when I was with my

lady friend I went back to the restaurant and complained. The one where we had dinner. So they gave me the spaghetti and meatballs to make up for my complaint. All I did was put them in the microwave.'

'The kids seemed to like them.'

'They would.' He paused and then went to the draining board where the plates were piled. 'That Willie is some kid,' he said. He picked up a small bone from the plate. 'See that?'

'What is it?' The bone was dry, almost black.

'Said he got it from the museum. If you read in the newspaper tomorrow that the brontosaurus has collapsed you'll know why.'

Dear Sir,
Ref. Mrs Sarah Boulting

Our client has instructed us today that when you had contact with your children on Sunday, you returned them to their home almost an hour later than arranged. Would you ensure that this does not happen in the future. Contact times had been specifically agreed by you and our client was caused unnecessary distress at the late return of your children, since you did not have the courtesy to inform her that you would be delayed.

In addition, our client has said that they were taken to your home. This should have been specifically arranged beforehand, the reasons for which have been fully set out in our client's statements.

Can we please remind you that the welfare of your children must take priority over all other considerations.

Yours faithfully,

Janes, Tarbert and Fawkes, Solicitors.

After he had read the letter Nicholas went for a three-hour walk around the streets of Paddington, Maida Vale and St John's Wood. He stared through the iron railings at the great emptiness of Lord's Cricket Ground. He knew how it felt. He returned to the flat. Sol was out making an offer to an actress. Nicholas sat down and dialled the number.

'Guy Fawkes, please.'

'You mean Mr David Fawkes.'

Nicholas even disguised his laugh. 'Oh yes, of course. Here at the golf club we always call him Guy.'

'Oh, it's the golf club.'

'Yes, the secretary.'

'Ah, Mr Manners. Just one moment.'

David Fawkes came briskly on the line. 'Hello, Henry. How are you?'

'Fine, fine, Guy.'

There was a suspicious pause. 'I thought it was Henry Manners. . . . Who is this?'

'Don't put the phone down or you'll be sorry,' said Nicholas succinctly. 'Sorry, I can't do the Scots accent. Not like Manners anyway. It's Nicholas Boulting.'

'I thought it might be. What do you want?'

'Listen, Guy of the Golf Club. Do you remember how we won the Fothrington Cup . . . ? '

'Oh for God's sake. Get off the phone. . . .'

'*How* we won it, I said.' He knew the message had got home. 'And you are next year's captain. Well, well. . . .'

'What are you saying, Boulting? Don't try to blackmail me.'

'It's not blackmail. But let me warn you. Another letter like I got today . . .'

'It's a formal letter representing our client's interest. Solicitors always write that sort of . . .'

'Not solicitors who might have something on their conscience. I'm not asking for anything special. Just don't write me another letter like that. Ever.'

A suspicion of autumn had come on the canal early in the morning. Mist was rising from the unmoving water around the moored barges so that they looked as if they might be smouldering. The trees were heavy too, dusty, weary after a long London summer and with a hem of brown on the lower leaves.

Nicholas had not been able to sleep and he sat moodily at the desk by the window. It had been daylight for an hour; now it was six thirty but little moved in the street. This was to be the moment when he was going to start to write again. An end to the false starts since *Lying in Your Arms*. He had reached a hundred and twenty pages, thirty thousand words, of *Falling from Grace* and another sixty pages of *Dancing with Delilah* before each had stuttered to an anguished stop. He had tried going from one to the other but neither could be kick-started. Now he was here, he was settled, he had to face up to it, he must begin again. He had his laptop on the desk and he lifted its lip like someone opening a casket of mysteries. The blank screen stared at him, waiting for him, challenging him to put some words on its face. He tapped out: *Owls of Desperation*. Then he stopped.

To his surprise he heard Sol moving upstairs. 'Want some coffee?' the American called down.

'Anything,' Nicholas shouted back. 'I've stolen one of your titles, Sol.'

'You're welcome,' responded Sol. 'Put some words to it. Like a hundred thousand.'

'I'll settle for a hundred,' returned Nicholas. 'It'll be a start.'

Sol brought the coffee down. Nicholas was still staring at the three words, his timid advance guard. The American looked over his shoulder at the screen. 'That's how far I got,' Sol sighed. 'There don't seem much you can add to *Owls of Desperation*.'

'It will do for a start,' insisted Nicholas without conviction. 'As long as I've got something, *anything*, on the page.'

'Sure as shit,' agreed Sol. 'The next part is the hard one. Why don't you write about a young girl going to visit her grandma and the wolf comes out of the . . .'

'It's been done,' smiled Nicholas. 'I'm almost sure.'

'So do it again. There are only so many basic plots, remember. Give her a nice name like Alice.'

'Mixing up two stories.'

'Okay, so you confuse people. They'll think it's new.'

It was his final contribution. He retreated up the stairs. At the landing he called: 'Tonight we're going to a party, Nick. A literary party.'

'What's it for?' Nicholas called back. Bravely he kept his eyes on the screen.

'What d'you mean, what's it for? It's for drinking and eating and meeting broads.'

'What's the "literary" content?'

'Oh, I get you. Some guy's written a book, can you believe. *Finished* the goddam thing. That's cause for a party any time. It'll be full of literary lions, so we'll be okay.'

'You've been invited?'

'Well in a way. For Chrissake, they ought to be pleased. A couple of literary lions like us.'

'So he cheated at golf. What's so terrible about that? If I played, I'd cheat.'

'But you *don't* play, so you don't understand.' They were in the taxi. 'It's a diabolical thing to do when you belong to a club and especially when you cheat it to win something like the cup we won. And Fawkes is going to be the new *captain* of the club.'

'So you got him by the balls?'

'Literally,' agreed Nicholas. 'I'm not vindictive and I'm not the club sneak but I've got that over the bastard. I'll teach him not to write his solicitor's letters to me. Not letters like that.'

'Lawyers are paid to think up shitty things to say'.

'This is different. He's . . . was a friend. He doesn't have to treat me like that.'

'How did he cheat?'

'Played the wrong ball,' said Nicholas dogmatically. Sol whistled. Nicholas continued seriously. 'He *knew* and *I* knew. He played *my* ball. We were partners and that would have disqualified us for that hole. We would never have won the Fothrington Cup.'

Sol shook his head: 'This is a whole new world.'

'Believe me, that's trouble at any sort of golf club. Major trouble. Cheating. I knew he'd done it and so did he, of course, and I think our opponents had a shrewd idea something had gone on but they wouldn't say anything like that unless they were absolutely sure. It's very serious. If it came out now . . . now he's going to be club captain . . .'

'But you're not going to tell.'

'No, I won't tell. I'm just as guilty as Fawkes but I'm not there any longer. I realised what had happened the moment it occurred but we were both desperate to . . .'

'Win the Fothrington Cup,' completed Sol knowledgeably.

Nicholas glanced at him. 'Right. God knows when I will play again so it doesn't matter. All he has to do is be civil to me.'

'You got him by the balls,' repeated Sol. He shook his head in appreciation. 'That's good,' he mused. 'That's very good.'

The taxi drew up outside the Garbo Club in Soho. 'Full of literary lions,' murmured Sol as Nicholas paid. 'Can't you just hear them roaring.'

There were two girls dressed in old ladies' clothes at an entrance desk. 'Do you have your invitations please?' asked one with professional sweetness.

'They got lost,' Sol told her. 'We get so many.' Nicholas found himself nodding.

'Names please,' said the young woman. Nicholas wondered why girls dressed like grandmothers. He heard Sol say: 'Hemingway, E.,' and to his astonishment heard himself add: 'Conrad, J.'

'Are Hemingway and Conrad on the list, Boony?' she asked leaning over towards the girl at her side. Nicholas and Sol exchanged glances. From the fringes of the crowded and noisy room came Paul Garrett, his glass held languidly, tipped sideways between two fingers like a cigarette. 'Mr Hemingway and Mr Conrad were invited by me,' he told the girls.

Both regarded him with a suffocated sort of admiration. 'Oh right, Mr Garrett,' said the one with the book. 'Mr Conrad, Mr Hemingway, will you sign here please.'

As they did so, with flourishes, a fussy young woman wearing black velvet with a lace cravat heaving frothily on her breast appeared through the entrance. 'Honey!' Sol exclaimed. 'You got here just in time!' He looked towards Garrett and then at the two secretaries. 'Miss April Day,' he announced grandly. The girls had given up. 'Guest of Mr Hemingway,' added Sol.

Garrett stepped aside and the three followed him into the room. A young man with a ponytail said: 'Isn't that Nicholas Boulting? What's he doing these days?'

'Not very much, I understand,' another man wearing a leather jacket answered. 'Apparently he's run out of steam.'

'Are you sure these are influential people?' Nicholas heard April Day whisper to Sol. 'I only want to meet influential people.'

Quietly Garrett said to Nicholas: 'How is living with Sol working out?'

'Wonderful,' said Nicholas. 'The only problem is a minor one – separating fact and fantasy.'

'Have you started writing?'

'Started today. Got the title down. It's called *Owls of Desperation*.'

'Splendid,' said Garrett unimpressed. 'I'll tell Mallinder's.' Nicholas picked up a glass of champagne from a passing tray. Someone tapped him on the shoulder and a woman's soft voice said: 'Mr Widdershins, I presume.'

It was raining thickly when they got out of the taxi. Nicholas paid the driver. She was already beckoning from the high porch as someone inside opened the door for her, letting an oblong of bright light out into the streaking dark. Nicholas hurried up the steps. A white-faced man, who seemed old, was holding the door open. 'Good evening, sir,' he casually said as if Nicholas was always arriving.

The man helped Loretta off with her coat. 'We'll have some coffee, please Mr Hethrington-Scott,' smiled Loretta.

'In the drawing room, Mrs Pollock?'

'In the drawing room,' she confirmed. The man went off swiftly with a strange clockwork gait. Loretta kissed Nicholas on his soaked face and said: 'Did you get wet?' She took his hand and led him into the drawing room. It was richly but comfortably furnished. 'He'll come and light the fire in a moment,' she said.

She indicated he should sit on a deep sofa and sat opposite him, her legs staring him in the face. She was better, more beautiful, than his shadowy memory from the night when she had left her telephone number on his buttocks. She was dark and slender with large, fine eyes and notable breasts. The lights of the room reflected in her eyes and on her knees. 'I'm glad,' she said, 'that now we know who we are. I don't think I would have wanted to continue with the Widdershins charade. It's such a stupid name. For either of us.'

'It was all right for one night,' he smiled. 'I didn't think I was going to see you again. You were definitely off me the next day. I think two years was the nearest I was quoted.'

She returned his smile. 'I get moods,' she admitted. 'And I'm always penitent when I go off the rails. I promise myself I will never do it again.'

'And do you?'

A shadow fell on her face. 'I do,' she answered in a low voice. 'I can't help it.'

The man who had anwered the door came in with a coffee pot and cups on a tray. 'Shall I light the fire, Mrs Pollock, madam?' he enquired.

'Please,' she said.

'I was afraid you might say that,' he grumbled. 'I find it very difficult. I don't appear to have the knack.'

'He blows himself up,' explained Loretta to Nicholas.

'All the time,' agreed the man morosely. He knelt in obvious fear at the fireside, turned the gas key and tremulously took a match from the box. Nicholas could see he had the timing wrong. The gas had been on too long. Anxiously Loretta glanced towards him. They both edged further along their seats while Mr Hethrington-Scott bent and struck the match.

There was, after a moment, a violent but controlled explosion. Flames puffed out from the appliance and then went like a red and yellow tongue up the chimney. Mr Hethrington-Scott fell back with a cry, overbalancing and ending up sitting on the hearthrug. When he turned, the front part of his bald head was black and red and his eyes were streaming. 'Fucking thing,' he said.

He stood up trying to regain some dignity, stared balefully at the now cheery fire and backed away from it. Scarlet-faced, black-blotched and with his eyes running, he turned slowly. 'Will there be anything else, Mrs Pollock?' he enquired loftily. 'If not I will go to my bed.'

'Please do, Mr Hethrington-Scott,' said Loretta. 'I think we can manage.'

The man wished them a sombre goodnight to which they responded, straight-voiced. Once he had left the room they remained tight-faced as Loretta put a finger to her lips. She was the first to give way, laughing silently and then having to smother the sounds. Nicholas began to laugh and put his hands over his mouth. Loretta said: 'Boom!' and mimed an explosion with her hands. She had to pick up a cushion to cover her mirth. With it still hugged to her face she crossed in front of the fire and almost fell on top of him on the sofa. He took the cushion from her and let it drop to the hearthrug. She slid against him and, still laughing, they kissed. Her hair, her perfume, herself, seemed to spill all over his face. They stopped laughing. His hands eagerly ran up to her dress above her waist. The tops of her breasts glowed. They kissed again. She began to move against him.

'Excuse me, Mrs Pollock, and sir . . .'

They peered over the back of the sofa, like lookouts in a trench at the sudden appearance of a raid. 'Yes, Mr Hethrington-Scott,' Loretta eventually said.

'I forgot to tell you, madam. Mr Pollock telephoned from the . . .,' he took a piece of paper from his inside coat pocket, '. . . the Central African Republic. He left a telephone number, Baonaroganda . . . that's B-A-O-N-A-R-O-G-A-N-D-A 27598201 that's . . . 27598201 . . . extension 43 or 44. He says you may have some difficulty getting through because the rains have set in. Perhaps you could telephone him at your convenience, he said. He was somewhat indistinct, Mrs

Pollock, but I understood him to say that he had been ill, malaria, I believe. And he will not now be home until November.'

'Thank you, Mr Hethrington-Scott, I will telephone him as soon as I can.'

'Thank you, madam. Goodnight. Goodnight, sir.'

The man made another exit. 'Perhaps I ought to go,' suggested Nicholas.

'Why ever would you do that?' she enquired kissing him again. 'He won't be home until November.'

They had a brandy and then she withdrew from him once more, going across to the chair on the other side of the fireplace. She sat facing him, the flames warming her face. 'I want to show you something,' she said slowly. Her eyes had become weighty. She lifted her eyelids and regarded him with a look that was almost one of modesty. 'Please remain where you are.'

Nicholas sat, glass in hand, his eyes on her. She leaned to one side towards the fireplace and pressing a switch, reduced the lighting in the room to a fusion of shadows. From somewhere music came, full, sensuous music. 'Smetana,' she said.

Loretta moved to the edge of her chair and began to unbutton her dress at the back. 'Don't move,' she warned him again throatily. 'I need you to watch.'

'I'm not moving,' he whispered, looking up at her.

When she had unbuttoned the back she slid the sequinned shoulders and arms away. Her own shoulders and arms were cream in the diminished lamplight. She was wearing a white lacy bra and she undid it between the cups, so that it fell away from her breasts, oval, fine, softly textured and coloured, the nipples smudged against her skin. 'What do you think of it so far?' she enquired.

'Wonder . . .,' he coughed and choked, '. . . wonderful.'

'Don't choke,' she said softly and seriously. 'I'm going to need your help.'

Nicholas remained transfixed. She still kept her distance. His clothes felt like lead. He sat on the sofa, as though they were conducting a remote drawing room conversation. And there she was, sitting naked to the waist, the light moving with the regular patterns of the artificial fire on her skin and with a sleepy, enquiring smile on her face. She seemed in no hurry to move. He stared at her, scarcely believing it was happening. It was obvious that she took pleasure in his voyeurism because she wriggled a little, replaced her smile with a frown and casually brushed an unseen fly from her nipple.

He thought it was time he made the next move. It was difficult standing up but she saved him the trouble. She knew the sequence. When he was only halfway to his feet Loretta held up her hand and said: 'Stay there. Don't move. I'll come to you.'

The sheer erotic theatre of it filled him from shoes to scalp. Standing with her dress held against her hips, her naked body moulded by the mobile light, she walked slowly towards him. 'I don't do this for everybody,' she said.

She took her time over the few feet from one side of the fireplace to the other. The gilt clock on the marble mantelshelf chimed twelve, although he was not counting. She gave it a glance and said: 'Five minutes fast.' She checked a slender golden watch on her fawn wrist. Then she was immediately before him, standing, still, eyes shining, her stomach in front of his face. Nicholas could feel her glow. He leaned forward and kissed her navel. It seemed the only thing to do. But gently she pushed him away. 'Not yet,' she whispered. 'No more yet. I'd like to keep you remote for a while. Try not to touch me.'

He sat on his hands. She stood, now a suggestion of a sway to the hushed music, the soft indent in her stomach moving only three inches from his nose. Loretta was aware of the moment. Without pausing in her sway she pulled the dress down over her hips and the short lace slip beneath it fell with the same movement. Her black stockings, supported by a frail suspender belt, looked as though they had been painted on her legs. She hooked her fingers in the top of her black pants and threw them aside as if she were truly glad to get rid of them. She smoothed her stockings, her hands moving up her thighs. 'I'm keeping these on,' she said as if he required an explanation. 'No point in getting cold.'

His hands climbed out like escapees from beneath his backside, and he slid them around her cool waist. His head returned to her belly, his nose pushing into her small copse of pubic hair. He sneezed violently on her stomach. She said: 'I do hope you're not allergic.'

As though to remove any risk of it she athletically squatted, her set face lowering itself to his. Now her eyes seemed as naked as the rest of her. His hands went to her hips in a manner of supporting her. She began to take off his tie. 'Nice,' she said. 'I like a good tie.' She looked at him uncompromisingly. 'Around my wrists.'

Nicholas muttered something unintelligible even to himself. She was busily unbuttoning his shirt. 'I simply cannot remember what your chest was like,' she murmured. 'It wasn't hairy, was it?' He reminded her that it was not and his fingers travelled up to her ribs to the underside of her breasts; her nipples were like pencil points. 'Not too much,' she pleaded seriously, suddenly falling against him. 'Not too soon.' Her eyes had an expression of pleasure and concern as she lifted her face. 'I must be one of the few women who suffer from premature ejaculation,' she joked. 'With me it's touch and go.'

Nicholas apologised but she did not listen. 'Let me get the rest of your things off,' she suggested as though pretending she did not care one way or the other. 'I need to keep myself in check, you understand,' she added smiling carefully. 'Otherwise we'll all be going home before the National Anthem.' She rose from her crouch and held out her hands to him, helping him to his feet. His whole body was pounding. 'You're hot,' she said feeling his glowing chest. She pushed her breasts against it. Her hair was under his chin flowing like a luxurious beard. 'It's very warm in here,' he groaned.

In her lazy, almost unconcerned way she unzipped him, put her hand in, and began to whistle tunelessly. 'There's no escape,' she said. She used both hands. 'He'll never get away. Not from me.'

He kissed her, her lips, her neck, her hair and one of her ears. Busily she pulled down his trousers and Jockey shorts. 'Kick your shoes off, darling,' she urged. 'Help out a little.'

When he was even more naked than she was, he allowed her to push him backwards onto the commodious sofa. She remained standing for a moment, looking down at him while he stared up at her. Her breasts lolled above him. 'Right,' she muttered adjusting her stockings. Her tone had become practical. 'Right, I'm ready. I'm going to impale myself on that implement. Just hold it steady for a moment, will you. While I climb on.'

He was in no state to argue. She climbed above him her face now held in a trance of expectation. 'God, I get so runny,' she complained to herself. She used both hands, holding him like a policewoman holding a suspect. She was steady now, supporting herself on her knees.

With a small cry from her and a gritting of teeth from him, she lowered herself to him. She wanted to do the moving and he let her do it. She eased herself up and down three times and then stopped. 'I've *got* to think of something else,' she said her face crammed with anxiety. 'Shopping. The Grand National . . . anything.' But with a moan she gave up and pushed down on him again. She began to gurgle. He was unable to keep himself back and they fell together in a frenzy of pleasure and perspiration. When they were done, they lay with her hair smothering his face, Smetana still playing, the clock ticking, the phoney fire guttering.

From behind the sofa, from the distance of the door, came the voice of Mr Hethrington-Scott. It froze them rigid. 'Madam,' he called sonorously. 'I forgot to mention . . . Mr Pollock said that if you fail to get him on the Baonaroganda 27598201 then you could try another number . . .'

In the morning he lay in the extravagant bed, eyes tight, like a boy pretending to be asleep. Intently he listened for her breathing but the only sound was the distinct, regular touch of the bedside clock. He ached everywhere. No one had ever had a night like that, he thought, but thinking again, he realised there must be others. He opened an apprehensive single eye. Her place across the wide bed was empty.

Like a man planning an escape, which he was, Nicholas, with his nose still below the sheet-line, examined the room. The curtains were drawn. They were long drapes down to the floor and he watched them; he would not have put it past her to be hiding, ready to spring yet again, with more surprises, more demands, more innovations, more songs.

'Loretta,' he croaked in a voice not meant to be heard. 'Loretta.'

Relief began to grow. He slid from the bed. Where were his clothes? His last memory of them was downstairs in the drawing room. There was a man's dressing gown hanging in the annex to the bathroom. It was a terrible purple-and-green florid thing, and rather short, but this was no time for worrying about taste. He put it on and with caution went out onto the galleried landing. The stairs fanned out gracefully. He remembered the stairs. Every one of them. How did she think up things like that? How could you do it on every stair, the finale on the top landing? 'A little now,' he heard her coaxing voice again. 'Then a little on *this* stair, and then on the next one.' He stepped down each one now and it came back to him how he had pleaded for a brief rest on the middle landing.

The front interior of the house appeared ordered and deserted. Strong sunlight was coming through stained-glass windows each side of the extensive front door lending an ecclesiastical flourish to the floor. Tentatively he peeped around the door of the drawing room and, more tentatively, went in. His clothes, fastidiously folded, even his socks, were arranged across the arms and back of the armchair in which last night she had sat so gloriously naked to the waist. Remembering her like that brought him a pang of pleasure. His shoes were precisely placed on the floor. He picked them up and examined them, then sniffed them. They had been cleaned. His trousers were pressed; they were still warm. Gathering the garments together he edged up the stairs again and back into the bedroom. A tray of coffee had materialised at the bedside, the spout of the pot steaming amiably. He looked around and out of the door on to the landing again but everywhere was a bright emptiness. A standing clock in the hall struck. It was ten.

Nicholas poured himself a cup of coffee. There were some select-looking biscuits on the tray but he did not disturb their formality. He went into the bathroom again, used the lavatory and touched the handle. It gushed like a melody. He washed his face and drank a glassful of water. Then he dressed swiftly and went down the stairs again. The softness of the carpet cushioned his steps.

Mr Hethrington-Scott was polishing a small, gleaming brass figure on a table concealed below the arch of the stairs. 'Good morning, sir. I trust you slept well.'

Nicholas performed a startled turn. 'Oh yes. . . . Good morning. Yes. . . . Thank you.'

'Mrs Pollock has gone riding in the park, sir,' said the man as though to save him asking. He looked straight at Nicholas and his pause was apparent. 'It's her bit of exercise.'

'Oh, yes. We all need a bit of exercise.'

'We do. That's very true.'

'Thanks for the coffee and . . . everything.'

'Please don't mention it, sir,' murmured Mr Hethrington-Scott beginning with slow purpose to walk towards the door which he opened. It framed the shiny September morning. Gratefully Nicholas moved towards the open air. 'Will you please tell Mrs Pollock that I will telephone her,' he said on the scrubbed stone steps. 'I have to go now. I have an appointment.'

'I'll tell her to expect your call, sir.'

Nicholas paused. 'Mr Pollock is returning in November, I believe you said?' he asked slightly to his own surprise.

'I did indeed, sir.' The expression on the man's face did not alter. 'Early November. About Bonfire Night I expect.'

Nicholas had reached the public pavement. 'Oh right, yes,' was all he could muster.

'Mr Pollock likes Bonfire Night,' continued Hethrington-Scott reminiscently. 'He enjoys the bangs.'

With a pale smile Nicholas gave a brief wave and strode out along the pavement. Then his groin went. He almost shouted in pain, put his hand to the place, and continued limping along the street. He looked back. Mr Hethrington-Scott was waving.

A taxi turned the corner and Nicholas hailed it like a vehicle sent by a relief agency. He gave Paul Garrett's office address and sat in the back, fatigued and crumpled. The office was in Soho and when he left the taxi a tout outside a strip club door invited him to see a bed show.

'A bed show,' repeated Nicholas to Garrett when he was sitting across from his desk. 'Who could possibly want a bed bloody show at this time of the morning?'

'Don't be unreasonable,' said Garrett in his mild way. 'Some men might only be able to go and see it at this time of the morning. Other times they're working or home with their wives and children.'

Nicholas eyed him suspiciously. 'Are you getting at me?'

'Not at all,' said Garrett in the same tone.

'I don't have a wife and I've hardly got a family,' said Nicholas sourly. 'At least I've only got them for one afternoon a week and then I get a solicitor's warning if I keep them out an hour late.'

'Some estranged fathers are only too pleased to get them back home,' argued Garrett. 'I was. I ran out of museums. We spent one wet Sunday afternoon at Liverpool Street Station, would you believe.' He waited. 'But I wasn't admonishing you about that, Nick. My concern is about your work. Are you doing any?'

'What about the film deal? Any news?'

'It's the usual obstacle course,' shrugged Garrett. 'I think I may get you the twenty thousand dollars up front. But that's not going to last long. Ex-wives are not so accommodating as current wives.'

'I've realised that already,' muttered Nicholas.

'Incidentally, you look appalling. I last saw you going off with that memorable woman. From the party.'

'I'm on my way home from that memorable woman.'

'Was she memorable?'

'I'll never forget her,' said Nicholas truthfully. He turned his miserable and baggy eyes on Garrett. 'Paul, what am I going to do?'

'About what?'

'My life of course.'

'What we all do, Nick. Get on with it.'

'Thanks.'

Garrett leaned over the desk. 'All I know is that you've *got* to start writing. You've now got somewhere to live. You ought to be sitting down there, getting on with your work, which *is* getting on with your life. You've got a contract and you've had money in advance.' He regarded him more sympathetically. 'You're simply *not* going home to start all over again. You've got to get that into your head. Not until she wants you. And then *you've* got to want to as well.'

'I do,' muttered Nicholas.

'Well, it's not on. Not at the moment. How much have you written since you walked out?' He moved his fingers on an invisible keyboard.

'Written? Well. . . .'

'How many words?'

'I've started on a novel,' Nicholas contended. 'I told you. It's called . . . er . . . *Owls of Desperation*.'

Garrett grimaced. 'How many words?'

'Three,' admitted Nicholas. 'Just those three. *Owls of Desperation*. The title.'

'Who thought up that. Sol Solomon? It sounds like him. He's tremendous for three words. That's all he ever does. Thinks up catchy phrases and titles. The trouble is he can't join them on to anything.'

'He seems to survive,' said Nicholas.

'By the skin of his word processor. Sol spends his life hanging on in there. He starts things, he never finishes them. . . . All he can do is talk. He talks the best novel in the business.'

Nicholas sighed. 'All right. Perhaps I ought to get right away.'

'You've *been* right away. For God's sake, you ended up in Torremolinos.'

'No. Somewhere I can *work*. Where I can settle down to it. Tuscany or somewhere.'

Garrett looked at him with gathering scorn. 'Go to "somewhere",' he advised. 'But not Tuscany.' He leaned fiercely across the desk: 'What the fuck would you do in Tuscany? Writing, mate, is about *writing*. Not about running off somewhere pretty to do it. You've got a roof, now sit under it and write.'

Nicholas sighed. 'I suppose you're right.'

'There's no *suppose* about it. Listen, Nick. *You have a contract from your publisher.* They've given you money. They'll want something for the money. That's not unreasonable, is it? They've postponed the deadline twice. Now you have a new one and its March 31st. Not April the first, not May the first; and *next year* not some time. If you don't write you don't live. And, incidentally, neither do I.'

'I know. I'm sorry, Paul. It's all been such a mess.'

Garrett regarded him grimly: 'And I am not going to represent any author who takes the cash and then fails to deliver. I can't do that. Nor will I. Even for you. For Christ's sake go and write something. If it's only your name.'

Six

He had come to wonder which was worse, facing a blank piece of paper, or facing a blank screen. He sat trying not to stare at the idle trees beside the canal, nor to trace the progress across the window frame of the procession of lazy airliners, losing height for London Airport.

He did not write anything that morning. Sol was singing Neapolitan songs above and cooking. He called down the stairs. 'Lunch! Come and get it!' Nicholas stood gladly and left the processor and the desk. Moodily he climbed the stairs.

'The microwave marvel does it again!' enthused Sol as the head of the Englishman appeared. He rejected the notion of making a note of the line with a critical shake of his face. 'Bacon, hamburger, fries, eggs every way,' he said. He stopped as Nicholas sat on the chair and studied his features. 'She damn nearly killed you, I can see,' he said with sympathy. He sat down on the opposite chair and eagerly leaned his elbows on the table. 'How was she?'

'How was June Noon?' responded Nicholas.

'April Day,' corrected Sol. 'Just great. Says she's an animal-lover and that's how she loves, like an animal.' He decided to note that and leaned over to the sideboard to record it on a pad. His face had changed when he returned. 'I'm lying,' he confessed. 'She wouldn't. Said I had not introduced her to enough influential people.'

'This is the would-be actress?' said Nicholas beginning to eat.

'So was it my fault that the Queen didn't show, nor Steven Spielberg, nor Sir Laurence Olivier . . . ? '

'He's dead, Olivier,' mentioned Nicholas.

'That's a good reason for not showing. Still, she's just a. . . . What d'you call it? A tart. That's it, a tart. Except she wouldn't be a tart for me.' He started to eat quickly as if to fill a deep need. Mouth full, he looked up. 'But you did okay? Okay?'

Nicholas nodded. 'I had your share as well.'

'Shit,' muttered Sol. 'Don't tell me. Okay, tell me.'

'I'm not going into detail,' said Nicholas primly. 'I may want to continue this relationship when I've had a few weeks' rest.'

Sol was reluctant to give up. 'It was that good?'

'Different,' conceded Nicholas. He paused, half a fried egg hanging like an ear from his fork. 'Sol, she had me singing.' He regarded the American soberly. *'Singing.'*

Aghast Sol matched the stare. 'Singing. You sang . . . while you . . . bang?'

'I sang.'

'Jeez, that's new. Singing.' He gazed at the prongs of his fork as if it were a microphone. 'What did you sing?'

'All sorts. "Michael Row the Boat Ashore" was one. She's a strange lady, Sol.'

'I must practise,' said Sol thoughtfully. 'I used to sing, you know. And I write songs. . . .'

'I don't think it was the song so much, not the words. It was the rhythm.'

Eventually Nicholas pushed his plate away and finished his coffee. 'Excellent,' he said. 'Thanks.' He rose. 'I've got to get some sleep and then I've got to start to write a book.'

'You got an idea at last?'

'No. I'll have to make myself think of one. Paul Garrett's been threatening me.'

'You could try *Michael Row the Boat Ashore,*' shrugged Sol with one of his thoughtful expressions. 'That's got a certain something.'

He slept the rest of the day and at six o'clock telephoned Loretta.

'Who is that?'

'It's me, Nicholas. Your singing lover.'

Her laugh was brief. 'You tease,' she said flatly.

'You were gone when I woke.'

There was a pause as if she were making signs to someone in the room or had a lot on her mind. 'Yes . . . well, I ride in the Park every day.'

'Good exercise.'

'Yes, it is.'

'Would you like to meet up this evening? We could go . . .'

'I'm tired,' she sighed. 'I need an early night.'

'Fine. I slept all the afternoon. Well, I'll see you for lunch tomorrow. . . .'

'No that's no good. I have a lunch appointment.'

'Oh, well, when?'

'When what? Oh, we could have lunch. Some time. I'm going away at the weekend and I won't be back until . . .'

'November,' he suggested.

'Why November?'

'That's when Mr Pollock returns from the jungle isn't it. . . .'

'There's no reason to sneer, Nicholas. He is doing a fine job out there.'

'You didn't seem to think so last night.'

'Last night was last night,' she said with a trace of apology. 'I can't see you again, not for a long time.'

'That's what you said the last time, remember?'

'Well, there are right times and times that are not right. You see, Mr Hethrington-Scott was a little upset after last night. He's a sensitive man and apparently we sang rather loudly. And the fire blowing up in his face and all that. I don't want to lose him. My husband would be most upset if he went. He looks after me . . . when my husband's away, if you understand.'

'I find it very difficult to understand,' admitted Nicholas.

He replaced the telephone and stared at the evening view outside the window. There were early lights in the restaurant across the canal. A man came from the hatch of one of the barges and began to water the plants and flowers on the deck.

Another man, smoking a pipe, walked a dog and spoke to the watering man, a car tooted and both men waved.

He dialled Paul Garrett's number. 'I'm going away,' he said firmly.

'Running away,' amended Garrett. 'Where to this time, Nick?'

'Not far. Not Luxor nor even Torremolinos. Not this time. I'm just going somewhere for a few days. I'll be back to take the kids out on Sunday. It won't be Tuscany, either. I simply want to go somewhere and sit and walk about and try to straighten a few things out in my mind.'

'Your new novel, I hope.'

'Yes. That's the primary reason.'

'Well, I told you this morning that the only way to write is to sit down and write. All the pretty countryside, all the hills, all the sunlit bays in the world won't make you write. The only view you ought to have is that screen in front of you. But if you need inspiration, thought time, then take it, by all means. But for God's sake use it, Nick. Stop being sorry for yourself. Stop mooning.'

'I know, I know. I won't go anywhere nice. I'll go somewhere miserable. It will suit my mood.'

'Come back with an outline and five thousand words,' said Garrett. 'Be a writer.'

Deliberately Sol put the coffee mugs on the table. His expression was hurt. 'I don't get why you're going,' he said sitting down and examining Nicholas's face as if he might find a grain of enlightenment. 'Was it something I said?'

Nicholas laughed quietly. 'Is there anything you *haven't* said, Sol?'

The American remained serious. 'Maybe not,' he said. 'You're just going to some place you don't even know? Just like that?'

'I'm coming back, it's only for a few days, for God's sake. It's the runaway in me.'

'Maybe I should come too,' breathed Sol. 'Maybe I could find some of this inspiration I hear about.'

'You're always inspired,' said Nicholas. 'Every day.'

'Sure, sure. I got inspiration in bulk.' He thought about it, took a folded envelope from his shirt pocket and, borrowing a pen from Nicholas, wrote it down. 'What I don't have is the application, the strength to put the inspiration on paper.' He had half-returned the pen but now he held on to it and wrote again on the envelope. 'It's like two mean guys in the ring, that word processor and me. We hate.'

'I know, I know,' shrugged Nicholas. 'I can't say whether I'm really going off to discover some answers, inspiration if you like, or whether I'm just running away from that bloody screen. Probably running away. It's an old habit with me.'

They had both finished the coffee. Neither wanted any more. Sol got up and put the mugs on the draining board. 'And you've got no idea where you're going,' he said flatly. 'You're just going to drive out of here, and go anywhere.'

'That's the general idea. Somewhere where the air will perhaps unclog my writer's block.'

'My writer's block, I love,' Sol said. 'I don't know how I would get by without it. The fight every day with that fucking dumb-faced machine, then knowing when I'm beaten. Doing something else. Cooking. Bumming around. Not writing.'

Laughing Nicholas said: 'But you make a living from it.'

'It ain't strictly honest, not delivering, like I do, but most of these movie people wouldn't know an honest man if they fell over him in the shithouse. I have no conscience about them. I trade lies and promises with them. And I really *mean* to get things done. All the time.'

Nicholas said: 'Maybe you *really* ought to come with me.' He regretted saying it at once but Sol did not even think about it. 'We'd get drunk,' he forecast. 'And I hate those fresh-air places. I like to have walls.'

'That's what Paul Garrett thinks I should do,' acknowledged Nicholas. 'You've got a roof, he says. Sit under it and work.'

'You'd better call me when you're there,' said Sol. 'In case anybody thinks they'll give you a million dollars all of a sudden.'

'All right. I'll let you know where I am. Sarah might ring about the kids, or the million dollars could turn up.' He rose and held out his hand, feeling a little embarrassed as he did so. But the embarrassment did not touch Sol. 'I've just got to straighten out my life,' said Nicholas. 'That's all.'

Sol ruminated. 'Nobody can straighten out their lives in a few days. It takes a lifetime.'

Nicholas handed him the pen and taking the envelope from his pocket Sol wrote it down. 'You're coming out with a lot of good stuff this morning,' mentioned Nicholas.

'Great. Some days I think I'm like Aristotle. But with me it ends there.' He tapped his shirt pocket. 'On the back of an envelope. I lose the stuff or when it comes up again I forget what it means. There's no real product.'

'Between us,' said Nicholas, 'we're not adding much to the world's store of great literature.' He picked up his packed bag and his briefcase and went towards the door. 'I won't be more than four days,' he said. 'I have to pick up Deborah and Willie on Sunday.'

'Kids equal responsibility,' said Sol. 'And I promise not to write that down.'

'I'll telephone anyway. When I get to wherever I'm going.'

Within two hundred yards of leaving Nicholas was faced with a decision. He sat in his car at the junction of Blomfield Road with Edgware Road and had the choice of going left and north or right and south. There was no other vehicle behind so he remained stationary and looked one way then the other. The gateway to his future remained unrevealed. Buses, lorries and cars went unconcernedly up and down. They knew where they were going. The people on the pavements were Asians, Arabs in robes, black and white Londoners, mostly on premeditated journeys. A boy balanced on a skateboard was curling among pedestrians.

It was a mild day and two young women having coffee on the small balcony of the café that overhung the canal with bravado, watched him, wondering why the car was unmoving so long in the middle of the street. A delivery van pulled up behind but the driver was in no hurry either and he examined his hairline in the mirror while Nicholas surveyed his options. Eventually the delivery man gave a languid touch of his horn forcing Nicholas into a decision. He turned right and went south.

That way the traffic, heading towards the West End, was heavy. He grimaced. He was not going to set out on an adventure only to be frustrated by successive jams at successive sets of traffic lights. At the junction with Marylebone Road, below the flyover, he turned left and east.

There were three lanes of vehicles but at least they were moving. Even so he chafed that his foray into freedom should be hindered by the volume of everyday traffic. He moved into the middle lane and decided to keep going as far as he could; until he reached the sea.

He went beyond Madame Tussaud's and the main-line terminals at Euston and King's Cross. As he passed the stations he entertained a brief fantasy of leaving his car and getting on a train, any train, and disappearing forever over the horizon. But there was nowhere to park. He drove on slowly.

Clerkenwell, Old Street, Bethnal Green. He had never realised London went on for so long. He kept the nose of the car pointing as near due east as he could. He wished he had a compass but the pale autumnal sun was on his right and he kept it there. He was pleased with that, navigating by the sun. Roman Road. Ah, that was more like it. Globe Town. That pleased him more. The journey was expanding.

He saw a sign to the Blackwall Tunnel and shied away from it. There were Chinese and Indians about. They gave the dun landscape a touch of exoticism. He waved to some sari-clad schoolgirls as he waited for them to cross a zebra crossing. They giggled and ran across, one of them giving him the finger and laughing. He was strangely cheered.

He arrived at London's encircling motorway, the M25, with a shock. He had forgotten it was there. At the first exit he turned off and gratefully headed east again. A sign said: 'Harwich.' He could almost smell the North Sea.

The road remained busy, bunched with heavy trucks heading for the North Sea ports. But eventually the urban landscape thinned and there were more trees than buildings. The countryside was flat, spreading far away like a misty green ocean.

By the time he passed Chelmsford his adventurous mood was evaporating. There was nothing like a solitary drive to make you think. He kept asking himself why he was doing this, running away again; mentally he thumbed back through the events of the past weeks. His wife was now an enemy and a stranger, his children, two uncertain particles from his past. Would he lose them forever? Irritably he turned on the radio and the singers lamented: 'When will I see you again . . . ? Awawa, wawa, wawa.' Tears came to his eyes and he almost missed a red light. A youth on a motor cycle in front, who had seen his unchecked approach and had frantically tried to move away from the oncoming bonnet, called over his shoulder: 'What the fuck d'you think you're doing, mate?'

'Crying,' Nicholas answered back.

The motor cyclist looked astounded but the lights changed and, treating him to the sign of the wanker, the youth drove off. 'You self-pitying bastard,' muttered Nicholas to himself. 'Stop it. Stop it *now*.' Savagely he turned the radio off poking his tongue at it. He straightened his face and his thoughts and kept going east.

Six miles short of Harwich he saw a sign indicating a small road to Littlehaven. He turned away from the main highway and down through thicket hedges and overhung trees. He put the car window down and at once smelled the salt. His spirits lifted a little. Surely Littlehaven would be a place for introspection, for dissecting past errors, and for trying to think of where he would go, what he would do. The mild sun had gone and low rain clouds were coming towards him. It would be a good place to suffer.

'You're wallowing in it,' he remarked fiercely. 'It's your bloody fault, nobody else's. It's up to you to get out of this.' He squared his shoulders even as he drove. To hell with them all. This would be the place to start a new life.

Littlehaven did not seem up to the task. It was smeared with rain and with fog drifting along its single street. The eves dripped, the trees shivered in the sea wind. It was more a place for wallowing. From along the coast a warning horn sounded like a bereft cow. He stopped the car by a small, empty, wet jetty. He got out and stood staring into the mist. The waves were unimpressive.

'Lost are you?' enquired a shaky voice. 'Took the wrong turn. People keep doing that.'

At one time he might have been a tall man but he was bent sideways as if by prevailing winds. His face was rheumy and his eyes like chalk. He wore an old macintosh and a flat cap. A damp dog appeared along the road and sat down beside him as if staking a claim. It stared at Nicholas and then cocked its leg against a rusty mooring bollard.

'No, I've always wanted to come to Littlehaven,' lied Nicholas.

Astonishment rearranged the wrinkles on the man's face. 'You have?' he queried. 'Littlehaven? Here? What for?'

'Just liked the sound of it,' answered Nicholas. 'Is there anywhere I can stay?'

The man searched his memory. 'There's Mrs Brinton,' he decided eventually. 'But she won't feed you. Anyway her husband's dying. Could be this week.'

'I was thinking more of a hotel or a pub maybe.'

'Hotels are miles away,' said the man. 'Why would they be here, I ask you? There's a pub and it's not too bad. Not for Littlehaven. They get fishing people and wildfowlers and such there. Not many just now I shouldn't reckon. It's just down there.' He pointed at right angles through the mist. 'It's called the Hope.' He cackled. 'About the only hope there is around here.'

Nicholas thanked him, gratefully got into the car and drove off. Littlehaven would have to be abandoned. Far better to keep driving. But half a mile along the wet road the Hope appeared out of the mist. Its windows were amber and the outer door was open. Outside was parked a big Citroen station-wagon with French plates. He decided to stop.

There was no one in the bar but there was a full fire in the iron grate and the room felt friendly. He put his bag down and rang the brass bell on the counter. A rounded man in a striped shirt appeared rubbing his hands. There was an ugly brass clock on the mantelshelf and it chimed four.

They had a room. 'Several in fact,' said the man as if he believed Nicholas might need more. 'It's quiet now.'

'Suits me,' said Nicholas. 'I need some time to think.'

'Thinking,' mused the landlord. 'There's plenty of time for that here.' He grimaced. 'In fact there's bugger all else to do.'

Nicholas had a beer and some sandwiches and the man showed him the room. There was a heavy bed and a flowered bedspread and a low window. Outside the afternoon dripped on. He left his bag unopened. 'I think I'll take a walk,' he said when he went down the stairs again.

'You'll need a coat,' said the man. His wife had joined him, resignation written all over her. 'You'll need one,' she echoed. 'It's damp and getting cold. There's an oilskin in the hall if you like. And some gumboots.'

'I should take it,' confirmed the man. 'It gets into your bones this damp does.'

'We want to go to Chelmsford ourselves,' said his wife. 'For good.' Nicholas went into the hall and the landlord came after him pointing out the gumboots. He took an oilskin from a hanger. There was a sou'wester too but the landlord said: 'You won't need that. You're not going out to sea are you.'

He gave an awkward laugh and Nicholas joined him. He put the oilskin over his sweater and jacket, pulled on his gumboots, and went out into the grey wash of the Essex afternoon.

The Citroen was still parked outside with his own car behind it. He walked in the opposite direction. The flat land was almost indistinguishable from the flat sea. The muted water was pushing over the shingle. There was a path along a low dyke leading into the unseen distance like a thread. He went that way.

It was eerie. The wetness of the air, the closeness of the mist, the brush of it on his face. There were no sounds, not even of birds, only the touch of the water on the unkempt shore. It was as if the landscape were aching for something to break the silence. He walked for half a mile along the dyke on the muddy path. He was glad of the gumboots. Every hundred yards was identical to the hundred yards before and that after; no change in the land, the air, the silence.

Then from the inland side he saw a spot of colour, a speck of red moving against the monochrome background. Someone was coming towards the dyke from the marshy fields. He continued walking and watched.

There must have been a flight of steps ahead, from the fields to the bank, because the red dot vanished and then reappeared coming in his direction. She was wearing a cloak, and huddled into it. She came near. Out there, in the isolation and the mist, they greeted each other. Her young face was dark and her eyes dark also under the cover of a heavy black headscarf. She took him for a local in his oilskin and boots. 'How many kilometres for the village?' she asked. There was a touch of accent.

'About one and a bit,' he answered.

She laughed. 'It is longer in this weather.'

As she spoke there came an abrupt honking and a low formation of geese on loud wings flew over. They both crouched and for a moment held on to each other. Then they laughed. ' 'Onk, 'onk, 'onk,' she imitated. 'I am so sorry. It was a shock.'

'They scared me too,' he answered. 'I am a stranger here as well.'

'You are well ready,' she said nodding at his protective clothes. She shook her cloak. 'I am glad I came with this.' She smiled at him again and then began to continue her walk. 'Goodbye then, I must go.'

Before he could think of anything else but 'Goodbye' she had continued on her way. He watched her go. After a hundred yards she turned and waved and he called: ' 'Onk, 'onk, 'onk,' making her laugh again.

That evening he had dinner in the otherwise deserted dining

room. Two men came into the adjoining bar but left after a few minutes. The landlord rubbed his eyes and said the weather made him tired. Nicholas rang Sol but there was no reply.

He went to his room. He was tired also. He lay back in the bulky bed and studied the beams on the ceiling. All the decisions and directions he had taken that day, from his first turning right instead of left at the very outset of his journey, to the leaving of the main road on seeing the sign, to the man with the dog directing him to the Hope, and his going into the inn, walking in the grey afternoon by the sea and speaking to the beautiful young woman in the red cloak; all those choices, those chances, although he was not to know it then, combined to form a fate, a story, which at that moment he could not have imagined. These things would change his life.

Rain was lashing at the tight window when he awoke, the morning as dark as winter. Around him the room was dim and he lay for a moment trying to consider where he was.

On the chest opposite was a tea-making tray, white crockery, a tall jug and broad teapot, squat cups, like a family of Eskimos. It was eight o'clock. He had nothing he had to do that day. Just be there. He decided to make an early start.

Twenty minutes later he went downstairs. It was almost as if the inn were a steady ship in a wanton tempest. Water was streaming down the windows, gusting at the panes. At the foot of the stairs was a beamed lobby. He could feel the cutting draught below the old front door. There was a notice-board with variously sized pieces of damp paper pinned to it. He read each one carefully, a man with time on his hands. It was strange that he had urgent work to do but that he was now in this vacuum; it was like digging a trench or constructing a fortification in front of a battleground and crouching there, hoping that the enemy would go away.

The notices told of the visiting hours of the mobile library and the doctor's surgery. There was to be a bring-and-buy sale at the church hall and on Wednesday the suspense and hope of bingo. Larry Evercreech advertised his fishing trips and you could, if you wished to make the journey, view a winter exhibition of teapots at Walton-on-the-Naze. At the centre of the informative collection was a timetable for the Harwich – Hook of Holland ferry.

In the dining room there was an early fire. A young black woman in a white apron was standing watching the log flames. 'Breakfast?' she said in a London Essex voice. 'You're gonna need it today. Tea or coffee is it?'

'Coffee please,' he said wondering what she imagined he was going to do to need a big breakfast. Swim to Belgium perhaps, or just go fishing with Larry Evercreech. Several tables were laid and one had been used. Four places had been occupied and there was a copy of the *Daily Mail* on one of the seats. He picked it up and went to a table near the fireplace. Outside he heard a car starting.

'She'll be back,' forecast the girl putting a pot of coffee on the table. 'I'll bring the toast. Two sausages was it?'

'Oh yes,' said Nicholas. 'I'd better put the paper back then.'

'Here she comes now,' said the girl.

Into the room came the beautiful young woman who had worn the red cloak. She smiled recognition and wished him good morning. She was wearing a grey sweater and black trousers. Her hair was tied in a ponytail. 'I'm afraid I've nicked your newspaper,' he said walking over and handing it back.

She laughed approvingly. 'Nicked is a good word,' she said. 'I know about the nick of time. But this nick means to take?'

'Stolen,' he said. 'Appropriated.' She had sat at the table for four again. 'Are your friends gone?' he asked. 'Would you like to join me? I am just about to start.'

'And I am complete,' she said. 'It was early.' She stood and walked the few paces towards his table. 'But I will take some coffee.'

When the waitress returned her eyebrows went up. She smiled. 'Might just as well get togevver,' she said. 'In this wevver.'

'I will have some coffee, please,' said the woman.

'Right, I'll get it,' said the waitress cheerfully. She turned to Nicholas. 'Do you want cereal?' she asked. She nodded. 'It's on the side table over there. You 'ave to 'elp yourself.'

Nicholas said he would not bother with the cereal. 'Righto,' responded the girl. 'I'll get your full breakfast and I'll get the lady some coffee.' She paused as if accustomed to giving advice, then said: 'You two 'ave a nice chat.'

They smiled at each other across the table. 'I think our nice chat must begin with introductions,' suggested Nicholas. 'I'm Nicholas Boulting.'

'And my name is Thérèse Bernet,' she responded. They shook hands gently across the cups.

'Why are you here, in this wet place?' she asked. She glanced at the rain-filled window.

'I don't know,' he said honestly. 'I . . . well, I just followed the road. And you?'

She shrugged. 'I also do not know. I came with my husband.'

'He went off with the others?' he said.

'Yes. To somewhere . . . to Wolverhampton. Right?'

'Right. That's a long way.'

'They have left me here,' she smiled wryly. 'They are busy men. Busy, busy, busy. They are engineers, you see. For electricity. For power stations. . . .'

Like someone who has perfected a plan the waitress returned. The face of another woman came around the partition and studied them. The plate was piled with bacon, sausages, eggs, fried potatoes, baked beans, mushrooms and tomatoes. Nicholas regarded it helplessly. 'This,' he said looking apologetically at his companion, 'was going to be a *solitary* breakfast. It's going to be difficult . . .'

To his astonishment, she said: 'I can help. I had only some small breakfast. Orange juice, coffee. Now I am hungry.' She picked up a fork and entranced, he watched her as she leaned over. '*Excusez-moi*,' she said spearing one of the sausages. She put it on a side plate. 'And perhaps a little bacon.' A rasher of bacon crossed the cloth before his eyes. 'And some *champignons* . . . mushroom, yes?'

'Yes,' he confirmed, watching her take them. 'Mushrooms.' Her fingers were white and slender. She sliced the sausage with delicate enthusiasm. '*Bon appétit,*' she smiled. He lifted a mushroom with his fork. '*Bon appétit.*'

The waitress returned with a rack of toast and blinked at what had occurred. 'Would Miss like a proper breakfast?' she asked her eyes going from one plate to another.

Thérèse smiled with her mouth full. She waved her fork. '*Non, non. Merci,*' she said.

'More toast?' asked the waitress. The head of the other woman came around the partition again and she shrugged back towards some hidden person as if indicating that the situation was getting beyond her. 'Yes, some more toast please,' said Nicholas. He paused. 'We're hungry.'

As though they had eaten together many times they consumed the food in silence. Eventually Thérèse pushed her empty plate aside and smiled at him. 'Your breakfast is nicked,' she laughed. He put his plate away also. The waitress, anxious to keep abreast of the situation, returned and took the plates, promising to return with more coffee.

'So,' said Thérèse like someone needing to catch up with news. 'You came to this place by going with the road? That is romantic.'

He responded awkwardly. 'I suppose so. I wanted to think about a few things and I thought this might be the place.'

She appeared understanding. 'For thinking this place is good,' she agreed. 'There is nothing else.'

'I am a writer and I thought . . .'

'Ah, that gives the reason,' she nodded. 'Writers must think. *Il faut penser.*' She tapped her forehead lightly. 'I understand. I am so too.'

'You're a writer?'

'*Non, non.* But I paint. Not important. But I paint. I sell even, a little. This is why I came with my husband.'

'You were going to paint while he was occupied with electricity,' he said.

'Very big electricity,' she corrected defensively. 'He and his colleagues have been at power stations here. Ipswich, Cambridge and other places. Now he goes to Wolverhampton.'

'And you still intend to paint.'

'Not very much, by the rain,' she replied glancing again at the window. 'It is water-colour.'

He laughed at her joke. 'It will need to be,' he said. 'When will he be back?'

'In three days,' she answered flatly. She gritted her teeth. 'I am angry with him. And also with myself for coming. I thought I could paint here. He said there would be nothing to paint in this place he has gone, Wolverhampton, only smoke.' She bit her lip gently. 'I think he is trying to . . . how is it? To send me to school. . . .'

'Teach you a lesson,' he suggested.

'*Oui*. Teach me a lesson. He told me always it was boring, his work. And boring for me to wait for him. I should have stayed in Paris.'

'Offhand,' said Nicholas, 'I would have said Paris was more fun than Littlehaven or Wolverhampton.' He glanced at the window. 'Maybe it will stop. Even here it can't rain for three days.'

'It did last week,' said the waitress confidently as she appeared to clear the plates. 'Never packed up.'

'I will look,' decided Thérèse. 'Perhaps some good weather comes.' She rose and he watched her walk, slim and graceful, towards the lobby. He heard her open the front door of the inn and her exclamation and the gust of chilly air as she did so. There was an interval before she returned. 'There is no light. It is rain and dark,' she said sitting down. Then she leaned towards him. 'What is this ferry to Holland?' she whispered. 'It is from near this place?'

'The ferry . . . well, it sails from Harwich. It's about seven or eight miles from here I think.'

She smiled like a plotter. 'You could take me there? In your car?'

'Yes, yes of course,' he replied with surprise. He moved nearer and whispered as well: 'You want to go on the ferry?'

She sat down and her fingers touched his wrists across the table. 'I think I will take a voyage, a cruise,' she confided. She scanned the edges of the room but the waitress and the prying woman were not to be seen. Thérèse stood up and went to the partition. She glanced around it and tiptoed back.

'It is my turn to teach the lesson,' she said. 'To my 'usband. I say to him that I want to return to Paris but he thinks serve the right . . . no, serve *my* right . . . yes?' Nicholas said: 'Yes.' She continued: 'Serve my right that I should stay here in the rain. Then I will not want to come with him on his business again.'

'He said you must not go back home.'

'*Non*.' She waved a slender finger, still smiling. 'He said that I must not put it into my brain to *fly* home. He said "*fly* home" you understand. In this way I could go home but I do not have to fly. I can go on the ferry and go on trains to Paris – no flying.' She looked quietly gleeful. 'That will be the lesson for him.'

Nicholas regarded her dubiously. 'He will be very annoyed,' he forecast. 'This is a long way to come back from Wolver-hampton.'

Her eyes met his fully. 'He must not leave me in this place,' she pouted. She put her hand on his. 'You will help Nicholas?'

'I'll take you,' he said looking at her eyes. 'But don't tell your husband it was me.'

She returned his smile. 'I will not. But we must be secret. I think perhaps the little black girl will . . . ?' She made a chattering mime with her fingers.

'Let's be on our way,' he said.

It took her ten minutes to pack. He was waiting in the car outside watching the blobs of rain hit and run down the windscreen, wondering, once again, what was happening to him. She came out in her red cloak and with two small cases. 'I will do it,' she told him hurriedly as he began to get out to help her. 'The little spy must not see you. Already she is asking.'

'She'll hear the car go,' pointed out Nicholas. 'And she'll see us drive off. Then I'll come back alone.'

Thérèse regarded him with sly seriousness. 'You must leave before my husband returns,' she warned. 'He is jealous.'

'Thanks,' he sighed. A sudden vision of Bonnie and her family came to him; and the old soldiers with their corpse of a comrade. Perhaps, adrift as he was, he was flashing a light to attract all manner of helpless, puzzled, cornered and fugitive people. 'We must go,' said Thérèse breaking into his thoughts. 'Or we will miss the ferry.'

The plural she used lurked in his mind as they drove along the rainy road and joined the main highway to Harwich, slotting into the long line of spraying trucks heading that way. 'Perhaps I should come with you,' he joked tentatively. A sign said 'Harwich 3 miles.' The rain and the traffic had thickened.

'Ah, but I thought you would,' she responded, her eyes widening and turning to him. 'That is good. We can take the cruise. We go to 'Ook of 'Olland. Then I go to Paris and you return here.'

'Oh, at least we could have lunch at sea.'

'That will be *fantastique*. How long is the voyage to . . .'

' 'Ook of 'Olland?' he mimicked.

She glanced his way in consternation but then laughed with him. 'It is difficult,' she said. Deliberately she repeated: 'Hook of Holland.'

They reached the ferry terminal with ten minutes to spare. 'Just as well you're not bringing your car, sir,' said the man at the ticket window. 'We've done loading.'

Thérèse insisted on paying for their passage. He watched her buying him a return ticket. She said firmly: 'I am the one on the journey, you are here to show me the way.'

'In case you get lost.'

'Yes. You are the guide . . . the . . . man who makes the course.'

'The navigator.'

'That is right.' She repeated it carefully: 'The navigator.' They had walked up the covered gangway and onto the vessel. Everywhere was wood and brass. They could see a dining room through a glass door.

'Serving lunch early today sir,' said a braided steward checking on a notice-board. 'Twelve noon.' He looked from one to the other as though he was not sure whether to tell them his news. 'It's going to get a bit rough, later,' he said darkly.

Thérèse glanced at Nicholas. 'How long does the crossing take?' he asked the steward. 'We only came on the spur of the moment.'

'Not a good spur of the moment, sir. It's eight hours,' said the man. He appeared to want to help them. 'There's still a couple of minutes, you could get off,' he suggested. 'Get a refund.'

'On no, this is not possible,' interrupted Thérèse. She squeezed Nicholas's elbow. 'We will not look at the waves,' she said. 'We must stay.'

Nicholas again faced the steward who shrugged and said: 'Why not have a drink? I'm just opening the bar. Just by the dining room, here, sir.' His bonhomie was ominous: 'Might as well have a drink or two.'

They followed him into the saloon. There was a scattering of apprehensive people sitting at the tables around the bar. 'The word's got around,' said the steward. He lifted the grille and announced so quietly it seemed almost to himself: 'Bar's open.'

'They do it on purpose,' Nicholas told her as he brought the drinks to the table. They had both ordered Martinis. Thérèse was pale. 'They like to set you up. Telling you there's a hurricane out there.' Glumly he sat down. 'I didn't think it took so long. Not eight hours.'

They raised their glasses in a subdued toast. 'Here's to the voyage,' she said. 'At least I will be going home.' She smiled. 'I am escaping.'

'I have to come back,' he pointed out dolefully. He rocked his hand like the motion of the sea. They both began to laugh. 'Let's have some lunch,' he said.

As they went into the dining room, with its white cloths set with glasses and silverware, and a ridge around the table edges to prevent them falling, the ship gave a nudge and began to move away from the pier. The splatter of the rain increased, streaking across the windows like restraining cables. Nicholas stood and looked out. On the quay a group of dockers were pretending to be sick into the water. Laughing, they pointed up at some passengers he could not see. 'Funny,' grunted Nicholas. 'Very funny.'

'There is a joke?' asked Thérèse.

'Not a repeatable one,' he answered. About half the tables were occupied. A florid man in a blue blazer arrived tugging at a distraught-looking woman. 'Eat,' he ordered loudly. 'Stuff yourself. At least you'll have something to bring up.'

'I don't know why we came,' the woman moaned putting her face on the table. 'It's going to be like last time. I thought I would die last time.'

Nicholas told the waiter that they would like to change their table. 'It's just as safe here, sir,' the youth said genuinely. 'They're all bolted down.'

'We'd like to move,' insisted Nicholas low-voiced. 'Away from other people.'

'Right you are, sir, madam.' The waiter led them to a place in a distant corner. The man who had been advising his wife to eat muttered loudly as they passed. 'You can't run away from the sea.'

When they had reached the new table Thérèse went to the ladies' room. The waiter, lowering his head and his voice even though there was no one within hearing, said to Nicholas: 'Have you booked a cabin, sir?'

'A cabin? No. Do you think . . . ?'

'You'll need one,' the waiter finished for him. 'It's blowing up a real bugger out there.' He studied Nicholas as if weighing up whether to go further. He decided to do so. 'Nature's uncontrolled violence, sir.' He handed over the menu. 'Don't reckon there'll be that many for desserts,' he went on. 'I'm sure your wife would be more comfortable in a cabin . . . when it gets to it.' Briefly he closed his eyes. 'Generally I have to lie down myself.'

Thérèse returned. 'If there is a storm to come,' she announced, 'then we must enjoy our lunch.'

'Right, madam,' said the waiter ominously. 'You might as well.'

They each had another Martini while they ordered. They could feel the ship being pushed by the wind. They began with duck pâté. Other passengers looked through the window and, some with expressions of disgust, some disquiet, watched them eating.

Thérèse said solidly: 'I will visit my mother when I get to Paris. I like to do that.' She looked up and asked. 'You have a mother?'

'No. She died some years ago. I have a father.'

'And you see him?'

'Sometimes,' replied Nicholas guiltily. 'He is very old now. In a nursing home in the north of England.'

She looked as if she were personally disappointed. 'Why does he not live with you?' She waited and then added: 'And your family.' There was another pause. 'And your wife.'

'I'm not sure that I have a wife and family at the moment,' he said. 'I am separated.' He thought he might as well tell her. 'I left home . . . I ran away.'

'Ah,' she responded with spontaneous brightness. 'This is me also. I run away. All the time.' Her fingers performed a running mime. 'See, I am running away now.'

As if it had been waiting for her to finish the sentence, the ship gave a lurch that sent the food, crockery and cutlery sliding to one side of the table where it was only prevented from plunging to the floor by the wooden rail at the edge. 'Oh, so soon!' exclaimed Thérèse with real concern. 'It is the storm?'

'Either that or we've rammed something,' said Nicholas attempting to appear flippant. The waiter came hurrying across. 'Will you still want your Stroganoff, sir?' He looked at them with a sort of pleading. 'Because I think I'd better get it now. While I'm still on my feet.' His face was like putty. 'I used to be in a hotel,' he added as if that were a full explanation. 'On shore.' Nicholas looked across at Thérèse. Her face was white with two doll-like spots of colour on her cheeks. The ship rolled again, lifted its nose and then its stern. Nicholas felt his stomach sag. 'I think,' he said to the waiter, 'that we had better take the cabin you mentioned.'

The youth appeared immensely relieved. 'Very wise, sir. I'll get the cabin steward. If you get along there a bit smartish I'll try and get some sandwiches to you.'

'Right, very kind,' said Nicholas trying to keep his voice normal. He had to help Thérèse to her feet. The ship rolled horribly again.

'Chicken or beef or pork, sir?'

'What . . . ? ' The floor slid away from below his feet. He clutched the table desperately. 'Oh, sandwiches . . . whatever . . .'

'Oh . . . oh,' cried Thérèse. She was heading for the door holding her napkin to her mouth. Sickened faces were pressed to the window observing her with grim satisfaction. A different steward came along the sloping floor like a skier. 'Come with me, sir, madam. We'll get you sorted out.'

They staggered after him clutching the rail as they went. Nicholas got a grey glimpse of boiling sea. 'Oh my God,' he moaned.

'*Mon Dieu*,' added Thérèse.

The newly arrived steward, striding on splayed legs ahead of them as if demonstrating how easy it was, opened a door and beckoned them into a cabin. Nicholas gratefully gave him twenty pounds. The man thanked him and handed him the key. 'It's all right, sir, we're not busy today.'

He closed the door on them. Thérèse was already hanging into the corner wash-basin. The cabin rolled like a dice. Nicholas tried to pat her gently on the back to comfort her but she motioned him away. There were couchettes in the cabin one above the other. He waited for Thérèse to finish at the wash-basin then indicated the bunks. Stricken-faced, she pointed to the lower tier, lurched towards it and rolled in. He took her place at the basin. Nausea swept over him. The ship was not still for a moment. An enormous pitch sent him tumbling across the small cabin. Thérèse, rolled into a moaning bundle, did not even look towards him. He hauled himself up and like a man crossing a ravine on a tightrope struggled towards the bunks. There was a short ladder to the upper tier. Gritting his teeth he went up it one hand, one foot, at a time. He was thrown first one way then the other; he hung out like an acrobat. He was sure the ship must capsize. His body would be found trapped in this cabin with a beautiful Frenchwoman. Oh God, oh God. He threw himself on to the bunk and clasped it. There was a diffident tap at the door. The voice of the upright steward who had led them to the cabin called into him.

'Your sandwiches, sir. Pork.'

By the time they reached their destination they were deep in exhausted sleep, one above the other. Nicholas awoke as the vessel was limping gratefully towards the Dutch pier. He climbed down, almost falling with unsuspected weakness. Thérèse was stirring. 'Always I have wanted to have a voyage,' she mumbled. 'But now, not ever.'

They hardly spoke again until they were on shore. They had staggered, like comic drunks, with the rest of the passengers down the gangway, and were standing on, almost feeling, the unmoving ground in the arrivals hall. 'Now you must go back,' she said her eyes unhappy. 'It is my fault. I am sorry.'

Nicholas felt the wind rattle the large building. 'I think I will stay here until the weather improves,' he said. 'I've always wanted to visit Holland. Do some mountaineering perhaps.'

Thérèse laughed almost shyly. 'You are a good man, Nicholas,' she said. She began to unzip one of her pieces of luggage. 'I have a little gift. It is for you.'

From the case she took a large, thick envelope. 'This is the only painting I did in England,' she said. She handed it to him. It was a pale water-colour. 'See if it has my special sign in the corner.' She touched with her finger. 'You see, a small bird on a tree. . . .'

Nicholas thanked her. He studied the painting. It was Littlehaven. The subdued street, the inn and the road in front of it. The bird was sitting at one corner. 'I will remember you when I look at it,' he told her. 'I hope we can meet again some time.' He looked steadily into her face. 'In Paris, perhaps.'

She did not reply, instead tapping the corner of the painting. 'My bird,' she said. 'You see, before I am married my name was Oiseau, Thérèse Oiseau. So I always have this bird.' She looked at him steadily. 'It will not be possible,' she said answering his enquiry. 'I do not think so.' Quietly she kissed him on both cheeks and he held her hand. 'I have given you much trouble,' she smiled.

'It was a pleasure. I can't think of anyone with whom I would rather share a storm at sea.'

She did not laugh but repeated: 'You are a good man.' Then to his surprise added: 'You must see your father. You must care for him. One day your father will be you.'

As if she thought it was the right moment she turned and walked away from him in her red cloak. He remained stationary, watching her crossing the concourse with her quick decisive steps. At the entrance to the building, at immigration, she turned and briefly waved.

Seven

Sol studied him doubtfully, his eyebrows and moustache drooping in unison. With little conviction he asked: 'Did you get to thinking out your life . . . or a plot . . . a poem, maybe a title . . . ?

To each of the enquiries Nicholas shook his head. 'Not a word,' he confessed. 'Even I'm beginning to think I'm a one-book man.'

'Okay, what did you do?'

Nicholas responded to his enquiry steadily. 'I went to Holland. . . .'

'Shit,' said Sol in a low voice. 'Holland.'

'I went with a beautiful Frenchwoman.'

'Double shit,' Sol whispered.

Nicholas shrugged. 'I can't even run away successfully.'

The American picked up a kitchen chair and turned it around, sitting and leaning over the back.

'And you met this French beauty out there in the wetlands of . . . where was it . . . ? Just like that?'

'Essex. Yes, she and her husband were at the pub where I was staying. She's an artist. They live in Paris.'

'And this Frenchman let you take his dishy wife to Holland?'

'He didn't know. He went off to Wolverhampton. . . .'

'You're losing me.'

'In the Midlands. He went there on business and she wanted to get back to Paris.'

'So she asked you to take her to Holland.'

Nicholas nodded: 'It was on the way. More or less. From Holland she went home.'

Sol rolled his eyes. 'Not not before . . . *amore*. . . .'

'Not before a force-twelve gale and a lot of vomit,' corrected Nicholas. 'God it was terrible, Sol. I thought the ship was going to overturn. There was no romance, believe me. . . .'

'Not even before the gale . . . ?' Sol looked crestfallen.

'Not even.'

'Let's fix the scenario. . . . This beautiful Frenchwoman, artist, comes up to you and says: "*Bonjour, monsieur*. Please take me to Holland".'

' 'Olland,' Nicholas smiled seriously. 'She said 'Olland. Like 'Ook of 'Olland.' He took the small painting she had given him. 'All I have of her is this.' He showed it to Sol who said: 'Nice.'

Nicholas took it to the alcove below the stairs and tried it against the wall. 'I'll get a frame and put it there,' he said.

With an excited clatter Sol turned his chair around. 'You've *got* to write it. It's a big romantic novel. Beautiful, neglected wife, a painter, a genius, a writer, big love, a big storm at sea. . . .'

'And a peck on the cheek and cheerio. . . .'

'*Au revoir*,' corrected Sol with a deep sigh. 'When will you see her again?'

'I don't think I ever will. It was just an incident, an adventure. She made it clear that she was closing the door.'

'After you'd vomited together?'

'I knew the score.'

'Jeez, you really are something.' It was half-admiration, half-scorn. 'And you're going to just drop it. Not even *try* to see her.'

'No point. It wasn't like that.'

'It's *always* like that,' muttered Sol. He ruminated walking over to make some coffee. 'Incidentally that other broad who never wanted to see you again . . . Loretta . . . what the fuck does she call herself, Wobbleshins . . . ?' Nicholas looked up quickly. 'Widdershins,' he amended. 'She rang?'

Sol shrugged. 'Said she can't live without you. She rang three times, for God's sake. She gave you the big brush-off, right?'

'Right. She has difficulty making up her mind.'

'She wants you to take her somewhere this weekend.' His eyes widened. 'Holland, maybe.'

'I can't take Loretta anywhere this weekend. I have a date with my kids.'

Sol put his head in his hands. 'I think I'm going to cry,' he said.

He took them to the same place for lunch, the Bedford Arms on Hendon Way. The same wry waitress was there and she led them to the same table. 'Here we are again,' Willie told her with bogus cheerfulness. She laughed and Nicholas tried to show a grin. 'You don't know how true that is,' said the woman. 'I see them all. They come in here, once, twice maybe, and then you never see them again. Father's got fed up with this access lark.'

Deborah told her stoutly: 'We're always going to come in here.' She looked at her father. 'We like it.'

'That's the plan,' said Nicholas. Perhaps the other fathers, or the children, had found somewhere better.

Deborah and Willie sat at the table. The waitress whispered to Nicholas. 'Later they come back with their mum and their mum's boyfriend. You can tell they've gone home and said they'd been here to Sunday lunch, so the mother brings them too. Not to be outdone, see.'

'There's a lot of psychology then, in a place like this,' suggested Nicholas.

'I'll say,' she said tightening her lips. 'I could write a book. I could tell a thing or two. I've been with my husband thirty years.'

'That's good,' said Willie brightly. 'Thirty years.'

She turned to Nicholas and lowered her voice. 'Hate the sight of the swine. But it's too late now. Couldn't afford it anyway. You have to have money to get rid of each other.'

She left them to study the menu. Nicholas sat between the children. 'She seems to know a lot about everything,' suggested Willie. 'Wonder why she has to work here?'

'She just likes helping people,' suggested Deborah kindly. 'Doesn't she, Dad?'

'Perhaps that's it,' grinned Nicholas. 'She's probably a registered charity.'

They had been standing outside the front door again when he had arrived at the house, two neatly turned-out figures, standing still, watching him approach.

'How is your mother?' he asked them when they were eating lunch.

'She cries,' revealed Willie bluntly. 'At night.' Fiercely Deborah smacked his wrist across the table and he withdrew it with a howl. 'She only cried because she fell down,' she affirmed turning to her father guiltily. 'Those little steps at the bottom of the stairs. That's all.'

'She was drunk,' muttered Willie studying his hamburger.

'She *wasn't*!' the girl shouted at him.

'She was drunk,' the boy repeated doggedly, still not looking up. 'She kept saying . . .'

Nicholas intervened but not before Willie had the last word. 'She kept saying she was pissed,' he said with the same bluntness. 'While she was sitting on the floor.'

Deborah stood, her pale cheeks running tears, and moved threateningly around the table towards her brother. 'You pig,' she cried. Nicholas put his arm out to stop her and gave Willie the opportunity to make for the door. He ran between the tables, still clutching his hamburger-loaded fork. As his father's attention was taken, Deborah broke free and went in sobbing pursuit. People stopped eating and watched. Nicholas stood and, attempting dignity, went striding after them. Other Sunday fathers grinned and nodded. One called: 'There's no accounting for kids.'

By the time Nicholas, at a trot, had reached the entrance of the building, Deborah and Willie had run around the corner to a playground dominated by a grotesquely grinning red tree giant. There were swings and a slide. He reached the gate just as Willie's head appeared at the tree giant's mouth. 'Shut up stupid!' he bawled towards his sister. She screamed something at him and advanced. Nicholas shouted at them. Willie waved the table fork like a weapon.

The girl charged in his direction. She ran to the back of the giant, shouting, sobbing that she was going to get him out of there. Willie climbed, face first, out of the giant's mouth and rolled on the ground. Nicholas tried to grab him but he swerved behind the swings. Nicholas, inwardly cursing his incompetence with his own children, attempted to reason with him. Deborah appeared from behind the giant and ran towards her brother. From the other side Willie pushed one of the swings at her and then the others as he moved along the line. 'Stop it, stop it, pig!' she screeched.

'Willie! Deborah! Both of you . . . pack it up! Stop it at once!'

Each child treated him to a separate but equally scornful look and continued. Willie escaped from behind the swings and, whooping, made for the slide. Enraged, his sister went after him. Again Nicholas tried to catch her but only delayed her enough to give Willie time to clamber up the steps of the slide. She began to follow him but Nicholas caught her, firmly this time. Willie was standing at the apex of the slide still holding the fork aloft while father and daughter stared up at him. Suddenly he stood and bawled at the top of his voice: *'My mum was pissed! My mum was pissed!'* A couple walking from the car park stopped and started laughing.

Deborah collapsed into tears. She hung on to her father. 'She *wasn't*, she *wasn't*,' she pleaded. Nicholas put her gently to one side. 'Come on down, Willie,' he said in a calm voice. 'We're going to the zoo.'

'Stuff the zoo!' Willie howled back. He was crying now also. Nicholas looked helplessly from one to another. As he did so, Willie, still standing, launched himself down the slide. Half-way down he swayed, hit the edge and tumbled over, falling with a heavy sound onto the tarmac.

'He did that on purpose,' sobbed Deborah.

At the hospital they were optimistic. Willie rolled his eyes horribly while they were examining his head but the black doctor believed there would be no permanent damage. They plastered the wound and gave him an aspirin and Nicholas with the quietened Deborah took him home.

'Do you think they get proper training in Africa?' suggested Willie holding his head in the rear of the car.

It was Deborah who answered: 'Stop it. Of course they do. Anyway it's only a bump.'

'It was your fault,' said Willie maliciously.

'No, it wasn't! You started it.'

'It was you . . .'

'Stop it!' shouted their father. He could see their startled faces in the mirror, Willie's even whiter than before. Immediately Nicholas felt ashamed. He lowered his tone. 'It happened,' he said. 'Whose fault it was doesn't really come into it.' He drove for another half a mile in silence. Eventually he said: 'Just *don't* tell your mother what caused the trouble.'

'About her being . . . drunk,' persisted Willie. He could not resist an opportunity.

'I'll kill you if you say that again,' said Deborah grinding her teeth.

''So you kill me,' shrugged Willie moving away from her on the seat. 'They'll bang you up for life then.'

'Daddy, tell him,' demanded the girl.

'Deborah's right,' said Nicholas over his shoulder. 'You'll only upset your mother, Willie. Just forget about the whole thing. You fell off the slide and that's all there was to it.'

Their wretched silence returned. They turned into the High Street and then along the road to the Old Vicarage. Sarah saw them coming from a window and she was at the door when they arrived. It was the first time Nicholas had seen her since their separation. Her face was hard. 'You're soon back,' she said accusingly. Then she saw Willie's plastered head and with a moan put her arms out to him and pulled him inside as if to get him away from a bad influence. 'He fell off a slide,' said Nicholas simply. 'At the hospital they said there's nothing to . . .'

'You've been to *hospital*!' Sarah almost squealed.

'He's all right, Mum,' put in Deborah firmly. 'The doctor said.'

'He was from abroad,' said Willie half-diplomatically.

Sarah had pulled both children into the house. Her bitter eyes returned to Nicholas. She closed the door in his face. He turned to walk disconsolately down the path between the yews. Then he heard the door open again and paused.

It was still Sarah. Her voice remained steely. 'Have you been to see your father?'

'No,' he answered looking back. 'Not recently.'

'Well you'd better, Nicholas.' She said. 'He's dying.'

'I heard them say I was dying,' mentioned his father. 'So I decided against it.'

Nicholas grinned leaning forward in the chair. 'I'm very relieved,' was all he could say.

In his private room at Rosedale Bernard Boulting, aged eighty-two, sat in bed, his hair shining and crisply parted, his face like crinkled paper. He emitted a combined cough and grunt. 'Mind you,' he said leaning forward as though he were keen to keep the matter to himself, 'I'm not all that bothered when I die. Sometimes I lie in bed and I'm so still I think it's already happened. When the bloody nurse comes in with whatever it is I've got to swallow I almost feel disappointed.'

'You seem to be fine,' Nicholas smiled. 'In . . . control.'

'Oh I am now. Today I'm all right. Sometimes I wander off in my mind. They think I've gone potty. . . .' He nodded towards the open door. A starched nurse crackled past. 'She's a big 'un,' the old man observed. 'Huge.' He snuffed and returned to his theme. 'I don't care if they do think I'm bonkers,' he continued. 'At least then they leave me alone. I just go off, back to years ago, when I was young, when everything was all right.' He glanced up sharply. 'How are you getting on anyway?'

Nicholas decided to tell him. 'Not that well, Dad,' he said. 'I'm living apart from Sarah.'

'That's your wife,' said his father as if reminding both of them. 'Well, she's no loss, I'd say.'

Nicholas returned the sharp look. 'What makes you say that?'

'Bossy boots,' muttered the old man. 'Never could stand her.'

'I've also got two kids,' said Nicholas defensively. 'Deborah and Willie.'

'So you have,' said his father as if he did not care. 'Forgot all about them.'

'That's the problem when you break up – the children.'

The old man waved a thin, airy hand. 'Oh, they'll survive,' he said. 'They'll grow up and have divorces of their own.'

'It's not a divorce yet,' pointed out Nicholas. 'But it's going that way.'

A young Indian in a white coat knocked and came into the room. 'This is the doctor,' said Bernard Boulting, waving his hand again. 'I forget his name.'

The man smiled and said: 'Peter da Souza.' He and Nicholas shook hands and then the old man insisted on doing so also, both with the doctor and with his son. 'It's a funny sort of name,' said Bernard.

'He had a bad turn,' said da Souza. 'But he's pulled around very well.'

'It's not easy to die,' grunted the old man. He regarded them challengingly. 'Bloody hard in fact.'

They both laughed and he turned his expression from one to the other. 'Anyway,' he said decisively, 'I want to go on a train.'

The two younger men exchanged looks. 'Why would you want to do that, Dad?' asked Nicholas.

'Why not?' argued his father. 'I used to like going on the train to the office. Same one every day there, and same one back. Same people on it. Loved it. Forty years I did that.'

'Tomorrow you can go out if you like,' said the doctor spreading his brown hands. 'It's not far to Harrogate.'

'All right. A train it is,' said Nicholas. He looked sideways at his father. 'If you're sure.'

'I'm sure,' said the old man frowning so deeply that his

wrinkles became clefts. 'That's why I said it. I'm fed up being stuck in here, everybody waiting for me to die.'

Bernard Boulting was all ready in his overcoat and scarf when the taxi arrived the following afternoon to take them to Harrogate station. He had refused to make the short journey in his son's car because he had never approved of the cautious way Nicholas drove. 'We can natter in the taxi,' he confided, like a promise. 'And I'll feel safe. Plodding along like you do is dangerous.'

He shuffled towards the reception area of the nursing home. The matron of Rosedale, Miss Southren, came smiling to them and said: 'Don't forget to come back, Mr Boulting. We'd miss you.'

'Never thought I'd end up in a big house like this,' ruminated the old man looking at the ceiling. 'What time of the year is it anyway? It's always the same in here and I keep forgetting to look out of the window.'

Gently Nicholas told him: 'It's autumn now. Pretty mild.' He recognised his father's scarf. It was in orange, green and purple, the colours of some rugby club for which he claimed to have played. Nicholas remembered him wearing that scarf. As a small boy the banded hues had attracted his attention, and his father had taken this as evidence that the child was not colour- blind. 'He knows which season it is,' said the matron as though it mattered. 'Don't let him fool you. He knows.'

The old man made a performance of getting the scarf properly wound around his neck and then unwound as he got into the back of the taxi. The matron walked inside. A plump young assistant came from the building. 'It will do him good,' she said quietly to Nicholas, and then more quietly: 'Don't take as gospel a lot of the things he says. He told us you were a priest.' She regarded Bernard seriously and said, 'It's the only thing they've got, the power of irritation.'

In the taxi, as it crunched down the gravel drive, the old man half-turned towards the house and announced loudly: 'I'm about the only one who doesn't fart in that place.'

The taxi-driver snorted as if trying to provide an illustration. 'It's true,' protested Bernard Boulting. 'Some of them spend their lives farting. Never stop. You see them going along in their pyjamas, farting as they go. Phut, phut, phut, just like an outboard motor.'

They reached Harrogate station and the old man stood and surveyed the exterior with an expression that said he was truly glad to see it. 'I used to like going on the train,' he repeated putting his hand on Nicholas's arm. 'Loved it. Every day, up and down, up and down. All the same faces. Very interesting.'

He fell to silence as they sat on a platform bench but, like a bird, watched every moment, a porter pulling a trolley of newspapers, a soldier drinking coffee from a plastic beaker, a woman sweeping, a small girl crying against her mother's skirt. 'It all goes on, doesn't it,' he eventually observed. 'All the time. Even when you're not there.'

At Rosedale they had planned the simple itinerary: local train to Didsworth Green, twenty-five minutes down the line, get off and sit in the waiting room until it came back on its return journey from York. 'Not much of a train,' grumbled the old man as it shuffled into the station. 'Only two carriages.' He examined it critically. 'And there's no engine. Where's the engine?' He glanced at his son sideways and decided Nicholas would not be taken in. 'Pity they don't have engines these days.'

They sat in the almost empty coach. 'They used to have nice brown pictures of seaside places on the walls,' recalled Bernard. 'Under the luggage racks. Bognor and places with people on the sands.'

Nicholas asked him if he had made many friends at Rosedale. 'It's not much of a place for that sort of thing, friends,' he replied solemnly. 'I have a sort of relationship with a woman there. We share a cough-mixture spoon. But that's as far as it's got.' He turned his eye towards the window. 'People spend a lot of time sleeping,' he said.

As if he had given himself a cue, his head began to nod to the rough rhythm of the train and Nicholas let him doze until they

147

were nearing Didsworth Green. He woke him gently and the old man blinked at the unaccustomed surroundings. 'We're here now,' said Nicholas. 'It's Didsworth Green. We get off.'

'What for?' asked his father. 'What's here anyway?'

'We change trains,' said Nicholas. It seemed to satisfy the old man. It was difficult getting him down on to the platform. A woman waiting to board the train tried to help but Bernard slipped sideways and knocked her backwards so that she sat down against the picket fence. Nicholas was caught between his swaying father and the shocked woman. His father did not seem to realise what had taken place and once he had steadied himself, moved towards her. 'Oh dear, oh dear. What *have* you done?' he admonished. 'Drunk again.'

Propping the old man against the fence, Nicholas managed to pull the solid woman upright and to make apologies. She said nothing but glared at them before getting onto the train, and continued to grimace through the window as it moved off. 'Plastered at this time of the day,' mumbled his father.

It was a small, damp station. There was a waiting room, as welcoming as a tomb, and they went in there and sat on the bench, side by side. 'It would have been better to go all the way to York. We could have had some tea,' said Nicholas. He looked at his watch. It would be twenty minutes before the train returned.

'It's all right here,' said his father looking around the forbidding walls. 'No crowds anyway.' He felt in his overcoat pocket and to his son's surprise brought out half a bottle of rum. 'Stronger than tea,' he said. He unscrewed the stopper with practised firmness and offered it to Nicholas. 'Have a swig,' he said. 'I take longer because I've got to take my teeth out.'

Nicholas accepted and felt the warm, sweet liquid burn his throat. 'I've never seen you drink before,' he said handing the bottle back. 'Nothing but a half of cider.'

'Me, I've wasted my life in all sorts of ways,' said his father taking out his teeth and putting them on the bench beside him. He took a substantial drink, watched anxiously by his son.

'Still,' he philosophised putting the stopper and his teeth back. 'Everybody does it, wastes their lives. You always know you could have done better.' He looked sideways at his son. 'Well, you've got shot of the wife and family. That's a good start anyway.'

'I ran away,' argued Nicholas. 'I'm not proud of it.'

'You must have got that from me, running away,' confided the old man. 'I was always doing it.'

'*You* ran away?'

'All the time. I was always running away from your mother. Then she kept running away from me. Sometimes we'd both go running off in different directions. In the end neither of us could think of anywhere else to go. So we just stayed.' A memory made him brighten. 'I ran away in the war too, you know. In the army. It was in North Africa and I decided to clear out. I met a German soldier and he had deserted as well. We hid up together. He spoke English. We decided that whichever side looked like winning we would surrender to them. Our lot started the advance so I took him in as a prisoner. Got a lot of praise for that, I did.'

Nicholas declined another drink of rum. His father removed his teeth again and set them on the bench just as a flushed woman in a purple plastic coat came into the waiting room. She sat down on the opposite bench and spotted the teeth at once. Bernard made no attempt to drink from the bottle. Instead he picked up the teeth, polished them on his sleeve and replaced them on the bench. 'You're not supposed to do that,' the woman said eventually. She looked from Bernard to Nicholas.

'What?' enquired Bernard. 'What can't you do?'

'Put false teeth on the bench like that.'

'Show me the regulation,' challenged Bernard. He picked up the bottle and took a drink. The woman shuddered and left the waiting room. 'She doesn't know,' said the old man. The train passed the windows, pulling up at the platform. 'This our train?' asked the old man.

Nicholas confirmed that this was. 'Good. Home we go,'

nodded his father. 'I've enjoyed it. I've had quite a good time in the circumstances.'

Again the old man slept in the train. Nicholas attempted to point out a church and a village and later a herd of cows but his attention was repaid only with snores. While he slept the creases eased from the worn face and the son sadly recognised a glimpse of the father he had known as a boy. The eyes, with the deep damage of age in and around them, were covered.

Bernard woke up just before they reached Harrogate as though he had paced himself, and muttered how the country-side had changed for the worse, even the cows were smaller. He was silent and appeared weary in the taxi, but once back inside Rosedale Nursing Home he came to life, strutting about familiarly and talking to anyone who would listen, and some who could not since they were deaf, pronouncing loud verdicts on British Rail, the state of agriculture, and the lack of humour and equilibrium in women.

'It's teatime,' he said as if eager to introduce his son to his own world. 'Let's go into the Big Lounge.'

Nicholas followed him into a spacious room. It had been recently decorated in pastel blue and white which served to accentuate the shabbiness of the furniture and the people sitting on it. But there was a robust fire burning in the open grate and the genial afternoon sound of cups and saucers. On each of the low tables was a silver bell and these were rung frequently by the querulous residents. Miss Southren, the matron, cruised reassuringly around the room and brisk young women in smocks distributed the tea trays.

'So nice to see you back home,' said Matron as though Bernard had been to Africa.

The old man rang his bell louder and more often than anyone and he was still ringing it when the plump motherly girl who had seen them to the taxi brought them a tray upon which was set a china tea service and a plate of cakes. He motioned Nicholas to sit in one low, small, armchair where his knees were pointed upwards to the ceiling, while he eased himself in the deeper one. The girl asked if they would like some fresh trifle but the old man waved the suggestion away. 'It takes hours to get it out of the gaps,' he said.

'Enjoy your outing, Mr Boulting?' enquired a lady with swollen joints sitting with four others at a table behind Bernard's back.

'Fine, fine,' responded the old man airily. He glanced at Nicholas. 'Just went out to make sure the world was still in order. My son here was getting concerned about it. But it seemed to be all right, within reason.'

The lady laughed politely but the companions did not seem to be aware of the exchange. There was a hush as they softly ate the trifle.

Bernard leaned closer to his son. 'She's the one I share the spoon with,' he confided. 'The cough mixture. Not bad is she?' Without waiting for confirmation he continued, whispering: 'Most of them are past it, though. I mean, look at them. Bags of bones and a handful of stuffing.' Carefully Nicholas glanced about them. 'You seem to be in the minority,' he observed. 'There's only a few men.'

'Men wear out quicker,' asserted his father. 'They have to work, don't they. That's why there are so many old women around.' He followed his son's survey of the room. 'Not that the men are much. Most of them just sit staring at the television. They don't even know what they're watching, laughing in all the wrong places, falling asleep with their mouths open.' He let his own mouth gape to demonstrate. 'Three or four of them at a time you see, heads back, mouths open, just like a coconut shy.' His laugh grated. 'See that one there with the odd slippers. Took more than a hundred of those vitamin pills, the whole pot, because he wanted to feel young again.'

The motherly girl returned and poured the tea, Bernard pedantically supervising her as if organising some obscure alchemy. She glanced at Nicholas and he saw the patience lying flat in her eyes. He thanked her but the old man did not, only sniffing and then tentatively putting his lips to the rim of his cup. He expected the tea to be too hot but it was not and he grunted as if deprived of a grumble. Then he picked up a square of fruit cake, first searching it like a minefield. 'Obstacles,' he confided. 'Cakes have obstacles.'

He was in mid-bite when the spoon-sharing lady at the next table cried out: 'A cockroach! Oh, Mr Boulting, do help! It's a cockroach!'

Nicholas stood but his father held out a firm hand and said: 'I'll deal with this.' He stood, replaced his cake on his plate and turned towards the table where the five elderly women were transfixed by a big cockroach standing, transfixed also, in the middle of the table. 'It's a nasty one,' moaned Bernard's lady friend. 'Please, *please*, do something, Mr Boulting.'

The old man did something. It was to pick up the serving spoon from the glass trifle bowl at the end of the table, to lift it like an executioner's axe above the cowering beetle, and to bring it down with a sharp crack on its black back. Nicholas was halfway to stopping him but it was too late. The cockroach was split and spread over twice its original body area. The ladies drew breath but none screamed. Their gazes were fixed, spellbound. One of them whispered: 'It's funny how they're so yellow inside, isn't it.'

Bernard nodded around as though taking a bow and then with some ceremony, like an executioner sheathing his sword, thrust the spoon back into the trifle bowl. 'That's dealt with that,' he announced. He looked towards his son for approval. 'Got him first shot,' he said. Some of the staff had gathered and watched with scarcely a glimmer of surprise between them.

'I'll get a dustpan and brush,' offered the woman who had requested help. She was forestalled by the matron, who lifted her eyes in a short, automatic prayer, and the motherly girl who, putting first things first, picked up the trifle bowl and carried it away. One of the ladies made a feeble motion to stop her. 'I was enjoying that trifle,' she complained to the matron. 'It is nice,' agreed Matron. Briskly the girl returned with the dustpan and brush and swept the cockroach off the table, wiping the spot with a cloth and suggesting that the ladies moved to another table. They did so grumbling. Bernard had returned unperturbed to his cake. The woman touched his shoulder and murmured: 'Very swift. And very brave.'

They finished tea, the incident apparently soon forgotten. The matron was at the door wishing each one a good evening. 'They'll remember it tomorrow,' said the girl who had taken away the cockroach. 'It will be the talking point at teatime.' All around the staff were cleaning the debris from the tea tables. There was the china clatter of broken crockery being swept up.

'You disposed of the body very quickly,' he smiled.

She returned the look soberly and said: 'You have to in this business.'

He drove moodily back to London. It was ten o'clock when he parked the car and walked under the chilly trees to the flat. Sol's light was projecting from his upper window out over the misted barges and the canal like an autumn lantern from a harbourmaster's look-out. A solitary car strayed up the street as if trying to discover signs of life. It stopped almost opposite the flat, backing into a parking space that had not been there when he had been searching a few minutes previously. It was an expensive car and shone smoothly under the street-lamps. The door opened and the long-coated legs of Loretta slid out.

'It's you, Nick, it's you,' she said in her theatrically throaty voice. 'I came to find you.'

She pushed herself against him and they kissed. 'Here,' she said with some urgency. 'Give me your hand.' She took his hand and fed it below her heavy coat. He felt the cool, bare flesh. 'I need you,' she said guiding his fingers to her naked stomach.

He kissed her again and pushed his nose against her face. 'Hang on,' he cautioned. 'The last time we spoke you never wanted to see me again.'

'That was before,' she said pushing herself against him.

'Before what?'

'Before I felt like I feel now. It's always the same. . . .' He withdrew his hand from beneath her coat and fed it around her waist. Even through the coat he could feel she was entirely

153

naked. She put her head against his shoulder seeking comfort, and they began to walk across the road. 'So this is where you live,' she said. 'With that mad American.'

'He's not mad, just crazy,' he corrected. She kissed his face as they reached the door. 'I could use you right now,' she said almost miserably. 'It's terrible isn't it.'

'It's confusing,' he confessed. 'Tomorrow you won't want to know.'

'That's tomorrow.'

He put the key in the door and turned on the light in the lower hall. 'That's better,' she said moving her shoulders. 'It gets cold walking around like this.'

They went up the short flight of stairs. Sol was looking down from the landing above, crouching as though considering a jump. 'Look who you brought in!' He could summon enthusiasm at will. He almost tumbled down the stairs. 'A drink is called for.'

Nicholas introduced them. 'We met at the party, at the Garbo Club,' reminded Sol. 'You wouldn't forget me.'

'We met briefly,' she said. She sat down on the settee her legs slipping from the hem of the coat. They looked as naked as legs ever looked. 'Let me take your coat,' said Sol moving forward.

'Oh no . . . no thanks,' said Loretta grabbing the coat against herself. 'I came out in a hurry.' She took in his expression. 'There's nothing underneath. No clothes anyway.'

For a moment Nicholas thought he detected a blush on the American's face. 'Well,' he said reaching for his stock response. 'I guess that *really* calls for a drink.'

They all had straight scotch as if they had been through some recent crisis. 'So this is where you live,' repeated Loretta looking around. 'It's really cosy.'

'I live upstairs,' put in Sol as if in hope.

'It's a good arrangement,' she said seriously. 'So you write up there and Nick writes down here, and if you run short of inspiration, or you can't spell something, you can always ask the other person.'

'That's the theory,' said Nick. 'Sometimes we turn out almost a whole sentence a day between us.'

At that moment he caught sight of Thérèse's small painting. It had come back from the framer's and Sol had put it on the wall below the alcove. He stared at it but then looked away.

'You're depressed,' said Loretta firmly. 'I can tell.'

'He's been to see his father,' provided Sol. 'Life rarely ends in a laugh.' He wrote it down.

'How was your father?' asked Loretta as if she knew him.

'Old,' shrugged Nicholas. 'They said he was as good as dead last week but he was pretty lively today. He spattered a cockroach with a trifle spoon.'

'That's lively,' agreed Loretta.

'Except for the roach,' said Sol.

He began moving towards the stairs. 'I was just starting a great novel when you arrived,' he said. 'Just got the title on the top: *Tigers Never Crap*. How about that?'

Almost primly he left them, mounted the stairs and closed the door above. Loretta began unbuttoning her coat. 'Do you want to look?' she asked. There were times when she was so uncomplicated.

She was opening it anyway. It parted like a black chasm with the glowing whiteness of her body underneath. He remainded at a distance, watching her. 'You're a voyeur,' she protested gently.

'You make it so easy.'

Smiling she eased the black coat over her shoulders and sat with it lying around her white waist. He turned and switched the main light off. The shadows on her body and her face deepened. Only her smile remained carefully lit. Her legs slid from the fur and she crossed them like a secretary about to take dictation. 'I'm starving,' she said, her eyes fixed on him.

He undid his tie with the alacrity of a contestant in a game with a time limit; she stood, her legs bending beautifully and, curiously, as it slid away, caught the coat and put it on again; she began unzipping his fly. She was avid. She peeled his clothes away and pulled him on top of her on the couch. 'You're wonderful,' he informed her honestly. 'You cheer me up no end.'

She slid from the couch onto the carpet and they rolled together. She hung onto him as if she were drowning. He struck his head on a castor of the couch, causing a small gash over his eye, but she would not brook any diversion. 'This carpet scrapes my backside,' she said. 'Nylon carpets do. Let's get into your bed. You do have a bed?'

He confirmed that he had. Holding a handkerchief to his forehead he helped her on with her coat and led her by the pliant hand to his bed. She climbed in familiarly. 'This is more like it,' she whispered, her breasts staring at him like twins from above the bedclothes. 'I prefer sex in comfort.'

Nicholas agreed although he was drained. He kept thinking that he should take his father from the nursing home and look after him. She wanted him again and he turned to her wearily. He was relieved that her eyes closed at once after that and she went remarkably quickly and soundly to sleep. He lay beside her, his body cooling. At one in the morning, the telephone rang. He picked it up. It was his wife.

She was crying. 'Nick,' she said. 'Please come home.'

He glanced sideways at Loretta's face in silhouette against the street-light coming through the curtains.

'Do you love me?' he asked.

'I don't know,' she sobbed. 'But you must come home.'

'I'm on my way,' he said.

BOOK TWO

Book Two

Eight

It was past two in the morning when he began to drive home. Lonely taxis still roved the London streets and lorries heading to the north were churning their course along the greasy roads. He blinked tiredly in the wet lights and he was full of thoughts; it was difficult for him to know how he truly felt. He was returning with uncertainty. In his mind he could still see a woman in a red cloak walking by the sea.

When he had touched Loretta on her sleeping, glistening face and said: 'I'm going home', she had scarcely shrugged, for sex exhausted her. She mumbled: 'That's fine, dear.' She half-lifted an eyelid as if to fix who he was. 'Just close the front door after you.' There was no point in reminding her that she was at his place. Against the coffee pot in the kitchen, the first place Sol would make for in the morning, he propped a note.

Now, driving through the void, reflecting streets, he himself reflected that this short journey was the beginning of a new life for him. Yet another. He sighed as he waited for the traffic lights to change colour. It was like a gambling game; as he approached another set he began to play it. Amber and red meant to proceed with caution, green was a good sign, red by itself meant he should turn around and go back for nothing was going to mend.

He had asked Sarah if she loved him and she had said she did not know, only that she needed him there. Now, presented with the unexpected choice, he asked himself the same question. Did he really love her, or did he miss the familiar married life? Shrugging, as he waited at another junction, he told himself aloud, with arm actions, that love mattered nothing. What was it anyway? A hook on which to hang a marriage. A taxi-driver gazing sombrely from the isolation of his cab witnessed his solo performance and, as if he knew the truth and understood, nodded sympathy.

Once he had left the main road he slowed. Approach with caution. Then at the beginning of the sodium lights of Boxley High Street he stopped altogether and pulled into the side of the road. He put his forehead on the wheel and tried to think logically. Did he really want to go back like this? Did *she* really want him back like this? Perhaps he should do a Dick Whittington, and go back to London. But Dick Whittington had a cat to ask.

'Good morning, sir. Are you all right?'

He had not seen the police car. Now one of its occupants was squinting through his window, an inch open at the top. His colleague in the patrol car was preparing the breathalyser.

Nicholas lowered the window. 'I'm not drunk, officer,' he said as if he did not want the man to worry. 'Just confused.' The policeman knew a sober driver. 'Lost are we, sir?' he enquired. Nicholas nodded. 'You don't know how much.'

'Where are we heading?'

He raised his eyebrows when Nicholas said: 'Home.'

'Home – and you don't know your way?' He eyed his colleague who had come with the blower set from the police car.

'Lost,' he whispered.

The second officer said: 'Ah. Where's he trying to get to?'

'Home.'

'Don't misunderstand,' interrupted Nicholas. 'I know how to get home. I'm just trying to make up my mind whether I want to go there.'

'Ah,' said the pair together as if they now understood the situation perfectly.

'I left a few weeks ago,' recited Nicholas. He did not know why he was telling them; except that they were available, that they seemed to be prepared, even eager, to listen and that, as constables, they might well be men of the world. 'She rang up tonight, an hour ago, and said she wanted me back.'

The first officer looked at his watch as he might to check an alibi. 'They do pick awkward times,' he agreed knowledgeably. 'Well, I don't know I'm sure. What do you think, Vernon?'

Vernon sniffed. 'Mine wouldn't notice if I went,' he sighed. 'Not until pay-day or she wanted some shopping.'

'It's the nippers,' said his colleague. 'You never know what they're thinking inside.' He glanced at Nicholas who nodded that he had children. A car appeared over the ridge of the High Street and snorted past them, half-lost in spray. 'A ton, Frank,' said Vernon with a sort of admiration. 'That's what he's doing.'

Another car, making a bow-wave, came over the brow of the slight hill and sped by. 'Trying to catch up with his mate,' he deduced.

The first policeman repeated: 'Yes, it's the kids.'

Vernon said: 'Well, I haven't got any. I don't object to sex, but I don't want kids.'

'I'd go home if I was you,' said Frank to Nicholas. 'You can always bugger off again if it don't work out.'

Nicholas thanked them for their help and company. They went back to their car and turning it in the road drove off sedately in the direction taken by the two speeding vehicles. They waved friendly waves as they went. He waved back, pursed his lips and restarted his engine. He drove up the shuttered High Street and turned into his road. There were yellow leaves on the pavement. He saw that she had left a bedside lamp burning. Like a light to guide him home.

He eased the car into the short driveway and got out. He turned and faced the house like a challenge, pushed his hair back, took a breath,and went towards the door. There was no need to knock. Sarah, wearing a dressing gown he had not seen before, opened the door and stood framed in the dim light from within. 'I saw the car lights,' she said in a low steady way. 'You're back.'

He stepped inside to the remembered warmth of the small hall. 'Yes, I am,' he said. 'I'm home.'

They stood close, almost against each other, for a few

hesitant seconds, then he moved his arms towards her and hers came to hold him. They clutched more than embraced, like two people who had just been dragged from disaster. He could feel her crying and he had to hold back his own tears. They hung close, swaying in each other's clasp, feeling each other's familiar shapes. 'Would you like a cup of tea?' she asked.

'No thanks. Nothing.'

They separated a little and he wiped the courses of her tears from her cheek with his fingers. She took the edge of her robe and dried his damp eyes. 'Let's go to bed,' she said. 'You must be tired.'

They slept, as they had often done when they were not quarrelling, curled against each other, her buttocks resting in his lap. They said little else once they were in bed, only kissing carefully, and folding down to sleep as they would at the end of a normal but late and busy day.

When he awoke it was to an overwhelming sensation of relief and reprieve. He saw the curtains and the shaded light beyond them, the kidney-shaped dressing table, the built-in wardrobes; he was really back home.

Sarah had risen at seven thirty to get Deborah and Willie to school. They already knew he had returned. They had heard in the early hours, but she told them anyway, without emphasis. 'Your father is home,' she said and then protectively: 'He's in bed sleeping.'

Deborah went up to the bedroom and he looked over the top of the duvet to see her standing shyly at the door. Without any words from either of them she ran to the bedside and, kneeling there, put her young, damp face against him. He kissed her and dried her tears on the duvet, mumbling that she could not go to school looking like that. Willie had loitered by the door and when Nicholas looked at him said: 'Jogga today and 'orrible double maths.'

Deborah looked at her watch and said: 'We'll be late.'

Willie said: 'See if I care.' He half-turned before going and said casually: 'Will you be here when I get home tonight?'

'I'll be here,' promised Nicholas. He felt ashamed.

He showered and went downstairs. Sarah was feeding a black cat that sometimes came over the wall of a morning. 'He still turns up,' said Nicholas for something to say.

'He knows when he's on to a good thing,' she replied. Her make-up and her hair were as careful as ever. There were small creases around her eyes. He could see that she thought the remark might have offended him and she came forward and kissed him. He returned the kiss. There was neither passion nor sorrow. They were just kisses. 'I'm glad I'm here,' he said smiling ruefully at her. 'I thought you'd got rid of me for good.'

'So did I,' she responded in a matter-of-fact way. She became busy. She poured him some coffee and he looked around the kitchen. Nothing seemed to have changed except her dressing gown. 'The children need you,' she said over her shoulder. 'They missed you.'

'I missed them,' he said. She turned and he looked at her. 'I won't do it again. Any of it.'

She patted his hand like a parent. 'Let's talk about it tonight. I have to help with the meals-on-wheels. I do that now.' The mention provoked a thought. 'You went to see your father.'

'Yes. He wasn't dead, far from it.'

'I know. I rang up. I spoke to him. He said you'd taken him out.'

'Yes. We went on a train. I'll tell you about it tonight.'

She smiled. 'We'll probably have a lot to talk about. Nothing like a marital crisis for improving conversation. What will you do?'

'Go and pick up my things,' he said.

Her eyes came up from her coffee. 'You'll come back?'

'Of course I'll come back.' He leaned over and kissed her on her pink cheek. 'I'm back and that's that. I've got nowhere else I want to be. Just here. I need a normal life, Sarah.'

'We all do,' she nodded. 'I've never felt so empty.' She put her cup down firmly. 'I've got a suggestion to make . . . but it will have to wait. This evening.'

He regarded her wryly. 'As you wish. It sounds intriguing.

I'll need to get my word processor and shut myself in that room upstairs and work.'

'No more offices in London?'

'No more offices. We're going to be broke if we're not careful.'

'Is it that bad?'

'Well, there's a film deal coming up, fingers crossed, on *Lying in Your Arms*. But I've got to get the next book under way. I haven't done a word. Paul is getting restive. And so are Mallinder's.' He stood up. 'But we'll talk about that tonight.'

She laughed thoughtfully. 'It's going to be quite an evening.'

'Promise we won't fight,' he said.

'I won't fight.'

'Nor me.'

He stood up and they kissed again, but not deeply. It was as though each did not want to frighten the other away. He went to get his car keys. Everything that had gone before must now be forgotten. Even Thérèse Oiseau. The first day of his new life had begun.

Sol looked disconsolate and said: 'Again, you ran away.'

Nicholas had never thought of it like that. 'But Loretta wouldn't mind,' he said. 'She was glad to see me gone, I expect.'

'Until next time,' said Sol. 'Anyway I didn't mean Loretta. I meant me. You ran away from *me*.'

Nicholas started to laugh but then saw the American's expression. He sat on a kitchen chair and shook his head. 'Christ, sorry pal. I didn't look at it like that.'

'I thought we were buddies. So some wife calls and you take off.'

'It wasn't *some* wife,' sighed Nicholas. 'It was my only one. And she was speaking for the kids too. You know I had to go.'

'I know it,' nodded Sol. 'Don't I just. Still it's a shame.' He moved side-on so that he could view Nicholas from the corner of his eye. 'You going to take the painting?'

Nicholas had already thought about it. 'Can I leave it here?'

he asked. 'I think she'll be better with you.' He walked two paces to the alcove below the stairs and touched the picture Thérèse had given him. 'Is that all right?'

'Sure. I'll look after her.'

'I must settle the rent too.'

'Shit, who cares about the goddam rent.' He lapsed into despondency. 'I was just getting to like you. Who can I turn to now? Who will I test my work on, my inspiration, my titles?'

Nicholas grinned and patted him on the shoulder. 'Somebody. There'll always be somebody, Sol. Maybe Loretta.'

'Please, no. Already I get her hate mail. She left here this morning and there was a note from her which I wouldn't want any nice person to read. It was about you, in the main, but it was addressed to *me*.'

'She'll be back,' forecast Nicholas.

'You'll still see her?'

'God, no.' He made a wry face. 'Maybe you could.'

'It's a nice idea but I don't think she's too well disposed in this direction.'

'Or any direction the next morning. You know how she is.'

'Sure, I know. But you're going home and being a regular guy, okay?'

'I have to. I've really got to put it together this time. I've got to grow up.'

Sol thought about it and said that growing up was always a pity. Nicholas packed his belongings and left a cheque on the bedside table because Sol said he wanted nothing to do with it, although he did ask where it had been left. They shook hands at the door.

'You've been a good friend,' said Nicholas. 'When I needed one.'

'If not a good influence,' said the American. 'Well, drop by sometimes. Don't just go forever.'

Nicholas promised that he would not. He had gone from the door and was almost on the street, but the American continued to hold it open. 'You said she likes you to sing?' he called.

'Loretta?'

'Sure. Who else? She likes a singing lover?'

Nicholas grinned. 'Simultaneously,' he answered.

Sol sniffed the autumn air. 'I sing, you know. And I write songs. Great songs.'

'Sing one to her for me,' said Nicholas.

He was home in time to meet the children leaving school. It was a duty he had undertaken only rarely in the past if Sarah was otherwise occupied and when the children were younger. Now it was not necessary for them to be met at the school gates, except that it was a twenty-minute walk. They walked home together often bickering, at other times unspeaking, or with Deborah hopelessly chasing Willie for some misdemeanour.

'You don't have to go,' Sarah said after she had made a cup of tea. 'They're fifteen and thirteen. The walk does them good.'

'I'll go,' he said decisively. 'I'll walk up. I'll enjoy it.'

Nicholas left and she washed the cups with an uncertain heart. It was not going to be easy. She picked up the telephone and began to dial a number. She hesitated, stopped, and put the receiver back. Then, biting her lip, she dialled again this time completing it. 'It's me,' she said sadly. 'Nick is back. Yes. He came home last night. So I'm just calling to say goodbye.'

She replaced the receiver. In two months she would be forty. She had been married for half her life. She and Nicholas had met at a party when she was working as secretary for a St Albans estate agency and he was a sub-editor on a local newspaper. They had danced closely all night and sunrise had found them walking silently by the Abbey Lake. In a year they had married. Getting engaged and married was something you did in Hertfordshire at that time. It was expected and accepted, as sure and routine as birth and death. Now she wondered if there had been a time when they were truly in love. And yet now there seemed no room for manoeuvre. Love was too difficult. Too complicated. She went to the bathroom, sat on the lavatory and cried.

Outside in the road she could hear the local children

returning from school. She dried her eyes, went down to the kitchen again, and began to prepare the evening meal.

Half a mile away Nicholas strode up the High Street like some landowner returned from a long voyage and walking his estate. He noted small changes in the shops; there were already warning notices about Christmas outside the newsagent's and the church; there was scarcely a leaf left on the trees.

Outside the school he fell into conversation with several mothers of junior-school children. Yes, he had been absent on business. Hollywood actually. Filming was scheduled for the spring. 'I used to act,' sighed one mother who looked as if she still did. 'I was thinking of taking it up again. Just small parts.' She put on a pair of sunglasses and looked at him deeply. 'If you've got anything that might suit me, let me know.'

She spotted her child and swaying her backside went away from him. 'You're not making a horror movie are you?' asked another mother who had been standing listening. They watched the former actress embrace her ten-year-old son theatrically. The boy wriggled with embarrassment and surprise. One of the wives mentioned that she would give anything, anything, to have a husband who picked up from school, and another invited him to an evening of charity poker.

Deborah and Willie came into sight from the direction of the senior school and, stopping at a distance, regarded him with something like suspicion, as if he might be the bearer of bad news. 'What's gone wrong?' enquired Willie bluntly as they reached the gates. 'You going off again?'

'Going off? What do you mean going off?' demanded Nicholas sharply. He was aware that the women he had told he had been in Hollywood were listening and making knowing faces. 'I've just come to meet you, that's all.'

Deborah hung on to his arm. 'I'm glad, Daddy,' she said. 'All day I've been afraid that you would have gone again.'

'Hollywood can wait,' he said strenuously.

Arms about their shoulders, he eased them away from the vicinity of the school. 'How was it?' he enquired.

'What?' they asked together.

'School. What did you do?'

'Jogga,' said Willie. He wriggled clear of his father's arm and kicked an empty plastic milk carton into the road. He added: 'But no maths. She's ill.' He brightened. 'She might even die.'

'You could get fined,' said Deborah. 'Littering the road.'

'I was just cleaning up the pavement,' answered Willie.

'I went to see your friend Sol today,' said Nicholas.

Immediately he had their interest. What was Sol doing? Did he look the same? Did he have anything else on television? Then Deborah stopped walking and said: 'You're not going to live there any more, are you?'

Nicholas shook his head and tightened his arm around her. 'No. Never. He's my friend and I'll still keep in touch, of course. He's a great guy.' He looked down at her face. 'But I'm home for good now.'

It was late, after the children had gone to bed, when they sat down to dinner. She had cooked it very carefully and they had had a bottle of wine from the special dozen they had kept from Italy the previous summer. Both felt out of place and uncomfortable, like strangers abruptly obliged to share the only table left in a restaurant, striving to discover conversation.

Then bluntly, she said: 'Do you think it's going to work?'

She surprised him but he was grateful for her directness. You could only talk for so long about the garden, household repairs, in-laws, other relatives and neighbours.

'If we *want* it to work,' he said. He reached for her hand across the table. 'I do. I wouldn't be here if I didn't.'

'So do I,' she said in a catchy voice. They leaned towards each other and kissed in an almost polite way. 'But it won't be easy, Nick. There's a lot of water under the bridge.'

'We've got to get back to normal and concentrate on it,' he said. He regarded her with serious fondness. 'It's not just our marriage, Sarah, it's our lives. I'm starting work tomorrow.'

'I'll get back to things,' she agreed. 'Everything's been let go a bit.'

'Has there been anyone else?' he asked looking at her straight.

'I haven't wanted anyone.' She laughed. 'I certainly didn't want you.' It was her turn: 'How about you? Anyone? Caroline?'

The name gave him an escape. He could be truthful. 'I haven't set eyes on her. She's gone somewhere. I'm not worried where.'

'We've got to try, Nick,' she said solemnly. 'For the kids. And for us.'

'It's no fun being on your own,' he nodded.

'But if it's too much of a strain,' she said looking straight at him, 'then we've got to be honest enough to admit it. It's no use either of us being miserable. I missed you, Nick, I missed you because I'm married to you.' She became a touch tearful. 'I missed having a husband.'

He looked down at his almost finished plate and said: 'There's no comfort for me anywhere else.'

They finished the wine tearfully and held hands across the table. Then Sarah dried her eyes and said with care: 'I have a proposal, an idea.'

'What's that?'

'I don't want us to be together being miserable, either of us.'

'Nor do I. We've said that. . . .'

'So I think we ought to make a bargain, a pact, and keep to it. We guarantee to stay together for a year.'

He sat back with astonishment. 'What an extraordinary idea,' he breathed. 'What in the name of . . .'

She continued strongly. 'In that time, we promise to keep all the rules. We stay together and try to make it work. We don't fight. We back off. And if it's obviously not working after a year,' she glanced at the wall calendar, 'at the end of November next year either of us can say they want out.'

'I've never heard anything so . . . What about the children?'

169

'What about *us*, you and me? If we're not happy with each other we're no good for the kids.'

She took his hand like a friend. 'I've thought it out very carefully, Nick,' she said. 'If we get through the year we can go on forever . . . until we die.'

Slowly he shook his head. 'You're an extraordinary woman,' he said quietly. 'More extraordinary than I ever imagined.'

She smiled frankly. 'Perhaps you never imagined before,' she said.

They lay in their bed, a little apart, isolated although together, just the rims of their feet touching, like some tenuous mooring, each waiting for the other to make the first move, put the first question.

Eventually from her own darkness Sarah asked: 'That night you went. What did you do? Where did you go?'

He was looking at the infinity of the ceiling. 'I had no idea where I was off to,' he laughed almost silently. 'I simply went down the road up the High Street, and to the station, the only place showing a glimpse of light. The last train was waiting ready to go so I got on it. I got off at Baker Street and walked down the road to a hotel.'

'How did you feel?'

'Terrible.'

'So did I. I got the children down and told them that you were going away, had gone away, and that from then on there would just be the three of us. It was quite exciting planning a new life like that, in theory. Holidays and all the rest of it. Then they went to bed and I sat up all night in the chair and wondered what was to become of me.'

'And what did?' he asked moving his head a fraction towards her.

'Nothing very much. Nothing that I care to remember.'

She was not going to tell him anything else. Instead she said: 'So you didn't see Caroline.'

'No, nothing,' he replied conscious that she had obtained an answer without conceding one. 'I never saw her from that day to this.'

He moved fully towards her and she in response turned her face to him so that they could each see the tip of the other's nose, their eyes tight as crevices in the bedroom dimness. 'Don't let's rake over old ashes, please,' he said warily. 'That's not going to help either of us.'

'What did you do?' She shifted. 'The children said you went abroad but they got the places mixed up. According to them you went to Egypt or Spain.' Nicholas grimaced in the dark. They turned onto their backs again.

'I intended to go to Luxor but I ended up in Spain,' he confessed.

'Why Luxor?'

'Oh, it sounded a sort of faraway – eastern, but not too far away. I wasn't brave enough to plan anything further afield, Australia, South America, the Far East. At heart I'm just a bloke who walks down to the shops.'

He thought she was going to comment but she refrained. 'But I didn't get anywhere near Luxor either,' he continued. 'Somehow, don't ask me how, I ended up in Spain, Torremolinos, for God's sake, with a fat blonde and her appalling kids.' He was blurting it out.

She gasped. 'You didn't! You've never been a man for fat blondes.'

'I wasn't for this one,' he answered. 'She and her family decided to adopt me. It was a nightmare. One of the twins kept crapping himself.'

Sarah began to laugh. 'Twins,' she said. 'Oh, Nick. What a bloody fool you are.'

'You can't tell me anything I haven't told myself,' he answered. 'And worse was to come. I landed up with a party of old soldiers who'd got to Spain by mistake and one of them died.'

'Deborah said someone had died. Willie came out with some yarn that you had to give the kiss of life. But I told them I didn't want to hear about anything you had done. I wasn't interested.'

Now Nicholas laughed. 'Willie should write the books. No, I was spared that, thank God. He was past the kiss of life when I saw him, long past it. But then I had to get his body back to England.'

She was giggling quietly, almost privately, again. 'What a husband,' she said. 'You can't even run away.'

'Don't tell me, I know. It all happens,' he grumbled. 'God, the other day when I went to see my father, he knocked some woman over on the railway station and then when we got back to the nursing home he bashed a bloody great cockroach with a spoon they were using to serve trifle – he splattered it all across the table in front of five old ladies, and then plonked the spoon back in the trifle dish. I can't tell you what *that* was like.'

Sarah became still. 'Perhaps we ought to have him come to live with us,' she said hesitantly. 'I've always had a conscience about it.' She turned to him again and he to her.

Nicholas kissed her calmly on the nose. '*You* might be able to handle it,' he said. 'But I'm not very sure about me. He seems quite okay there, he grumbles of course but that's part of being eighty-two.'

They were fully facing each other again. He could feel her breasts lolling warmly against him under her nightdress. His arms went around her waist. 'You've got slimmer,' he said.

'Getting myself into shape for life and whatever it brought up,' she answered adding: 'Or whoever.'

He kissed her and she returned the kiss. 'It's so foolish,' she whispered brokenly. 'Just packing it in, just not caring enough. It was my fault too. I'm not backing out of it. It was just it was you who had the soap in your ears.'

'Is Nicholas Boulting there, please?'

'That's me. Oh . . . is that you, Paul?'

'Yes. Oh, sorry Nick. I was merely being cautious. Sol said you'd gone back but you never know how accurate Sol is, or life is for that matter, and it didn't sound like you.'

'Sarah rang me and I came home. It's the only place I can be.'

'There's nowhere like it,' said Garrett. 'Home.'

'Anyway I'm working. I've written five thousand words of a novel.'

'That's good news.'

'It's about a man who meets a Frenchwoman, loses her, and how he tries to find her afterwards.'

'Big romance, eh? Looking for someone always makes for a good plot. And you're slogging away.'

'Every day this week. I'm up there in my little attic, looking out of the dormer window at the roofs of the houses and the tops of the trees, and I put my hands on the keys of the typewriter and *make* myself write.'

'What happened to the word processor?'

'I've gone back to the typewriter,' answered Nicholas. 'It makes it seem more like work.'

'Ah, a penance,' observed Garrett. There was a pause. 'Can I see some of it, the novel? After ten thousand words, say. I'd like to reassure Mallinder's. Newby is getting restive.'

'Of course,' said Nicholas. 'I'll tell you when I've got to ten thousand.'

'You've got a title?' asked Garrett.

Nicholas said: 'It's called *Lost in France*.'

'Love it,' said Garrett. 'I hope the lady is beautiful as well as mysterious.'

Nicholas paused. 'Yes,' he said eventually. 'I can promise that.'

The Christmas party Sarah suggested for the night before Christmas Eve did not appeal to Nicholas but Sarah was sure. 'It won't be just a party,' she told him. 'It will show the people around here.'

'Show the people around here what?' He was sitting in his work room, the typewriter keys staring up at him like an eye-bank. Outside the roofs were wintry, the treetops like old fingers. Sarah had brought his coffee. 'Can I see?' she had asked leaning across his shoulder. She read the typed page in the machine. 'Intriguing,' she observed.

'That was yesterday's,' he said to her. 'I haven't written a word today. I was just trying to think of some.' He took the coffee from her and she sat chummily on the stool at the side of the desk. 'You ought to get a secretary,' she said fitting her bottom more comfortably. 'But she had better have a small behind.'

'What other sort would I choose?' he said looking at her sideways.

'*I'll* choose,' she corrected. 'You see if she's up to it professionally and I'll give her the once-over for other things.'

'I'm not having some fat bat,' he responded.

'I didn't say you were,' she said sipping her coffee primly. 'A fat bat wouldn't fit on this stool. You want somebody efficient and nice but plain.'

'I won't bother. I've managed without up to now. I can always get someone temporary from an agency.' He paused and added: 'Why do we have to have this party?'

'To show them that we're still together . . . back together.'

'Who knows any different?' he argued. 'I was only away a few weeks. I might have been on a business trip. I told one nosey woman at the school that I'd been in Hollywood writing a script.'

She appeared admiring. 'Oh, that was a good let-out,' she said. 'It gives you some kudos as well. I wish I'd thought of that.'

'What *did* you think of?'

She cocked her head sideways like a cat, as though summoning a thought, a habit that irritated him. 'Well, I sort of mumbled about you being out of town and so forth. But people around here read between the lines.'

'Most of them probably read better between the lines than along them,' he commented.

'Don't be cruel. They're not unintelligent. They can't help it if a lot of them are just housewives. It's not a mind-bending occupation.'

'You think they sussed us, eh?' he said backing off again.

'Child's play for them. I've never been invited to so many

coffee mornings. I didn't care what they asked in the end. Most of their husbands wouldn't have the guts to do something like that. Run away. And they know it.'

He smiled ruefully. 'It wasn't guts, it was anger.'

'At being found out,' she added. It was her turn to withdraw. 'The men around here, in general, wouldn't have the initiative to actually clear off. And if they did they'd be back, tail between the legs, the next day. Or get lost.'

'I went to Torremolinos,' he pointed out. 'I didn't intend to.'

'All right. So you did.' She looked reflective. 'I quite enjoyed the notoriety in a way. For a while. Out shopping, women would point me out. I could *feel* them doing it. If you turned around quickly you could catch them. Some would even watch how much food you were buying at the supermarket.'

He laughed outright. 'It gives a new meaning to the phrase "check-out". God, who would have thought it.'

She regarded him seriously. 'The kids had to cope with it as well.'

Her husband lowered his coffee mug. 'How did they cope?'

'Willie had two fights. One was in the classroom. There was blood all over the other boy's desk. And he caught the other one after football. In the shower.'

Nicholas grinned seriously. 'I see.'

'He came home and cried.'

'I'm sorry.'

'So am I,' she said in her honest way. 'It takes two. It was my fault as well.'

'What about Deborah?'

'She had to put up with some spite at school. But she can handle it. She's a woman.'

'With a lifetime of coping with spite in front of her,' he suggested.

'She might have. On the other hand she might escape, she doesn't have to live like we do – here. She's bright. She wants to write like you. But perhaps she'll be a lawyer and profit from the spite of others.'

Nicholas avoided the subject of lawyers. 'So you want

to invite these wagging tongues to our Christmas party,' he said.

'Absolutely. It will show them that our marriage is resilient and that we can handle our differences.'

'We could dance together all night,' suggested Nicholas slyly. 'Close together, gazing into each other's eyes.'

'You don't want the party,' she said flatly.

'Let's have it by all means,' he reassured her. 'Let them all come.'

It was a strange journey for Paul Garrett and Sol to make, out into the London suburbs two nights before Christmas. Twice Paul, who was driving, lost his way because he had never been to Boxley. To Sol it was a new, endless, landscape of semi-detached houses, parades of small shut shops, outer railway stations and brick pubs. Pavements were damp and eerily vacant under pale yellow street-lights. He felt like the co-pilot on an uncertain mission. 'I think I'm going to have a nosebleed,' he muttered.

They arrived in Boxley early. They were the party's first guests. Garrett had wanted to be there to talk with Nicholas. 'Can I see what you've written so far?' he asked.

'The novel?' said Nicholas.

'The novel.'

Sol was as glad to see the children as they were to see him. They were going to spend the night with school friends at a house a mile away. He had brought a video. 'In this one,' he said in his expansive but confiding fashion, 'I *act*. You didn't know I was an actor too?' He was apparently enchanted with Sarah. He slotted the video into the television. 'I just put in a cameo performance.'

Few people could so blatantly brag and at the same moment be as convincingly modest as Sol. Willie and Deborah sat with him while the video played. 'There! That's me!' exclaimed Sol pointing. 'My acting début!'

'But it's Father Christmas,' protested Willie pointing. 'How can we see if . . .'

'. . . it's you?' completed Deborah. She gave him a soft push.

Sol's moustache became agitated. 'But it *is* me,' he protested. 'I'm telling you. Forget the whiskers. Just tell me. Who else acts good like that?'

They laughed and watched with him. Neither wanted to leave for their friends' house, but Sol went with them and screened his acting début to the family there.

Paul climbed to the attic room where Nicholas had been writing. He looked out of the winter window above the desk. 'Can I see how it's progressing?'

'Of course,' responded Nicholas. 'It comes to about fifteen thousand words so far.'

'Which reminds me,' said Garrett reaching to the pocket of his jacket. 'Twenty thousand dollars from Herald International Films for the option on *Lying in Your Arms*.' He looked momentarily embarrassed. 'Less ten per cent. I didn't know whether I should give it to you downstairs.'

'That's wonderful and welcome,' said Nicholas. 'You needn't have worried about Sarah, it would have been all right. Everything is above board with us now. We're really giving it a try.'

'It's all you can do,' nodded Garrett. He handed an envelope to Nicholas who opened it, took out the cheque and waved it. Garrett sat on the small stool, the only seating for which there was any room apart from the typing chair which Nicholas used, and began to read from the first page of the manuscript. '*Lost in France*,' he recited with a shake of his head. 'It has a sound, a feeling. I like it.'

'I hope you'll keep liking it,' ventured Nicholas. 'It's about time I turned out something you thought was some good.'

'Sir Handley Mallinder will be relieved, not to mention Henry Newby and the Mallinder accounts department,' murmured Paul without taking his eyes from the page.

Nicholas said: 'I'll leave you to it, Paul. I've got to sort out the booze and get myself ready.' Garrett glanced up and fingered his tie. 'Did I come properly dressed?' he enquired.

'Yes, fine. They tend to put on their best clothes around here. Later the middle-aged ones tend to take them off.'

'*I'll* need to take off about midnight,' mentioned Garrett. 'I'm going to Los Angeles tomorrow. I'll take Sol back to London with me if he's not in love by then.'

'Midnight should give him plenty of time,' smiled Nicholas. He crouched under the attic door and went down the steps to the bedroom landing. Sarah was dressing in the bedroom. 'He's going to like it,' said Nicholas. She was standing in her bra and a black evening skirt.

'It's time he approved of something of yours,' she said casually. She was holding out a lace blouse. 'After a bestseller like you had, you'd think he would have found it easy to sell the next book.'

'He has *sold* it,' Nicholas reminded her. 'I . . . we . . . had the advance. It's just that I haven't actually *finished* anything since.'

'Maybe he's too choosy,' she said. 'I read things all the time that are a lot inferior to anything you've written.'

He took the cheque from his pocket. 'He's just given me this – the money for the *Lying in Your Arms* film option.'

Her hand shot out like a beak. She plucked it from his hand and grinned as she looked at it. 'Eighteen thousand bucks,' she said. 'That's more like it.' She rammed the cheque in her handbag.

It was gone as he blinked. 'I'll sort out the drinks,' he said going out of the bedroom.

'Put plenty in the punch,' she called after him. 'That get's them going.'

In the kitchen he took a book of party recipes from her shelf and began mixing the ingredients for the punch. Everyone would be handed a glass as soon as they arrived. He was stirring it when Sarah appeared, dressed and carefully made-up. She was wearing her pearls at her throat. He enjoyed her looking like that. She sniffed at the punch then unhesitatingly picked up a bottle of gin and poured the contents into the bowl. 'I hate it when they take an age to get started,' she said.

Nicholas went upstairs. He climbed into the attic just as Garrett was placing the pile of manuscript on the desk.

'When you're ready, when you've finished rewriting, I'd like to take this much,' he picked up the sheaf. 'And show it to Newby at Mallinder's.'

'You like it?'

'Terrific,' nodded Garrett seriously. 'This one is really going to work.' He nodded at the typescript and sat down on the small chair. 'Who is she?' he asked. 'This lady? This Cécile Frenet? She seems real. Someone you know?'

Nicholas smiled ruefully. 'Someone I met,' he acknowledged. 'Briefly.' He saw the question in Garrett's face. 'Nothing like that. It's not her real name, of course. She is called Thérèse Oiseau. She was just staying in that place I went to in Essex, near Harwich, when it rained all the time. You remember, when I did that most recent bit of running away.'

'Yes, I remember.' His voice dropped with caution: 'You were with her, were you?'

'Not "*with*" her", not like that,' Nicholas said. 'We were just, well . . . together. It's a long story. She was going to Paris, back to her home, and her husband. Eventually.'

Garrett grinned and tapped the manuscript again. 'She seems to have made a deep impression on you. She's so lifelike. You write as though you're in love.'

'She's only fiction now.'

'Does Sarah know? About the story I mean. Have you shown her this?'

'No.'

'Don't let her see all this until you have to,' advised Garrett. 'She'll know. Women do.'

Nicholas frowned. 'I'll tell her the same as I've told you,' he said. 'Cécile Frenet is fiction. Now she'll always be fiction.'

They left the attic, Garrett having to bend almost double to get out of the door. They met Sarah on the landing. 'I'm glad he's writing again,' said the agent like a doctor reporting the start of a recovery.

'So am I,' returned Sarah. 'Otherwise he would have to go back to work.'

Nicholas said: 'The twenty thousand dollars should keep us from the poorhouse for a couple of weeks.'

'Eighteen thousand,' corrected Sarah. She smiled at Garrett. 'You have to have your cut.'

'Otherwise *I'd* have to find myself a job.' He smiled gently.

'It goes into the bank tomorrow,' she said firmly. 'They'll be glad to see it.'

There was a sounding of the front-door chimes. Nicholas went and found Sol standing there. 'I got lost,' said the American as he entered. 'It's a different world out there.'

He glanced at Sarah who said: 'It's the world we know. We like it.'

Sol looked embarrassed. Then he said: 'The kids wanted to come back.'

'They had better not,' said Sarah archly. 'Parties around here tend to be grown-up.'

Nicholas raised his eyebrows towards Sol and then did the same to Garrett. 'I don't know why she's like this,' he shrugged when Sarah had gone hurriedly to the kitchen. 'She's not usually so sharp, so aggressive.'

'It's because *she* knows *we* know,' suggested Sol.

'About me? About clearing off?'

'I think so. That's how women are.'

'But all the neighbours know,' argued Nicholas. 'According to Sarah. She's invited some of them tonight, to demonstrate that we're together again, that we've made up.'

Garrett sighed: 'Ah, but there's a difference, Nick.' He peered with a frown into the seething punch bowl. 'These neighbours knew you had gone away but they didn't know where, and possibly didn't care.'

'To them you were just a void,' nodded Sol. 'But to her *we knew* what you were doing. You lived in my apartment. And Paul knows things about you. That's how she figures it.'

'Perhaps she even thinks *we* put you up to it, encouraged you,' grinned Garrett mischievously. He lifted the punch ladle and smelled the brew. 'But she's certainly convinced we know about other things that she *doesn't* know.'

'Sarah doesn't want to know,' said Nicholas gingerly. 'I've told her about some things. Nothing, you know . . . incriminating. I told her I never saw Caroline, which is true.'

'And she believed you?' asked Garrett.

'Yes. I'm sure. We've tried to put everything behind us. We're giving it a chance.' He almost added: 'For a year', but the mellifluous chimes sounded again. Garrett stopped himself wincing.

'Go will you, Nick,' Sarah called. 'It'll be the Deares. They're always first.'

As though conforming to some prearranged tactic, Paul and Sol moved towards the back of the long room as Nicholas made towards the front door. 'The Deares are always first,' ruminated Sol. He glanced at Garrett hopefully. 'That's one hell of a title.' Garrett asked: 'What's the story?'

Sol looked peeved. 'What do you want, a title *and* a story?' He repeated: '*The Deares are Always First*' and took out a notebook to write it down. There was a decanter with glasses on a tray. Garrett poured a straight scotch and Sol followed suit, watching for Sarah as he did so. Garrett raised the drink: 'Send it to me when you've added another hundred thousand words.'

'Okay.' Sol responded to the toast. 'Once I've fixed the title the rest is easy.'

Sarah had forecast correctly. The duffle-coated Deares came in like bulky Eskimos greeting Nicholas at the door. Frank Deare, a purple-faced fruit wholesaler, hugged him like a Hollywood phoney flapping his arms and hugging him again. 'Glad you're back, lad,' he said standing back to study the host's face as if searching for permanent damage.

'Stay with us now,' whispered his tiny, bright-eyed wife. She clutched his biceps with steely fingers. Nicholas winced. They expressed curiosity about the punch but said they would prefer something else first. A scotch and vodka. The chimes sounded again.

An irresolute-looking couple, the man blinking and tall, the woman pinkly timid, waited in an attitude which suggested they might make a dash for it any moment. Nicholas did not recognise them but they said they were new to the area, Nigel and Thelma Bevins. Once he had welcomed them and taken their coats, they quickly made themselves at home, recognising the social territory, the country of estate agents, minor computer men and people in a small way of business. They saw the Deares sipping spirits and asked if they might have the same. Sol appeared from the interior and offered to get their drinks. Sarah came down the stairs, making an entrance despite the limited audience, smiling an overall smile, followed by individual hugs and kisses and introductions.

Guests started arriving quickly now, some as if they had been lurking behind the hedges until more people had rung the chimes and gone through the door. Sarah ushered the Deares and the Bevins with their drinks to the distant end, hoping that the new guests would be satisfied with the punch. Few were. The plum-coloured mixture remained undisturbed until a Mr and Mrs Crope accepted it meekly and remained, unspeaking and unspoken-to, through most of the evening. They went early. Sol, always socially willing, conversed with Bert Alexander, a Boxley car dealer and his wife, Marie. 'Don't any singles turn up for these events?' he enquired jovially. 'Everybody's got somebody before they get through the door.'

'We swap,' Marie Alexander told him skittishly. She had a face like one of her husband's used vehicles.

Bert said profoundly: 'Part-exchange.'

The room was becoming full and warm. A younger wife smiled with her eyes at Garrett. Her computer-sales husband kept coughing and saying that he wanted to go home. 'For Christ's sake, go,' she hissed and repeated it as he coughed again. 'Where do *you* live?' she asked Garrett turning to him with an instant smile as she did so.

'Pimlico Road,' said Garrett.

'Oh yes,' she tried to think. 'By the Lion's Head?'

'I'm afraid I don't know the Lion's Head.'

'It's on the Watford Road.'

He told her he meant Pimlico in London and she became

deeply attentive. She learned that he was a literary agent. 'I *used* to write,' she said as though she had given it up as too easy. 'For the school mag.'

Her husband had retreated to confide in another guest, coughed and repeated that he wanted to go home. 'Him,' she almost snarled to Garrett. 'Works in computers. Comes home and talks computers. I don't know what the hell he's going on about. Goes on about bytes, whatever they are.' She flickered her lashes. 'I wish somebody would bite me.'

Sarah had taken care with the music. Enya first, so that people could come in and feel easy, then Elton John and Phil Collins. The guests having eyed each other were beginning to dance. Later it would be the Beatles. It was a known programme in these parts. Sarah came through the crowd to dance with Garrett, making the woman with the computerised husband scowl. They danced, closed in by the others and he felt her full and warm against his jacket. 'I'm glad Nick has seen sense,' she said near to his ear. 'He wanted to come home all the time.'

'And who wouldn't?' he said suavely.

A neat, decent woman who lived alone in a flat, danced with Nicholas, glanced across at Sarah and whispered: 'Your wife should be glad. Good husbands don't often come back. Only the crummy ones.' She eased away and smiled genuinely. 'And you're a decent man.'

Around them the guests were getting drunk. The music was still low but louder. 'I wish mine would come back,' she confessed. 'It's no fun by yourself and it's hard for a woman over forty to find anybody. Anybody worthwhile. If men aren't married then there's a reason. There are not many un-discovered treasures.'

She said her name was Yvonne and she asked him where he had gone when he left home. He told her briefly. Before the dance was over she said: 'She should really *try* with you, Nicholas. Some women won't forget, won't leave it alone, a break-up, even after they're back together again. And that's dangerous. It's like the old tale of the man sitting on a branch that he's busily sawing through.'

Then she said: 'Will you introduce me to your friend?'

'Sol?' guessed Nicholas, glancing his way. The American was making three people laugh at the kitchen door, eating food from a plate and using his fork to impersonate an aeroplane. 'No,' Yvonne corrected quietly. 'Your other friend.' Paul Garrett was pretending to be absorbed in a book he had taken from a corner shelf, drink in one hand, book in the other. 'What's his name?' she asked.

'Paul Garrett,' Nicholas answered. 'He's my agent. I'll introduce you. He looks as though he needs to be introduced.'

He held her fingers briefly to lead her towards Garrett. 'Good,' she smiled. 'I like tired-looking men.'

They reached Garrett. He laid down the book. 'Paul,' said Nicholas. 'This is Yvonne.' The lady extended her hand. 'Pattison,' she added.

At once Nicholas was caught by a fat and insistent male hand. 'Some advice,' mumbled the man as if he were selling it from a tray. 'I've got some good advice.'

'I'm not really in the mood for advice,' returned Nicholas. He did not recognise the man and he tried to brush him off but the fat hand would not let go. 'Who are you anyway?' Nicholas asked. He checked his watch: it was eleven thirty. The party had been going more than two hours.

The advice vendor had a failed and florid face. 'I arrived in with the others,' he pointed vaguely.

'Which others?'

'Your wife said we could come in. We're from a party down the street. They ran out of booze.'

'I'm not surprised,' said Nicholas studying him. 'All right, let's have the advice.'

For a moment the stranger appeared to have forgotten what it was, but eventually he managed to focus and said: 'Get your head down, man. Consolidate. That's the way to mend a marriage.'

Nicholas reacted testily, decided he could not be bothered and walked away, surprised that his own first step was a stagger. The music was very loud now and unremitting, everyone seemed to be drunk. Suburban party drunk. People were hanging onto each other, clutching as they danced. He caught a glimpse of Sarah laughing in the kitchen. 'You pissed off, you did,' muttered a woman close to his arm. 'And you told me up at the school that you'd been to Hollywood.'

He remembered the face that designer glasses could not save. 'I pissed off to Hollywood,' he said. She demanded a dance and caught hold of him. She sagged like a dead albatross and he trawled her into a corner and let her slide into a heap.

He leaned dizzily against the wallpaper. How much had he drunk? How long? He took in the thick scene, the haze and heat of the room, the mindless music, the harsh laughter, the stumbling, the pawing. They were middle-aged men and women. He wondered what their children would think if they could see them. What would his own children think of him and Sarah? What *did* they think?

Around midnight a woman threw up all down the sequins of her dress and a man attempted to wipe it off with the sleeve of his jacket. Somebody laughed and somebody screamed. Nicholas could see neither Sol nor Paul. A flushed man with a loud tie was telling a plump woman that God did not exist.

'You seem to know everything,' she sneered.

'I sell encyclopaedias,' he said. 'I could get a set for you.'

Nicholas heard Sarah's high laugh from the kitchen. Creeping sideways he went up the stairs and into their bedroom. He was almost surprised to find it unoccupied. Unsteadily he undressed and put on his pyjamas, then went to the bathroom. The din from the party was swelling up through the floor. 'For Christ's sake,' he muttered miserably. 'Go home. The bloody lot of you.'

As though in defiance, the din increased. He heard the front door slamming and a couple bawling obscenely at each other on the path outside. Staggering with booze and fatigue he retreated into the bedroom and flopped on the quilt. More people arrived from somewhere, probably another failed party. The thudding music seemed to be regularly lifting the carpet. He got up, put on his dressing gown, stumbled along the corridor to the back of the house and opened the door of Deborah's room. The curtains were open and insipid moonlight drifted across the bed. Her childhood teddy bear, arms welcomingly wide, was propped against the bedhead. He patted it fondly on the head and lay down. Before his eyes had closed, the door eased open and he heard a man's urgent whisper: 'In here. This will do.'

Two sniggering people began to creep into the room. Nicholas reached out his naked foot and slammed the door back violently against them, shouting: 'Bugger off!' The woman squealed. The man cursed and apologised. They went.

He clenched his eyes and his teeth. From below, even over the music, came the crash of furniture toppling, and screams followed by more screams of laughter. Nicholas got up and went along the corridor. He reached the top of the stairs. Down below it was like a pool of bubbling mud; there was no room between the heads. Where had they all come from? Bodies crushed together, clutching, laughing, screeching, stumbling. The Beatles, the pride of the elderly, were singing: 'Get back! Get back! Get back to where you once belonged!'

'Shurrup!' he bellowed from the landing. 'Shurrup!'

His voice was so violent that everyone paused for a couple of beats, frozen in attitudes. 'Go home!' he shouted at them, flinging his arms out. 'The party's over. Fuck off!'

There was no sign of Sarah. 'Fuck off yourself!' called a male voice. 'Rude bugger.' In a moment, as though he was no concern of theirs, they were at it again, shrieking, bouncing, embracing, kissing, feeling, uncaring. A conga line formed and a bottle was being passed along it. Furiously Nicholas turned from the landing and strode to the bathroom. From the cupboard he took a plastic bucket, half-filled it with water and returned to the landing. Looking down on them he felt like Gordon at Khartoum. They saw him and all began chorusing savagely: '*Get back! Get Back! Get back to where you once belonged!*'

They belted it out, turning their wild, perspiring, painted faces towards him, and jabbing their fingers: '*Get back to where you once belonged!*'

With an almost ghostly yell he produced the bucket and threw the water over their upturned faces. One woman, mouth agape, had it filled. Then he threw the bucket after the water.

There was bedlam. One man tried to advance on him up the stairs, reached the third tread but paused, as though he had forgotten what he intended to do, and then toppled back.

Triumphantly, Nicholas wheeled and marched down the upstairs corridor to the back of the house. In Deborah's room was a rope fire-escape ladder. He opened the window. The ladder hooked to the sill. He flung it down into the garden and then climbed out. He swayed like a clown on the rope but he reached the lawn. Then, in his pyjamas, dressing gown and sheepskin slippers, he ran away.

Nine

Outside the seventeenth-century Crown and Sugar Loaf, one of the original buildings of Boxley, Isobel Smeaton, the landlady, and Xavier were wishing a convivial goodnight to friends following a late and extended session in the bar. They were both swaying and smoking, Isobel a cigarette, Xavier a cigar, blowing the fumes into the chill air of the early hours.

They had waved the car away and were about to return to the warmth of the inn to lock up for the night when Isobel saw a man in pyjamas, dressing gown and slippers running irregularly towards them along the pavement.

'Jogging,' she guessed.

'Funny sort of jogging,' responded Xavier. He examined his watch. 'At one in the morning. Who is it?'

'Might be Wee Willie Winkie,' suggested Isobel still swaying a little. She leaned from the waist, peering at the nearing figure. She coughed achingly.

'It's what's-he-called, that Nicholas Boulting, that writer chap,' she observed trying to smother her splutters. 'In his jarmas.' They could hear his feet flapping on the paving stones. 'And slippers,' added Xavier. 'He looks like somebody's after him.'

They waited until, panting, Nicholas drew near. He pulled up distraught, breathless and still drunk. 'Merry Christmas,' ventured Xavier with a blink. Isobel studied the plaid dressing gown, the sheepish slippers and the two leg sements of striped pyjamas.

'Yes, yes of course, Christmas,' Nicholas smiled faintly, still trying to recover his breath. 'You too.'

'Is it for charity?' asked Isobel in her deep, rasping, sixty-a-day croak.

'Charity? Oh I see. No . . . . It's just . . . I got locked out of my house.' Their expressions shaded. 'Have you got a room I can have for the night?'

Xavier said slowly: 'It's not something we do, let rooms.'

'But we've *got* one,' said Isobel with a moment of decision and excitement. 'Come on in. You'll catch your death.' She began to cough convulsively and Xavier hit her on the back with the palm of his hand.

Gratefully Nicholas ducked under the lintel where it said: 'Brian and Isobel Smeaton, Licensed to sell Beers, Spirits, Wines and Tobacco.'

The empty warmth of the low room closed around them. Isobel turned up the gas fire and Xavier opened the flap and went behind the bar. 'How about a night-cap,' he said, pointing, laughing, at the bare head of the other man. 'It's about all you haven't got.' He measured out three straight scotches and they briefly raised the glasses. 'I suppose you'll not be wanting to talk about it,' Isobel said throatily to Nicholas.

'What's that? . . . Oh, me like this.' He looked down the front of his dressing gown to his striped pyjama legs with his bare ankles showing between them and the slippers. 'Well, to tell you the truth I get a bit claustrophobic at this time of the year. Christmas parties and all that. I wasn't locked out but I just found it necessary to get out of the house.' He smiled in hope at them. 'You could call it Santa Claustrophobia.' Neither showed any reaction for a moment and Xavier said: 'We feel like that sometimes don't . . .' He turned for Isobel's confirmation but was met with her nudge. 'Xavier, didn't you get it? *Santa Claustrophobia.*'

Xavier gave an unsure guffaw. 'Oh I see. Right. Very good. For this time of the morning.'

'Xavier's a trifle on the dull side,' put in Isobel. 'Personally I thought that was *very* clever. That's what comes of being a writer.' She coughed gratingly. Xavier poured another round.

'Put these on my bill,' said Nicholas unsurely. He patted his empty dressing gown pockets. He did not need another drink. 'You'll have to trust me until I pay.'

'Of course we'll trust you, dear,' rasped Isobel. She held on to his elbow. 'You'll be wanting to go up, I suppose. You must be knackered. Running all that way.'

Nicholas nodded. Her grip increased. 'I'll show you,' she said. 'Xavier will be clearing up down here.' She let go of his elbow with a final squeeze and led him up a tight spiral staircase. Her bottom wagged before his eyes. 'Here's the room,' she coughed. 'There's no key.' She turned towards him on the landing, her stomach an inch away from his dressing gown cord, her hollow eyes glowing expectantly. 'But I don't expect you'll mind.'

Nicholas desperately avoided her emotive gaze. 'No, I won't mind. I'm flaked out.'

Isobel pushed herself nearer, the knot in his cord digging into both stomachs. He could smell smoke and whisky on her breath. 'He's not *really* my husband,' she cackled nodding towards the sounds of glasses from below. 'My former Brian went off with a tart from Hayes and Harlington.' She had gathered breath to accentuate the aspirates.

'Down by the airport,' Nicholas added desperately. He fumbled for the door knob.

'The bed's freshly made up.' She peeped around the edge of the door and switched on a dingy light. 'I could come an' keep you comfy. Once that one's gone to bed.' She jerked her head towards the bar.

He was trying to get into the room and keep her outside. She convulsed again, almost doubled up with it. God, why was it never Bassinger? 'Thanks,' he said. 'But I can't. I need some sleep. I'm desperate.'

'So am I,' she rasped. She fell off-balance and he put out his hand to save her. She squeezed it with fingers like pliers.

'I've got a heart condition,' he mumbled.

'My liver is shot to smithereens and just listen to my chest,' she wheezed, quickly abandoning carnal desire for an exchange of disabilities. 'I'll let you get to bed then,' she said defeated. 'Kiss me goodnight.'

Her lips drew together like strings and he attempted to get away with kissing her lightly. Instead she crushed her face to him, almost gnawing his lips. 'Goodnight, darling,' she moaned. Crimson lipstick was spread like strawberry jam across her mouth and his. With glinting eyes she turned and staggered down the thin stairs. Nicholas shut the keyless door quickly. He studied his black-eyed, pallid, lipstick-spread face in a mottled mirror on the dressing table. There was a frail chair and he jammed it under the door handle. The room was chill and the bedclothes meagre. He got into the single bed still wearing his dressing gown and put his head on to the paltry pillow. His body and his mind ached. He had done it again. He had run away.

Unfamiliar morning sounds from the street woke him. For a few moments of immobile panic he lay in the tight bed gazing at the grubby ceiling, the walls, the emaciated curtains and the bare furniture of the room. Where the hell was he now? Groaning, he shifted his aching body. The bed was as hard as a coffin. His knee was sore where it had been pressed against the frame. His head throbbed. He remembered.

His cases must even now be standing on the Old Vicarage doorstep. He moaned again and imagined his return home, with Sarah's frosty face at the window and the children looking down from upstairs, shaking their heads at his hopelessness. Stiffly he sat up, the bed creaked, and he looked at his watch. It was almost noon. Keeping his knees together he swung his legs to the floor.

The poor curtains dangled within reaching distance and he lifted an edge cautiously as if he expected a face to be looking in from outside. An uncompromising grey sky was decorated by dots of rain on the glass. 'Sod it,' he chided himself. He saw himself throwing water over his exuberant guests. Now he could never go home.

He went out into the corridor. There were downstairs voices, the click and hum of the bar. He had no clothes apart from his pyjamas, his dressing gown and the slippers. He located a grim bathroom, and his pulling of the chain brought the landlord.

'You're feeling terrible,' forecast Xavier.

'In all sorts of ways,' confirmed Nicholas. 'For a start I haven't got any clothes.'

Xavier was concerned. 'She's already told everybody in the bar.' He nodded over his shoulder. 'Had them in fits.'

'I'm pleased,' muttered Nicholas. 'Anything to cheer up Christmas.'

'I'll get you out the back way.'

'Thanks.' He held up the patterned arms of the dressing gown. 'How do I go out in the street like this?'

'Not to worry,' said the landlord. 'I'll take you home in the car.' He surveyed Nicholas sympathetically. 'I wouldn't mind escaping myself,' he confessed. 'But she's too crafty for that. I hope she didn't bother you last night. She gets randy. Thinks she's Brigitte Bardot.'

He promised to return in five minutes and he did. Nicholas opened the door. The landlord's cautioning finger beckoned him. Xavier led the way down the passage towards the back of the building and they descended another turning staircase, emerging into a cold courtyard behind the inn. Among the stacked steel barrels was an old Ford. Nicholas climbed in and Xavier opened the gate. 'If anybody asks about your gear we can always say I've brought you from the hospital,' he suggested. He drove into the High Street surging with Christmas Eve shoppers, Chamber of Commerce lights swinging in the wet wind. 'Crouch down if you don't want to be spotted,' suggested Xavier. Nicholas crouched.

With a resigned sigh Xavier said: 'She'll carry on something terrible because you've gone. She's like that. Thank God I'm not married to her. I lived down at Hayes and Harlington, near the airport, and I was quite happy, married and everything, and then my wife cleared off.' He jerked his head backwards. 'With *her* husband, in point of fact. Not that I blame *him*. *My* big mistake was to get in with *her*. She reckoned it was pooling our sorrows.' He snorted. 'Doubling mine.' They were going towards the Old Vicarage now. Apprehension filled Nicholas. Xavier, sensing it, said: 'You could make out that you don't know where you've been,' he suggested with a minimum of hope. 'Lost your memory.'

Nicholas said: 'Unfortunately she won't have lost hers.' They were outside his house now. Xavier stopped the car and Nicholas prepared to get out. Through the yews on the path he thought he could see a face in a window. 'Well, here goes. Into battle.' He shook the driver's hand. 'Thanks, Xavier. I'll come around and settle what I owe.'

'It's not Xavier,' the landlord admitted as if anxious to get it off his chest. 'She reckoned Xavier was more romantic. It's Norman.'

'Well, thanks Norman,' said Nicholas shaking the again proffered hand like a bond forged in mutual adversity. He got out of the Ford and shut the door firmly, waiting and waving as it departed. Then he revolved, standing straighter than he felt, and walked towards the house.

He had no opportunity to ring before the front door was opened by Sarah. He almost ducked but she was grinning at his nightclothes. 'Sleep well?' she asked.

She stood back to allow him to enter. Carefully he walked into the kitchen and sat down on a stool. She poured him a mug of coffee. 'The kids are out doing their last-minute shopping,' she said. 'You know what Willie is like. Deborah went with him to make sure he behaved himself after what he did last year.'

'Knocked over all the dolls in Harpers,' recalled Nicholas with great caution. 'Cracked heads everywhere.'

He looked up from the coffee. 'I'm sorry, love,' he said. 'About the bucket of water.'

'Where did you go?' she asked. 'I'll get some lunch and then perhaps we can both do some shopping.'

'Fine. I'd be glad to.' He was feeling his way. 'I ended up at the Crown and Sugar Loaf. They gave me a bed.'

'Didn't they think it a bit odd you turning up like that?' She nodded at his dressing gown.

'I told them I'd been locked out by accident,' said Nicholas. 'The chap is very decent. He brought me back in his car.'

'I saw it.' She stood up and went to the fridge.

'I'll have a bath first,' he said. 'And get some gear on. I feel rough.'

Sarah nodded. 'So do I.' She bit her lip. 'It got completely out of hand. I don't understand why people go so over the top. They left the punch until last and that *did* it. Normally they're all so bloody boring.'

He sniffed. 'What about my bucket of water?'

'I doubt if they noticed. They soon forgot anyway. They were rolling our dirty laundry basket down the High Street at three this morning. My knickers were found outside W. H. Smith's. Nobody would go home. I almost called the police. I thought the place was going to be wrecked, set on fire or something. We would have needed more than one bucket of water.'

When he was in the bath she brought him a glass of white wine. 'I thought I'd be back with Sol by now,' he confessed, regarding her from the suds. 'Soaking the guests at your own party isn't the best behaviour.'

'Nobody was on their best behaviour,' she said. To his surprise she leaned over and kissed him lightly. 'It was bloody funny actually. Funnier than the laundry basket.' Her look became serious. Her eyes were dark and blodged. 'In any case we have an agreement,' she said solemnly. 'We overlook things, remember. We try and understand. I've bought you a present you'll like. I hope you've got a nice one for me.'

'Several,' he said. He looked at her speculatively. 'Shall we go to bed for half an hour?'

'I thought you felt awful.'

'It might do me the world of good.'

She pushed at her hair. 'I look awful,' she said. 'A mess.'

'It brings out something in me.'

'Oh, you like a bit of rough.' She laughed outright and splashed the bathwater in his face. 'All right,' she said. 'I've only just made the bed.'

*

That evening Nicholas at last felt at home. In the chair before
the gas log fire he enjoyed the smug comfort of the returned
traveller, the explorer, the prodigal; he had a drink in his hand
and the *Daily Telegraph* on his lap. Sarah was sketchily singing
carols in the kitchen. Upstairs Deborah and Willie were
wrapping presents. In the hall, its lights reflecting on the
window, was a decorated Christmas tree sprouting from a pile
of ribboned parcels.

'We should get a dog,' he called to Sarah.

'Why is that?' she called back easily. 'Do you want a dog?'

'It would complete the picture,' he suggested. 'Domesticity.
I might even take to smoking a pipe.'

'The dog I wouldn't mind, the pipe I would,' she responded
putting her head around the door. Her face was pink from
cooking. 'It's a pity I've already bought your present. I can
picture a Great Dane licking your face tomorrow morning.'

'So can I,' he agreed. 'But there's not that much urgency. I
just thought it would be a good idea. The kids would like it.'

She had returned to the cooking. 'Until it came to taking it
for walks,' she called. 'Then whose dog would it be?' He asked if
she wanted another drink. Before she could answer the
telephone rang. Sarah picked it up and leaned back thinking
about the possible dog. She did not finish the call but came to
the door. 'It's your father,' she said quietly. 'You'd better
speak to them.'

He got up from the chair and went to the telephone. When he
had finished he put it down slowly. 'They say if I want to see
him I had better go now,' he said to Sarah.

'People can't choose the time they die, not as a rule,' she told
him.

Nicholas shook his head. 'The old so-and-so is quite capable
of it,' he said. He faced her and they put their arms on each
other's shoulders. 'You've *got* to,' she said. 'You'll have to go
now.'

'Right. Thanks,' he said. 'I ought to.'

Sarah took her hands from his shoulders and they kissed

briefly. She turned and made for the stairs. 'I'll get some things together for you.'

She passed Willie on the landing and said: 'Daddy's going away.'

'Not again!' exploded Willie. He almost fell down the stairs. 'You can't run away on Christmas Eve,' he confronted his father. 'What about our presents?'

Nicholas laughed and held him guiltily. Deborah was at the top of the stairs staring down in disbelief. She descended a fearful tread at a time. Sarah was trying to call to them that it was all right, but her daughter did not hear. 'You're *not* going?' she whispered. 'Not again?'

'It's not like *that*,' he protested. He studied their faces. 'Your grandfather's very ill. They don't think he'll live over Christmas. I'll have to go and see him.'

They said: 'Sorry' almost together. Sarah appeared with shirts over one arm and pyjamas over the other. 'Your father has to go,' she told them flatly. 'You have to realise.'

Efficiently she packed his overnight case and he found the car keys and went to the door. The children stood silently. When he was almost at the car he went back and kissed them. 'I might be back tomorrow,' he said. 'He could recover. He's done it before.'

'Thank heaven you've only had one drink,' said Sarah going to the car with him. She had been carrying his case and now she handed it to him. As if she knew what he was thinking she said: 'It's a nuisance for him too, I expect,' she said. 'I've often felt guilty, Nick, that we did not have him living with us or close to us.'

'I don't think I could have stood it,' he replied.

'You have to go now,' she said. 'You are all he's got.'

Nicholas kissed her again and she patted him with both hands on the lapels of his jacket. 'I'll get back as soon as I can,' he promised. 'I'll phone anyway, of course.' She went back but remained in the doorway while he climbed into the car, started the engine and turned on the lights. 'Drive carefully,' she called. The beams leapt out contorting the yews. He waved finally and drove out into the street. In the mirror he could see her and their children standing under the porch light.

It was nine o'clock. The decorations hung dumbly in the High Street. Everyone had gone home for Christmas. There was little traffic and he quickly reached the motorway, then drove steadily north. Once into the country the blackness of the night closed in. Domestic windows blinked across fields, and illuminated Christmas trees glittered in the M1 service areas. Lights moved towards and around him like space stations travelling through the sky. An hour passed, then two, then three.

At midnight he left the motorway and took the M18 east of Sheffield then onto the A1 at Conisborough, driving due north past Adwick le Street, Pontefract and Wetherby to the A59 through Knaresborough to Harrogate.

The journey took four hours, an hour less than when he had last driven it. In front of the Rosedale Nursing Home was a widespread cedar which had been sparsely hung with coloured bulbs. He stopped in front of the door of the old building. Inside he could see another tree glittering silently. Everywhere was still. The old people would be asleep, the old man might be dead. He tried to pick out the window of his father's room.

As he went through the main door he became aware that someone was sitting, watching, in a small alcove within. It was the plump and motherly girl he had seen on his last visit, the one who had removed the squashed cockroach. She had been waiting for him. She stood up and came out of the niche with a quiet smile. 'You got here,' she said. 'He'll be pleased. I'll tell Matron.'

'He's still with us then,' said Nicholas.

'Still. He says he is not going to die until tomorrow. Not until he's heard the Queen's Speech.'

Dr da Souza appeared along the corridor with Miss Southren, the matron, and a nurse. 'He is sleeping,' he said kindly. 'But I'm afraid he will not be among us for long.' He looked directly at Nicholas. 'He doesn't seem to mind,' he added with a slight

sideways smile. 'He told me he is rather looking forward to it.'
He led the way along the hushed passage. The matron asked if
he would like some tea and sent the nurse to get it. The plump
girl stayed with them. There came the sound of regular
breathing from some of the side rooms and someone had a fit of
spluttering. A door was open and Nicholas saw a large woollen
stocking hanging on the bottom of the bed. The matron
followed his glance and said: 'They don't forget it's Christmas.'

They walked a few more paces along the dimmed corridor.
'Others do forget,' observed the Indian mildly. 'They have it in
their heads that Christmas is only for the Brits. Each year I am
on duty right through, Christmas Day, Boxing Day, New
Year's Eve. But, as it happens, I am a Christian. I would like
some time off.'

'You ought to tell them,' Nicholas said.

The small man shrugged. 'Then by next year they would
forget again. Do you want to see your father now?' asked the
doctor. 'While he is asleep.'

Nicholas hesitated, then said: 'I'll just look in.'

Dr da Souza turned aside and gently opened a door.
Nicholas followed him carefully and went into his father's
room. Bernard Boulting seemed hardly to be breathing. The
doctor backed away and Nicholas looked at his father's
sleeping face, then went quietly from the room.

He followed the doctor and the matron along the corridor.
The matron opened a door and led the way into a bed-sitting
room. 'You will be comfortable in here,' murmured the doctor.
The plump girl had made a quick decision and now she
appeared with a vase of holly. 'Ah, well played Rina,' said the
Indian.

'It will make it look a bit Christmassy,' said the young
woman. She faced Nicholas and blushed. He thanked her and
put his overnight case on the floor.

They went out. Rina put her head around the door again and
said: 'Would you like a sandwich or anything with the tea? It's
coming now.'

She turned and took the tea tray from the arriving nurse

saying: 'I'll see to Mr Boulting.' She came into the room and poured a cup for him asking: 'Is there anything else you need?'

'Nothing, thanks,' he answered. 'I'm demolished. I just want to sleep.'

'All right then,' she responded cheerily. There was a moment's hesitation. 'He's lovely, your dad,' she said.

'Is he?' he said with genuine surprise.

'Yes. Didn't you know? He's funny.'

'Oh yes he is,' agreed Nicholas cautiously.

'Goodnight then. Happy Christmas.'

'Happy Christmas,' he responded.

She closed the door but immediately reopened it. 'By the way, I don't think Dr da Souza told you. He almost had a fight today.'

'Good gracious. Dr da Souza?'

She giggled. 'No, silly. Your father.'

'A fight. But he's dying.'

'That wouldn't stop him, not someone like him. No, the old boy we call the Vicar, although he really isn't one according to his records. He upset your dad and it nearly came to fists.' She closed her own full fists and pumped them. Then she went out again and he slumped on the bed. There was a big old-fashioned television set in the room. He took his shoes off. To his consternation the door began to open again. There was no knock and he watched as a sparse tortoise-like head came around it. 'You're in,' creaked a voice. There was a clerical collar ringing his thin neck, despite his being in pyjamas and dressing gown.

'I am,' sighed Nicholas. 'You must be the Vicar.'

'Yes, and I've come to complain about your father. He really is most aggressive, you know.'

'I understand he's dying,' pointed out Nicholas. 'That's why I've come. Dying probably makes people aggressive.'

The man took it in craning his head from side to side. 'Not everybody,' he eventually said defensively. 'The meek shall inherit the earth, remember. Goodnight sir.'

'Goodnight,' responded Nicholas thankfully. The door closed and he stood up and locked it.

Five minutes later he was lying between the starched sheets. It was the second, strange, narrow and comfortless bed he had slept in on successive nights. He sighed and began to go to sleep. He slept and woke repeatedly through the night. His dreams were full of ghosts and journeys and he rolled and groaned until he fell from the bed. On his hands and knees in the darkness, on the floor, he crawled around, frightened of the dream. Climbing back into bed he went to sleep slowly. His knees were sore from his fall. He was roused by a knocking on the door. Grumbling, thinking in his confusion that the bogus vicar had returned, he unlocked it. Rina was there with a cup of tea. It was daylight.

'He's still asleep,' she said putting the cup on the bedside table. 'It's eight thirty. He generally doesn't come around until about ten anyway.' She looked at him as though wondering whether to tell him something important. 'It's Christmas Day,' she said ultimately. 'Happy Christmas.'

'Oh, yes, Happy Christmas to you,' he returned. He picked up the teacup gratefully. She again appeared hesitant but then said: 'The patients have their Christmas dinner about twelve. We start early because they're slow eaters. Then this afternoon they have their visitors and there's a concert, some people from the town come up and give a bit of an entertainment.' There was another pause. 'I thought I'd warn you. If you fancy having Christmas dinner in the staff room, I'll be having mine about three thirty.'

'After the Queen's Speech,' he said carefully.

'Oh yes.' She appeared embarrassed. 'After that.' She regained her composure. 'There's breakfast in the staff room. You just help yourself.'

Twenty minutes later he looked in at his father's door. The old man was sleeping, snoring mildly, on his back, mouth open to the ceiling as if hoping to catch something. There seemed no point in remaining in there. Nicholas went to the staff room and had some toast and coffee. Rina came in when he had almost finished. 'He's awake,' she reported quietly. 'He knows you're here.'

Nicholas went along the corridor with her. Frail old ladies, seated in a circle, were tossing a coloured ball to each other, their faces void. A man was grimacing at a jigsaw puzzle. A radio played somewhere, a choir singing carols. There were starched nursing staff carrying sheets and exchanging greetings. He followed the plump girl into his father's room.

'Mr Boulting,' she said, 'you have a visitor.' She went out and closed the door behind her.

Bernard Boulting was propped in bed, his face pared to the bone, his eyes bright and savage. 'Oh, it's you,' he said in a rallying voice. 'I wondered when you'd get here.'

Nicholas stood at the bedside not knowing whether to kiss his father. The old man remained motionless now looking ahead without expectation or interest. Nicholas patted him on the stretched skin on his head. 'It's Christmas Day,' he said.

'I know,' grumbled the old man. 'Sodding Christmas. That's what I've always said. Why did you come? Did they tell you I've had it?'

'I heard you weren't very well,' said Nicholas guardedly. 'But you seem all right now.' He made an attempt to laugh. 'I gather you were ready to have a fight yesterday.'

'Fight?' queried his father. 'Fight? I can't fight. I can't get out of bed.'

'With the Vicar,' Nicholas prompted.

The expression brightened with pleasure. 'Ah, that old farter,' recalled Bernard. 'Yes, I did threaten him. You couldn't blame me. Coming in here with his dirty dog-collar. He cuts that out of a Daz packet, you know, he's not even a real vicar. He came in here to see if he could watch me die. Well, I wasn't having any. Standing there farting as he does. I wasn't going to die with somebody letting off like that.'

'Sarah and Deborah and Willie are thinking about you,' said Nicholas deliberately. 'They send their love.'

'Who's that then?' asked the old man apparently keen for details of anyone who loved him.

'My wife, Sarah, and the children, Deborah and Willie,' Nicholas told him.

Bernard ignored the information. 'I had a fight with your mother once,' he said screwing up his face to recall the details. 'I mean a proper punch-up, not just words. By God, she caught me with her skinny fist. Like being hit with a bone.' He regarded his son with a hint of apology. 'We weren't very happy.'

'I'm back home now, with Sarah and the kids,' persisted Nicholas. 'You remember I told you we had parted company.'

'Oh yes. Well you don't want to be by yourself over Christmas, do you,' said Bernard. He seemed to remember something. 'They have a concert here this afternoon,' he said concisely. 'They had it last year.' He shot a glance that could have been accusing at his son. 'I've been in here two years now, you know.' He remembered the concert again. 'Bloody appaling it was. I'm glad I don't have to listen to that row. What time is the Queen's Speech?'

'I think it's three o'clock,' repled Nicholas tentatively.

'I've told them I'm not going to die until I've heard what she's got to say.' His voice suddenly became weaker, diminishing in moments to almost a whisper. Nicholas looked anxiously behind him for help. Rina was hovering outside the door and she came in. 'You'd better rest now, Mr Boulting,' she said firmly. She began to rearrange his pillows. Nicholas realised how frail his father was. Like a frayed old piece of rope. 'You have a bit of a sleep,' said the girl. 'Your son will come in when you're having your lunch. It's Christmas dinner today, remember.'

'All right,' said Bernard resignedly. He seemed to avoid looking at Nicholas. 'Turkey – but not too much stuffing.'

Nicholas remained a few more minutes before going outside into the corridor. The Vicar, now dressed in shabby clerical black but with one end of his collar flying loose like a broken hinge, was waiting. 'Did he tell you?' he enquired. 'About our confrontation?'

'He mentioned it,' said Nicholas resignedly.

The man made a sulky face. 'I only went in to see how he was getting on,' he grumbled. 'And he accused me of making antisocial noises.' His eyes came up to ascertain that he had been understood. Then, as though to demonstrate, he emitted a precise fart. 'Perhaps I do have a tendency to emunctory moments, but so do many elderly men. Your father was most aggressive.'

'He's dying,' pointed out Nicholas helplessly.

'Impending death is no excuse for bad manners,' recited the man. He realised his dog-collar had come adrift. After a brief attempt to fix the flying end, he asked Nicholas to do it and Nicholas eventually found the safety pin and fastened it around the gnarled tortoise neck. The Vicar shuffled away.

The seated ladies were persevering with their ball game but the ball was now being passed in the opposite direction. A nurse came past them and tried encouragement. 'Now the *other* way,' she suggested heartily. The ball fell to the floor in the confusion. It rolled colourfully towards Nicholas and he picked it up and made to hand it to one of the circle. Each woman was waiting with her hands stretched out. He handed it to one. The woman gravely thanked him but glowered towards the nurse. 'She always spoils the game.'

Nicholas went to the public telephone in the entrance hall and called Sarah. 'He's still hanging on,' he said. 'Awkward as ever.'

'Poor you,' said Sarah. 'And poor him. Have you been able to talk with him?'

'Oh, he's full of conversation, he's full of life for that matter except that they say he's dying. His heart is scarcely ticking over but that did not stop him trying to have a punch-up with another patient he accused of letting off.'

'Letting off what . . . ? Oh I see.' She laughed. 'He's still got some spirit then.'

Nicholas said: 'He says he doesn't intend to snuff it until after the Queen's Speech this afternoon.'

He heard her muffled laugh again. 'He's priceless isn't he.' The tone dropped. 'Perhaps we should have known him better.'

'Perhaps *I* should have,' he corrected. 'What are you doing?'

'Just about to have lunch. The table is set. Deborah's done that. I told her she'll make a great silver-service waitress one day and she was most insulted. Our Willie managed to flood the bathroom this morning practising with his snorkle outfit. I'll get them to the phone.'

When Deborah spoke to him she said: 'Dad, I loved it.'

'Laying the table?'

'Don't mess, I mean my present. The shoes and the dress and the other things.'

'Your mother chose them. I bet you look nice.'

'They're really super. Here's Willie. He flooded the bathroom. When are you coming home?'

'As soon as . . . as soon as I can,' he said.

'How is Grandad?' Her voice dropped as if she were reluctant to ask.

'He's being himself. But he's sinking.'

'I'm sorry.'

'He's an old man.'

'Yes, but I'm still sorry.'

'Don't worry. Enjoy Christmas.'

'All right.'

'Hello Dad,' said Willie in his matter-of-fact way. 'We've had a bit of bother.'

'The bathroom flooded.'

'How d'you know that? Oh, they told you. Mum and Deborah. Women will talk. Anyway it's getting dry. Thanks for the snorkle stuff and the other things. How is Grandad?'

'He's sinking.'

'Poor old Grandad. I suppose he's very old.'

'He's eighty-two,' said Nicholas.

'That's very old.'

Sarah came back on the phone. 'We'll see you when we see you then,' she said. 'It's a pity you can't be here.'

'I could have been there, but I didn't know. Even now I don't know. He's awkward to the last.'

He put the phone down and went into the lobby. He could hear the patients in the dining room. There was the explosion of a Christmas cracker and some screeches. He went towards the door. The patients, some wearing paper hats and puzzled expressions, were at the long tables supervised by the staff. They were eating with varying degrees of enthusiasm and efficiency. Someone was playing a piano at the far end, lustily but not tunefully. A pair of ladies almost in front of him tried to pull a cracker but had insufficient strength. Nicholas made a movement forward and Rina appeared. 'Take the other end,' she insisted. He put his arms around the frail shoulders of one of the women. Her bones were projecting through her dress like a coat-hanger. He helped her to tug. Rina took the other old hands in hers and pulled too. The cracker split with a bang and there were cries of delight and broken laughter. 'I haven't laughed for a long time,' said the woman Nicholas had helped. 'Hardly at all.' She looked at him more keenly. 'You *are* Mr Boulting's son, aren't you?' she said. She pushed her plate aside and half-turned in her seat. 'You were here the day he so gallantly killed the cockroach.'

'Yes,' agreed Nicholas. 'I remember.'

She lowered her voice. 'I hear he's dying,' she said. Her eyes went around cautiously.

'I'm afraid so. That's why I have come.'

She pulled her eyebrows together. 'Don't let him die today,' she warned as though he had the power to order the time. 'Not Christmas Day.'

Visitors, ushered in by Matron and the staff, arrived after the meal and the concert party began setting up their stage. The old people and their relatives sat on rows of chairs and waited. Nicholas saw Rina glance at him and he followed her. 'We can have our dinner now,' she said. 'While they're listening to the singing and trying to work out the jokes. They like the conjuror best. The good bit is watching the relatives. They can't get away quick enough.' As they went along the corridor, her wide backside in front of him, she half-turned and said: 'We'll take a peep and make sure he's all right.'

They went into the room at the same moment as his father opened his eyes. Rina recognised the look. 'Stay here,' she said quietly but urgently. 'I'll get the doctor.'

She went out swiftly. Nicholas, his heart sounding, went towards his father. 'Has the Queen spoken yet?' Bernard Boulting asked. His voice was a croak.

'Not yet,' Nicholas told him.

'I can't wait around for her,' said the old man as though impatient at someone late for an appointment. He held out his skinny hand. Nicholas took it, pulled up the chair and sat by him. His father's eyelids dropped as he attempted to locate the pulse.

Bernard opened his eyes to glistening slits. 'Son . . .'

'Yes Dad, I'm here.'

'I want to be buried at sea.'

Nicholas felt his mouth sag. 'At sea?' was all he could say.

'Yes, if it's not too much trouble.'

'Hello, Sarah. He's just died.'

'Oh I see. I'm sorry Nick.'

'He asked to be buried at sea.'

'At . . . at sea? But . . . good God . . . he's never . . .'

' . . . Been to sea, I know. The nearest he's ever got to it is the cross-channel ferry.'

'He would, wouldn't he.' Her dry laugh came over the telephone. 'Difficult unto death.'

'And beyond it,' added Nicholas. 'He said if it wasn't too much trouble. They were his last words.'

'The final one being "trouble"?'

'Yes.'

'What are you going to do?'

'I could drive back but I'd have to return here the day after tomorrow and I feel drained. There's the registrar of deaths, all that business, and even the undertakers are not open over Christmas, although they do have an emergency service, so I believe. But this hardly qualifies as an emergency.'

'I see. I didn't actually mean that. I meant what are you going to do about him wanting to be buried at sea?'

'God only knows. It's got to be complicated.'

'You can't take him seriously, even with his dying words.'

'Sarah, I can't think about it now. I'm exhausted. I didn't have much sleep and this sort of thing takes it out of you. The doctor has been to see him for the last time. They have to make sure.'

Her voice softened. 'You should try and get some rest.' A burst of haphazard singing came from down the corridor. Sarah said: 'Whatever is that noise?'

'They've started to sing,' he said. 'The patients.'

'Have you had anything to eat?'

'Not yet. I'm afraid Christmas dinner has been upstaged. I can go into the staff room and have it there but somehow I don't feel in the mood for party hats and reading mottoes out of crackers.'

'I don't imagine you do. Why don't you try and get some sleep.'

'I will. How are the kids? Have you had a good day?'

'The usual. We're just settling down to watch the television. We missed the Queen.'

'So did the old man.'

'We should have known him better,' she said again.

'I know. *I* should have.'

'Call me later. I'm sorry Nick.'

'Thanks love. It's not his death I feel sad about right now. It's his life.'

'Don't blame yourself. He was a difficult and . . . well, unfriendly old man.'

'I know . . . . But he was my father.'

Nicholas replaced the telephone. The patients were singing 'Ten Green Bottles'. 'They'll run out of breath after a while,' forecast Rina appearing in the corridor. 'I'm sorry about your dad. I'd got to like him.' Her rounded face was low. 'But that's why people come here, to die.'

Together they walked along the corridor. 'Ten Green Bottles' was flagging. 'And if one green bottle should accidentally fall . . .'

'It will tire them out,' she forecast. 'They'll be asleep by six o'clock, seven at the outside.'

207

'Like small children,' he said.

'That's right.' She laughed. 'What about when your dad smashed the cockroach and then put the spoon back in the trifle?'

He smiled and nodded. 'It seems he's remembered for that.'

'What will you do now? Are you going back home?'

'I think I'll stay . . . if it's all right. I've got to make the arrangements and it will have to wait until the day after tomorrow. I'll go into town to a hotel.'

'Do you want to?'

'I thought you might need the room.'

'Oh no, that's all right. We only use it for cases like yours, when somebody has to stay because of a patient's condition. With a bit of luck this lot will all see the New Year in.' She thought a moment and said: 'Barring accidents.'

'Thanks, if that's all right. But I'll move out tomorrow. I'll go to a hotel then. At the moment I think I could do with a sleep.'

'You have some,' she encouraged. 'I'll give you a call this evening. About nine. We have supper in the staff room. When everything's gone quiet. You'll need something to eat by then. You've missed your Christmas dinner.'

'You're kind, Rina. Thanks.'

'It's all right. I feel sorry.'

He went into the room where he had slept the previous night. It was too warm. Taking his shoes off he lay on the bed and tried to sleep. For a few minutes he did so but then woke with a start at the sound of carols being sung outside his door. Wearily he got up from the bed and opened it. Four old women and two men were in the corridor singing 'Good King Wenceslas' in cracked voices. They ran out of words or breath and stood frozen in their attitudes with embarrassed smiles. The gaunt lady who had praised his father's bravery with the cockroach was at the centre and it was she who spoke. 'We have heard that your father had passed on,' she said steadily. 'So we thought we would cheer you up with a carol.'

'Thank you . . . ,' he blinked. ' . . . Very kind.'

'Well, that's it,' she said decisively. 'Off we jolly go.'

Obediently the group trooped away. The lady leader remained for an extra moment, leaning forward. 'I was very fond of your father, you know,' she confided. 'We had a lot in common. We shared a taste in cough medicine. If only we had been a little younger.'

There was no regret in either her voice or her face. She made the statement like a fact and then turned briskly and went at a loping walk after the others. Rina appeared with a cup of tea. 'I couldn't stop them,' she said apologetically. 'They wanted to sing to you.'

She walked into the room and put the cup and saucer on the table next to the bunch of holly she had brought. Already some of the berries had fallen and she swept them up with a practised hand. 'The television works,' she said. 'It's ancient but it works.'

'I think I'll try and sleep,' he said. He thanked her for the tea.

'What will you do tomorrow?'

'I haven't really thought. I'll go to a hotel. Maybe I'll watch the box then.' He thought about it. 'On the other hand I may just get into the car and spend the day driving around.'

'Where?'

'Oh, anywhere. Across the moors. It really doesn't matter. Driving is very good for thinking.'

'Yes, I suppose it is. I don't drive, but I think a lot.' Almost in the same breath she said: 'I've laid out your father. He looks very rested.'

He barely understood. 'You've . . . oh yes, I see. You have to do that?'

'It's part of my job. I'm used to it.'

'How old are you?'

'Twenty. You think it's young for doing this kind of thing, I expect.'

'Well, it does seem like that.'

She laughed quietly. 'The old people here, the old chaps especially, think I'm like a film star, glamorous, you know. I know different but they only see things through their eyes.' She went out and he sat on the bed drinking the tea. He turned on the television. There was a comedy show on one channel, a Yuletide game-show on another, the repeat of something he remembered seeing on a previous Christmas on the third and on the fourth a black-and-white film with subtitles. He was confronted with a scene on board a sailing ship. The crew were gathered and the captain was reading aloud. Nicholas moved with a sort of horror towards the screen. They were burying a man at sea.

Ten

'Sarah. How are you?'

'How are *you*, that's more to the point. We've been thinking about you.'

'Thanks. Well I've just seen the old man. They've laid him out.'

'Was he peaceful?'

'A good deal more peaceful than he's been for most of his life. More content.' He paused. 'I really ought to drive home now.'

'No. You stay. There's no point in your driving home just to drive back again. Will you just stay there?'

'They say it's all right if I want to. They've given me a room here but I think I'll find a hotel.'

'Is it very depressing?'

'It's sad. We don't know how people live.'

'Burial at sea is a nightmare,' she told him suddenly. 'Just to make the arrangements. It takes ages and a million miles of red tape.'

'Who told you that?'

She hesitated then said: 'David. David Fawkes. He rang to wish us a Happy Christmas and I told him.'

'David Fawkes rang?'

'Oh come on Nick. He's a friend.'

'He's no friend of mine.'

'Perhaps I shouldn't have told you he called. He was only doing his job, you know, when we were heading for a divorce. They have to do unpalatable things, solicitors. They have to be thick-skinned. He only had my interest and the children's interests at heart. He may have been wrong, but he was only doing what he was paid to do.'

'Good old Guy Fawkes,' he muttered.

'Now stop it. You're tired and upset. I wish I'd never mentioned it.'

'So do I.' He breathed deeply. 'All right, Sarah. Maybe I am oversensitive and I don't feel very good. I'll call you tomorrow. Love to the kids.'

'Yes. All right, Nick. Goodnight darling. Try and sleep.'

He put the phone down and stared along the corridor, deserted and dimmed. David Fawkes. All he needed now was David Fawkes.

That evening at nine o'clock he went to the staff dining room. All the lights were on but it was almost deserted. In one corner was a group in white overalls, workers from the kitchen. Some distance from them Rina was sitting by herself in the centre of a long table upon which were the remains of several meals, cutlery, plates, glasses and cups. 'I waited for you,' she said. 'I'll get you some food. It's only cold.'

'That will be fine,' said Nicholas. He took a chair opposite her. The white-coated people ceased their conversation and looked towards him. One waved in an embarrassed way, an acknowledgement of professional sympathy. He thanked them with a return wave. Rina came back with two plates. 'I've got a bottle of wine in my room,' she said. 'I'll go and get it.'

She had put turkey and ham, cold potatoes and salad on the plate and various pickles were on the table. He realised how hungry he was. She returned with the bottle of white wine already opened. 'Yugoslav Riesling,' she said, examining the label. 'I hope it's all right.'

'Perfect,' he smiled. He let her pour two glasses. They raised them. 'To your dad,' she said quietly. 'He gave me this wine.'

She saw his expression. 'It was the only present I got this Christmas,' she went on. 'He gave it to me three days ago. Just in case, as he put it.'

'Here's to him,' he said. 'Wherever he's got to.'

'I wonder if you can grumble in Heaven,' she mused. 'Probably not much to grumble about.'

'He'll find something,' he smiled. He studied her round face across the table. 'What is Rina short for? Irene?'

'I wish you hadn't asked,' she said looking down at her food.

'I'm sorry.'

'It's dead embarrassing.' She leaned closer, a piece of turkey and a pickle on her fork. 'My father's fault. He was a Fascist, see . . . well, a Nazi, to be honest. He got it from my grandad who got interested in the Germans during the war. Finished up believing they were right and our side was wrong. Anyway my father got it all from him and he got to be a Nazi, no denying it.'

'So he called you . . . ?'

'Hitlerina,' she mumbled. She looked up sorrowfully. 'Terrible isn't it. But it stuck. I had to shorten it of course. At school they let me use my second name Eva. Then I found out that was after Hitler's lady friend.'

Nicholas said: 'What a dreadful thing to do.'

'Mad. Mad *as* Hitler he was. My mum cleared off somewhere. God knows where and he had his skull cracked in a pub fight and was never right again. Died three years ago and good riddance. I'm on my own. That's why I work Christmastime.'

'You haven't got any other family?'

'Oh, there's my brother Adolf but goodness knows where he is. If I could only get off tomorrow I'd have liked to go with you on your ride, just to get out, but I can't get anybody in. It's a pity. I would have liked it.'

'Yes,' he said thinking about it. 'It's a shame. I planned to do it alone. Time to think. But you would have been welcome.'

'I wouldn't have been in your way,' she promised. 'We could have just been quiet together. I think you're lonely.'

The man behind the desk at the Yorkshire Grey Hotel, Harrogate, was surprised to see him on Boxing Day but recovered sufficiently to ask if he was having a nice Christmas.

'Mixed,' said Nicholas. 'Do you have a room for tonight?'

They had a room. 'Well that's not too bad – mixed,'

philosophised the man. 'When you think what it *can* be like.' He shook his face sorrowfully as if thinking of the consequences of some natural and, worse, recurring disaster. It was a moment before he brightened. 'Anyway, I can promise you a fine old time tonight. We always have a bit of a do on Boxing Day night. People are getting bored by then. The guests enjoy it, some of them reckon it's the best part of their Christmas. And we get people coming in from all around, Leeds even. It gets quite noisy.'

'I'm going to be out all day,' Nicholas told him as he signed the register. 'And I won't be back very early.'

'It goes on late.' The man took the register and turned it around to read the identity of the stranger who would be out all of Boxing Day and be unlikely to return for the evening fun. 'You're a long way from home,' he said. 'Over Christmas.'

'It was necessary,' said Nicholas. He thought he might as well tell him. 'My father died yesterday. He was in a nursing home here. Rosedale.'

'Oh I see. That was bad luck.' He seemed uncertain as to who had suffered the bad luck. 'I'll take you to the room,' he decided. 'All the best rooms are gone, it being Christmas, but this is not too bad. Good views of the cricket ground.'

'That will be useful,' said Nicholas. The man said: 'It's nice in the summer. You can watch them play while you have a lie-in.' Nicholas followed him. He always seemed to be walking into strange rooms. This one was bleak, the curtains framing a mousy landscape. 'I'll turn the rad. on,' said the man. 'It soon gets warm. But you'll be going out, you say.'

'Yes.'

'Difficult your dad passing away over Christmas. Making the arrangements and that.'

'That's why I'm staying. I'll have to wait until tomorrow.'

'I can recommend a good undertaker,' offered the man. 'Does a nice job. Did with my old dad. Neat and proper. No fuss. Ernie Pallister. In fact he'll be here tonight for the do. He always comes with Dilly, his wife and his boy Arthur, who helps in the business. They're a great laugh off-duty. Lovely family.'

'Oh right.'

'Get back a bit early and have a word with him. You could kill two birds with one stone.'

Not for the first time in his recent history he did not know where he was going. Now he was almost alone on the road which left Harrogate in a sedate, suburban manner, but once outside the town, almost as if relishing its freedom, began to climb steeply.

The countryside was void. There were a few fields and villages at first but once the route began its earnest ascent, there were gathering hills and on the hills there was snow. He felt a small exhilaration, the hint of an adventure when the sun appeared and brushed the wintry land with a silver light; but neither the view nor the mood lasted.

Before leaving the Yorkshire Grey he had telephoned Sarah and the conversation had been uncomfortable and disturbing. 'There is no way he can be buried at sea,' she had said as if she had made up both their minds. 'Nor any reason. He was just being difficult as usual.'

'Well, he won't be difficult any more,' Nicholas had pointed out. 'I'll ask the undertaker about it, that's the least I can do. If it's going to mean delaying things and all sorts of red tape then I think he'll have to give us the benefit of the doubt. Not that he's got much say in the matter. Not now.'

They were choosing their words. But she could not sustain it. 'Where will the funeral be if it's not in mid-Atlantic?' she asked. 'Up there or down here?'

'It might as well be up here. He doesn't, he didn't, know anybody down there.'

'He didn't know many people anywhere,' she pointed out. 'I doubt if anybody in Reigate remembers him sufficiently to go to his funeral. The majority of people he knew there he upset.'

'I know,' Nicholas sighed. 'I'll put a notice in the local Reigate paper and if anybody is interested in coming, which I doubt, not all this way, or sending some flowers, then they can.'

'So you think it would be better up there?'

'Well, at least he knew the people in the nursing home. They'll come, I expect. They'll make up the numbers.'

'I could never understand why he insisted on going up to Harrogate in the first place. He didn't have any connections there did he?'

'None as far as I know, certainly not recent. He'd had a holiday up here years ago. Perhaps with Mother, when they were speaking. Maybe he had fond memories.'

'Or he was just being cussed,' she amended. 'Knowing it was a long way for you to go to visit him.'

'Or putting enough distance between him and me, us, so that he wouldn't be bothered with visits.'

She sighed. 'He should at least have come to live *near* us, if living *with* us would have been difficult. He would have got to know some people then.'

'So we could get a quorum,' he said.

'We're not getting on very well this morning are we?'

'No, if it's my fault, I apologise,' he said. 'I'm dog-tired, that's all.'

'I'm sorry too,' she said reasonably. 'What will you do today?'

'I've checked into a hotel, the Yorkshire Grey at Harrogate,' he said. 'This is where I am now. I think I'll drive around a bit. The countryside is nice. Fill in the day.'

'I thought you were tired.'

'There will be nothing on the roads. It's very isolated north of here at this time of the year.'

'It's raining here. The Boltons are having a Boxing Day drinks party. I'll go to that. The kids are going roller-skating this afternoon.'

'I'm sorry you're by yourself,' he said.

'That's all right. So are you.'

As he drove up through Wharfedale he recalled their edgy conversation almost sentence by sentence. He went higher, through a hamlet with no visible inhabitants. The sky had closed in again, the hills with their cladding of snow standing against the deep day. He passed a church where an old woman, carrying a spray of holly, was stumbling into the churchyard. He wondered if churches allowed people from outside the parish, visitors, to be buried among their homely graves.

He passed only two cars in the next hour, one hurrying downhill, the other an old van labouring up. There was a signpost pointing to Hubberholme and Yockenthwaite off the main road. On impulse, as he had with Littlehaven on the Essex coast, he turned the car and followed that way. There was a spread of snow from the hills to the fringe of road now. He drove on, mile upon mile. It was amazing in crowded England how you could be so alone. His thoughts wandered homelessly, his mood was low. He saw a light as the road climbed over the shoulder of another rise. A further mile and he saw it was an inn, solitary, far from anywhere, but with lights in its windows, framed by the stone of the walls. There was a snow-rimed sign which said 'The Silent Wife' illustrated with a picture of a gagged woman. He stopped the car, got out, went to the door, and pressed the latch. It clattered open.

The stone room was vacant except for a man intent on a newspaper behind the bar. He scarcely looked up as Nicholas entered, as though people were coming in all the time. There was a robust fire in the grate and comfortable benches and solid tables around the walls. From the beamed ceiling hung some old lanterns and a pin-ball machine stood abandoned in one corner.

'Know any jokes?' asked the man when Nicholas was seated with a whisky. His voice was slow, deep Yorkshire.

Nicholas was slow to respond. 'Well . . . jokes. Let me see. I can't remember them as a rule.'

'Nor me, that's t'trouble. On New Year's Eve we have a right time in here. Every year we have a right good time. But I have to tell a couple of jokes. The wife is singing. It's all amateur. But I can't think of a joke. I know two but I used them up last year and I've only got a few days left.'

'Perhaps they'll not remember,' suggested Nicholas.

The man, who had pink broken skin and watery eyes as if he spent a lot of time in the wind, looked astonished. 'Not remember? Not remember? Oh, they'll remember all right. If it kills them. It's all the same crowd and they'll know.' His animation stopped abruptly and worry crammed his face. 'Nay, I've got to get some new material.'

'What about limericks?' suggested Nicholas. Was there no one in the world without problems?

'Limericks?' said the landlord leaning hopefully across his counter. 'Funny rhymes you mean?'

'That's right. "There was a young lady of Crewe." That sort of thing. They're not difficult to make up. You could use some local places. What have you got around here?'

'Hubberholme, Yockenthwaite,' recited the man. 'Oughter-shaw.' His voice lost optimism. 'Heckmondwicke.'

'Hard,' conceded Nicholas. 'Difficult to rhyme.' He put his glass on the bar and the barman poured another scotch. 'Have this on me,' he said. 'For trying.'

'I heard a joke,' ventured Nicholas raising his glass. He was oddly grateful for the diversion. The man had not asked him what he was doing there, or where he was going. Now the landlord looked immensely pleased and, as if to put their relationship on a partnership basis, he held out his thin hard hand. 'My name's Tom Burton,' he said.

'I'm Nicholas Boulting. This man walked into a pub . . .'

'Wait, wait,' urged Tom Burton. 'I'll write it down. I'll only forget, else.' He turned over a beer mat and picked up a stub of pencil, licking its end. 'Right. Man walks into pub . . .' He wrote feverishly and then looked up expectantly.

'He had a chihuahua on a lead. . . .'

'A what? Oh yes, I see.' The stub of pencil hovered, then halted. His face rose again. 'Won't "dog" do?'

'It has to be a chihuahua,' said Nicholas.

'All right. "CHEW-WA-WA." That'll do. Right, go on.'

'He walks in and the barman says that they don't allow dogs apart from guide-dogs. But the chap has got his eyes closed. "I'm blind," he says. "I've just bought this new guide-dog." The barman looks at the chihuahua and says: "But guide-dogs are usually Alsatians or Labradors." And the man feels out and says: "What have they sold me?" '

Nicholas laughed hopefully. Tom Burton was still writing it down. He perused it. 'Yes, that might do,' he said without a particle of a smile. From the back of the bar, pushing the curtain aside, came a stranded-looking woman who nodded at Nicholas. 'Mr Boulting has just given me a joke for New Year's Eve,' Tom Burton said with a hint of achievement. 'Listen. . . .'

Reaching from the beer mat he recited the joke laboriously to her. She remained unsmiling and said: 'The dog was too small.'

She retreated behind the curtain as though it was part of an act. Nicholas had a turkey sandwich. Tom Burton said stolidly: 'Somebody else did tell me one but I don't know whether to use it.' Anxiously he studied. 'Could I try it out on you?'

'Go ahead,' said Nicholas. He sat down and waited.

'Old people's home,' said the landlord slowly. 'Old lady says to old man: "If you come to my room I'll make you a nice cup of tea and hold your willie." ' His anxious expression intensified. 'You understand?' he asked. Nicholas said he did. Tom Burton took a deep breath. 'I've got to get this right,' he mumbled. 'That's right . . . ! "A nice cup of tea and hold your willie." And the old man says: "I can go to Mrs Jenkins's room for that." And the old lady says . . .' He checked his small script carefully again. 'She says: "What's Mrs Jenkins got that I haven't?" and the old man says: "St Vitus's Dance." '

Nicholas found himself laughing. The whole nightmare of the past few days, his father's dead face, the old lady who was his father's last friend, his own sins of omission, were jumbled into the joke. He went out still laughing so that the man would hear him. Outside the door he was abruptly confronted by the massive sweep of the snowed countryside, the hills and the clefts and the road rising cold and uncaring to an apparent nowhere. Bleakly he walked towards his car.

As he drove away he caught a glimpse of Tom Burton looking at him through the window, perhaps just wanting to see what sort of car he had. Would he have any more customers that day or would he have to wait until the right good time on

New Year's Eve? Nicholas was still driving north. A snowy sign told him he had crossed into Cumbria. The countryside became more muscular, the hills drenched with winter clouds, snow layered to the edges of the road, the day already darkening. But he could not go back yet. There was nowhere to go back to. He thought of Sarah at the Boltons' drinks party and wondered, as she undoubtedly would wonder, why he was not there with her. Enquiries would be made as to where he was and some would conclude that once more he had run away. Perhaps he had.

The nose of the car was pointing up like a small, brave, ascending aeroplane. To complete the illusion he drove into cloud before dropping again into a valley, empty but for the snow and the wind. He could see a crossroads ahead with a telephone box and directional sign standing, arm extended, like a thin, dutiful man. When he reached it he stopped the car. He ought to ring Sarah. He looked at his watch. It was just past three. Perhaps she would not be home yet. Boxley parties were often extended. She would have had champagne at the Boltons'. They always served Spanish champagne which they boasted was as good as French any Boxing Day. Nicholas decided to postpone the call.

Sitting at the crossroads in the car he saw, against the snow, far away, a red dot. It startled him. A red dot in a monochrome landscape; like Thérèse walking the path on the grey and green Essex shore. He watched the speck of colour intently as it moved towards him. It was so far away at first that it took five minutes before he saw it was a cyclist wearing a red anorak. The cyclist drew level and stopped. They were like explorers meeting by chance in some Arctic wasteland. 'Afternoon,' said the man cheerfully. 'Going far?' He took out one ear-piece of a Walkman.

'Just driving,' Nicholas said realising he did not know how far. 'Looking at the scenery.'

'That's what I do,' said the cyclist. Each word came out with a cloud of vaporised air. 'I'd rather have this . . . ,' he swept one arm around the horizon holding onto the bicycle with the other, '. . . than people any day.' Pushing back his woolly hat he revealed a forehead brown and pitted as a loaf. He removed the other ear-piece of his Walkman. 'Can't stand Christmas, any of it,' he said. 'I just get out.'

'How long have you been on the road?' asked Nicholas as one tramp might ask another.

'First light Christmas Eve,' replied the man. 'I've been pedalling all that time with the music going.' He tapped the Walkman. 'Marches, military marches.'

Nicholas had not touched the button of the car radio or the tape during his entire journey. 'In the summer,' said the man, despite his rejection of the world, apparently happy at some human contact, 'I bike all over Europe. I get the wind charts, you know the prevailing winds, and I get them at my back as far as I can. I've biked hundreds of miles like that.'

'I must try it some time,' nodded Nicholas.

'I can't afford a car,' said the man sniffing at the vehicle. 'Or I'd have one.'

He pulled his hat down and adjusted his Walkman before pushing on the pedals again and moving away towards the north. Nicholas shook his head and watched the diminishing red dot in the driving mirror. He wondered where Thérèse was now.

He thought about it for a moment then left the car and went into the telephone box. Through the glass he could see the contours of still and silent snow. Picking up the handset, he put his finger towards the buttons. As he did so he was thoroughly startled by a knocking on the glass behind him. He turned swiftly in the confined space and saw that the red-anoraked cyclist had returned and was peering urgently through the window. He opened the door. 'Are you going to be long?' asked the man.

'Well . . . no . . . actually. I don't really know. Go first if you like.'

The cyclist smiled toothily. 'As there's only two of us,' he said. Nicholas began to exit from the box and the red man sidled in. 'There's nobody else likely to jump the queue is there,' he said. Nicholas stood outside in the gaunt wind as the cyclist dialled. While he waited for a response he opened the door a fraction and confided: 'I clean forgot to post my pools. I'm ringing my auntie to do it. Ah, there she is.'

He closed the door privily and Nicholas waited, watching the day dying on the pallid slopes. The man had an extended talk with his auntie and emerged apologetically. 'She natters on a bit,' he explains. 'Nagging me because I left her by herself at Christmas. She knows I like to get on the bike.'

'You should get a tandem,' suggested Nicholas as he took the cyclist's place in the box.

'No. I wouldn't want her behind me. Nag, nag, nag,' insisted the man. Again he studied the car. 'I'm having one of them when my pools come up,' he said.

Nicholas watched him mount his bike and trundle away. He rang the operator and asked for the number for International Directory Enquiries and dialled it. It was some time before there was an answer. 'We're busy,' apologised the operator. 'People always lose the numbers of their long-lost relatives in New Zealand on Boxing Day.'

'It's not New Zealand,' Nicholas assured her. 'It's Paris.'

For some reason she said: 'Good,' as if she meant it. He heard her make an aside to someone near. 'That's good,' she repeated returning to him. 'You see, because it's Christmas we're having a bit of a sweepstake here. It makes up for us having to work today. Everybody puts a pound in the kitty and you use the initials of the places people ask for. The first one to make up the word "HAPPY" as in "Happy Christmas" gets the jackpot. And Paris is one of the Ps.'

'Oh, I see. How many letters do you need now?'

'Just the H and the other P,' she said. 'I got lucky with Yokohama.'

'I could call back asking for Hanover and then Phnom Penh,' he suggested.

'No, I need a P not an N. There's no N in HAPPY, silly. Anyway that would be cheating.' She became businesslike. 'What was the name in Paris?'

'Bernet,' he said without hope. 'Thérèse Bernet.'

'Have you got an address? There's hundreds of Bernets.'

'No. I knew it would be difficult.'

'Difficult?' she said glumly. 'Hopeless more like it. Masses of Bernets, no Thérèse Bernet.'

'It has an H in it,' he suggested.

'I could do with an H for the jackpot,' she interpolated. 'No. Nothing with Thérèse with an H either. Anything else?'

He was wishing he had never made the call. 'She may have an art gallery,' he tried. 'Could you look under galleries?'

'I am,' she replied as if to demonstrate her quickness. 'No. Not a thing. Sorry.'

'That's all right. I knew it was a long shot. Thanks for trying.'

'It's all right. It's a change from trying to find somebody's auntie in Auckland.'

He replaced the phone and peered out of the window of the phone box to the desolate darkening snow. When he opened the door the wind caught him as though it had been awaiting the opportunity. Outside the box he looked around, a single figure in a landscape. 'God,' he muttered. 'What the hell am I doing?'

He got in the car and sat motionless. Why could he not simply forget her? Undoubtedly she had forgotten him. He was merely an incident from her life, a man she had met and with whom she had shared a few unusual hours. But Nicholas often saw her face, her coat, her smile, often heard her voice. Every day as he wrote about the fictional Cécile, Thérèse had become more real. He played a game of how they might meet again and be together. She inhabited his reverie and his dreams. Sarah, his real, live wife, was a stranger in this fantasy but he had little conscience about that. It was only fiction. Sarah was fact.

After ten minutes he roused himself but, unable to decide even on the way he should take, he got out again and peered at the signpost. The word 'Harrogate' was just discernible in the lace of snow on the directional arm. He took that road.

It was a demanding journey in the profound darkness.

Occasionally an isolated light showed, from some cottage or farm, blinking in the night like a navigational beacon. There were steep bends in the road, climbs and drops in the dim white runner of snow. He turned on the car radio and caught the announcer's words: 'Mussorgsky. "Night on the Bare Mountain".' He turned up the volume.

After two hours of driving, face almost against the windscreen, he found himself descending on to a plain of scattered lights. Harrogate, a signpost promised, was five miles. He was fatigued and, deep in his mind, he still did not know where he was going. After Harrogate, where? Phnom Penh perhaps.

Now the road was yellow-lit and there were illuminated trees and decorations in the windows of suburban houses. Cars were going in either direction but few people walked on the pavements. It had begun to rain.

He was returning to the Yorkshire Grey Hotel with more misgivings; could he get a drink and something to eat before the threatened jollities of Boxing Night began? He was in no mood to play games or enjoy acts, nor to exchange talk with off-duty undertakers. He wanted to go to bed and pull the bedclothes over his head.

Then he saw what he thought at first was a bright shop but, as he passed, realised was a restaurant. At the next roundabout he did the full circle and went back. It was a Chinese restaurant. The Happy Land. He left the car and went in. The waiter near the door seemed glad to see him. 'Early yet,' he said checking his watch. 'But not many people today.'

'Well, you've got me,' said Nicholas taking off his coat. He ordered a whisky. He felt hungry. It was six thirty.

He sat at a corner table in the empty place. There were some decorations on the walls and ceilings, glinting orientally.

The waiter brought the scotch and the menu and said the trimmings were for Chinese New Year in February. Nicholas drank the whisky at once and ordered another. When he had the menu in front of him he glanced over its upper edge and his eyes went to a telephone on the wall. He ought to ring Sarah now.

She took a while to answer. 'I've only just got in,' she said in a muffled way. 'And I might as well tell you I'm a bit pissed.'

'These lunchtime parties do go on.'

'This one turned into three parties, different houses, one after another.'

'Well you're back now. You sound as though you ought to lie down.'

'I'm all right. I've been drunk before you know.'

'What are the children doing?'

'Oh, they're watching television. They've got the leftovers. It is a pity you weren't there today at the party.'

'Which one?'

'All of them. What have you been doing?'

'Driving around. Up through Wharfedale in the snow.'

'Everybody wanted to know where you were. I felt a bit embarrassed. You should have come home, like you said, after he died.'

'It's a four- or five-hour drive, at night,' he sighed. 'And then I would have had to come back tomorrow.'

'Why didn't you let them, the nursing home people, look after things? They could easily have done. The registrar and the undertakers.'

'He was *my* father not theirs.'

He sensed she was holding back a remark. Instead she said: 'Well, I was telling them about him wanting to be buried at sea. That raised a few laughs.'

'Oh, you've been drinking out on it, have you?'

'Don't sound like that. Just because you choose to moon around up in bloody Yorkshire on Boxing Day.'

'Instead of guzzling the Boltons' Spanish champagne,' he retorted.

'You're really shitty sometimes.'

'So are you, Sarah. I'm putting the phone down now. I hope that when we speak next you will have sobered up.'

He did it angrily. As he went back towards his lone table he realised there were tears blocking his eyes. If he had not already run away, he would have run away now. He sat at the table, drank the second scotch, and picked the menu up so savagely with both hands that he tore it. The waiter, watching from near a Chinese screen, calmly brought him another. 'Having good time?' he enquired.

Nicholas looked again over the ridge of the menu, straight at the telephone once more. He stood up and went towards it. The waiter winced and retreated behind the screen. Nicholas found the number of the Rosedale Nursing Home in the directory and rang it.

'Is Rina there?' he asked. He realised he did not know her other name. Scant of breath she came to the phone. 'Are you finished for the day?' he asked.

'Yes. I'm off duty at last. Why?'

'I'm at a restaurant in Harrogate, a Chinese, called the Happy Land. I wondered if you'd like to come and have something to eat. Do you know it?'

'I've seen it,' she replied quietly. 'All right, I'll get a taxi. It will only take a few minutes.'

She arrived pink-faced, swathed in a duffle coat. Nicholas took it and handed it to the waiter. She said she would have a glass of wine. 'This is ever so nice and unexpected,' she said when they were sitting down. He was sorry he had drunk the two scotches so quickly and was now halfway through the third. He pushed it a few inches aside. She followed the action and said: 'Been drowning your sorrows?'

'Yes,' he confessed. 'But I'll stop drowning them now.' He smiled at her. 'How are the patients?'

'They've got through another Christmas.' She looked embarrassed. 'Except one.'

'Another milestone?' he said.

'Another milestone. They set themselves targets, their birthday, Christmas, August Bank Holiday and so on. It's like an obstacle race.'

The waiter, smiling now, relieved that Nicholas had company and he was rid of the burden of a prospective drunk, came and took their orders. Nicholas ordered a bottle of white wine. 'It's strange how you are . . . well, so involved in the place,' he said.

'What else would I do?' she said with a touch of surprise. 'It gives *me* a home as well as giving them one. It's a settled life, a roof. There is nowhere else I could go.' She stared at the wall ahead. 'Anyway I'm fond of them although it's hard going sometimes.'

'I can imagine.'

'At night,' she said. 'You should hear the chests. The whole building wheezes. Like babies crying.'

'What interests them?'

'Money,' she said decisively. 'They love their money. They count it, go through their bank statements with a tooth-comb. They're always complaining they've been robbed. I heard an odd noise one night and found one old chap with his light on and the room piled up with money. I mean, *piled* up. There were stacks of notes and premium bonds, National Savings and share certificates and on his dressing table, bunches of coins. He was counting every last penny, complaining that he was eighty-five pence short.'

'Avarice, the last pleasure, eh,' said Nicholas.

'All that's left,' she said. Her rotund face had become thoughtful but now she made herself brighten and asked: 'What did you do all day?'

'I went to the Yorkshire Grey Hotel,' he said. 'Where I was promised a big knees-up tonight. I don't think I could face that.'

'We've always got your room,' she said hurriedly. She blushed and said: 'I hope you haven't been cooped up in that hotel all day.'

'No, I went on my exploration. God knows where I went altogether. I went into the Dales, in the snow. I only met three people. The landlord of the pub and his wife getting ready for next week's New Year's Eve extravaganza. She sings. He wrote down a joke I told him. Then I met a chap on a bike, in the wilderness. He had renounced the world but forgotten to post his football pools.'

'You do have adventures, don't you,' she giggled.

'Too many sometimes. They seem to lie in wait for me.' Through the meal he told her of his running-away, how he had become entangled with Bonnie Ware and her family, and the old soldiers in Torremolinos. She listened entranced. 'God, I went to Spain and nothing at all happened to me,' she said. 'Except sunstroke and gyppy tum.'

The evening went swiftly. They had a second bottle of wine. She had a port and he had another scotch. Other people came into the restaurant. As they left Nicholas was surprised to see how it had filled up. 'You shouldn't drive,' Rina told him. 'We ought to get a taxi really.'

'All right,' he said. The waiter said his car would be all right outside and telephoned for a taxi. They sat in the back, and Nicholas put his arm around her plump shoulder. Her head dropped tiredly against his lapel. Neither spoke. When they reached the nursing home with its gaunt cedar tree decorated with the mocking lights, she half-turned and half-kissed him. He kissed her soft cheek. 'You're a good man,' she whispered.

The taxi dropped him outside the Yorkshire Grey Hotel. 'They're having a right old time in there,' said the driver with envious relish. 'I've already had three trips here tonight. Listen to them.' Nicholas could hear it. The blaring chorus of 'You'll never walk alone' was issuing from open windows on the lower ground floor. With a heavy heart he went in.

'Ah, there you are!' enthused the man he had seen that morning. 'I was worried you'd miss the fun. They're going strong.'

'I thought of going to bed,' said Nicholas dubiously. 'I've got a lot to do tomorrow.'

'Ernie Pallister, the undertaker, is in there,' pointed the man. 'You could have a bit of a chat with him. Come on in. Have a drink. My name's Frank Grainger.'

Nicholas allowed himself to be led into a large and heavily overcrowded room. The air was hung with smoke and alcohol. There must have been three hundred people around bottle-strewn tables and in chairs along the walls. A fat young man in a velvet jacket was just leaving the stage at one end, smirking at the wild applause.

'That's Ernie Pallister's lad, Arthur,' said Grainger. 'Phil lad, get this gentleman a drink. . . . How about a scotch, sir. It's on me. It's nice to have somebody from the south.'

'They don't know how to enjoy themselves down south,' said the barman lugubriously handing the scotch over like a challenge. Nicholas eyed him, drank the whisky at a swallow and asked for another, and one for Grainger. He finished the second drink more casually and surveyed the turmoil. Men and women were laughing, some bellowing, kissing fiercely and embracing. There were howls as the whole table full of drinks slid over. 'Boxing Day,' said the barman shaking his head. 'They do have a great time.'

'Come on lad. I'll introduce you to Mr Pallister,' offered Grainger.

Nicholas was trying to estimate how much he had drunk. He ordered another scotch and bought one for the barman. 'Tha's not bad,' said the barman. 'He ain't too bad, is he Mr Grainger?' he repeated as though seeking a second opinion. 'For a southerner.'

Beckoning Nicholas with his finger Grainger led the way through the throng. The air was as overpowering as the noise. A two-man band, a trumpet player and percussion, were gathering their resources for another onslaught. 'Did you 'ear our Arthur singin'?' asked the undertaker's wife when they were introduced. ' "You'll never walk alone." '

Feeling himself swaying and trying to bring the whole group into focus, Nicholas admitted he had. 'The pallbearers' song,' whispered the obese son. His father grimaced and said: 'You never know who's listening, lad.'

He turned to Nicholas. 'I gather you want us to look after your dad?'

'Yes,' said Nicholas slowly, unsure now he had seen Arthur that this was so. 'He wants to be buried at sea.'

'We don't have much call for that around here,' said Mr

Pallister without appearing ruffled. 'Seeing as we're about as far as you can get from the sea in England. But happen we can make the arrangements.' He was drinking black stout in a pint glass, the froth like lace. 'But we won't talk about it now; I don't care for business with pleasure. Have a drink, lad.'

Nicholas accepted and afterwards bought a round for the entire table. After an illustrative burp, Mrs Pallister said she only drank champagne and apologised, but the bar had champagne on tap. The two man band started up again and there was rowdy community singing. The undertaker sang without a detectable sound emerging. 'I've learned that over the years,' he confided in Nicholas. 'Practised it.' A loud man in a huge dinner suit who was acting as Master of Ceremonies but had apparently, at an earlier stage, fallen from the stage, was now operating again. 'Right, everybody!' he bellowed into the microphone but clutching his ribs with his free hand. 'We're going to play Hi-ho!' There was immense enthusiasm; shouts and hoots and encouragement.

'Hi-ho?' enquired Nicholas hazily. 'What's Hi-ho?'

'You'll see,' promised Ernie Pallister. 'By heck, it's a laugh.'

'*You've* got to play!' demanded Dilly, his wife pointing at Nicholas. 'Go on, lad, it's a scream. You go with our Arthur.'

Arthur was already on his feet and wiping his mouth. 'Aye, come on,' he encouraged. 'Stay by me,'

Unsteadily Nicholas got to his feet. It was as if he had no resistance. Mrs Pallister guided him out behind Arthur who, in his puce coat, was already making his way like a gladiator to the centre of the floor. Under the orders of the MC, still clutching his ribcage and coughing, a wide space was cleared. Tables and chairs scraped aside. Glasses crashed. There was hysterical laughter. People fell on the floor and could not get up. Two teams of men were being formed, seven in each. Mr Grainger, the hotel man, was counting them. He saw the stumbling Nicholas and called: 'See, I knew thee'd 'ave a good time.'

'Get down on th' knees,' instructed Arthur taking charge of Nicholas. 'Like I'm doing.' The other competitors were kneeling upright, in two lines of seven, each man holding the waist of the team-mate in front. Nicholas got down like a dromedary. Having coaxed him to the floor, Arthur took the next place in the line. He felt the big coffin-carrying hands around his waist.

'Right!' bawled the MC over the excitement. He went along each team counting. 'One, two, three, four, five, six, seven.' He used his fingers to show the audience, pushing a late entrant aside. 'Snow White only had seven dwarfs,' he bellowed. 'You can be the witch!'

Nicholas felt his knees hard against the wooden floor. His head was foggy, the room whirled before his eyes. He needed the support of the man in front to stay upright. The man wriggled and he relaxed his grip. He thought of Sarah. He thought of his father in the mortuary. Oh God.

The MC had regained the stage. 'Right,' he shouted again, still massaging his ribcage. 'All ready. When I give the signal by waving my hankie you start moving. Not before.'

Someone fell sideways in the other team dragging three others with him. Nicholas was amazed to hear himself laughing madly. Eventually the fallers were righted and both teams were ready. The MC called for silence and the noise dropped although another table collapsed resoundingly and had to be righted. Nicholas wondered how long he could stay in this position. 'Don't give up, lad,' warned Arthur from behind. 'There's a lot of beer on this. Left knee first remember.'

'I won't,' promised Nicholas drunkenly, flagrantly, over his shoulder. 'I won't. Left knee first.'

'Hi-hooo!' the Master of Ceremonies called echoingly. The competitors, Nicholas apart, echoed: 'Hi-hooo!'

'Again! Not good enough!'

'Hi-hooo!' they sounded. Nicholas joined in weakly. 'Hi-ho.'

'Hi-ho . . . and go!' urged the man on the stage. He waved his crimson handkerchief.

The parallel teams stuttered forward, upright on their knees, left knees, then right. They sang as they shuffled.

> 'Hi-ho, Hi-ho,
> It's off to work we go!'

It was agony. Attempting to sing with his team, Nicholas could hardly contain his cries of pain as his knees struck the floor like pistons. The room was in uproar, shouts of encouragement, ridicule and blame. He thought he was going to be sick but he held it back because he could see that the man in front was wearing his best suit. They only went twenty-five feet but it seemed like miles.

> 'We do our best,
> Then take a rest,
> Hi-ho, hi-ho, hi-ho. . . .'

They reached the stage and Nicholas fell forward releasing his hands from the waist in front and falling forward onto them. 'Coom on!' shouted Arthur pulling him upright. 'We've got to go back yet!'

Nicholas remembered making the turn-around, the tail of the crocodile becoming the head and the knees beginning to bump in the other direction, but how they got to the end of the race he never recalled. When the others had risen to their feet to the wild acclaim of the room, the other team having won the beer, Nicholas remained on the boards crouched like a praying mantis. 'Lift him up,' he heard Mr Pallister say like a boxing referee. 'He's had enough.'

He had no remembrance of being taken to his room, only the throbbing of his knees through his drunken dreams. At four in the morning he had to go to the lavatory. He could hardly stand and he dared not crawl. He cursed and fell and cursed again. He took off his trousers and bathed his knees in cold water.

At ten he was awakened by a knock. A woman came in with a tray of tea. 'Mr Grainger said you might be needing this,' she said studying him kindly. 'Are you all right?'

'Yes, thank you,' he lied weakly. His expression contorted as he tried to move in the bed. 'It's my knees.'

'Aye, he said it might be,' she nodded. 'There's a chemist two doors down. It's not far.'

He decided to drink the tea before examining his injuries. When he did his eyes extended in horror. His knees were black with bruises, the skin was blistered and broken. 'Oh God,' he moaned again.

Somehow he managed to get to the bathroom. It took him ten minutes to put his trousers on. Every touch was agony. When he walked it was like a man on short stilts. He was cursing himself now. What a fool, what a cretin, what a banal bastard. He could not bring himself to ring Sarah, not suffering like that. He went stiffly down the stairs. Mr Grainger was standing with guilty solemnity behind the desk. 'It weren't fair,' he said shaking his head. 'They shouldn't have done it.'

'I can only blame myself,' Nicholas said mournfully.

'Aye, but those lads *know* what they're in for. They'll all have done it before. They pad their knees. They have those pads that carpet-layers and the like use. You didn't.'

He declined a late breakfast. He felt too sick. 'I've got to go to the Registrar and to see Mr Pallister,' he said.

Mr Grainger looked at the clock. 'I'd better ring him for you,' he decided. 'He gets busy after Christmas.' He reached for the desk telephone and dialled. Nicholas sat down heavily on a lobby chair. The hotel man spoke into the phone and then replaced it. 'He says if you hurry around now he can see you. Otherwise it will have to be after four. I knew he'd be busy.'

'Is it far?' asked Nicholas pitifully.

'Not that far. Ten minutes . . .' his voice diminished. 'But . . . with your legs . . . I'll get a taxi. It won't take a minute.'

Nicholas rose from the chair. It was difficult to know whether his knees hurt more standing or sitting. It was a separate, different pain. At a slow strut he went towards the front of the hotel and stood there stiffly. The taxi was mercifully prompt. Mr Grainger came out to open the cab door and help him in. 'Go steady with him,' he advised the driver. 'His legs are gone.'

It took only three minutes but the driver was sympathetic. 'Have you had it long?' he enquired.

'Last night,' Nicholas told him. The man nodded as if he understood and thanked him for the fare and the tip. Nicholas shuffled around to confront the premises of Pallister and Son. There was a black window, a middle panel of clear glass and a bunch of flowers in an urn. As he watched a disembodied hand appeared with a small plastic jug and poured water into the vase. A bell rang solemnly as he went through the black-and-gold door. Mr Pallister came through a silently sliding door and came towards him with a fittingly tight smile. He offered a long white hand. 'How are the knees?' he whispered.

'Not at all well,' said Nicholas. 'They're killing me.'

'I'm sorry to hear it,' murmured Mr Pallister professionally. He put his arm on his visitor's shoulder. 'Come in and have a seat.'

He opened the door and frowned broadly as Nicholas went in at his cautious strut. 'You do seem in a poor way,' he said as though sensing a potential client. 'I blame our Arthur. He gets carried away.'

'That's a change,' suggested Nicholas with weak wryness.

'Trade joke, I'm afraid. This business has more jokes than most, Mr Boulting. You need to be a comedian to be a funeral director. My father always used to say that you had to remember that the first syllable of funeral is "fun". Not that you would let it spoil people's bereavement.'

'No, I suppose you couldn't.'

'Now your late father. You would like Pallister and Son to make the arrangements?'

'Yes.' He had a vision of Arthur carrying his father's coffin single-handed.

'And you mentioned that he expressed a wish to be buried at sea?' The mourning eyebrows were fractionally raised.

'He did. I think he was just being mischievous. It's complicated, I imagine.'

'Very. Being well inland here we do not have much of a call for this sort of ceremony but I have made some enquiries and last year at the National Conference a lad from Cornwall gave an interesting talk on what the procedure is. Apparently they have quite a lot of marine burials down there.'

'What has to happen?'

'Well for a start the coroner has to be informed. Two coroners in fact. Here and the coroner of the area where the burial is to take place.' He looked up quizzically. 'Did he mention any particular area of the sea? Any preference?'

'No they were his last words. He just said: "I want to be buried at sea. If it's not too much trouble." '

'Not too much trouble,' ruminated Mr Pallister. 'Well, that might be your let-out. Your conscience-salver. People often say strange things as their last words, believe me. First thing that comes into their heads sometimes. Do you think he was serious?'

'I think it was just his natural awkwardness. A sort of joke in a way. He's probably sitting up there laughing now.'

'We need to get the coroner's permission,' repeated Mr Pallister as if he did not enjoy the thought of a ghost laughing at him. 'Then the Department of the Environment, civil servants, red tape, I'm afraid. You can't go dropping bodies in the sea off Blackpool, for example.'

'You could ruin somebody's swim,' nodded Nicholas.

'Yes, it's understandable.' He brightened a touch. 'One thing you will save on is the coffin.'

'Oh?'

Mr Pallister leaned forward as though glad to have some good news. 'We don't need one. In fact any casket weighted down sufficiently to keep on the seabed would be so heavy that it could not be handled. It would probably sink the boat that was taking it out to sea. You'd need a crane. So we'd have to use what the sailors of old used, and still do for that matter. Weighted, I believe, with chains. Canvas. It has to be a canvas shroud. And . . .' He hesitated. 'The final stitch of the sewing-up must be put through the nose.'

Nicholas reacted with horror. 'Why? Why is that?'

Mr Pallister regarded him nervously. 'It is so that if the . . . er . . . remains should be somehow washed up on the shore the authorities would realise everything was proper and there had been no underhand business. Murder, for example.'

'This is becoming complicated,' said Nicholas.

'I'm afraid it is going to be. And these things take time. Time and tide you might say in this case. And that means . . . er . . . storage.'

He studied the other man's expression. 'Listen,' he suggested helpfully. 'Would it not suit everybody's requirements, including that of your late father, if instead of being *buried* at sea, there was a cremation and his ashes were scattered on the waves?'

Nicholas regarded him with appreciation. 'Do you think that would be all right?' he pressed.

'Oh, I think so. It would most certainly be a good deal simpler. And he expressly said: "If it's not too much trouble." You could keep the ashes at home and when there was a suitable day you could hire a boat, take them out to sea and scatter them. I don't think he would object to that.'

'You don't know my father,' said Nicholas. 'I mean you *didn't*.'

'No. That's true. One of the oddities of this profession, Mr Boulting, is that very often the first time we meet people is after they have ceased to be.'

'At least they can't argue,' said Nicholas. He made the decision. 'I think we should do it that way. A cremation and then scatter the ashes at sea.' He paused: 'You don't need special permission for that, do you?'

'Not too near the beach,' advised Mr Pallister. 'Especially when it's busy. There have been one or two complaints about that sort of thing, so I have read in the trade journal. But not if you take a boat out at a reasonable distance. The dust of people has been deposited in all sorts of places, the greens of the favourite golf club, the goalmouth of the local football ground, and so on.'

Nicholas felt relieved. 'Right, thank you,' he said. 'When should it be?'

Mr Pallister consulted his diary. 'Monday of next week,' he

suggested. 'Two o'clock. It gets dark so early at this time of year. It makes it very miserable when it's dark.'

Eleven

His knees ached all the way down the motorway. Sarah had been apologetic on the telephone. 'With decent champagne I wouldn't have been like that,' she excused herself. 'I'm sorry.'

When he arrived he sat down stiffly while she made him a cup of tea. She appeared smiling from the kitchen and put the tea on a table beside his chair. He could see she was playful. 'Let's go away,' she said. 'Let's have a holiday somewhere hot.'

She did something she had not done for a long time. She sat on his lap. Nicholas emitted a cry of pain that howled through the house and made her leap up in alarm. 'Good God, what's wrong?'

'My knees,' he said faintly avoiding looking her in the eye.

'What's the matter with them?'

He rolled up his right trouser-leg and displayed the blackened bulge. She stood away, speechless.

'And the other,' he confessed in a mutter. He rolled up the left trouser-leg. 'Jesus,' she breathed. 'What have you been doing?'

'Hi-ho,' he said simply and miserably. 'Playing Hi-ho.'

His eyes went slowly up to meet hers. 'What,' she enquired, 'is Hi-ho?'

'It's . . . well, it's a game . . . it was Boxing Day night. I was smashed.'

Sarah sat down still with her eyes fixed on him. He described Hi-ho while she remained motionless and unsmiling. 'You must be mad,' she said eventually.

'Don't tell me, I know,' he muttered. 'I was just very depressed. I'd been driving around all day, and I had a meal

238

and drank too much wine and then when I went back to the hotel I was pressed into having a few scotches. My own fault, I know. And one thing led to another and I found myself in one of the Hi-ho teams.' He explained further then, as though in mitigation, he added weakly: 'The undertaker was there.'

'The undertaker? Our undertaker?'

'Mr Pallister,' he nodded. 'I thought I could discuss the funeral with him, the business of being buried at sea and so on, but he was off-duty and his son, Arthur his name is, got me into this ridiculous game.' He paused sorrowfully. 'And that's when I did my knees.'

'And your father . . . was . . . lying . . . dead.'

'Don't. I know.'

She searched for words. 'We've just *got* to stop this, Nicholas. Both of us. I know I was in a state and I'm not proud of it.'

'It was Boxing Day,' he shrugged.

'All right. So it was. But are we trying to press the "self-destruct" button? On this marriage, I mean.'

'I know. It seems to happen despite everything you do to try and keep things straight.'

To his surprise she got from the chair and moved towards him. Primly he covered his knees and his eyes were pleading. She emitted a dry, wry laugh. 'What a mess. Bruised knees.' She shot him a look from the corner of her eye. 'You're sure it wasn't doing anything else?' she asked. 'Hi-ho *not* ho-ho?'

'It wasn't,' he said. 'I know it looks bad but what I've told you is the truth.'

'I believe you,' she said flatly. She got up and took his cup. He was surprised to see that he had drunk his tea. She went towards the kitchen and called to ask if he would like another. He accepted and she came back with it. 'All right,' she breathed. 'So the funeral is on Monday.'

'Two o'clock,' he said. 'Mr Pallister thinks it gets too gloomy after that.'

'We wouldn't want that to happen. So he's cremated and we keep the ashes and when the weather gets better we can take them on a day trip and scatter them on the sea. It sounds like a good compromise. Very sensible.'

'Where will we keep them?' he asked shiftily surveying the room.

'Anywhere. In your study. Anywhere but the kitchen. We don't want accidents.' She had poured a cup of tea for herself and she stirred it and said: 'So after the funeral shall we go on holiday?'

'Why not?' He regarded her hopefully. 'How about France?'

She looked aghast. 'France? In January?'

'It's pretty mild down on the Côte d'Azur. Nice. Menton.'

'I thought of somewhere like the Caribbean.'

'Yes, I know. It's just that I've got to a point in the novel, Sarah, when Robert, the main character, goes to France to find her, the Frenchwoman, Cécile. Everything so far has been set in this country. If we had a couple of weeks in France it would help me with the background. I mean, I know some of it obviously, but I need to fill in the details.'

She sniffed. 'What's the matter with filling in the details in June or July?' she asked.

'I'm writing it *now*,' Nicholas told her firmly. 'It's got to be delivered to Mallinder's by April, remember. And the action takes place in winter. I need some winter background.' He attempted to encourage her. 'We can go to Paris and stay at a decent hotel and go to restaurants and stuff, and then go down to Nice and Grenoble, places like that. We could go up to the ski slopes.'

'We don't ski any more,' she pointed out. 'Neither of us.'

'But the snow is nice. There's other things to do. Après-ski. It's very smart up there.'

'I'd rather go to Antigua,' she said.

He moved forward, groaning a little with even the slight bending of his knees as he did so. 'Listen, I promise we'll take a real holiday in the spring. When the book's finished.'

'Somewhere hot?'

'Somewhere baking,' he said.

'All right,' sighed Sarah. 'I'll get my thermals ready.'

'Good girl,' he enthused. 'We can have some terrific meals and there won't be a soul on the roads and we can sleep in a four-poster in a château. All that business.' He held out his hands and she responded after a slight hesitation and caught his fingers in hers.

'I love you,' he said.

'Me too. I love you.'

They kissed. From the kitchen door Willie who had just come into the house watched them without them seeing him. He sighed and went upstairs, still unobserved, shaking his head.

His father, he felt, would have thoroughly approved of the day. It drizzled from noon and when they were walking from the car through the cemetery to the crematorium, a low wind began to hum and blew the drizzle in their faces. The inside of the chapel seemed even bleaker. Mr Pallister was at the door, black topper in hand. Arthur and the other pallbearers were only faces set in the windows of the hearse. They had already carried the casket into the chapel. Arthur gave him a scant thumbs-up.

He had thought that there would be only five mourners; himself, Sarah, Miss Southren, the matron from Rosedale, Rina and Dr da Souza, so he was astonished to see that two well-distanced chairs at the rear of the crematorium were occupied by two elderly women who, it was apparent even to a brief glance, were identical. Nicholas and Sarah both smiled dutifully at one and then the other and then returned swiftly to look again at each other. Sarah raised her eyebrows. Nicholas shrugged. The ladies, heavily in black with the same hats, responded only minutely, each raising a single finger.

The service was soon over. Mr Pallister had enquired about suitable music that morning when Nicholas had gone to see his father's body. There seemed to be a slight touch of triumph on the lips as if he were aware of the trouble he was causing. Did the deceased, asked the funeral director, have any favourite hymn or sacred tune? Nicholas could think of none; he could not remember one occasion when he had heard his father sing, hum or whistle. They had settled for 'The Lord's My Shepherd' to the tune Crimond and now the tremulous handful of mourners sang it. The two strange ladies at the rear appeared to be loudly trying to out-do each other. The officiating clergyman had mud-caked golfing shoes under his cassock and a pencil behind his ear. He mumbled the obligatory words and eyed the coffin poised before a pair of red velvet curtains like a wooden ship awaiting launching. Nicholas found himself almost mesmerised by the box now containing his father, and felt both guilt and sadness. He knew so little of his father's life; he wondered how much had been wasted.

At the end of the clergyman's incantation, they sat waiting embarrassedly for something else to happen. Music warbled painfully but then straightened itself out into a reprise of 'Crimond' and the coffin began to slip horribly towards the curtains. Nicholas and Sarah dropped their heads. Three people cried, Rina and the two elderly ladies at the back.

Outside the drizzle had reluctantly ceased but the early afternoon was winter dim. 'It was very kind of you to come,' Nicholas said to one of the strange ladies. 'You are sisters, I take it.'

They were standing nowhere near each other, edging away in fact, to keep their distance.

'Yes,' replied one. 'Unfortunately,' added the other.

Nicholas looked towards Sarah who was thanking Miss Southren, Rina and the doctor for being there. He returned to the ladies. 'Well, er . . . I'm afraid I don't know your names. I'm Nicholas, Bernard Boulting's son.'

'We know,' the women said, this time together. They glared at each other. 'I am Beryl Harris,' said one swiftly.

'And I am *Mrs* Bertha Nobbs,' put in the other with a pipe of triumph.

'And you knew my father?'

'Yes,' they said in emphatic unison. 'In Reigate,' said the married one like a dagger thrust before the other could open her mouth. But her sister compensated: 'I knew him *very* well.'

242

'So did I,' said Mrs Nobbs. '*Very* well indeed.'

Sarah came across the wet gravel. 'These ladies were friends of my father,' Nicholas said helplessly.

'In Reigate,' said the spinster getting in first this time. It was like a verbal game of Snap.

'Oh, how kind of you to come,' said Sarah. 'You saw the notice in the local newspaper I suppose. You must come to lunch with us. You've travelled a long way on a day like this.' She leaned a little sideways. 'We should really get going,' she told Nicholas. 'Rina, Matron and Dr da Souza will go in his car.'

'I'll come with you, if I may,' put in the married sister firmly.

The other woman looked huffed but said nothing. She merely turned and went towards Dr da Souza's car calling: 'I'm coming with you, if I may.'

With deepening misgivings, Nicholas helped Mrs Nobbs into the back seat. Sarah got in beside her. 'You surely must be twins,' she said sweetly. Nicholas started the engine and motioned to Dr da Souza to follow him.

'We are,' said the elderly woman brusquely. Her lips were working. 'Worst thing that ever happened to me, being born with *her*.'

Nicholas sensed Sarah flinch behind him. 'Oh, that's a pity,' struggled Sarah. 'You don't get on very well then?'

'We don't get on at *all*,' snapped the other uncompromisingly. 'In fact we hate each other. We haven't spoken for twenty-five years.'

'But you came to the funeral together,' said Sarah desperately trying to fashion a compromise.

'Not by choice. She was on the same train. And wearing the same *hat*. That was a shock, I can tell you after all this time. Ratbag old spinster. She's always been jealous of me.' She emitted a little purr. 'Just because I have a way with the men.'

Thankfully Nicholas turned the car into the forecourt of the hotel that Mr Pallister had recommended as being nearby and having good food served late. He had reserved for five which he now increased to seven. 'As long as I don't have to sit near *her*,' said Bertha Nobbs.

Nicholas was already making sure of that. They sat along a wall seat so they did not face each other and with Miss Southren, Rina and Dr da Souza between them. Sarah and Nicholas took the end chairs. They were the only people in the restaurant. 'Keep off the subject of your father,' whispered Sarah to Nicholas before they took their places. 'Try not to mention him.'

It was difficult since Bernard Boulting was the reason they were there. The lunch was surreal with every topic skirting the obvious. The single sister had apparently told Rina and the matron and doctor her side of the hatred and the professionals from the nursing home fenced skilfully with the conversation.

Eventually, however, it could not be avoided. 'I was deeply in love with your father,' announced Beryl sonorously. Bertha, caught with her mouth full of apple tart, shouted: 'So was I! But he loved me back!'

Helplessly everyone sat while the twin sisters craned their heads along the line to grimace at each other. 'All that must be a long time ago,' suggested Sarah feebly.

'Years, surely,' reinforced Nicholas.

'It seems like yesterday,' asserted Beryl. 'I was here with him in Harrogate.'

Nicholas felt himself pale. Every eye now turned to the married sister. She was not found wanting. 'He had a better time with me,' she rasped. 'Nineteen forty-eight. I took him from you! *And* you never knew.'

Beryl slammed her spoon down. 'I loved him!' she howled.

Bertha snarled back: 'But you couldn't keep him! Nor any other man. That's why you're a scratchy old maid.'

Beryl picked up the last spoonful of pie and, appearing to eye it regretfully at first, flung it towards the far end of the table. It caught the shaken Dr da Souza on the shoulder. Matron got it off with her own spoon and napkin.

'Ladies, ladies,' pleaded Nicholas rising pathetically. 'If you cared at all for my father, you would *not* be doing this. We've only just cremated him.'

'I'm off anyway,' snorted Bertha simultaneously rising from the table. 'I'm not going on the same train back as *her*.'

She seemed almost to snap to attention. 'Goodbye,' she said stoutly. 'I want you to know that I loved him deeply.'

'And Tony Bingham, and Billy Hall, and Ivor Kettle!' rasped her sister.

'Ivor Kettle!' bawled Bertha from the door. 'He hated you. Hated your corsets.'

Rina, who had been watching the exchange with a little less horror and amazement than the others, now became professionally active. Getting the nod from Miss Southren she rose and took Bertha with friendly firmness by the elbow. 'I'll get you a taxi to the station,' she told her. 'There's a train in half an hour.'

'Fall under it!' howled her twin.

It was the parting shot. Rina propelled Bertha from the restaurant. Nicholas thanked God it had been empty. Beryl suddenly crumpled into tears. 'Oh, she's always been terrible to me,' she sobbed. 'Bernard told me I was his only love.'

They left the restaurant more sombrely than they had left the crematorium. 'I hope everything was all right,' ventured the waitress, anxious after seeing what had happened. 'Everything wasn't,' confessed Nicholas. 'But the meal was fine.' He added under his breath: 'It was the people eating it.'

Rina reappeared and Nicholas thanked her for removing Bertha from the premises. 'She's used to them,' the matron put in quietly.

Out of doors, Beryl had lapsed into a sulky silence, her eyes, now dulled, travelling around the group as though in search of someone else she could harangue. Nicholas felt she was his responsibility and said that he and Sarah would take the old lady to the station. Dr da Souza checked his watch and said: 'By now the way should be clear. The four ten has gone.'

'Over her, I hope,' repeated Beryl grimly.

Miss Southren said that they would have to leave. Cagily she shook hands with Beryl, studying her as if she might prove a fruitful if difficult subject for study, and then with Sarah, saying she was glad to have met her. Sarah thanked them for being there. Without looking at her Rina shook hands with Sarah and then she turned and put her arms about Nicholas. His arms went to her wide waist. She hugged him and kissed him on the cheek and he returned the kiss. She said nothing but turned quickly and got into Dr da Souza's car with the matron and they drove away. The others were left in silence.

Nicholas opened the rear door of his car for Beryl and she squeezed in. Sarah sat in the front passenger seat. Nicholas drove towards the station.

'I can't tell you the shock I had this morning when I saw her on the train,' muttered Beryl overcoming her silence. She gave a small private sob. 'I didn't realise it was her.'

'But you must have recognised her,' pointed out Sarah testily. 'You look just like her.'

'I hope not!' retaliated Beryl hotly. 'Not now. She's aged much more than I have.' She gave a sniff. 'No, I meant I didn't realise it was *her* all those years ago. With Bernard. I suspected he had someone else but I never realised it was my own sister.'

'Good God,' mumbled Nicholas.

'No, I didn't, not ever. All these years. Not until I saw her this morning on the train. Then I realised. I wasn't even aware that she *knew* Bernard. We never went to our house because he was married and our father would have found out, picked it up in a minute.'

Nicholas felt Sarah turn towards him. He kept his eyes on the road.

'But I might have guessed,' the woman continued. 'She was always trying to get one up on me. If I had a doll, she had to have a talking doll, if I won a prize, she had to win a bigger prize. It was she who strangled my cat. Never proved but I know she did it. Daddy said we could only have one cat in the house and she refused to share. If she couldn't have it, then I wouldn't.' Beryl began to cry more freely. 'It was ever such a nice cat too. It was called Manky.'

With relief Nicholas saw the signs to the station. 'And as for men,' pursued Beryl. 'She was like a shark. That's why I kept Bernard a secret. Or so I thought.' She gazed at the houses and hotels of Harrogate through her tears. 'We had such a lovely, loving time here,' she whispered. 'I didn't keep him secret enough.'

'Harrogate station!' exclaimed Nicholas loudly, like a platform porter. Gratefully he got from the car and opened the door for the old lady. Sarah said goodbye and hoped she would have a pleasant journey. Nicholas took her as far as the booking hall, shook hands and fled back to the car.

'Jesus,' he said angrily. 'That's all I needed. Stupid old cow.' He corrected himself: 'Cows.'

'The sins of the fathers,' muttered Sarah looking straight ahead.

'Don't you start, for God's sake.'

An exhausted void fell between them. Nicholas watched the dark, rainy ribbon of the road. Sarah eased her seat back and closed her eyes. He drove on. Even with her beside him he felt he was alone again.

The lights of the motorway swam by, signs and exits succeeding each other. It stopped raining and further south a quarter moon rose, a bent traveller among dingy clouds.

Eventually Sarah stirred, her dark lashes lying on her puffy cheeks, her head half sideways towards him. 'That Rina seemed very fond of you,' she said still without opening her eyes.

'Did she?'

'It looked like it.'

His face was to the road, her eyes remained shut. 'She's a lonely girl,' he said carefully. 'In that place with all those old people.'

'Why doesn't she leave? Do something else?'

'It's her home, she says. She hasn't got anywhere else to go.'

'I imagine not.'

'What does that mean?'

'She doesn't seem the sort to be able to fit in anywhere.'

Nicholas sighed. 'Does it matter?'

'Not really,' said Sarah. Now she opened her eyes. 'You took her out to dinner last week didn't you?'

'What makes you think that?'

'I was sending your jacket to the cleaner's.'

'And what did you find in the pocket?'

'A bill for a Chinese restaurant. The Happy Land, was it?'

'It was.'

'For forty-two pounds. Even *you* can't eat that much fried rice.'

'So I took Rina to the Chinese restaurant. It was Boxing Night, she'd been working all through Christmas and she was very good to my father.'

'Was she good to you?'

He saw a services exit on his left and swerved so violently that he threw Sarah protestingly to one side and had the car behind honking in anger. He pulled into the parking area, stopped the car, and turned to face her: 'Sarah, shut up,' he said quietly. 'Nothing improper has taken place between me and that girl, nothing. I'd been driving all day and I found myself sitting alone in an empty restaurant, so I telephoned her and she came over and we had a friendly meal and I took her back to the nursing home, said goodnight, and that was that.'

'What about your knees?'

'Oh, for fuck's sake!'

'Exactly.'

'Don't be so bloody clever,' he bit back angrily. 'I bruised my knees playing Hi-ho.'

'Not on some bare floor. . . .'

'It was a bare floor, that was the point. . . .' He glared at her and then dropped his anger. 'All right, let's go and have a cup of coffee. I'll prove it to you.'

'How are you going to do that? Show me how it's played.'

'I'll prove it,' he persisted tightly. 'Let's go and have some coffee. I could do with it.'

'All right.' She had reduced her tone also. It was as if they were too spent to fight. She picked up her handbag and her coat and opened the door. They walked a yard apart to the lit entrance to the services building. No one spoke until they reached the corridor leading to the restaurant. Then Nicholas caught her arm: 'Just wait a moment will you.'

There was a pay phone on the wall. While she watched he fingered a number which he took from a card produced from his inside pocket. She did not realise until he spoke. 'Ah, Mr Pallister, good evening. It's Nicholas Boulting here. Yes, I thought it was all you could have done. Thank you.' He felt Sarah's embarrassed clutch on his arm, but he continued: 'Mr Pallister, my wife Sarah is here. We're at the motorway services. I wonder if you would explain to her the game of Hi-ho and tell her how we played it on Boxing Night. Yes, that's right. . . . Yes, Hi-ho.'

He was holding his wife firmly. She shot a furious and embarrassed glance at him but he gave a pull on her wrist and, after a pause, she stepped doggedly forward and said: 'Hello.' She listened for a full minute and then said: 'Thank you. I'll hand you back to my husband.'

Ashen-faced, she gave him the phone. He thanked the funeral director again and put it down. They stood unspeaking, both heads hung for a moment as if they were praying. Then he said: 'Do you still want a coffee?'

He could see she was going to cry. She turned and stumbled out. He followed her. The car park was all but empty at that time of night, at that time of the year. He caught up with her, held her around the waist and turned her around. Tears were coursing on her face, reflecting in miniature the vapid standard lamps. Her mouth trembled. 'I'm so sick of everything,' she sobbed.

'So am I,' he returned. 'It's hopeless.'

She was going to break away but somehow in the same movement they came together and embraced as though trying to protect each other from their mutual despair and misery. They held on to each other desperately, turning slowly so that they might have been dancing on the wet tarmac. When they stopped revolving he loosened his arms and they confronted each other, their wet faces inches apart. 'I'm sick of it,' she repeated softly.

249

'I know,' he said gently. 'I am too.'

'Let's go home,' she said.

'Right. Let's stop it and go home.'

They put an arm around each other's waists and, like lovers, walked towards the car.

The Monday postman walked up between the regular yews with a cubic registered package. Sarah signed for it and, eyeing it sceptically, carried it up the stairs to the attic where Nicholas was writing. 'I think it's your father,' she said.

She set the package down on the desk then stepped a pace back as though taking part in a rehearsed and ordered ceremony. Nicholas remained seated. Both regarded the package with a kind of distrust. 'We ought to open it, I suppose,' suggested Nicholas.

'We *must*,' Sarah said decisively. 'We can't just leave him wrapped in brown paper.'

'Shall we leave it until after lunch?'

'Why? We ought to do it now.'

'There can't be much air in there,' joked Nicholas grimly. 'All right. You undo the string, you're good at that.'

'And you open the box,' she appended.

'Yes, yes. That's my duty.'

'Willie said he wanted to be here when we did it,' mentioned Sarah cutting through the binding tape.

'I bet Deborah didn't.'

'She said she's going to live with her friend Julia, if we keep the ashes anywhere in the house. She's afraid your father will come to haunt us.'

'I wouldn't put that past him,' said Nicholas. She had now cut through the tape and opened the wrapping. A slightly disappointing plastic box was revealed. There was a label fixed to one side which said: 'Bernard Boulting.' There were some numbers which Nicholas at first thought must be some sort of EEC code but then realised was the date of death.

He picked up the cube and drew it towards him. There was a small catch at one side and he undid it and, with a brief pause, lifted the lid. Sarah retreated again and, wide-eyed, looked over his shoulder. There was not much to see. The casket was about two-thirds filled with grey granular ash. 'That's him all right,' nodded Nicholas.

'Don't joke,' she said in a low voice and added: 'You don't amount to much in the end, do you.'

He closed the lid firmly and re-hooked the catch. 'I'll keep him in the desk,' he decided thoughtfully. 'He'll be all right in there. It will remind me not to waste my life.'

Sarah said: 'I can't see why you think he wasted his. If there was one thing he didn't grumble about it was the past, except about your mother. By the look of his ex-girlfriends at the cremation he hadn't been idle.'

Nicholas nodded. 'Not many men can boast of identical twin lovers.'

'It couldn't have been much of a change,' suggested Sarah. She regarded him seriously and then, with no alteration of expression, the casket. 'When do you think we'll take him . . . you know . . .,' she made an undulating motion with her hand, '. . . out to sea?'

'Soon.' He smiled revealingly at her. 'I thought on our way to France.'

'But . . .,' her face and voice dropped, 'we're not going on the *ferry* are we? Not this time of the year? It will be two hours of hell.'

'I thought we might go from Harwich to Hook of Holland,' he said.

'God, how long does . . .'

'About eight hours. But it's not *always* rough and we can have dinner and a cabin. Very civilised. And after dinner, after a good bottle of wine and a couple of brandies, we can throw the old man overboard.'

'But . . . why go to . . . Harwich?'

He patted the manuscript on his desk. 'Because that's the way the story goes,' he told her. 'The lovers go that way to escape her husband, and they go on to Paris . . . where she vanishes.'

251

Sarah looked as if she did not believe him. 'And that's why we have to go that way?' she said.

'It is. It will be all right.'

'I don't understand really,' she confessed. 'I always thought the idea of fiction was that you made it up.'

'Not all of it. A story needs a background.'

'All right,' she said eventually but firmly. 'If you say so.'

'*You* don't have to come that way,' he conceded. 'I could take the car across to Holland and drive down to Paris and you could fly and we could meet up there.'

Sarah thought about it. 'No, I'll come,' she said. 'I think I ought to. Otherwise you'll only get into trouble.'

She left him with his novel and the ashes of his father. He sat looking at the plastic casket and then surveyed the room. He went to the bookcase and made space alongside his run of the *Encyclopaedia Britannica* and put the container there. Then, after a moment's consideration, he picked it up again and moved it to a place between two volumes, one ending with Bolivar and the other beginning with Bolivia. 'Near enough,' he told himself. He patted the box and said to his father: 'You'll be all right there.'

Returning he sat pensively at the desk, grimacing at the page he was heavily rewriting in felt-tipped pen. Why was he involving Sarah? She had never asked, nor had she ever been asked, to help with his work, by reading and giving opinions; by suggesting paths for the story, nor accompanying him on working journeys. Paul Garrett had warned him against showing her the text. But now he had slotted her into the plot, his own real, vague plot, and he did not understand why he had had done it.

Sarah had not regarded his writing of *Lying in Your Arms* as a serious endeavour, only something to keep him occupied at home in the evenings. He had kept it to himself, plodding away in a corner of the living room of their former house, when his normal day's work was over, with Sarah watching television with the volume down, or up in their bedroom reading or asleep. He had never confided in her over the plot nor the characters nor his hopes for *Lying in Your Arms* and she had not enquired. She was surprised at the novel's publication, and amazed and pleased at her husband's success. It was later that she became afraid of the new world into which they were being drawn.

Their relationship since that time had been so fragmented that there had scarcely been the climate to involve her in any of his further work; she had not read a word of the aborted *Falling from Grace* nor the abandoned *Dancing with Delilah*. Now with *Lost in France* he had continued to keep his writing private, almost secret, giving her only hints of the story, and she had not asked anything further. She was keeping to her side of the fence.

But now Sarah was going with him. He had brazenly asked her and she had taken up the challenge. He was taking her to the place where the tale began, to the marshes of the Essex coast, to the dampness of Littlehaven and across the sea from Harwich. He gave himself a choice of motives; one to exorcise the memory of Thérèse, a memory that had grown into a presence; at first written as a character into the pages, she had gradually become real and was bothering his thoughts and lately his dreams. To be with Sarah in those same places might possibly erase the facile memory, replace a fantasy with a solid person, and bring some sense to his life, and hers. There was also the hidden, unacknowledged anyway, thrill of having Sarah with him there. And to go once more to where Thérèse had been, their meeting place.

In London he had talked to Sol about it. 'I always fell for it,' Sol had agreed. 'It's the romantic in guys like us. In writers. I would take my wife to somewhere I had been with another girl. Or a *girl* where I had been with another girl. I couldn't figure it out myself. Jesus, once I even flicked over the hotel register to where I had signed my own name a week before, and said hello to the waiter and the porter just indiscreetly enough to give my wife the clue that I had been there. Man, it was like the murderer returning to the scene of the crime, compulsion, but taking the Chief of Detectives along too. It gave me a charge, a feeling of danger.'

'Did she notice?' Nicholas had asked.

Sol looked disappointed he had mentioned it. He shook his head. 'No, never,' he complained. 'None of them did. That was a disappointment. Maybe they didn't care enough.'

Nicholas was now playing the same game and would do so, he realised, probably with less flair, a less confident touch than Sol. Now he had talked Sarah into it he knew she would be with him whatever; she would not back away from the challenge. He did not know whether it was the right thing, but it was going to happen. She was coming with him. Would he briefly find a trace of the fantasy Cécile, a scent of the real Thérèse?

Going to the alcove below the stairs in Sol's apartment, Nicholas had taken down Thérèse's small painting. Sol said: 'She's still on your mind?'

'I'm afraid so. I can see her as I write about her. The two women, the one in the book, Cécile, and Thérèse, the real one, they're one person now.'

'That's why you're writing so good,' said Sol. 'You've got to pay for everything in the end.'

'I'd like to see her again – just once. To see if she's real.'

'Meanwhile it's Sarah you're taking to France.'

'Yes. Maybe we're both playing a game of dare.'

As they drove away from the house Willie and Deborah appeared, heads together, in an upstairs window both waving flags. They had kissed their children on the doorstep but by the time Nicholas had driven the car from the drive, the pair were swinging the Union Jacks in farewell.

'Do you think it's safe to leave them?' wondered Nicholas as they drove towards the High Street. Sarah was looking over her shoulder through the rear window at the flags. 'We have to leave them at some time,' she said. 'After all, Deborah is sixteen and Willie has promised not to give her trouble, and my mother and father will be over at the weekend.' She sighed and turned to the front as they went into the High Street. 'It will be interesting to see how the whole thing turns out.'

The meaning was not lost on him. How would this journey

be for them? In more ways than one they were venturing beyond their everyday lives and the familiar suburban London into an unknown territory. They drove silently but when they were on the main route going towards central London Nicholas nodded to the roadhouse with the tacky giant in the playground.

'That's the Bedford Arms where I used to take the kids to lunch,' he mentioned.

'I know,' she replied still looking ahead. 'I went there with them too.'

'You didn't tell me.'

'I forgot to mention it,' she answered easily. 'And I told them not to. I just wanted to see inside the place. Strange, isn't it, curiosity.'

'Yes,' he nodded. 'It's strange.'

She glanced to the back seat. Wedged between their two suitcases was the squat box containing Bernard Boulting's ashes. 'We couldn't have put him in the boot,' said Sarah. 'It really wouldn't be right.'

They drove as far as the motorway junction and then headed east. Sharp January sun reflected from the tarmac. Clouds hung in layers on the horizon ahead. They conversed little. Sarah turned on the radio and they drove to pop music.

After a few miles she said as though she had been thinking over what had happened to them: 'This time we're running away together.'

'It makes a change,' he said. Perhaps they were both running away from themselves.

The road was much as when he had last driven it; huge vehicles trundling towards the east-coast ports, cars edging through the drizzle that had begun as soon as they reached the Essex flat country. 'Why ever did you have your lovers meet in a place like this?' asked Sarah. She peered through the smeared side window. Bare trees waved like seaweed. 'It's hardly romantic.'

'Unpromising,' he agreed. 'That is what I mean to convey, the greyness of it. She wears a red coat and she is in the distance when he first sees her, a bright dot in the landscape.'

Sarah glanced at him sideways. 'I really *must* read this.'

'I'd rather you waited until it was finished.'

'I'll wait.'

He knew by the distances to Harwich on the road signs that they were approaching the Littlehaven turning. He pretended to see the arrow for the first time. 'There,' he said. 'This turning looks promising.'

He was aware that she was regarding him oddly but the moment passed. 'Littlehaven,' she repeated. 'Well there's got to be something down here if it's only a little haven.'

He drove along the single road, dripping hedges close on either side, mud churning from the wheels. The sky was low and fast, coming in bands from the direction of the sea. 'What a place,' Sarah grumbled. 'Can you imagine anyone coming here, let alone living here?' She looked at his profile. 'What are they here for, by the way, your star-struck lovers?'

'She's a painter and he has come here to go fishing,' he said.

'Let's see if it's as you made it up,' she said quietly.

He was driving into the village, along the shore, by the jetty and the mud-flats. With a start he saw a limping man walking a dog and remembered how they had been there before. Why was he playing this game, taking these risks? Why had he not told her in the first place? He could have mentioned his visit without revealing Thérèse and their journey across the North Sea. Now it was too late. He was already feeling an underhand thrill at the deception.

They slowed outside the Hope. 'Looks like the only pub,' he said.

'We can have some lunch,' said Sarah, 'That's something.'

'Why not,' he found himself saying. This was madness. Imagine bringing her *here*. He got out of the car and surveyed the desolate coast, the sea coming to the shore like a miser, a little at a time, the dirty sky pressing down on the grubby water. A single lost bird was piping. He screwed up his eyes and peered along the sea-path where he had first seen Thérèse. It was disturbing, almost frightening, the way she was growing in his imagination, the place and the woman in the red cloak. He turned back to the car. 'I'll make sure they're doing lunch,' he said. He told himself he would return to the car and say they did not serve it. But in his heart he knew he was going to dare it. She remained in the car and he went in.

It was scarcely three months since he had been there but he was almost surprised to find things were in the same place. The low lobby with its notices on a board, the timetable for the Harwich–Hook of Holland Ferry, the selections for the darts team. He bent his head and went into the bar. The registration book was lying open by a brass bell on the counter, just as it had been that day last year. No one was there. He was about to ring the bell but his hand went to the book and he quickly turned back the pages. It was not necessary to turn many. There was his name and the date, and just above it four signatures the last of which was that of Thérèse Bernet. He was still staring at it when a woman appeared. He had never seen her before.

'Ah,' he hesitated. 'Are you doing lunches?'

'We generally don't in the winter,' she said. 'But how many is it for? We could do something.'

He should have escaped then with no conscience but instead he heard himself say: 'There are two of us.'

'That's all right then. If you'd like to give us a few minutes, have a drink, and I'll see what we can manage.'

'How long have you been here?' he asked.

'Since after Christmas,' she said. 'The last people have gone to Chelmsford. They found it a bit cut off. Have you been here before?'

'Oh, no,' replied Nicholas hurriedly. 'No, just generally interested.'

She appeared perplexed that he should have enquired at all. 'I'll tell my wife,' he said as she frowned. He went out. At least the landlord was not there to recognise him. God, what a ridiculous game. 'We can have something,' he said opening Sarah's door. 'They don't really do lunches in the winter but they can manage.'

'That's all right,' she said preparing to get from the car. He held the door for her. She added: 'After all we can have our romantic dinner on board tonight.' She sniffed towards the murky sea. 'At least it's flat,' she said. 'At the moment.'

They went into the inn. 'Funny spot,' whispered Sarah as she had to bend below the lintel. 'Can't think why there's anything at all here. Not in a place like this.'

'In the summer I expect it's quite busy,' he suggested. 'And out of season they probably have wildfowlers and birdwatchers and people going fishing.'

'And ladies coming to paint,' she added slyly. He led her to the bar and the woman returned and said that they could have fish and chips or ham salad. They chose the ham salad and Nicholas ordered two gins. 'It won't be long,' said the woman. 'Why don't you go in and take a table.' She gave a short laugh. 'There's plenty of them.'

Almost as if the action were beyond his control, he directed her to the table where he and Thérèse had eaten breakfast. As then, there was a fire in the grate but today it was low and sluggish. Sarah sat surveying the room, the ceiling beams, the brass, the copper, the dim firelight. 'Is this where you'll have them meet?' she asked. 'Yes,' he replied, looking around him. 'I think it might fit.'

'What are their names again?'

'He's Robert,' he said steadily. 'And she is called Cécile.'

'How romantic.'

Nicholas studied the room and said cagily: 'It's near enough.'

She was smiling. With Sarah you never knew.

They finished their gins. Nicholas was professionally and explicitly dissecting the room when from behind the screen at the end came the black waitress. Nicholas knew his face had drained. He had taken the ultimate risk. 'Oooo, 'ello!' she exclaimed in her perky London voice. 'Fancy . . .'

She saw his panicked eyes and astutely turned towards the vaguely smiling Sarah. 'Fancy . . . a nice piece of cold pork instead of the 'am?'

Nicholas felt his breath return. His smile was grateful. 'Oh, yes. Yes please, that would be nice.' He glanced at his wife. 'How about you, darling.'

'The ham, I think,' Sarah said slowly as if half-aware that she had missed something.

'Right you are then,' said the girl. Her bright smile again startled Nicholas. 'Nice to see you . . .' she changed course once more, '. . . on a day like this.'

She cut short his mumble by turning lightly and going back behind the screen. 'She's a bit funny, isn't she?' said Nicholas to fill the silence.

'Yes,' she anwered casually. 'It was almost as if she recognised you.'

'She was just being chirpy,' he said.

Then he became aware of a peeping head emerging from behind the screen; the same enquiring middle-aged woman's face that had spied around it when he was there with Thérèse. She was pasty-skinned, her hair tight, her expression displeased. To distract Sarah he indicated some copper tankards on the mantelshelf: 'They look pretty ancient. I wonder if they are.'

'I wonder,' echoed Sarah with no interest. She sensed the scrutiny of the woman spying from the screen and looked around swiftly just as the head was withdrawn. 'Was that someone having a look at us?' she asked.

'Where? No, I didn't see anyone,' he mumbled. 'Ah, here it is.'

The waitress, full of smiles, came around the screen with two plates and was followed by the disdainful woman with a dish of boiled potatoes. As she laid it carefully on the table she studied Nicholas closely and then moved her censorious expression to Sarah. Slowly she backed away.

'Funny woman,' mentioned Sarah.

'She's a bit potty,' said the waitress collecting condiments from the next table. 'She thinks she's seen things before. Like . . . what's it called?'

'*Déjà vu*,' suggested Sarah.

'That's it. I knew it was French.' She smiled sweet and teasing at Nicholas. 'Any wine?'

'Yes, two glasses of white I think.'

'French?' she asked cheekily.

'French,' he muttered.

He was cursing himself for taking the risk. How damned stupid to come here. A murderer returning to the scene, as Sol had said, and taking the police with him. He sat silently and began to eat. The waitress returned eagerly. 'Two white wines,' she said putting the glasses down. 'French.'

She loitered as though wanting to be of further use until Nicholas said: 'That's fine, thank you. For the present.'

She went away jauntily but then the other waitress returned with a small dish and a spoon. 'Apple sauce,' she intoned, her eyes piercing Nicholas. She set it down and transferred the scrutiny to Sarah who smiled nervously. Eventually she retreated still looking over her shoulder and finally disappeared behind the screen only to look back again from around its edge. 'She is potty,' muttered Nicholas. 'Really.'

'Inbreeding, I expect,' confided Sarah. 'There must be some funny things go on around here.'

He grunted agreement and went on eating. 'We shouldn't be too long,' he cautioned. 'The ferry is at four and they don't wait around.'

'Don't they?'

'Not if they can help it. Especially if you've got a car. It's not so bad if you're just passengers . . . so I've been told.'

He took her in across the table, lifting his almost empty glass. 'I'm glad you came, Sarah,' he said.

'So am I,' she replied lightly, responding with her glass. 'You don't like being on your own, do you. And . . .,' she breathed in with satisfaction, 'so far it's been interesting. I'm enjoying myself.'

They did not delay for coffee. 'You're terribly anxious to get going,' commented Sarah. He repeated that they needed to be at the ferry in good time. The waitress came with the bill and he settled it as they left, going to the bar to sign the credit card slip. Both waitresses stood framed in the window and waved as they left.

'She *was* friendly,' mentioned Sarah archly as they drove through the wet and straggling village, the afternoon light already diminishing. 'Still, I expect she would be with the tip you gave her.'

'How much did I give her?' He was so heavily on guard now that he barked the question almost before the end of her sentence.

'I thought I saw ten pounds changing hands.'

'Trust you,' he grumbled. 'It was simply that the drinks go on a different bill and I'd filled out the total on the credit card slip before she remembered. So I paid her cash for them. Eight eighty, keep the change.'

That was sharp, he thought with satisfaction. Sarah said: 'Sorry,' and he shrugged: 'Don't mention it.'

They drove in silence, hemmed in by the lane, spindly branches touching the roof of the car like knocking fingers. The lorries on the main road had their headlights on. He turned the car to join the traffic and headed north-east. In half an hour they were in Harwich. Nicholas contrived a performance of finding the way to the ferry terminal although it was blatantly signposted. Sarah impatiently duplicated the direction of the posted arrows with her nail-varnished finger. Once more she studied him sideways but this time time said nothing. 'These places are hell to find,' muttered Nicholas.

'They would be if you've never been in the area before,' she agreed casually. 'Look *there* it is, follow that enormous sign. See it? Where it says: "Ferry Terminal" in huge letters.'

He grunted that he had detected it and added: 'It's simply very difficult while you're trying to avoid the wheels of a German juggernaut.'

They reached the dock. Nicholas put his hand out of the car to collect the tickets. Sarah bent forwards to smile extravagantly at the uniformed man. 'Thanks, *bon voyage*,' called Nicholas over her shoulder.

'You *are* confused,' she observed as he drove up the ramp. 'He's not going anywhere. We are.'

'Oh, yes. But, listen, love, let me get this car aboard. It's a difficult manoeuvre.'

She was unable to resist it: 'Not for you.'

They stopped on the ramp. There was a cargo loader beckoning him on but he applied the handbrake and turned to Sarah. 'Now listen, darling,' he said succinctly. 'If you want to get off now, I suggest you do so. It will be difficult after we sail.'

To his surprise her expression dropped and she said: 'All right. Sorry.'

'Good. Thanks.' He released the handbrake and the car began to slide backwards down the ramp. He cursed and cursed again as the vehicle behind hooted urgently. He applied the handbrake again before increasing the power and climbing the incline. 'Nearly changed your mind,' said the loader affably. Nicholas apologised but the man added: 'I've seen them all. Counted them on and counted them off.'

Nicholas negotiated the car into a space indicated by another loader. They did not get out immediately but sat there. He closed his eyes with his head on the back of the seat. 'We're not going to have much fun on this trip if we keep trying to score off each other,' he told her with exaggerated patience. 'We're on a collision course. We've got to pack it up now before we seriously quarrel.'

Once again she nodded and said he was right. 'Shall I take your dad up?' she asked immediately as if they had settled all disagreement. 'Or do we leave him in the car?'

'Oh . . . yes. We'd better leave it . . . him . . . for the time being. Nobody's going to steal him. They'll be sorry if they do.'

She laughed and they were both aware of the relief. He leaned towards her and they kissed lightly. 'We've made up,' he said.

'Yes. We've made up.'

He opened his door and went around to her side. He was surprised how crowded the car deck was. 'We can't just cart that casket around the deck until we're sorted out with our cabin. I think it would be just as well to leave it in the car until we . . . er . . . need it.'

'After dinner,' she said.

'After dinner. We'll give him a jolly send-off.'

They took their light luggage from the back seat and he held her hand as they climbed the metal staircase from the car deck. 'I hope it's a good restaurant,' she said.

'The grill room is very good,' he said. Then: 'According to the brochure.'

The sea lay serene, the night was not even cold and a scrap of moon was showing when they went out on to the deck with his father's ashes. Wrapped in their heavy coats they stood at the rail, both tipsy from the gins, the wine and the brandies, passing the casket from one to another. 'You do it,' he suggested woozily. 'I don't like the idea. Not my old man.'

'No, *you*,' Sarah protested swaying as she pushed the box back towards him. 'It's not my job.' Tenuously they held it between them for a moment. 'Perhaps we shouldn't have drunk so much,' she suggested trying to steady herself. 'It doesn't seem proper. And the air's getting to us now.'

Nicholas rolled against the rail. There was no one else on the deck. The lights of another ship were in the middle distance, voyaging in the opposite direction.

'We've got to take account of the wind,' advised Nicholas. 'They could blow back.' He licked his finger and held it up to the breeze. Sarah did likewise. Between them they dropped the box.

It fell to the deck and burst open spreading the meagre portion of grey ashes over the boards. 'Oh shit,' moaned Nicholas. 'Now we've done it.'

'Oh God. What can we do?'

The ashes lay in a grey pattern, those at the fringe slightly ruffled by the air. Horrified they faced each other. 'I'll get a broom,' said Sarah.

'Where?' he asked his eyes darting around. 'Perhaps I can push him over the edge with the side of my shoe.' He shaped to do it but she pushed him back with some force and he stumbled away as the ship rolled. 'No, no, Nick,' she pleaded. 'It's not fair. A broom is best. We'll get all of him over that way.'

She staggered off leaving him holding on to the rail and

staring at the grey unregulated ash on the deckboards. He looked up in concern as he heard someone approaching. Two ship's officers were strolling towards him. With a swift sideways kick he sent the plastic casket over the side. He shielded the ashes with his shoes, standing pigeon-toed in front of them. The two men neared. They regarded him with surprise. 'Fresh evening, sir,' suggested one. They halted, their hands behind their backs.

'A bit,' responded Nicholas with a voice he hardly recognised. 'Needed the air.'

He realised they were studying his strange stance. He shifted uncomfortably, the movement revealing some of the ashes previously concealed by his toe-pointing shoes.

'It's all right,' said the second of the officers. 'This is a smoking deck.'

'You'd be better off on the leeward side, though,' suggested the other.

Thin-lipped he thanked them and, after treating him to a joint curious look, they continued on their way almost colliding with Sarah emerging from below with a broom. She distractedly returned their wishes for a good evening and swerved around them in the same movement. Their puzzled eyes followed her. 'Let me do it,' she muttered to Nicholas darting a look over her shoulder. He shifted his feet, shuffling sideways while the officers, ten yards away, remained transfixed. With a swift sweep of the brush, Sarah pushed the ashes over the side. 'There,' she said. They both turned satisfied faces towards the officers.

'There's no need to do that,' called one. 'The deck will be washed down in an hour.'

'Don't like to leave a mess,' responded Sarah with huge sweetness. 'It's not fair on other people.'

The quartet found themselves staring each other out. Nicholas and Sarah remained stationary and it was the officers who eventually revolved and left the scene with perplexed farewells.

Nicholas looked down at the spotless deck and his feet, then at Sarah, then at the broom, and eventually at the flowing sea into the sky. 'Sorry Dad,' was all he could say.

They made love that night in the gently swaying cabin, rolling under the blankets, kissing and holding, as though they were afraid. They were emotional and tearful, glad and giggling. They seemed to be full up. Eventually they lay naked and close and the ship breathed quietly. They were quieter than the ship. It was better than it had been for a long time. Both feared that it might never be the same again.

Twelve

Sarah woke him as they were entering the port. They went up on to the deck and looked out at the colourless, low-lying land, the red-roofed Dutch houses, the cars of people going to work. They stood holding hands wrapped up against the sharp, salt air.

They spoke little, as if they feared they might disturb the mood of the night before. They had coffee and croissants and went down to the car when the loud-hailer summoned drivers. Sitting, almost huddled, they waited and watched the high bow doors of the ferry open to admit a widening channel of grey light.

'Enter Mr and Mrs Nicholas Boulting,' he announced. She squeezed the arm of his coat.

They drove first towards Rotterdam, after which they had breakfast in a steamy café between Breda and the Belgian border. It was crowded with shop- and office-workers filling the space against the bar, conversing in subdued morning voices at the tables, sending skeins of smoke into the already thick air.

They drove over the frontier and on into France. Sarah was at the wheel and he was muttering into a pocket recorder. 'I don't know what you see to say so much about,' she told him when they had lunch at Valenciennes. He spread his hands: 'Buildings, streets, countryside, canals, bridges, rivers and above all people. The man with all the pots and pans on his bicycle, the nun eating the baguette as she trundles along, the old woman shooing the geese, the businessman in his car eating a cake and attempting to look important.'

'I'm sorry, Nick,' she remarked genuinely. 'But I just don't understand your work. I never have done.'

'They're bit players, well some of them. Background. Figures in a landscape.'

'It's your own private world,' she said. 'You make it up.'

'As you go along,' he agreed.

They reached Paris in the late afternoon, left the Périphérique and headed for the centre. Sarah had made reservations at a hotel off the Champs-Élysées in one of the quiet, dark streets almost at the heart of the city. 'Do you know what you're going to do?' she asked him when they were in the room.

'No,' he admitted. 'I am just going to wander around and see what happens, if anything. The lady, Cécile of the book, being an artist would probably live and work on the Left Bank or somewhere like that.'

'Do you want me to come with you?'

He smiled. 'Do you think I'll get into trouble otherwise?'

She looked embarrassed. She had taken off her dress and was sitting in her slip at the dressing table. As he went over to her she moved up on the stool and they sat side by side conversing in the mirror. 'I thought you might like the company,' she suggested quietly. Then mischievously: 'Even if you are looking for a lady.'

'A fictional lady,' he amended. 'Which means I can find her where and when I please. That's one of the plusses of being a novelist. You can arrange people, arrange their births, their lives and their deaths, for that matter.'

'That sounds very powerful,' she said to his reflection.

'Then you realise it's only a story,' he said.

'And does he find Cécile in Paris?'

'I think so. But much later. His search is a long one.'

'I'm beginning to like it.'

He had his arm around the silk slip on her waist and he began to rub her ribs and then the side of her breast. 'Tell me a story,' she said half-turning. 'About us.'

They went to the bed and he lay naked next to her. He could feel the warmth of her body through the silk. 'Once upon a time,' he said, 'there was a man and a woman who were happy when they allowed themselves to be.'

'Go on,' she said. She eased herself on top of him and they made love that way.

'It's difficult telling a story from down here,' he said.

'Let's concentrate on the real one,' she said.

They lay for a long time afterwards. He closed his eyes and slept. She pulled the bed covers up around them. Within her there was a deep sadness. While he breathed in sleep she lay looking at the shadows passing the winter window. She felt treacherous and afraid and she wondered what was to become of them.

They went to the Left Bank in the morning. The day was clear but the air was chill and the grey wind sifted along the Seine. They were both in heavy coats walking the lanes, between the empty carts and barrows turning the corners and peering into galleries and windows. There were few people about, the occasional shuffler along the cobbles, people grouped, as though for warmth, in cafés, artists working in studios warmed by gas heaters and oil stoves.

They went into some of the galleries in the Boulevard Saint-Germain and the Rue de Seine, glad of the relief from the sharp wind. One had an extended room displaying the work of artists in sections on a long wall; and they progressed slowly around the exhibits. Sarah, trying to be interested, pointed to canvases and made short comments. 'This is the sort of place where your Cécile would sell her work, is it?' she eventually asked. 'She would not have a gallery of her own?'

'No. She paints and she tries to sell her work and sometimes she does. But Robert comes to Paris and begins to look for some clue to her . . .,' he paused involuntarily as his eyes caught something, 'whereabouts.'

They left the gallery and went to a muggy café, the heat from the urns clouding the windows. They sat at a round, marble table with iron legs. 'Do you want to stay here for a while?' he suggested. 'Have another coffee?'

He felt underhand in doing it. She said she would be glad to stay. 'I won't be long,' he promised rising from the table. 'I'll just mooch up to the end of the street and back. Then we'll have a cognac *before* lunch.'

With a quickening pulse he went out of the café and along the Rue de Seine. He re-entered the last gallery they had visited and then swiftly moved along the exhibits. He stopped and surveyed the paintings displayed on one wall. There it was! He almost crept closer to look at it. It was a countryside scene, water-colour wash. In the corner was a small bird.

His eyes covered the gallery. A woman, who appeared to be in charge, was talking to two other people in the distance. He bent towards the painting again. There it was, a tiny bird, *l'oiseau*. He touched the frame and peered at the painting closely as if he were an expert making a detailed examination.

'*Monsieur?*' It was the woman who had been in conversation at the far end of the gallery. She was awkwardly angular with long, blonde, streaked hair. She nodded when he asked if she spoke English and said: 'A little.'

'I wondered if you could tell me where I can find the artist who painted this?' he asked. He glanced guiltily towards the door as though Sarah might appear. 'Her name is Thérèse Oiseau. Her married name is Bernet. See, she puts a bird in the corner.'

The woman bent her long back to see. 'Ah, *oui*,' she said. She craned up again. 'I do not know this artist,' she shrugged. 'But the person for this gallery . . . the director . . . is not here today. Tomorrow she is here. You must come then.'

Nicholas thanked her. He touched the frame of the painting once more and then went out into the street. He felt a fierce and enclosed excitement. He knew he was going to find her.

That evening did not go well for them; it was as if they had run out of both conversation and stamina. For two hours they had sat in a restaurant, eating without relish, and passed whispers to each other about other diners or passers-by outside the window, the last resort of people who have nothing further to say. Finally, they had given up doing even that and had sat sombrely holding hands in an arranged surrender.

Nicholas did not sleep until long into the early hours. Thérèse was in this city, not far away, perhaps in the next street. Sarah was curled with her face away from him breathing deeply. He woke at eight with a sense of anticipation and guilt. When he was in the bathroom she called to him sleepily. 'I must get going,' he said putting his head around the door. She was leaning on her elbows in the bed, her face pink, her eyes puffy. 'I'll do some shopping,' she yawned. 'Where are you going?'

'I have only a general idea,' he said tugging on his overcoat. 'You can't measure this sort of thing. There's nothing logical about it, it's accidental.'

She folded herself beneath the duvet again. He went to the side of the bed, leaned over and kissed her on the side of her warm face.

'Will I see you for lunch?' she asked.

'All right. Why don't we meet back here at twelve thirty?'

'I'll be here.' She eased below the cover again. From there she said: 'Perhaps you'll find your Cécile today.'

'It's possible.' He attempted a firm laugh. 'If I don't, then I'll have to make her up.'

Heavy with thoughts, he left the room and went down the stairs. Insipid January light was drifting through the circular front door of the hotel. He smiled a touch as he waited for a woman carrying parcels to revolve the door and come through. 'Widdershins,' he remembered aloud. She looked at him oddly.

He took a taxi to the Left Bank and walked along the deviating street to the gallery. A notice on the door said it opened at ten thirty. He grimaced and went to the café where they had been the day before. He was reluctant to use his miniature recorder in places like that. It gave the impression of snooping, so he wrote random notes about the surroundings, the outlook from the window, and the people who came and left, on a sheet of hotel notepaper. He drank two cups of coffee and then went for a cold circular walk around the echoing cobbled streets arriving at the gallery door at ten forty. Inside, towards the back, was a woman drinking coffee and adding figures behind a cluttered desk. She glanced up and smiled professionally. '*Monsieur?*'

'I wonder if you can tell me where I can locate Thérèse Oiseau?' he asked. 'You have one of her paintings over there. With the bird in the corner.'

She appeared puzzled and scratched her forehead with her glasses but the mention of the bird cleared her brow. 'Ah, Oiseau,' she said. 'Yes, I know. You would like to buy that painting?'

'Well, no, I'm sorry. I am travelling and I can't take it with me.'

'We can send it.'

'No. I really want to contact the artist herself. Perhaps I will be able to buy it at another time.'

'It will still be here,' the woman shrugged. 'She is not popular.'

'I would like to contact her,' he repeated evenly. 'Do you have an address?'

Impatient now, the woman puffed out her cheeks and said: 'Somewhere there must be.' With some reluctance she opened a ledger. Nicholas waited while she frowned over the ledger. 'There is a gallery,' she said eventually. She reached to the desk and picked up a card and a pen. She wrote on the back of the card. 'This,' she said showing it to him and then handing it across the desk. 'Galerie Tissot, Avenue Mozart. It is near the Trocadéro.'

He took the card and went out into the street, glancing at the water-colour landscape as he passed it. 'It is very nice,' the woman called forlornly after him. 'We could take a smaller price.'

'I'll be back', he promised. She closed the ledger, walked over to the picture and scowled. 'Oiseau?' she queried. '*C'est un rossignol.*' A nightingale was what they called a painting that never sold.

Nicholas hailed a taxi and gave the driver the address. He watched Paris go past, grey on grey. He wondered where Sarah was shopping. He felt mean and unhappy. Then he thought of Thérèse in her distant red cloak. He had to see her again. Just once.

The taxi arrived at the gallery. 'No,' he said across the driver's shoulder. 'Please, a little further.'

The driver shrugged and said:' Galerie Tissot, Avenue Mozart.'

'Yes. But a little further.'

The driver glanced at his meter and drove a further hundred yards. '*Là?*' he sniffed. '*Oui, merci,*' responded Nicholas. He left the cab and walked guardedly towards the gallery. There were paintings in the window. He loitered by a newspaper stand. A couple went in and a young woman came out but it was not Thérèse. He took a deep breath and made for the door. The two people who had entered while he was watching were coming out into the street again and he stepped back to allow them to pass. He peered through the glass. There were several vague shapes at the back of the room. Still looking, he felt for the door, pushed it open and stepped inside.

At once he saw three of her paintings. He stood looking at them and a softly smiling man came towards him. 'Thérèse Oiseau,' said Nicholas. 'Please, is she here?'

The man indicated the water-colours. 'The paintings but not the artist, *monsieur,*' he replied. 'Maybe this afternoon. Sometimes she comes in the afternoon. Did you wish to purchase a work by Thérèse Oiseau?'

'Not at this moment. But I would like to speak with her.' He paused. 'I am an old friend.'

'She has many,' smiled the man. 'You must try in the afternoon. There is a message perhaps?'

'Thanks, but I'll come in later.'

Across the avenue was a restaurant. He went inside and ordered coffee, sitting by a table in the window which gave a good view of the Galerie Tissot, only obstructed by the corner of the newspaper stand. He sat for almost an hour, watching across the traffic. He then went back to the hotel. Sarah was just descending the staircase. 'Any luck?' she asked.

'Not bad,' he answered. 'I've covered a lot of ground. I ended up in the Avenue Mozart, near the Trocadéro. It's quite lively along there and there are several galleries and that sort of thing. It's not as arty as the Left Bank. I found a restaurant.' He waited, then plunged, even as he did so wondering why: 'We could go and have lunch there.'

Sarah grumbled at the Paris traffic and the length of time it took to reach the Avenue Mozart. Nor did she like the brasserie for it was now crowded and they had to share a table with a couple who kept laughing.

'I'm glad they've gone,' sighed his wife when the pair finally departed, still mirthful. 'I wonder what the joke was.'

'It's annoying when you don't know,' he agreed.

'You keep thinking it might be *you* they find so amusing,' she said. Nicholas tried to appear not to be watching the gallery across the street.

'Why does this research have to be so detailed?' enquired Sarah. 'Wouldn't *any* restaurant do, *any* art gallery? Couldn't you have just made the whole thing up?'

'I *am* making the whole thing up,' he pointed out pedantically. 'But if you're going to tell lies, even if it's in a novel, then it's as well to get the lies right.'

At that moment he saw her. Thérèse standing on the far pavement. There was no mistake. Thérèse. He dropped his fork and by the time he had picked it up again she had vanished. Sarah said testily: 'This gets very intense, doesn't it. When I read this book I'll appreciate how much agony has gone into it.'

'There's no need for sarcasm,' he retorted in a low voice. 'I'm sorry you don't have my undivided attention.'

'All right,' she sighed. 'We seem to spend a lot of time apologising to each other. When are we leaving here?'

He almost choked. Thérèse was crossing the street, heading for the door of the brasserie. 'Quite soon,' he muttered. Sarah sighed again and dug her knife fiercely into her Chicken Kiev. The melted butter oozed out. Nicholas forced his eyes from the door and fixed them on his plate. He heard the door open. Thérèse had come in. Her voice was greeting someone. Inch by inch he raised his head.

There she was. Beautiful. She was laughing and wrapped in a deep brown coat. He glanced briefly towards Sarah who was dissecting her floating chicken. He dragged his gaze away from Thérèse and looked down at his plate. 'This is so greasy,' commented Sarah.

'Yes, it often is,' he heard himself say. He glanced at her. 'Chicken Kiev.'

Thérèse had sat down. She was now out of his view but he could hear her laughter. The place was slowly clearing. The couple at the next table left and then the four businessmen beyond that. Now her slender back was in his view. She had taken off her coat revealing a fawn sweater. She was talking animatedly to another woman who was wearing a hat, using her hands to illustrate a story. He heard Thérèse laugh again. Oh, God.

'I don't want anything else,' said Sarah pushing her plate away. 'Not even coffee.' She regarded her empty plate unhappily. 'Considering this is Paris, I didn't think much of that.' The waiter arrived at her elbow and asked if she had finished. She gave a truly false smile. 'Yes, *merci*. It was very nice.'

Nicholas paid the bill. Their route to the door would take them directly past the table at which Thérèse was sitting. 'Shall we go?' said Sarah scraping her chair. He helped her with her coat, having to manoeuvre her so that he did not face Thérèse.

'Whatever are you doing?' demanded Sarah. 'Spinning me around like this?'

'Sorry. I was in an awkward position.'

She regarded him with annoyance. 'You're strange sometimes, Nick,' she said.

He repeated his apology absently. She was already making for the door, brushing by the table occupied by Thérèse and her companion, turning impatiently waiting for him to catch up. He went past the table like a crab, shuffling towards the exit, his face kept away from the occupants, like a man with a stiff neck. For a terrifying instant he thought she had spotted him. Conversation at the table ceased. Accidentally he nudged the other woman's chair and said '*Pardon*' over his shoulder. He reached the door and, still moving as though performing some awkward and complex dance, opened it for his wife. They went out into the wintry air of the avenue. Sarah was standing regarding him oddly. Through the window of the restaurant he glanced and saw her again. He caught his breath. He thought she was staring back.

They left Paris the following morning and drove south. It rained thickly on the *autoroute* and the heavy traffic hemmed them in. Sarah said she had not slept well and now she was curled up on the back seat. He could hear her deep breathing and he was glad she was not sitting unspeaking beside him. She woke once and asked: 'Where are we?'

'On the *autoroute*. Just approaching Auxerre.'

'Raining still?' she grumbled.

'Still raining,' he confirmed.

He thought she had gone back to sleep but she may have been awake. He drove resignedly on and they reached Lyons in the early evening drizzle. They went to a big, modern hotel because Sarah insisted that she wanted a television. She had room service that night and watched the satellite channels. He went down to the bar and then, alone but relieved, he ate in the coffee shop.

'This has got to be the most boring road in the world,' she grumbled the following morning when they continued their journey.

'The rain's not so thick,' he pointed out.

'The traffic is,' she said. Spray smeared the windscreen as they overtook another eight menacingly revolving wheels.

'It's rarely short of interest if you're driving,' he added.

'I'm sure it's worse than our motorways.' Another toll area materialised out of the drizzle ahead. 'And you have to pay.'

'After Grenoble we'll take the N85, the Route Napoléon,' he said.

'That was in the guide-book?' She was sitting up now.

'I read it in the coffee shop last night.'

She bridled. 'There was nothing stopping you having room service like me.'

'I didn't feel the need to watch *Hollywood Lovers*.'

There was snow lying heavily to the east. Sarah said: 'Is it up there we go?'

'Sort of up there, but not quite. The road goes south to Nice. It's hilly so there will probably be some snow. You wanted a change of scene.'

Sarah peered again at the mountains. The snow lay on them dull and threatening against the drab sky. 'I'd prefer the change of scene to be somewhere in the West Indies,' she remarked.

He laughed slightly. 'Oh, come on. Don't be churlish. When we get beyond Grenoble we can have an early lunch.'

'You seem to think that all life's grumbles can be solved by having a knife and fork in your hands,' she observed. She was looking more anxiously now at the rising road. Outside the car the air was grey with cold.

'I ought to write that down,' he said. 'About the knife and fork.'

'Don't be so shitty,' she answered.

This time nobody apologised. They sat dumbly until they came to a wooden chalet, more Swiss than French, its roof projecting like a crown. He pulled the car into the area in front of the building. 'Lunch,' he said. 'Now cheer up.'

Next to the chalet was a tourist bureau and having established Sarah over a gin and tonic, he went in there returning to the restaurant with some brochures. He sat opposite her at the table. It was only just after noon and the place was almost empty. An open fire was flying up a wide brick chimney. 'They said there are no problems on the road, the Route Napoléon,' Nicholas said. 'Normal winter driving.'

'No chains?'

'No chains. And about ninety kilometres on there's an *auberge*, just off the road, which they recommend. A place called St Jean de Valle. Great views of the mountains, no trouble to get there, good food, nice rooms.' He looked at her hopefully. 'It's an easy drive. Doesn't that lift your spirits?'

'Not as much as Barbados would,' she said but then smiled. 'All right, I won't say I'm sorry because we promised not to. But anyway we're here in the mountains in the snow and that's that. Let's look at the menu.'

More than an hour later they drove on to the main highway. The sky and the road were both grey, separated by bands of deep white. Other vehicles slushed by. Sarah seemed to have gone to sleep again. He drove phlegmatically for eighty-five kilometres and then began to search for the sign for St Jean de Valle. It was nearly dark now and he leaned over the wheel attempting to see beyond the headlights. The traffic, which had been considerable around Grenoble, had thinned and he could hear the wind whistling. Sarah roused herself and sat blinking at the black and white through the windscreen.

Twice he thought he saw the St Jean de Valle sign on the left but by that time it was too late to turn. Then he saw a third. He turned the car abruptly in slush, throwing Sarah sideways. Ahead it was suddenly narrow and dark. 'Where are we?' she asked.

'I think it's just along here,' he answered without conviction. 'St Jean de Valle. . . . I think.'

They felt the car slither. He cursed and she held her breath. The headlights staggered around a narrow bend. The wheels went sideways. 'Go back,' said Sarah sharply. 'Get back on the main road.'

'I can't turn,' he grunted. 'There's no room. It can only be along here.'

The car drifted again, this time the other way. Sarah emitted a small squeak. He said: 'You're not helping by squeaking.'

'I'm squeaking,' she replied tartly, 'because there's probably a five-hundred-fucking-foot drop on each side of this road.'

'It's banked with snow,' he snapped. 'And there's no need to swear.'

'I'm frightened, that's why.'

'For God's sake, Sarah.'

He was travelling as slowly as he could but the wheels kept losing direction. The headlights gleamed against the relentless white, wind moaned down the culvert. Nicholas stared ahead. Sarah had clenched her eyes and cowered back in the seat. 'You ought to stop,' she suggested through tight lips. 'Stop before we go over the edge.'

'We can't just stop. It's probably around this bend.'

The car snorted as they turned the corner. Facing them was a wall of snow, tall and complete. Impassable. The headlights stabbed at it impotently. Nicholas stopped the car. 'God damn it,' he said.

He squeezed his eyes against the windscreen. The view was filled, edge to edge, corner to corner; unbroken white. Anxiously he opened his door and took in the scene through the aperture. The cold cut into his face. He closed the door hurriedly. 'Blocked,' he moaned. 'Bloody blocked.'

Sarah regarded him in the dimness with a sort of fatalistic triumph. 'What do you propose to do?' she enquired.

'God only knows. I can't get out and shovel the bleeding stuff away.' He looked at her and caught her expression. 'Unless you'd like to.'

'No thanks. You got us in here.'

He stifled his retort. 'We can't just stay here,' he said instead. 'And we can't turn around. We'll have to back down the road.'

'Around those bends? We'll never do that.'

'Or we could walk,' he amended looking staight into her face. 'Fancy a nice walk?' He put his head wearily on the rim of the steering wheel. 'Oh fuck it,' he groaned.

'Now who's swearing,' she replied. She was still curiously triumphant. 'Fucking it is not going to solve anything.'

Ignoring her he attempted to be rational. 'One of us is going to have to get out and guide the other.' He saw her face fall. 'Which one do you want to be?'

'I'll drive it,' she said decisively. 'I'm not going out there.'

'Right, you drive,' he said. 'Try and reverse – very carefully.'

She sniffed. 'I know I'm not in Boxley shopping centre,' she said. 'You'd better get out before it sinks.'

He clambered from the car and pulled his overcoat out after him. The air was stiff, the wind threatening. Sarah moved over to the driving seat. 'Take it easy, for God's sake,' he warned. 'Don't go running me over.'

'I'll try not to,' she said without confidence. Nicholas wound down the window and then closed the door. She shuddered but said nothing further. 'I'll be right behind you,' he said through the window. 'When I shout put her into reverse.' He almost lost his balance as he backed down the confined road but somehow recovered. 'Can you see me all right?' he called to her.

'I can see your face,' she bellowed through the window. 'Just.'

He tried to calculate the car's angle. As a last hope he looked back down the confined road. All behind him, all around, except for the rear lights of the vehicle, was black and white. 'Right, start reversing.'

She came back gingerly to his orchestration. It worked until she reached the bend and then, in her nervousness, she pressed too hard on the accelerator and the vehicle slewed. Nicholas jumped wildly out of the way and staggered about like a novice skater trying to keep his balance. Sarah's anguished face appeared from the window, now almost side on. 'I can't do it,' she cried. 'I'm terrified!'

'All right, all right,' he said advancing on the car like a drunk. 'I'd better drive. You get out.'

She looked at him pleadingly. 'Can't we just walk down to the main road, Nick? It can't be that far. We'll never get out like this.'

'It's too far,' he replied. 'Let me have a go.'

'It's so cold,' she moaned getting out. She tugged her bulky coat around her. 'I'm shivering.'

He hugged her briefly around her coat. 'Perhaps we needed this crisis,' he said half-mockingly. 'It will bring us closer together.'

'Oh, shut up,' she retorted. 'Get in the bloody car.'

He climbed behind the wheel and watched her in the mirrors as she stumbled like a woolly bear down the road. He thought she was going to tip over but she managed to right herself. Eventually she turned and called hoarsely: 'Come on.'

Nicholas managed to get the car out of its twist. The wheels whirled sending up waves of slush. He heard her shouted protest. The manoeuvre succeeded in straightening the vehicle and he called from the window: 'Okay . . . I'm coming back.'

With extreme care he reversed along the snow road with Sarah backing away, calling and gesticulating. He negotiated the next bend successfully and was beginning to feel elated when he noted that she had vanished from his view in the mirror. He stopped the car. 'Sarah! Sarah, where are you?' He opened the door and his feet slid away from him but he held onto the handle and arrested the fall. Bit by bit he stood up and shuffled toward the rear.

His wife was lying in the snow on her back, her legs kicking weakly, her face frozen, her eyes sharp with tears. 'I want to go home,' she moaned. 'I've *got* to go home.'

It was a woman, prosaically walking her small dog, who found them and took them to her house less than a hundred yards away. Her husband was watching a football match on television and hardly acknowledged their distressed arrival. He gave a half-attentive wave, almost one of dismissal, and returned to the thrills on the screen.

The woman called a taxi for them. It was quickly there and the driver easily drove them back to their car. Nicholas had failed to apply the handbrake and it had slipped sideways into the bank of snow at the roadside. The driver eyed it and muttered: '*Merde.*' They got gratefully into the taxi again and he drove them to St Jean de Valle, a further kilometre along the main road.

They had baths and, exhausted, got into the bed with half a bottle of brandy from the room refrigerator. They drank it between them and went to sleep.

By ten o'clock in the morning the car was retrieved and keeping to the main road they reached Nice by evening. It was raining miserably, the streets streaming, the lights along the Promenade des Anglais swinging morosely in the wind. They found a hotel and went to a restaurant where they had a mostly silent meal. When they were in bed again Sarah said: 'I meant it, Nicholas. I want to go home.'

'I'll put you on the plane tomorrow,' he said.

It rained all the way along the seafront, sluggish waves hitting the promenade. Clouds clogged the sky. At the airport Sarah said: 'I'll go on straight through. There's no point in you waiting around.' Their kiss was perfunctory.

'I'll be back by the end of the week,' Nicholas promised. 'I'll mooch around here today and start driving tomorrow.'

'Don't rush,' she said. 'Do what you have to do.'

'I will.'

She went towards the departure lounge. He waited for her to turn and wave but she did not. He returned to the car and spent the rest of the morning driving through the disconsolate downpour. He had no plan. Sometimes he picked up his tape recorder and muttered hopefully into it about the drizzle swallowing the sea, about the mountains made ragged by the clouds, about the soaked streets and the hunched and hurrying people. He drove up on to the Corniche. The town and the coast were invisible from there but he could see into the hills and beyond them the brooding snows of the mountains.

Moodily he thought that his aimlessness illustrated the aimlessness of his life. He knew that now Sarah had gone he would drive to Paris. He had to see Thérèse. Already he felt the guilt and the anticipation.

At lunchtime he returned to the hotel. He went to sleep in the afternoon and woke up in the dim room, the curtains heavy over the wet windows, once more wondering where he was. As if it had only been waiting for him to wake, the telephone rang.

It was Sarah. She was crying. 'I got home and found Deborah in bed with a boy,' she said starkly.

Nicholas was shocked. 'Deborah? It can't have . . . How do you mean?'

'She was in bed with a *boy*, a *youth*,' she sniffed. 'That kid I used to employ to help when you went off. I've had a terrible scene with her.'

'She's sixteen,' he said slowly, realising.

'She's our daughter,' amended his wife sharply. 'I don't care about anything else. They were in *our* bed.'

'Our bed?' he repeated aghast as though it mattered.

'Our bed. She said there was more room. Little hussy.'

Nicholas closed his eyes. 'Do you think it was . . . well, a one-off?'

'For a writer you don't choose your words very well at times. If you mean was it the first time, she says it was, but I don't believe her.'

'What are you . . . we . . . going to do?'

'What can we do? It's happened now.'

'God, she could be pregnant.'

'She says there's no chance of that. But I don't believe that either.' She began to cry again. 'Nick,' she said. 'I can't tell you how upset I am.'

He said: 'I'll come home. I'll start driving now. I'd fly but I can't just leave the car here.'

He was surprised to hear her say: 'Don't break your neck. It's not as though she's been raped or anything. She was a willing party.'

'What's the kid's name, the boy?'

'Dean Biddescombe,' she sniffed. 'He's unemployed.'

That night, when he was in bed, he telephoned her. 'How are you feeling now?'

'Pretty miserable,' she breathed. 'I've had a long talk with

282

her. She's terrified that I will tell you. I didn't let her know I already had.'

'I'll have to pretend I know nothing about it,' he said. 'After all it's not going to make it any better.' His voice descended to doubt. 'And she won't do it again. Not yet, anyway.'

'She's promised it will stop here and now. But I don't know. We ended up hugging each other.' She laughed wryly. 'I think Willie is wondering what he's got to do to get attention like this. He doesn't know of course. . . . At least I don't think so.'

'Willie somehow finds out about things. It wouldn't be so bad if it were him.'

'That's a typical man's thinking,' she said but with no emphasis. Then she said: 'At least it's taken our minds off our own problems.'

He paused, then said: 'Have we got problems?'

'If you haven't noticed then you're dimmer than I think you are,' she said evenly. 'You know we're just not getting on, Nick.'

'It's difficult to be compatible when you're lying on your back in the snow in the French Alps,' he said.

She laughed drily. 'You can say that again. Really, I should never have come with you. You're better on your own. What did you do today?'

'Drove around in the rain.' He shrugged as he spoke. 'Up on the Corniche, around the sodden streets. Every now and then I made some comment to the pocket recorder.'

'It's a funny sort of job, isn't it.'

'I suppose it is. Wandering around talking to yourself.'

'It wasn't just an excuse for running away again? This trip?'

'You were with me,' he pointed out.

'You need company even when you want to be by yourself. I don't understand you, Nick.'

'Nor me,' he admitted. 'But don't worry about us, Sarah, I know it's been difficult. There have been tremors.'

'We've both felt them,' she said.

'I know. We'll get through it. Don't worry.'

They said goodnight and he put the phone down. They were

like swimmers, he thought, trying to reach out to each other, but with strong currents pulling them apart. And there seemed nothing they could do about it. Except reassure each other with phonecalls and falsehoods.

Before leaving Nice in the morning he called her again. 'Deborah's gone to school,' she said. 'It seems odd that they can go to school *and* have sex, doesn't it.'

'It does to me,' he said heavily.

'I bet she's not the only one.'

'I doubt if she is.'

'It's just that she's *our* only one,' said Sarah. He could hear her sadness over the phone. 'Are you starting back today?'

'Yes. I'm just about to check out. I'll come straight up the *autoroute*.'

'Not the way Napoleon went?'

'No,' he smiled. 'He was no judge of a road. I'll spend a morning in Lyons, because I want to work something into the story. If it gets late I'll stay there.'

'Will you stop at Paris?'

'I might.' He tried to sound calm. 'On the other hand I may just come straight up the motorway. I'll see how it works. When I'm driving, particularly that sort of driving, I can work things out.'

'But it should be the weekend.'

'I'll be home Sunday, latest.'

'Good. We'll have roast beef.'

'I'll look forward to that. Love to Deborah and Willie. What's Willie been doing?'

'I don't know,' she said. Then, as if she had not meant to tell him: 'He keeps disappearing.'

'How do you mean, disappearing?'

'Well, he goes off for hours. You know he used to shut himself in his room and listen to his records. Not now, he doesn't. He just vanishes. He comes back but he doesn't say where he's been. I did actually ask him and he just said very grumpily: "With my friends." I hope he's not up to anything.'

'Well, at least he can't get pregnant.'

'I wish you wouldn't joke like that.'

'Sorry.'

'I know. But you shouldn't.'

'I said "sorry". I'll call you tonight from wherever I am.'

'All right.'

Moodily he replaced the telephone and grimaced at it. Why could things be misunderstood so easily; why did lies sound like the truth and the truth like lies?

He paid his bill and picked up his car from the hotel garage. The rain had stopped but Nice was chill, the sea glowering, the buildings dank. The fountains in the gardens by the Casino had been turned off. There was enough water without them. He was glad to get into the car and begin the journey to the north.

He was relieved that Sarah was not beside him. It was better to be by himself; he could be alone and he could think. He thought about the pointlessness of this journey. Had he learned anything? Had he even sketched in the backgrounds he had said he required? The tape in the pocket recorder had not run through one side.

He reached Lyons in the late afternoon and went to a hotel in the centre of the city. He walked around in the evening with no special plan or direction. A prostitute in split red shoes tried to solicit him as he returned to the hotel but he refused her politely, saying: '*Fatigué, très fatigué.*'

'*Moi aussi, je suis fatiguée,*' she told him and limped away along the damp pavement. After a few yards she took off her shoes and walked without them.

He called Sarah and told her where he was. 'Deborah's doing her homework,' she said. 'She's taken on a sort of saintly look.'

'I hope she's not thinking of being a nun,' he said. She did not pick him up on it, however, but merely said: 'I doubt it.'

'Is Willie there?' he asked. 'Maybe I ought to have a word with him.'

'He's only been in ten minutes. I've told him it's too late to

285

be out in the week. He says he's been with his friends. He's running a bath so I should leave it now. See what you think when you get back. I don't think it's anything terrible. He doesn't seem furtive. When he came in tonight he said that it was time we had a dog.'

They were both silent. 'Are you there, Nick?' she said eventually.

'Yes. Sorry. I was thinking about the dog.'

She said: 'It's another member of the family.'

'I'll talk to him about that too. It's a responsibility.'

'A commitment,' she said quietly.

When they had finished speaking he lay back on the hotel bed and thought about it. A dog was serious. A dog lasted.

He could see the early evening lights of Paris from miles to the south, like a halo in the deep January sky. As though he and the car were programmed to do so they unerringly found the Avenue Mozart. He parked only a few yards from the gallery; it was still open, he could see the shapes of people moving about against the lights. He went towards the door. Would she be there?

Inside was a group of people holding glasses of champagne and leaning towards paintings. There was a girl with an open book sitting behind a table near the entrance and she caught his eye as he went in. '*Monsieur?*'

'Ah . . . yes. E. Hemingway,' he said blandly. 'Friend of Joe Conrad.'

The young woman vaguely examined the list. 'No,' she said, it seemed to herself. She looked up seeking help. Her eyes were going around the room. She came back to him. 'From London?' she asked.

'Of course.'

She turned the book so that he could sign. His travelling clothes, his car jacket and open shirt, were unremarkable in the room of artists. A waiter appeared with a tray of champagne glasses and he took one with a quiet '*Merci.*'

He moved into the crowd, pretending to give some attention

to the paintings, but surveying the faces. He could not see her. At the end of the room was the man he recognised from his last visit, smooth in a dark suit, handing out catalogues from a gilded desk. Moving unhurriedly through the crowd Nicholas approached. '*Bonsoir, monsieur*,' he recited. The man handed him a catalogue. 'Is it possible that Mademoiselle Oiseau, Thérèse Oiseau, will be here this evening?'

'You came before to ask for her,' remembered the man. 'A little time ago.'

'That is correct. But I did not see her then.'

The man shrugged. 'It is possible,' he murmured looking around the assembly. 'She would have an invitation. Maybe she will come.' He pointed towards the desk by the door. 'Ask Marie,' he suggested. 'She has the list. Maybe she has been and gone away. I have not seen her.'

Nicholas returned to the desk and asked the receptionist to check the list. Then, as he repeated: 'Thérèse Oiseau', someone arrived outside the door and he looked up and saw it was her.

She was alone, engulfed in her brown coat. For a moment she stared through the glass at him. He tried to smile but it did not reach his face. She continued to gaze at him through the oblique glass, the door a little open on her gloved hand. Eventually, she pushed it. He took the handle and she stepped inside. Now she was smiling. 'You're crazy,' she said.

Thérèse could hardly believe that he had searched for her and had found her. 'It is like a detective,' she said shaking her head. They sat in the restaurant across the Avenue Mozart at the place where she had been when he was there with Sarah.

Now she was with him, sitting opposite, her composed face only two feet away, her smile deep. Eventually she asked: 'But *why* did you want to find me?'

'I wanted to see you,' he told her. 'You've been on my mind. I have been writing about you.'

Again she was astonished. 'About me? Writing? But what do you write of me?'

'In the story . . .'

'It is a story?' Her eyes were wide. 'I am in this story?'

'Yes. It's a book. A novel.'

She laughed outright. 'But this is crazy. There was only the time we met in that place in England and on the ferry and that was all. How could you write about me?'

'You are one of the two central characters,' he related seriously. 'You are called Cécile. The man is called Robert. . . .'

She put her face in her hands and regarded him studiously. 'And this Robert is you.'

'He is. He follows her to France.'

'Why does this Robert follow this Cécile . . . that is a terrible name . . . why would he follow her to France and try to find her?'

'Because he is in love with her. The book is called *Lost in France*.'

Her expression became serious. She looked into her wineglass. 'But,' she said slowly, 'this is not true. It is not life. It is romantic but . . . it is not true.' Her eyes came up and fixed him. 'What about your wife?' she said.

'I am back with her now,' he said. 'We have tried to mend the marriage. We have two children.'

'That is good reasons.'

'But it is very hard. For both of us.'

'Marriage is always hard,' she said.

'What about your marriage?'

She shrugged. 'It was too hard. It is finished.'

The waiter arrived and Nicholas paid for the wine. It was all she would have. He said: 'Sarah was here with me, in this restaurant.'

'Here?' she blew out her cheeks. 'When was this time?'

'Only last week. On Friday. You came in and sat at this table with another lady. . . .'

Again she was amazed. 'Your wife and you . . . in here when I was here with Claudine?'

'We sat at the table at the end of the window,' he said indicating over his shoulder. 'You came in and sat here.'

Thérèse looked as if it were all beyond her. 'But . . .' she could not finish. She spread her hands.

'It was Robert looking for Cécile,' he said.

'It is too difficult for me,' she said. 'How did you know?'

'Where to find you?' He told her how he had discovered the painting with the bird and had gone to the gallery and then to the restaurant. 'This is serious,' she said shaking her head. He reached over the table and put his hand on hers. 'I came to find you,' he said.

'With your wife!'

'We passed within inches of you as we left,' he said. 'I almost touched you.' His fingers remained touching hers.

'Now I remember,' she nodded slowly. 'I imagined there was something. I tried to see you from the window.'

'And now I am here.'

'Nicholas,' she said patiently. 'I cannot get all this into my mind. I have plans. . . . What about your marriage? You are trying to make it . . . mend it.'

'We have said for one year,' he told her. 'It was Sarah's idea. We would stay for a year. It's been difficult but we have tried to keep to it.'

'And when is the end of the year?'

'November,' he admitted lamely.

'This is January.'

'I know. But I had to see you.'

Suddenly she seemed to make up her mind. 'We must leave,' she said. 'You have made a long journey.'

They went out into the damp street. It was still only nine o'clock. 'I live close,' she said beginning to walk. She put her arm in his and they walked silently. His heart was racing. Her face was set, looking straight ahead. They turned down a quiet street with trees and benches and old houses. She stopped and they turned to face each other. 'I must tell you something,' she said.

'Tell me.'

'I have someone else,' she said. 'He is not here now, in Paris. He has gone to Des Saintes, in the French Caribbean. It is small

289

islands, near to Guadeloupe. He has a boat. I am going there tomorrow.'

Nicholas felt his mouth drop. 'I'm too late,' he said.

'It is so.' She looked concerned. 'I think that it is an unbelievable thing that you have found me. I cannot say how I feel about that.' She patted the front of his coat. 'I am only amazed and very flattened.'

'Flattered,' he suggested sadly.

'Yes. That is it. Flattered.'

'I'm the one who is flattened,' he added. He regarded her with diminishing hope. 'And you *must* go . . . tomorrow.'

'There is nothing for it. It is all fixed.'

'Do you love this man?'

'I think so. But I don't know. Love is a hard thing to say. My husband does not care for me now. I used to love him, I think. But now he is jealous of Henri, my friend. Crazy jealous, although he has not loved me himself for a year. He told me this.'

'I see. So there is no hope for me?'

She tapped him with her finger. 'I think you must go home,' she said. 'You have an arrangement, a bargain. It is a promise to your wife, to you also, and you must keep it. Even if I did not know Henri and I was not going away, I would say this. One marriage broken is enough.' She leaned forward and he thought she was going to kiss him. But then her eyes came up over his shoulder. 'Oh, non!' she cried.

Before he could move Nicholas felt a hand grasp the collar of his coat at the back. It tugged him around and confronted him with a stocky man wearing a Homburg. The man uttered one angry word, '*Salaud!*' before lifting his hat and butting his head into Nicholas's chest. Thérèse cried out: '*Non! Non! Albert!*' Nicholas felt the breath wheeze from his body. He crumpled at the waist and his assailant gave him a fierce push which sent him staggering back, landing him neatly into the middle of one of the iron seats ranged along the pavement.

His shoulders hit the back of the bench, knocking any further air from his lungs. The force of his fall caused the bench to tip and, as he emitted a hollow howl, it capsized depositing him in the street. Through the sudden mist that fell he heard Thérèse berating her husband as she stamped up the short garden path to the door of the house. With a final shout she slammed the door. Nicholas was still lying in the road. The man strolled over and peered down at him. 'You are English?' he asked.

Nicholas could only move his jaw.

'Thérèse says you are not the man,' he announced adding: '*Pardon, monsieur,*' before striding away.

Nicholas waited until his breath had returned. Using the seat as a prop he got to his feet. His back and chest ached. A window opened in the third floor of the house. Thérèse's silhouetted head appeared against the room light. 'Nicholas,' she called weakly. 'Are you all right?'

'I wouldn't say that,' he gasped. 'But I'm on my feet.'

'I am so sorry. He is mad. He thought you were Henri.'

'So I understand.' He was standing up without support now, but swaying around. He held on to the seat again.

'Nicholas,' she called again. 'I cannot come out. He will try to kill me one day. I do not want trouble like this.'

'No,' he called up shakily. 'I can understand.'

'Go to Sarah,' she called. Her voice was emotional. 'And I will go to Henri. That is the only way. Goodbye *chéri.*'

He had to lean against the overturned bench again. 'Goodbye Thérèse,' he waved haplessly.

She closed the window and he began to hobble away. Then, when he had gone some distance, he heard the window open again. Her voice came after him: 'Nicholas, you are wonderful! Goodbye!'

He waved with difficulty. 'I know,' he said almost to himself. 'Thanks.'

Thirteen

He had lost his dream and there were bruises on his chest and back; his journey home was painful. On the morning crossing from Calais to Dover a turbulent sea rose and a spiteful wind. He spent the voyage in the bar and the passenger lounge. Many of his fellow passengers were staring into paper bags. He drank two double brandies, ate a tough pork pie and then had another two brandies.

As he drove from the ferry and out to the Dover dock gates, a policeman leaning against a patrol car beckoned him down and gave him the breathalyser test. It was positive. 'Officer,' he pointed out. 'I've only driven fifty yards.'

'That's all it takes, sir,' mentioned the policeman. Nicholas regarded him pleadingly. 'It was a terrible crossing,' he said. He undulated his hand. 'I had to have something. A couple of brandies, that's all.' He tried a sporting offer: 'I'll find somewhere to lie down for a couple of hours.'

From behind them came a sharp, loud impact and the police car was violently shunted along the road. The officer looked aggrieved. He snap-closed his notebook and began to stalk back to where a bulky French estate car was nuzzling the rear of the patrol vehicle. He grimaced at Nicholas. 'Go and get your head down somewhere.'

Gladly Nicholas drove two hundred yards along the sea front and stopped at the Straits View Hotel, the first of a line of single-fronted stone houses. Outside it said: 'Vacancies.'

A downcast woman was in the front lobby dusting an artificial plant. 'I'd like a room, please,' prompted Nicholas.

'Thirty-five pounds,' she said unerringly. Swiftly she

deposited the key on the counter. 'Number three. Sea view.'

He gave her a credit card. 'There's a television in that room,' she confided. 'Eric Portman film this afternoon.'

He went upstairs and into a large, doleful room. A bay window overlooked the chaffing sea. He stripped to his shirt and climbed into the bleak bed. He could not sleep. After two hours he sat propped up and watched the Channel; it seemed as though it were in the room with him. Cold and un-comforting.

Eventually, still sitting, he lolled into an edgy sleep and was woken by the sweep of wind against the window. He lay startled, wondering once again where he was. Groaning he climbed from the bed. He stood at the bay in his shirt-tails looking over the long, wild, unchanging sea, then washed his face in the basin. On the dressing table was a plastic tea-making set. He made a cup of tea. It was three o'clock. Afterwards he went downstairs. There was a pay phone in the corridor and he rang Sarah. 'I'm in Dover,' he said heavily. 'I was breathalysed.'

'Oh no! Was it . . . ?'

'I managed to get out of it.'

'So where are you now?'

'In a hotel . . . of sorts. . . . I've had a sleep.'

'You get to the oddest places, Nick. Were you over the top?'

'Brandies on the ferry,' he said. 'It was choppy. Anyway I've slept it off. I'll get a sandwich or something and then I'll start back.'

'I need to talk to you.'

'Oh? What now?'

She would have preferred to postpone it but she said: 'It's Willie. He's been seen with a strange woman.'

'Oh Christ. Not *him* as well!'

'She's in her forties. He's been seen . . . *holding her hand*.'

'But, that's ridiculous.'

'I know it's ridiculous. But he has. I'm going to watch him today. When he comes out of school.'

'Are you sure she's not one of his teachers?'

'Can you imagine Willie holding hands with one of his teachers?'

When Deborah came to the door and threw her arms about him extravagantly he bellowed with pain. Sarah was halfway down the stairs.

'I'm a bit bruised.' He tried not to look at her.

'Not again,' said Sarah her eyes hardening.

He thought Deborah was going to cry. She went upstairs. Sarah gave him a hard stare. 'You haven't been playing Hi-ho have you?'

'No I haven't.' He attacked quickly. 'You don't seem to remember a few days ago when you were lying flat on your back in the snow and I fell over getting out of the car.'

'No. I don't remember you falling over.'

'You were poleaxed,' he pointed out. 'I fell down and then the car door caught me. I'm black and blue.'

She swallowed her doubt. 'You didn't say anything then. . . .'

'The bruises didn't come out until you'd gone off from Nice. I've been in agony. Now, what's all this about Willie?'

Sarah beckoned him into the kitchen. They sat down on two stools. She started to cry and he handed her a square of kitchen roll and then another, tugging them from the wooden peg. 'I've seen her,' she sniffed. 'With him. With our Willie.'

'But this is crazy,' he said. 'He's a schoolboy. And she's in her forties, you say.'

'At least,' she put in tartly. 'And very ordinary.' She put her face in her hands and sobbed: 'He was carrying her shopping!'

Deborah came to the door and called through it. 'Please don't quarrel,' she sobbed. 'Is it about me?'

'It's not about you,' her mother sniffed back. 'And we're not quarrelling.'

'Oh, all right.' The girl's voice softened. 'I'll go back upstairs.'

'I'll come and talk to you soon,' called Nicholas. 'There's nothing wrong.'

'She's not from around here,' said Sarah. 'I was in the car

and they were standing on the pavement, by the shops. By the time I'd found somewhere to park, they'd vanished.'

As if on cue Willie's voice came from the hall. He called up the stairs to his sister. 'Is she out?'

'We're in,' Nicholas said going to the kitchen door.

'Ah,' said Willie. 'So you are.' His attitude dropped when he saw they were confronting him. Nicholas turned a kitchen chair and leaned over the back.

Willie asked for a piece of cake. Sarah hesitated but cut a slice from a chocolate sponge.

Willie said: 'I'm hungry.'

'You would be,' responded his father. 'You have a busy life.'

Willie bit into the cake spreading chocolate around his mouth. His mother bit her lip. Nicholas said: 'What's been happening with you?'

'Nothing much,' answered Willie through the sponge and chocolate. 'Just the usual.'

'The usual being what? You've been out late. And who is the lady you've been helping with her shopping?' Nicholas tapped the back of the chair.

'Oh her,' said Willie as though relieved that they knew nothing more serious. 'That's Mrs Preece. I help her.'

'Where is she from?' interrupted Sarah. 'It gave me a bit of a shock just seeing you with her.'

'She lives over on Broadmead,' Willie said. 'On the council estate. I go over there and watch the television.'

'With her children?'

'They've not got any children. Mrs Preece has got bad eyes.'

Sarah shruggled for words. Nicholas said slowly: 'No children?'

'They've got a dog. He's called Lassie.'

Nicholas leaned closer: 'But tell us what you do over there.'

'I go over after school and she gives me chips or fish fingers or something and I just sit and watch the television with them and Lassie. And then I take Lassie for a walk and then I come home.'

'But why didn't you tell me about going there?' asked Sarah angrily.

'I didn't think you'd notice.'

Nicholas felt Sarah stiffen. 'I asked you where you had been when you came in late,' she protested. 'And all you said was that you'd been with friends. But I took it you meant friends from school.'

'What about Mr Preece?' enquired Nicholas.

'He sits and watches the telly too.'

'Yes, but who is he? What does he do for a living?'

'He's a policeman,' said Willie. 'Well, he was. He's just retired because some bloke hit him with a lump of wood and he gets dizzy spells.'

The parents sat defeated. He had worked his way through the chocolate cake and was glancing towards the rest. Sarah cut another piece. Nicholas said: 'But didn't it occur to you that it's a bit odd going around to somebody else's house and just sitting there?'

'They didn't mind,' said Willie. 'They like me going there. So does the dog.'

'I think we must meet Mr and Mrs Preece and have a talk,' said Sarah decisively. 'We obviously have a lot in common.'

Willie studied her over the cake as if he doubted it. 'I'll introduce you,' he offered.

The school was crowded; careers advisers were in rooms, with books and advisory leaflets and coloured wall charts. There was a disabled man from the army. One of the teachers gave guarded guidance on teaching. Parents, with pupils trudging behind them, wandered hopefully from classroom to classroom seeking the future from these who were past it.

In the assembly hall almost every row of chairs was filled for the talk by a careers officer. As Nicholas was about to sit he realised he was next to David Fawkes. He manoeuvred Willie into the chair so that the boy was separating them. Willie said: 'Hello, Mr Fawkes. Mum's over there.'

The careers officer progressed through his subject tediously. An hour drifted on. Nicholas knew he would have to face

Fawkes at the end. But almost before the reluctant applause for the address had expired, Sarah approached.

Fawkes got in first. 'Playing golf?' he asked Nicholas.

'I've more or less given up.'

'I've resigned the club captaincy,' said Fawkes casually. 'I'm going to Chicago next week. I'm joining an American firm.'

Sarah turned away and went back to Deborah. Fawkes said: 'It's initially for two years, but if I like it I'll probably stay.'

They had not shaken hands. Fawkes glanced in the direction of Sarah. 'Is everything working out?'

'We'll be all right.'

Sarah returned standing awkwardly in the aisle. She stepped forward and she and David kissed each other on each cheek. She said: 'Have a wonderful time in Chicago.'

'I'll try,' he said walking towards the exit.

Sarah turned to Nicholas: 'That Mr and Mrs Preece are here. Willie has gone to sit with them.'

People were moving from the hall. He followed Sarah down to the front. Willie was wedged between a man and a woman, both clad in anoraks. The woman wore thick glasses. The man was balding and overweight. Willie was talking to them, and although he saw his parents approach, he continued. The couple looked up with a touch of surprise as Sarah and Nicholas halted. Willie turned his attention to the empty platform. 'I'm this young man's mother,' announced Sarah carefully. She extended her hand almost formally towards Nicholas. 'And this is his dad.'

The two people were astonished. The woman leaned forward as if to focus them. The man's mouth opened. 'So you're back,' said Mrs Preece eventually. She glanced sideways at Willie who was scanning the distance. 'Lance didn't say.'

'Lance?' asked Sarah faintly. Nicholas covered his eyes. 'Who may I ask is Lance?'

'Me,' owned up Willie. 'I like the name Lance.'

'Isn't Lance his name?' enquired the former policeman.

'His name is William,' Nicholas told him. 'Willie for short.'

'Never liked Willie,' muttered Willie. He stood up. Nicholas retained him gently by the shoulder. 'I think you'll be needed here for a couple of minutes,' he suggested. Willie sat down.

'He's your son?' asked Mrs Preece, her voice fainter than Sarah's.

'Yes.'

Mr Preece seemed to be trying to phrase something. 'Don't have a spell, Ben,' warned his wife.

'You've come back from South Africa,' Mrs Preece faltered. 'Capetown.' Willie had a trapped expression.

'I've never been in South Africa,' Sarah said. She eyed Willie.

'And your husband . . . ,' the woman suggested timidly, 'has not been in Alabama?'

'Never,' confirmed Nicholas.

The woman took off her glasses and wiped them. 'I don't know what to say.'

Mr Preece looked searchingly at Willie. 'You made it all up?' he asked. 'The auntie who looked after you. The uncle in prison. Your dog you lost and never found.'

His wife added almost as in a reverie: 'Capetown, Alabama.'

'It was just something to say,' shrugged Willie. 'While the commercials were on.'

'I don't know whether to laugh or cry,' said Sarah. 'Just imagine it.'

'He did,' Nicholas reminded her. 'Vividly.'

She put her drink on the kitchen table next to his. Deborah and Willie had gone to bed. Sarah decided to cry but only slightly. Nicholas passed her a piece of kitchen roll. 'It's terrible,' she sniffed. 'The fact is he preferred their company to ours. He liked their council house better.'

'The dog was a big factor,' muttered Nicholas. 'We'll have to get him a dog.'

'Get *us* a dog,' she said like a reminder. 'A family dog.'

They regarded each other dejectedly. 'A dog might do us good,' he said. 'One that we can all look after.'

He shook his head and laughed mirthlessly. 'I still can't get over it. He just went off and adopted another family.'

'Parents,' she corrected. It was difficult for her to share even his solemn amusement. 'We should have heard warning bells clanging everywhere. What with him and Deborah.'

He finished his drink. 'I ought to do more with Willie,' he said. 'We ought to go to football matches or cricket.'

She shook her head. 'He'd hate that. So would you.'

She took the glasses and put them in the dishwasher. 'Let's go to bed,' she said.

They slept only until two. He woke and was lying with his thoughts. She said: 'Are you awake?' She knew he was.

'I think I'll go and look through the manuscript,' he said. 'It's on my mind. I want to see where the bits from France can slot in.'

'It's almost finished?'

'Another month and a bit.'

To his surprise she said: 'I'll get up and make some tea.'

They went downstairs in their dressing gowns. It was a windy night and the yew trees in the front garden agitated like people nervous in the dark. The kitchen was warm. He brought the manuscript down. Sarah made the tea and they sat silently with their mugs. After a while she said: 'Did you ever find her?'

'My heroine?'

'Cécile.'

'Did *Robert* find her,' he corrected. 'Well, yes and no. I decided that he would trace her but that by that time she had found someone else.'

'How sad.'

'That's the way the story goes.'

'Perhaps he finds her again some time.'

'I don't think so. Unless it's in another book.'

She was watching him carefully. 'Will you read me some of it?' she asked.

Nicholas looked up. 'Now?'

'Why not. We're not doing anything else.'

'All right,' he said still doubtfully. He shuffled through the pages. 'Let's see. This will do. It's the part where he first sees her. When she's walking along the path by the sea.' He paused and looked up.

She said: 'I'm listening.'

He took a sip from the mug. And he read: 'The land and the sea were almost one, grey against grey. There came a smattering of rain and the wind that came from the water pushed the reeds and grass aside and rifled through the end buildings of the village. The top of the church spire whistled, there were few birds; they must have been hiding. It was a desolate and lonely place and afternoon. He was convinced that nobody would be about who had no need to be. Except him. But, as he walked the path along the broken shore, he saw, in the distance, inland among the dark reeds, a dot of bright red, a moving figure, vivid against the twilight country. . . .'

He paused. 'Enter Cécile,' he said looking up.

'Go on. I can hardly wait to see her,' she said. He read for another ten minutes. Without saying anything she picked up the cups and took them to the dishwasher. He folded the manuscript.

'I've never read it aloud to anyone,' he said.

'It was beautiful,' she said in a strange voice, reluctant, sad, and with realisation. 'You must read some more for me.'

'Not now.'

'Not now,' she agreed. 'Let's go to bed. We'll both be tired in the morning.'

They put the lights out and went up to their bed. Sleep did not come easily for either. They lay a little apart each listening to the suburban wind and each with their separate, different and remote dreams.

By the middle of April the book was finished. He sat gazing at the words 'The End' and then picked up the telephone slowly, not taking his eyes from the final phrase, as if he feared it might vanish. He dialled Paul Garrett's number almost by touch. 'It's done,' he said. 'Every last rewritten word of it.'

'Wonderful. When can I see it?'

'Now, if you like.' Nicholas looked at his watch. It was eleven in the morning. 'I'd almost finished it last night. "The End" – they must be the loveliest words in the English language.'

Garrett laughed. 'For an author. Can you get here for lunch?'

'I'll come on the train.'

He went downstairs. Sarah was out, the house was empty. He wanted to tell someone. The new dog was in the kitchen, a mongrel which Willie had found and which gazed from its basket hardly able to credit its luck.

'Right, Jenkins,' Nicholas said to the dog. 'I've finished. It's done.' He waved the thick manuscript and the dog ducked. 'See that, mate. That's taken a lot of blood and sweat and tears and mucking about.'

The name Jenkins had been chosen by Willie in memory, he said, of a boy who had been at the school but had died in a motor-cycle accident. 'Good guy, Jenkins,' he had reminisced. 'Went off to be a stunt rider. Hit a rock in America. Splat.' He slapped his palms together.

The dog was an unkempt black-and-brown mongrel with a reprieved expression. Nicholas put down the manuscript and lifted him from the basket. 'You'd better take a trip to the garden before I go, son,' he suggested. 'God knows when anybody else will be back.'

Jenkins was suspicious. Believing he was going forever, he whimpered and struggled. Nicholas took him under the apple tree at the end of the short back lawn and waited reassuringly. The dog obliged then made a dash for the open kitchen door. 'At least somebody likes being at home,' said Nicholas.

He put on a suit. It was a spring day, windless and warm. He walked through the sunshine with an upright step, his manuscript in a plastic bag. The same threadbare employee who had been on duty on the night he ran away was at the station, kicking the ticket machines. 'Bastards,' he grunted.

Nicholas sat on the train his carrier bag smugly on his lap. It was the middle of the day and there were few passengers. At Baker Street he got out and took a taxi to Garrett's office. Soho was dusted with sunshine. 'Ah, *there* it is,' said the agent rising and holding out both hands. Nicholas took the manuscript from the bag and handed it across the Victorian desk. Garrett glanced at the first page and the last and, a little to the author's disappointment, put it in the desk drawer which he locked.

They went out and walked through the patterned streets to the restaurant. 'What do *you* think about it?' asked Garrett.

Nicholas said: 'I don't know. I've been with it for so long.'

'Will you miss her?'

He laughed wryly. 'Cécile? I'm sure I will.'

'She's very real,' pursued Garrett. 'Even in the first chapters I read.' He glanced sideways at his client.

'I went to try and find her in France,' Nicholas said. 'With Sarah.'

Garrett hummed. 'A novel within a novel.'

'I suppose it is. I was searching for a figment.'

'But all the time you were looking for a real person.' Garrett smiled privately. 'No wonder it reads as it does. From the heart.'

They went into the restaurant. The head waiter showed them to Garrett's normal table. They sat along the wall. 'I actually found her,' Nicholas mentioned. Garrett whistled soundlessly. 'You did? And you had Sarah with you?'

'I even saw her when Sarah was with me, in the café in Paris, but I couldn't speak to her. Then Sarah came home and I went back to Paris and found her again.'

'My God, it gets better. I didn't think she would stay merely a dream.'

Nicholas sighed. 'She is now. She doesn't want to know.'

Garrett began to laugh, his head against his thumbs. 'Don't tell me any more,' he asked. 'Let me read it.' He shook his head: '*Lost in France*.'

Nicholas said: 'So here I am without even an imaginary lover. Safely married. Her, me, the kids, the dog.'

'Ah, you have acquired the dog.'

'I know, I know. It's called Jenkins.'

'Cementing the marriage,' nodded Garrett. 'Perhaps I should get one. As a precaution.'

The waiter arrived with the main course. Nicholas waited until he had gone: 'You're . . .'

'Getting married,' finished Garrett. 'I met her at your Christmas party. Yvonne Pattison. She was the only sober person there. It's in June.'

'Why didn't you mention it before?' Nicholas smiled at him.

'I've scarcely had the opportunity,' pointed out Garrett 'With your dramas. And anyway I wanted you to finish your novel. One romance at a time is enough.' He grinned and confided. 'Things are happening for Sol too.'

'Sol's . . . don't tell me Sol's getting . . . ?'

'Married?' Garrett completed. 'Oh, no. Nothing dangerous like that. But he's going to have a bestseller like you.'

'He's actually written something?'

'Crime stories for children,' nodded Garrett. 'Animal crime stories. You know how he always had animals in his titles, giraffes, elephants. Well, he came up with the Detective Fox. I thought it had a certain sound to it and I stood over him while he wrote it. There's Puss the Cat Burglar, and a smash-and-grab raider who is a centipede. I got him a publisher and I got him an advance and, best of all, I even got him to work.'

When Sol opened the door he elevated his eyes for caution and led Nicholas upstairs. Loretta was draped across the sofa, posed to the tip of her cigarette. She blew smoke like a temporary screen. 'Hello,' she murmured when it had cleared. 'My name is Loretta. What is yours?'

Both men stood hushed. She spread another skein of smoke and behind it Nicholas contrived to compose himself. 'I am Nicholas Boulting,' he said feeling odd. 'We *have* met.'

'Perhaps.' She narrowed her eyes as though squeezing her memory. 'I meet so many people.' Sol headed towards the drinks, his standard retreat in trouble. 'Nothing for me, darling,' Loretta called sweetly. 'I must go.' She consulted a beautiful watch on her slim wrist and unwound herself from the sofa. 'Life calls,' she sighed.

Nicholas solemnly shook hands with her and she kissed Sol

luxuriously before he took her to the door. He returned a little shamefaced. 'Sorry she didn't recognise you,' he said. He continued pouring their scotch.

'You'd think she might.'

'You mean because you've shagged her up and down her staircase,' said Sol.

'Sort of,' returned Nicholas. He looked up. 'Anyway I'm glad you're looking after her.'

Sol shrugged. 'If I don't some other guy will. That's why she pretends not to know you. It's one of the games she plays. It's to kid herself that she's faithful to one lover at a time.'

They sat down and Sol said: 'Her husband came home from somewhere and went off to somewhere else. To find out why there are no penguins in the Arctic or something.' He looked up as though seeking justification. 'They have a celibate marriage. They keep ten thousand miles apart.'

Nicholas said: 'I hear you're a top author. Paul Garrett told me.'

'He's a slave-driver,' grumbled Sol good-naturedly. He leaned forward. 'Do you realise what it's done to me, success. It means I have to *work*. When I was a failure nobody expected anything. Now I don't have a choice, I've *got* to goddam write. It's terrible.'

Nicholas said: 'I think the Detective Fox is a great idea.'

'The Law with the Brush,' murmured Sol. 'I've gone animal crackers, Nick. I'm just writing a mystery called *Spot the Leopard*. Jeez, how did I get into this?' He looked bleak. 'Do you realise, I've had to stop cheating. God, it's just awful. Animals talk in my sleep.'

'You always had animals in your titles. And you're good with kids. My kids still talk about you.'

Sol's eyes lit. 'How are they? Glad to have their dad home I bet.'

'They don't say. But I think they're all right.'

The American's moustache drooped with seriousness. 'And is everything okay? You and your wife?'

Nicholas shrugged. 'As good as most married couples.'

'That don't sound very promising.'

'It's been difficult. But we're getting through it.'

Sol rose and went to the alcove below the stairs returning with the small framed picture. 'And how is the *oiseau*?' he asked. 'Any news of the little bird?'

'I saw her,' Nicholas told him. He took the painting and studied it reflectively. 'But she's flown.'

'Gone? Where?'

'To the Caribbean. But she's safely inside my novel.' He made the motion of closing a book. 'She won't escape from there.'

'You've finished it?'

'Done. I took it to Paul today. A hundred thousand words.'

The American groaned and shook his untidy head. The rim of grey hair was shaggy. 'Jeez, and I have nightmares over a few lines spoken by a fox,' he said. He looked up. 'What's it like?'

'I can't tell. It's like your wife committing adultery. You're the last to know.'

'Is your wife committing adultery?'

'No.'

Sol looked thoughtful. 'I'm glad you're okay,' he said sincerely. 'In every way. You'd never have finished a novel here. You'd have been writing about robber mice like me.'

BOOK THREE

Fourteen

The completion of *Lost in France* left him, illogically, and at once, bereft. He cleared his desk, ordered his books on the shelves and replied to waiting letters. Then he sat looking out of the window at the eternal triangle of the Boxley housetops and predictable trees filling from suburban spring to suburban summer.

'Now you've got nothing to do,' said Sarah bringing him his morning coffee.

'It's very odd,' he admitted. 'Like being bereaved.'

She returned from the door when she had almost left the room. 'Now your Cécile is gone forever,' she teased. 'You'll have to find another lady.' She reached the door again and added: 'Or do a sequel.'

Their life together had become steady in the extreme. They rarely argued, only skirmished, backing off quickly. Nicholas joined the Neighbourhood Watch and, from his eyrie, spied for criminals in the street. 'The Detective Fox,' he mused as he sat. 'The Law with the Brush.'

'Are we going on holiday in the summer?' Nicholas asked Sarah.

'August? I hadn't thought about it,' she said.

They avoided looking directly at each other. 'With the children,' he added swiftly.

'I suppose so.' She had doubts. 'We ought to have a holiday with them before it's too late.' She coloured. 'I mean before they go off. Before they leave school.'

'It could be our last chance,' he agreed. 'You choose. Where?'

'I don't mind. You choose.'

'Italy,' he said firmly. 'I think we ought to rent somewhere. One of those old farmhouses you read about.'

'But near the sea,' she said.

'Right,' he told her with a firm smile. 'A farm near the sea in Italy.'

'It sounds romantic,' she said.

'Perhaps it will be,' he answered.

Sometimes they went out to dinner with friends; always Sarah's friends for he found, to his surprise, that he suffered from the writer's curse of self-imposed insularity. His acquaintances had been on the golf course and he no longer played. One afternoon he had gone up to the club. The spring sun was enticing, the fairways new and green. There were strange faces in the clubhouse, one of which had succeeded to his lapsed membership, and those he recognised from the past did not appear to have noticed his absence.

He tried to become interested again. He hired some clubs, paid a green fee, bought six golf balls and walked out alone. From the first tee he struck his drive into a deep neighbouring lane, his next fell in thick gorse and he never saw the ball again. By the tenth hole he had only one of the balls left. He took no care. He unleashed an angry drive that flew longer than he had ever hit a ball before. It soared into the washy sky and went on and on, far out of sight, out of the course, out of orbit for all he knew. He glared down the verdant tongue of fairway. There was no one in sight. It was as empty as death. He slung the bag across his shoulder and muttering: 'Who cares?' strode back to the clubhouse. The secretary bought him a drink.

'It's a great shame you let your membership lapse,' Henry Manners said in his kindly Scots. 'You won things, didn't you. The Fothrington Cup with Guy Fawkes. He's away somewhere now.'

'Chicago,' provided Nicholas.

'So he is. It's a constantly changing scene, a golf club you know, although it always looks the same.' He paused reflectively. 'It's somewhere for men to go.'

'Like a monastery or a strip club,' added Sarah when he went home.

Jokes were their refuge. They sometimes shared them with a sort of desperation or handed them to each other like gifts. They provided a way out, an escape from reality or confrontation.

That summer Deborah was to leave school to begin a journalism course in London. Willie was only interested in leaving school. 'But you must have some idea what you want to do,' Sarah encouraged.

'You must have,' insisted Nicholas.

Willie, cornered by both, promised: 'It will come to me in a flash.' He tried reassurance. 'You won't have to keep me. I'll get the Social.'

Once his secret family had been exposed he lost interest in them. Mrs Preece had telephoned. She said the dog missed him. Jenkins, the new mongrel, occupied little of Willie's thoughts or time. The real Jenkins, it transpired, had never been a stunt rider, was not dead, and had never been to America.

'It must have been somebody else,' shrugged Willie. 'I'll try and remember who it was. Then we can change the dog's name.'

It was late. There were no lights in his attic apart from the illumination from the screen of his word processor. It glowed like an altar lamp. He was comfortable, safe, and isolated there and outside he could hear the dark summer rain among the trees. A few windows showed squares of light but most of Boxley was in bed. The telephone rang. It was a low purr and did not sound anywhere else in the house. He picked it up. It was Paul Garrett.

'Is it too late to call you?' he asked. 'Now I've done it.'

'Not at all. I'm sitting up working.'

'On what? I thought you'd finished. Don't try to gild the lily. It's too late for this lily anyway.' He paused thoughtfully. 'Don't tell me you're starting another book?'

'Well, tinkering with it. It's just an old idea.'

'Good. The more of them you have the better. Have you got a title?'

'You know I have.' Nicholas laughed quietly. 'It's the best part of it.'

'It's the shortest part. What's it called, or don't you want to tell me?'

'I don't mind. You'll remember it. I tried to write it before but I couldn't. It's called *Falling from Grace*.'

'Yes, I remember it. And *Dancing with Delilah*.' He sounded doubtful. 'Do you think it will work this time?'

'I can't write another like *Lost in France*,' said Nicholas.

'A one-off was it? You'll never find another Cécile?'

'Nor look for her.'

'Right. Well, it's a good thing you're in that frame of mind because I've been having telephone conversations with the film people, Herald International. They've just called me from Los Angeles. They think because they're awake everybody else in the world is. They now think they need an English scriptwriter for the movie of *Lying in Your Arms*. After all it's an entirely English book. And I've suggested to the man there, Joe Brewson, that you ought to do it.'

'Me? That's great,' responded Nicholas slowly. 'But I've never written a script, Paul.'

'It's only putting words on paper. You do that all right. It won't be a shooting script, so you don't have to worry about angles and movements and shots and all that. You do the scenes and the dialogue. They'll probably have to bring somebody else in afterwards but so what? They always do that anyway. Sometimes two or three or four writers. I don't see why you can't have a stab at your own story.'

'It would be terrific,' said Nicholas with a whispered enthusiasm. 'I'm in a sort of vacuum now. I just cut the lawn and take the dog for a walk. I really don't know what to do with myself. It's strange.'

'Post-novel depression,' said Garrett. 'Quite usual. This will fill the gap. Probably more than you'd bargained for. Anyway,

I've had a few conversations about this and I've persuaded Joe Brewson. He's on our side now. He has to get others at Herald International on our side as well. But we should hear in a couple of weeks.'

Nicholas went down the short flight of stairs to the landing. There was still a light on in their bedroom. Sarah was propped against the pillows with an open magazine. 'Midnight telephone calls, is it,' she said. 'I could hear you talking.'

'It was Paul. The film company want me to write a screenplay of *Lying in Your Arms*.'

Her interest was immediate. 'How much will that be worth?' she asked.

'I don't know yet. It's still got to be okayed by someone at Herald International in Hollywood.'

'So it's not certain.'

'Not yet. We should know in a couple of weeks.'

'It will keep you off the streets,' she said without edge. 'You've taken to mooning around.'

There was a sounding of the front-door chimes. They looked at each other and then at the bedside clock. 'Who can that be?' said Sarah.

'God knows. I'll go and see.'

Deborah, in her nightdress, was already on the landing. 'It's late, isn't it,' she grumbled.

'It certainly is.' He looked into the kitchen as he passed. Jenkins was curled and sleeping. He went to the front door and opened it.

Astonished he saw Willie standing there; Willie wearing a track suit and drenched from the rain. 'It's pissing down,' he said walking in.

'What the hell are you up to? We thought you were in bed.'

'I was. But I thought I'd get up and do a bit of training. I forgot my key. I'm in the four-forty on Friday.'

'Where? At Ascot?'

Willie had gone to the downstairs cloakroom and had begun to dry his hair with a towel. Sarah in her dressing gown came down the stairs. 'I wish you'd moderate your language,' she said to Willie who looked puzzled. 'What did I say?'

'Pissing down,' Nicholas told him.

'Oh, sorry. Pouring.' He looked at his parents in turn, challengingly. 'It's the school sports on Friday. I'm in the four-forty metres. You said you'd come. Remember?'

Neither did. 'I told you ages ago,' he said.

'All right,' said his mother. 'One of us will come. But why go out running in the rain at this time of night? I just don't understand you, Willie.'

'I know,' he said bluntly. 'Anyway I thought I do some training while there was nobody on the streets.' He regarded them just as bluntly. 'Don't forget. Friday. The four-forty at two thirty,' he said.

Garrett rang the following morning. 'Herald called me again, after I talked to you,' he said. 'But by then it *was* too late.'

'It would have been all right,' answered Nicholas. 'Willie was out training.'

'Oh. Well . . . this man Brewson called back. On Friday one of the vice-presidents of the corporation, a man called Bert Zaltpepper, which can't be made up, is arriving at Heathrow. He's on a visit of a few hours, literally flying in and out. He has a meeting in London and then he's off somewhere else. I've suggested that you meet him at the airport and talk about *Lying in Your Arms*. Give him some of your ideas for the script. So he knows *you*. So you're not just a name. That should clinch it, Brewson thinks. And Zaltpepper will be briefed.'

'That's good news, Paul. Good old you.'

'His plane gets in at eleven from Los Angeles. I'll call you later with all the details. Make sure you're there. Take *Lying in Your Arms* so he'll recognise you. Hold it up so he can see it.'

He had taken the call in the kitchen. Sarah was making coffee. 'That's Friday,' she said. 'That's Willie's sports day. I can't go. I've promised to take my parents to lunch. It's their anniversary, remember. I can't change that now. You know how disapppointed they get.'

'The sports are at two thirty,' he said.

'Mum and Dad eat slowly, you know that. And they like to chat. I can't change anything.'

Nicholas sighed. 'It will be all right. I wouldn't want your mother to do without second helpings.'

'Nicholas.' Her voice was a sigh.

'All right. I said I would be there at the sports and I will. This man is arriving at eleven so I should have ample time to be there at two thirty. I won't let Willie down. But Mr Zaltpepper is important.'

'He certainly sounds it,' she sniffed.

He drove to Heathrow and put the car in the short-term car park. Inside the terminal he checked the Arrivals indicator. The flight was an hour late. He glared at the board as though he could make it change. It did not. At the Enquiries desk the man shrugged: 'That's what it says. That's what it means.' He detected the agitation. 'In fact it may be even later. Traffic is heavy this morning.'

The plane landed at twelve thirty and it was one o'clock when the passengers began to emerge from the Arrivals door. He stood attempting to pick out a suitable face for Zaltpepper. He held *Lying in Your Arms* flat across his chest. He checked it was the right way up. Then he heard the name being called: 'Mr Zaltpepper, Mr Zaltpepper.' One of the line of waiting drivers, holding a board, was attracting the attention of a man in a sagging suit, a man with a surly expression behind ugly glasses. Nicholas went, almost crept, towards him.

A capped chauffeur took the American's suitcase. Mr Zaltpepper was annoyed. 'Fucken' airline,' he said. The driver said: 'Yes sir.' Nicholas hung back but as the pair headed for the exit he moved quickly. 'Mr Zaltpepper,' he announced. 'I'm Nicholas Boulting.'

'So what?' said the man creasing his face. The chauffeur frowned protectively.

Nicholas said: 'It was arranged that I meet you here. Mr Brewson fixed it. I'm the author of . . .'

'Brewson,' muttered Bert Zaltpepper. 'That fucken' . . . He fixed what?'

'With my agent, Paul Garrett . . .'

The American impatiently checked his watch. The driver was hovering at the door. 'Get in the car,' decided Zaltpepper without enthusiasm. 'We'll have to talk in the car.'

Nicholas swiftly thought of three things: his car in the short-term car park, the Boxley School sports day, and the script of *Lying in Your Arms*. 'Yes, of course,' he heard himself saying. 'I'm with you.'

He was motioned into the seat beside the driver. 'I've got to have some room,' said Zaltpepper from the back. 'There was no fucken' room in that plane.'

They began to drive. Zaltpepper fidgeted and breathed laboriously. He took his time. They made for London along the motorway. Traffic was light. 'Okay,' said Zaltpepper eventually. 'So I'm in London. I've got four hours to get through this fucken' meeting and back to that fucken' airport and on another fucken' plane.'

'About the script?' said Nicholas.

'I don't want to talk about it. But I have to.'

'Thanks. I'd appreciate it.' He turned awkwardly to face the American, but Zaltpepper waved him back again.

'Sure. It's got to be a big script, you know what I mean,' he said. 'It's got to have feeling, love, lots of love interest. Maybe even a fucken' dog.'

'A dog?'

'Dogs are box office. Big dogs are big. The bigger the fucken' better. If you can get this script right, mister, there's nothing going to stop us going ahead this year. That's if you can *get* it right, and I never knew one fucken' writer do that in my whole fucken' life.' He continued with the monologue. 'We need to get to locations,' the American confirmed swiftly. 'And we need to change the main location. It's no good where it is. Fucken' Burma is not box office. Fucken' India maybe . . . but maybe not now. Mexico would be my guess. Until some other mother-fucker has some clever fucken' ideas. . . .'

'It's not set in Burma,' pointed out Nicholas desperately turning again to face the American.

'Burma,' insisted Zaltpepper. 'I read the fucken' thing myself. Fucken' Burma. Who ever heard of Burma? I thought it was Bermuda. Burma is no go. We could get it made in Mexico for less, providing the fucken' Mexes don't have a fucken' revolution and fuck it up.'

'My book, the script I came to see you about,' Nicholas gulped, still looking at Zaltpepper, 'is set in London.'

'Shit!' he said for a change. He stared at Nicholas as though seeing him for the first time. 'What's it fucken' called?'

'It's called *Lying in Your Arms*,' muttered Nicholas. 'You've bought the film rights.'

'We have?' grunted Zaltpepper. 'Well I've never fucken' heard of it.'

The driver grinned nastily as he let Nicholas off at Hyde Park Corner. No one said goodbye. The car roared off as if anxious to put distance between them. Nicholas thrust two enraged fingers up at the receding Bentley. It was ten minutes to two. He almost choked. Sod it!

He waved down a taxi. 'I want to go to Boxley,' he said.

'Where's Boxley when it's 'ome?'

'Hertfordshire.'

'Not with me, mate. Just going off duty. South of the river.'

He halted three cabs before one took him: 'How long will it take?'

'Can't tell. Middle of the day. Maybe an hour.'

He climbed into the back and sat cursing. Mr Fucken' Zaltpepper. There was a traffic build-up in the West End, through the Baker Street area, in Finchley Road, and an accident on the Hendon Way had halted all three lanes. The taxi-man had a slanging session with a truck driver. Nicholas fumed. At last, they were on clearer roads; the London cab panted up Boxley High Street and stopped at the school gates. It was three o'clock. As he paid the forty-pound fare he could see the crowd of parents.

Nicholas hurried through the school gates and skirted the buildings to the fringe of the playing field. To his overwhelming relief he saw Willie was on the track. He charged forward calling encouragement.

'He won't come off,' said a man who stopped him. 'He just keeps running.'

Nicholas looked again towards the track. No other competitors were in view. 'He's been going around now by himself for twenty minutes,' said the man. 'When we tried to get him off he turned violent, very nasty, so the headmaster said to leave him. We're waiting to start the hurdles.'

Nicholas ran on to the track after his son. 'Willie! Willie!' He called. Spectators laughed and pointed to the man in the suit, tie flying. He panted. The loping boy did not hear. Not for two hundred yards. The distance was increasing. Breathless, Nicholas halted in the middle of the track; the onlookers cheered. Someone shouted 'Shout!' Nicholas cupped his hands. He could scarcely breathe in. 'Willie!'

The boy slowed and stopped, sinking to his knees on the grass. His father staggered towards him. Willie was crying. Nicholas, filled with shame, reached him, stood and caught hold of his hands. Willie's face looked up at him. 'Where've you been?' he sobbed. 'I'm knackered.'

He waited until Sarah was out before making the call. It was picked up at once. 'Hello, Sol.'

'What's been keeping you?'

'Sorry. I did ring a couple of times but you weren't there. Loretta keeping you busy?'

'Not for one moment momentarily,' replied Sol regretfully. 'She's blown me out. About three weeks ago. Haven't heard a thing.'

'Oh, she'll come around, she always does.'

'Not this time.'

'Well, that answers my question actually. I was wondering if you were taking her to Paul's wedding.'

'No chance,' said Sol. He realised. 'Oh, I get it. You'll be there with Sarah. And you don't want any . . .'

'Exactly.'

'She didn't recognise you last time,' pointed out Sol. 'When you were right here in the apartment. After all you'd been through with her.'

'You know what she's like. Next time may be different.'

'Don't worry, pal. She won't be there. I don't think she'll ever be there or anywhere else I am, not from now. It's a shame. I enjoyed her company. It was a neat arrangement too, her husband out in the boondocks, showing his wedding photographs to the natives around the camp-fire.'

'What went wrong?'

'One of those crazy things, Nick. We were going to Rome. She has friends in Rome and she wanted to show me off to them, I guess. But we drank a load of champagne before even getting to the airport and then more at the airport. I got smashed and I went to the men's room and somehow I pissed on my boarding card. And they wouldn't accept it at the gate. Loretta was hysterical. We missed the plane. Big confrontation. No Loretta. Lonely me. She won't be at the wedding.'

'It's a relief.'

'I hear your novel is something.'

'I'll tell you when it's published. The critics didn't bother to review the last one. This time they'll be lying in wait. How is Foxy the Detective?'

'Kids love him. And grown-ups.' He sounded droll. 'But I'm running out of mice.'

Paul and Yvonne were married in Chelsea on a June day when even the Thames shone. The reception was on a river steamer which sailed from Westminster to Greenwich and returned in the evening; there was a lady harpist, and a band which played on the stern. Nicholas, standing near the rail as the vessel sailed, saw a figure in pink getting out of a taxi, fiercely holding her hat, and squealing for them to wait. The captain had to reverse the engines and put down the gangplank so she could make an extravagant boarding. 'Darling!' she howled. Sarah was standing near and Nicholas turned away quickly towards the far bank of the river.

Loretta made for Sol looking like a Mississippi gambler in his grey morning dress. They threw their arms about each other and kissed exuberantly. 'You nearly left me behind.' She pointed a long pink finger but her smile was overwhelming. She picked his silver top hat from his hand and skimmed it over the side of the boat like a Frisbee. 'Whoever is that?' asked Sarah.

Loretta fussed over the bride and groom apologising for missing the ceremony. 'I simply didn't realise that Caxton Hall had been closed for so many years.'

'She's Sol's girlfriend,' Nicholas told his wife in a low voice. 'His responsibility.'

'Why are you whispering?'

'I'm not,' he said raising his tone. 'It's just that she's pretty outrageous. You never know what she's going to say next. Or do.'

'Do you know her well? You've never mentioned her to me.'

'Oh, I don't know her much really. Sol's been keeping her company for some time. She's just one of those crazy women.'

'DARLING!' howled Loretta focusing him for the first time. 'My darling, WIDDERSHINS.'

Nicholas felt Sarah stiffen although she was a yard away. Sol tried to head off Loretta by frantically pointing out the view of St Paul's. She got to Nicholas. Sol stood back.

'Widdershins,' repeated Loretta longingly. She pressed against him for a kiss.

'What,' asked Sarah succinctly, 'is widdershins?'

'Anti-clockwise,' Loretta informed her sideways as if she were an interloper. 'Or against the seasons and the stars.' Again she kissed Nicholas deeply.

'Loretta,' he muttered easing himself away. 'This is Sarah, my wife.' The words sounded like a drum beat. 'Sarah, this is Loretta, Sol's ladyfriend.'

'Not since he urinated on his boarding pass,' amended Loretta. She glanced at Sol. His moustache drooped. Loretta

320

held up her champagne and eyed the sun through it. It made a golden shape on her face. 'Although a few more glasses of this and I may change my mind.'

Sol put his arm around her and led her to the rail. 'What an interesting woman,' murmured Sarah.

'She's crazy,' repeated Nicholas. 'There's no knowing what she will do next.'

'Apparently not,' agreed Sarah slowly raising her glass. She also held it up to the sun as Loretta had done. Her eyes came around to her husband. 'Widdershins.'

The band on the stern began to play, the music drifting over the evening water. The boat anchored off Greenwich as the satin of a fine London evening settled around it. The buildings on the shore became as soft to the eye as in an old painting. Eventually the vessel turned and began her up-river journey. Dancing began on the deck.

Sarah was being shown the navigation instruments by a young and eager ship's officer. Loretta nudged Nicholas. 'Darling Widdershins,' she said. 'Let's dance.'

With a glance at the bridge where he could see Sarah's hat, Nicholas extended nervous arms and she folded herself genially into them. 'I wish you wouldn't call me Widdershins,' he pleaded. 'Not in front of Sarah.'

'But it's my pet name for you.'

'I don't want my wife to know you *have* a pet name for me,' he argued. 'I'm surprised you remembered.' Her eyes were growing mischievous. 'Oh, come on Loretta,' he pleaded. 'Be a sport. I'm trying to keep my marriage together. It's all right for you when your husband is miles away.'

Her expression changed. 'How do you know he's miles away?' she asked.

'Well, he usually is. I'm not saying it's not a good arrangement. Some of us would love it. But he is, isn't he.'

'Miles away?' she repeated.

'He's in Africa or up the Orinoco or finding out about penguins,' persisted Nicholas. 'And I'm not saying it's not useful work. . . .'

She laughed drily. 'Nicholas,' she said her eyes now sober and hard. 'My husband is seventy-six years old. He lives permanently at his club, the Adventurers', only half a mile from the house which he rents for me.'

Nicholas studied her. 'Then all that telephoning from Africa . . .'

'It's fantasy,' she completed solemnly. 'For him and for me. I have lunch with him once a week on Wednesdays. He's a dear, generous man, and all he has of me is a photograph taken on our wedding day. He's quite happy and so am I.' She glanced towards the bridge. Sarah was descending the steps. 'And here comes your wife, the lovely Mrs Widdershins.'

Fifteen

The house in Italy was south of Naples overlooking Porto Lovino. Its name, La Serena, was hung in sun-faded tiles on the stones of a half-fallen boundary wall. Outside it was white and pink, the plaster falling away; the terracotta terrace, around three sides, afforded an ancient coolness. There was a balcony projecting from the main bedroom and above that a roof terrace. On the ceilings of the main rooms were old, slowly clanking fans.

The balcony, its rails of patterned ironwork, gave a long view of the red corrugated land, sloping to a stripe of hard blue sea. There was a stone-strewn path leading down through olive trees to the rough beach, a place of lizards.

There, in August, the sea was as unmoving as the sky. The heat hung over everything. Every afternoon Sarah was prostrate, sprawled on the bed with the fan shuddering, thinking wistfully of the summer coolness of Boxley.

The land surrounding the house was dry and brittle, the haunt of noisy insects. Anyone approaching in a vehicle could be seen far off by clouds of parched dust. On their third day they saw a donkey and cart approaching. They watched it near. It arrived carrying a thin woman in her fifties, her features sharp and without colour under a wide canvas hat, and wearing an old flowered dress. Her name was Harriet Thurston.

'We're across the hill,' she said in a squeaky upper-class voice. 'We've taken the house every summer for twenty years now. It would be very nice if you could come across for a little food and some wine. Perhaps when you are all settled.

Towards the end of the week, shall we say.' Deborah and Willie were standing watching on the terrace. 'We have two young girls, our nieces. The children could play together.'

They sat in the long afternoon shade of the terrace. The sky was hot, the landscape transfixed by August. They were stirred by the bumping of a band, the sound coming from the village by the sea. The jolly music continued while the sun eased into the evening; when the air had cooled the family walked together down the sloping path towards the shore and then along the beach to the little port.

The stone square was crowded with people in shiny best clothes, sitting at the tables of the cafés that spilled out on to the cobbles, gathered in eagerly chattering and laughing groups, the old people wagging their fingers while recalling something from long ago or telling again an ancient joke; others dancing to the pumping band below the illuminated trees.

At the centre of the scene a bride and groom sat with awkward formality; their families surrounding them as if reluctant to let them go. They watched the dancing and nodded at the laughter but remained as though required to be spectators. They waved with shy smiles, acknowledging the waves and wishes and jokes of the dancers and others in the crowd. Old people came to give them advice. The bride had a composed, pale face with deep eyes and black hair. Her veil hung over it like a cloud, and her dress was an almost ghostly white in the evening light. Her groom looked ungainly in his rigid suit, his face dark and thick, his eyes gentle but uncertain. Each had a small glass of wine on the table before them.

The feast was over by then. Savagely gossiping women shook tablecloths and carried clattering crockery in the background. The band played on heavily but heroically, the cheeks of the brass players red, their eyes bulging; the banging of the drum raising half-hearted flights of pigeons from the roofs.

Sarah was wearing a long red peasant dress. Nicholas turned her in a waltz. They had been eagerly invited to join the party and the Italian people smiled and nodded approval as they danced among the guests. Deborah and Willie watched bemused. 'Fancy dancing like that,' observed Willie scornfully. 'Just going round and round.'

'You jump up and down,' pointed out Deborah.

'So do you,' responded her brother. 'Not always to the music either.'

Nicholas felt Sarah's body warm through the thin dress. 'Remember our wedding, Nick?' she asked.

'Like yesterday.' He smiled close to her face and she returned the smile seriously. They put their cheeks together as they waltzed to the unflagging music; her earring bounced against his nose.

'All right,' she said challengingly. 'What was the name of the church?'

'Ah now . . . yes, it was St James'. The Less. Or was it the Great? One of them. Wembley High Road.'

'Very good. I'm surprised.'

'Ask me another.'

He felt her grin form against his cheek. 'You ask me.'

'Right. What was the name of the vicar?'

'The Reverend Bunny,' she laughed. 'I'm not likely to forget that.'

The band stopped abruptly as though the musicians had all run out of breath at the same moment, and everyone began to clap. Nicholas and Sarah stood apart. Then, gathering itself, the waltz began again. 'May I?' he asked her with a small bow.

'Of course.' They began to revolve again. From the corner of her eye Sarah saw a young man approach Deborah and invite her to dance. Deborah rose, blushing, while Willie grinned. Nicholas followed Sarah's look as he turned her in the waltz. 'I hope she can *do* a waltz,' said Nicholas.

Sarah said: 'She'll give it her best shot.'

'Do you remember the terrible band at our reception?' said Nicholas. 'The pianist couldn't play at all. He just came to get tanked up.'

'That's when he started to play,' she laughed. 'And what about that awful best man of yours. What was his name . . .?'

'Percival Powell-Pont,' recalled Nicholas. 'You mean his jokes.'

'About the poor Reverend Bunny and all the rabbits,' she giggled. 'I wonder what's happened to Percival Powell-Pont.'

'Went to Australia,' he said. 'Never heard of since. Where is the Reverend Bunny now?'

'It was a long time ago,' she said quietly. 'It goes so quickly.'

'Twenty years,' he said. He kissed her cheek and she kissed his. 'Take a look at Deborah,' she whispered. He searched the whirling dancers and saw his daughter at the edge of the floor, deliberately and with difficulty, making the steps of the waltz. The youth held her waist at a distance and she held his. 'She's learning,' observed Sarah. From behind them they heard Willie sucking demonstratively through a straw projecting from a Coca-Cola bottle. They both laughed.

Towards the end of the evening Willie won a round cheese in a skittles game and they bore it back triumphantly. From the sea, and as though it had been awaiting them, rose a ripe moon. It climbed the sky theatrically, flooding the stony countryside spread before them. The house stood white and clear in the shining night.

They all held hands and began to sing together. They sang: 'By the light of the silvery moon' and tried to dance to it. Willie dropped the cheese and it rolled away from them down the sloping path, bouncing and running. Shouting, Deborah and Willie both pursued it and caught up with it at the foot of the hill. 'Not even a dent on it,' said Nicholas examining the covering rind. He put his arm around Sarah's waist, feeling her skin through the cotton dress. Her arm went around him too and, happily, they all walked towards the house in the light of the widespread moon.

Harriet's husband, Grenville Thurston, leaned back against his wooden seat below the evening trees. Supper was finished. At a distance an Italian youth was chopping logs noisily and Grenville called to him to stop. 'One has to get the boiler going if one wants a hot bath,' explained Harriet. Grenville wore a coloured blazer, the stripes faded like those of an old canvas canopy, a stiff collar and a food-stained old school tie, clumsy grey flannels and open-toed sandals.

'The parents of Catriona and Philomena,' he intoned, 'that's my brother and his wife, have unfortunately split up. The girls went to live with their grandparents in Hereford.'

'But then *they* split up,' said Harriet in her squeak. 'The grandparents.'

'A final, desperate, leap in the dark,' sniffed Grenville. 'God knows what they hope to find at their time of life.'

'Everyone hopes to improve on their lot, I suppose,' reflected Harriet. 'The grass is greener attitude. Annie, that's the girls' mother, said she had found a man with huge testicles.'

'Some people don't *have* a reason for splitting up,' ventured Nicholas.

'They try to find one,' added Sarah.

The two girls came from the stone house with a bemused Deborah and Willie walking with them. Willie spread his hands towards his parents. Deborah shrugged. Catriona and Philomena were wearing nightdresses. They had bare feet and they danced diaphanously to the pop music from a radio which Philomena held. 'They're free spirits. They won't wear anything under their nighties,' said Harriet awkwardly. 'It's supposed to let the air circulate.'

'It ventilates,' observed Grenville. 'It's good for them.'

'We're going down to the port,' announced Willie. Deborah glanced at her parents. 'Is that all right?'

'The girls can go if they get properly attired,' decided Harriet. 'They cannot go like that. It would be tempting fate.'

'Not to mention the local chaps,' put in Grenville.

The girls shrieked and began dancing unashamedly, their young bodies sliding against the thin nightdresses, their breasts protruding. 'Bring on the local chaps!' shouted Philomena.

'They don't mean it,' said Harriet unhappily. 'They're just being brazen.'

*

Porto Lovino was lit and lively. It was only a sloping walk and they could see the figuration of lights around the square as they descended. Music floated up in the close night. The young people went first, hurrying down the rough road. Grenville and Harriet had decided not to accompany them because it was Grenville's night for a hot bath; the Italian youth had lit the boiler and poked the hot-water system of the dilapidated house. Harriet wanted to bake bread. Catriona and Philomena, she said with no confidence, could be trusted to make their way back before midnight. 'I have issued serious threats if they disobey,' said Harriet vaguely as though trying to remember what they were.

Nicholas and Sarah reached the cobbled centre. A fragile breeze wandered from the harbour sidling among the buildings and brushing the low, round-topped trees in the square. There were cafés and restaurants with their striped tables outside under the trees and the balconies. Music came from somewhere and there were people moving in the lit rooms above so that, viewed from across the street, it appeared like a frieze.

They had a glass of wine each. As a refuge from silence they began to talk about the children. They could see Deborah in her white cotton dress sitting with a group of young people around a table at one corner of the square. Willie was with the two young girls on a bench, their bare brown legs swinging below it. An old Italian woman sat on the other end of the bench looking into space.

'I hope our Willie is not going to be trouble,' said Sarah, 'now he's getting older.'

'He may change,' said Nicholas without much hope. 'Perhaps he'll just grow out of it.'

Sarah sipped her wine. 'I'm frightened about him. He's like a time bomb,' she said in a low voice. It was as if she thought it was time she made the point. Nicholas regarded her with concern. 'I can just hear him ticking away, Nick,' she went on still looking towards their son. 'You just see. I hope he doesn't disrupt people's lives.'

'He told me he fancies being an actor,' Nicholas said defensively.

'Perhaps he should. He could work out some of his fantasies then.'

'As long as he doesn't just drift,' she said. 'That's what I'm afraid of.'

'What about Deborah?' he said.

'She'll be all right, I think,' responded Sarah carefully. 'She's someone who cares; I'm afraid our Willie isn't.'

'What do you suggest we do about him?'

'I've tried to think,' she said seriously. 'I've watched him and I've wondered. But what Willie wants to do, he'll do. It's going to be difficult to *train* him for anything.'

They had another glass of wine and then went for a walk alongside the harbour, the boats lolling in the dark warmth, the music from the square drifting over the rooftops. 'Do you want to eat something?' he suggested.

'Yes, I do. Harriet's "a little food" was really a *little* food. They're an odd pair, aren't they. They're not like anybody we know.'

'I certainly can't see them in Boxley,' he said.

They went towards a restaurant on the harbourside. It was almost deserted. 'Let's go back to the square,' said Sarah.

They rounded the corner and went once more into the activity. The lights on the round-headed trees made the leaves glow bright green. There were more people now and as they sat at a table a band struck up at the distant end. They did not talk.

Twice while they ate spaghetti Willie came to them to ask for money for pizzas and drinks. Deborah arrived, her face warm and excited, with a handsome, olive youth. Sarah was sure it was the boy who had invited her to dance at the wedding. 'Can I go to the disco?' she asked. 'There's a crowd of us.'

'Another night,' said her mother. The girl's expression dropped.

'It's midnight now,' said Sarah. 'We'll be walking back soon. You can go another night and your father can pick you up.'

The girl turned wordlessly and said something to the youth. They walked away through the people. 'We're going shortly,' repeated Sarah calling after her. Deborah half-turned and waved in a dismissive way. 'Hussy,' said Sarah.

'Let her go to the disco,' suggested Nicholas. 'She'll be all right.'

Her eyes were unexpectedly bright. 'I said she can go another night. And you can arrange to pick her up.' She took her mirror from her handbag and studied her make-up. 'Nick, did you see that boy? He's not a kid. She *is*. As far as I'm concerned she is anyway. She's sixteen, we don't know that boy, she didn't even introduce us.'

'Probably didn't know his name,' shrugged Nicholas. 'Young people don't introduce themselves.'

'Exactly. I want to know what she's doing and who she is with. We don't know any of that crowd. They may be perfectly all right but as far as I am concerned she's still a child.'

She stood decisively. He paid the bill and they walked through the crowded square. Willie, Catriona and Philomena were surprisingly obedient. They only found Deborah after a search. She was sitting in a café in a small garden with half a dozen others. 'We're going now,' Sarah told her. The others turned their faces toward the girl as if they expected her to argue.

Deborah seemed about to say something but did not. Instead she regarded her mother and slowly stood. The others remained silent. The boy she had been with looked embarrassed and lifted his glass of Coca-Cola. Deborah turned and mumbled: 'Goodnight. *Buona notte.*'

In her white dress she walked apart from them through the square with Willie and the two girls half-running ahead. Catriona and Philomena both kissed him laughingly at their gateway and they ran up the path to the house. 'They're going to be actresses,' announced Willie oblivious to his own family's silence. 'And when I'm an actor we're going to get a show together.'

They reached the house and Willie had some lemonade and went to bed. Deborah had gone to her room immediately. Sarah and Nicholas sat on the terrace. They heard Deborah's door open and she went along the wooden landing to the bathroom. When she returned Sarah called: 'Goodnight, Deborah.'

There was no response.

'I said goodnight, Deborah,' insisted Sarah loudly.

They heard the girl slam her door. 'Right,' said Sarah getting a little unsteadily from her chair. He rose too and touched her arm.

'Sarah,' he said firmly.

Above them the girl's door opened. She came out onto the railed landing in her blue nightdress, her hair long, her cheeks wet.

'Goodnight Mother,' she replied her voice shaking. 'And thanks for nothing.'

Sarah started forward but Nicholas caught her arm more firmly and this time she did not shake him off.

'You,' sobbed Deborah. Her neat fists pounded the banister. 'You two! You're great for telling people what to do. You can't even put up with each other's company. You want everybody to be miserable like you are. You only brought us here with you because you can't bloody bear to be by yourselves!' Willie, brown-bodied, appeared from his room wearing a pair of underpants and stood listening with surprise, softening to pleasure.

His eyes went from her to his parents like a spectator at a tennis match on two levels.

Sarah was rooted now. 'Thank you, Deborah,' she said. 'I'm not trusting you, because I haven't forgotten the last time.'

Horrified, the girl's eyes went from her mother to her father. 'You told him,' she accused. 'You promised, you promised. . . .' Sobbing she turned and went towards her room. 'Goodnight!' she shouted over her shoulder.

'Goodnight,' said Nicholas under his breath.

'Goodnight,' said Willie cheerfully like someone who has enjoyed a show. 'Sleep tight.'

Sarah's face was stretched and pale. 'I'm going to bed,' she told him.

'So am I,' he said quietly.

Nicholas turned out the lower-floor lights and they went to their room. Sarah almost stamped up the stairs. His steps were slow. The night was airless and, lying below the single sheet and the clattering fan, neither could sleep. After an hour he heard her crying softly and turning in the bed attempted to comfort her, putting his arm over her.

'No,' she whispered. 'It's too hot.'

He lay for another few minutes and then got up. 'I'm going to sleep on the roof,' he said.

She did not reply although he was aware that she was still awake. He was wearing pyjama trousers and now he put on the jacket and went outside and up the steps to the roof terrace. The stars were low and astounding, the sky milky with their incandescence. He lay on one of the sun loungers and studied them. They provided no answers, no illumination except their own.

There was a canvas chair and eventually, sleeplessly, he got up and sat in it, almost at the edge of the low wall around the roof terrace. He remained there looking out to the luminous and soundless sea.

Exactly below him, on the balcony, Sarah sat in another chair, also staring blindly out into the night. Neither was aware that the other was there. Someone looking from the garden would have seen them in their strangely parallel isolation. Two faces looking out towards the night sea.

Deborah lay awake sweating, eyeing her bedside clock. The night was humid, motionless. It was a week since her bitter quarrel with her mother and the incident had not been mentioned since. It was as though it had never happened; a bad dream shared by all of them. Now she knew the risk she was taking but nothing was going to get in her way. Tonight she was going to be with him.

She watched the luminous minute hand shift to two o'clock. Until that moment she would not allow herself to move. Naked under the sheet she lay with only her face exposed. She was a precise person and at exactly two she put her feet to the bare floor. There was a diffuse light coming through the door which opened on to the balcony. As she went like a shadow across her long mirror she caught sight of herself and paused, examining how she looked at almost seventeen. Her body was brown. She put her hands below her breasts and gently pushed them up, then rubbed her stomach and down to her thighs. She pushed her hair away from her face. Then she cleaned her teeth allowing the water to come from the tap in a noiseless dribble. She had already put out her black swimsuit and now she pulled herself into it. She was ready.

There was an iron staircase from the balcony but to reach it she had to pass her parents' open door. She could either go that way or creep down through the interior of the house and let herself out by the noisy kitchen door. The front entrance was locked at night. She had already decided which way to go.

Even her naked feet seemed to make a noise as she edged along the balcony. The moon was behind her and it threw her shadow forwards so that it advanced before her across the space in front of the wide door to her parents' room. She listened carefully, but briefly. If she was caught she had already made an excuse that she had been hot and restless and had decided to go for a lone night swim.

Her father was breathing deeply but her mother was stirring. Deborah heard her speak but, after a startled moment, realised that she was muttering in her sleep. She trod across the gap and made for the balcony stairway.

It was Willie who saw her flit across the front of the house. He was lying awake in the airless night and he had gone to his open window at the moment when his sister was passing through the olive trees. He pulled on a pair of shorts and followed. She was almost at the beach when he caught sight of her again, standing, slight in silhouette. Then, abruptly, she went from his view.

He advanced like a spy and lay flat and peered over the rim of the grass and rock. His sister was posed at the centre of the moonlit space. He could see she was watching not merely standing. She looked around her. Willie watched intently. Catching his breath he ducked as another figure appeared only yards to his right. The young man's eyes were on the beach and he did not see Willie.

Deborah turned and, saying something Willie did not understand, the youth ran eagerly to her. They embraced passionately, the boy's arms pulling her greedily close to him. Willie recognised who he was and almost bit a mouthful of gritty sand when they parted, and the young man reached out and eased the straps of the swimsuit away from his sister's shoulders. Her breasts were distinct in the moonlight. Willie had only seen them once before by accident when he had gone into her bedroom without knocking. Years before he had tried to spy on her through the bathroom keyhole but she was obscured by steam. After that he had not bothered.

Now she kicked her swimsuit away and stood naked, smiling in front of her lover. The youth was pulling his shorts off. They embraced deeply again. Willie had an erection and a crick in his neck. The young man eased himself down to the sand and gently but strongly like a confident acrobat pulled Deborah on top of him. They were kissing and arousing each other with their hands. They caressed and grappled and eventually quietened and began to make love. Willie had never realised you could do it with the woman on top. His eyes were wide. He craned his head higher. Deborah's white buttocks were heaving. Then he heard his sister cry out happily and heard the boy soothing her. They lay still for several minutes and then got to their knees. They stood and began to walk towards the sea. The youth suddenly laughed and picked up the slim naked girl and carried her to the shoreline. Willie, stuffed with excitement, crept away.

He had been waiting for fifteen minutes, wondering if she would appear when *both* of them arrived. 'Why did you bring her?' he asked Catriona.

'She wanted to come. She's experienced.'

'I'm experienced,' called Philomena who was already busily blowing up a Lilo some distance away.

'We both are,' said Catriona primly.

'But *two* of you,' argued Willie. 'I mean, it's embarrassing. . . .'

'Not necessarily. She can watch. I said she can if she doesn't talk.'

The sisters were both in their nightdresses. It was one o'clock in the morning. A touch of breeze pushed at Catriona's hair. 'It's done,' said Philomena eventually. 'I've blown it up.'

'It's good practice,' said her sister brazenly. Willie said: 'What for?' then blushed. Philomena dragged the Lilo towards them and now she arranged it in an almost motherly way and said: 'All right. Are you ready to start?' She peered at him enquiringly. 'Did you bring a torch?'

Willie said he had remembered and produced it and shone it on her face. He could easily see that she wore nothing below the slight nightdress. Slowly he took his eyes away and looked up at the overhanging bluff. 'It should be okay here,' he said. 'Nobody can see.'

'Well let's start,' urged Philomena.

'You promised not to talk,' pointed out Catriona. 'So don't.' She smiled in the night towards Willie. She pulled the nightdress around her so that her breasts were sharp against the material. He learned forward and she allowed him to push them tentatively. 'Have you got much on under this?' he enquired.

'Not a thing,' Catriona said. 'Do you want to see?'

'I wouldn't mind,' answered Willie in a voice so low that he choked.

'All right, you shall,' she promised. 'Use the torch.' She lifted the garment up to her knees then over them. 'You can peep now,' she said. 'But you'll have to get closer than that.'

Willie was on his hands and knees and he crawled forward to peer between her legs by the torchlight. She opened her knees wider. He whistled. 'Don't whistle up there,' she said.

Willie withdrew his head.

'I'll show you mine,' put in Philomena.

'She'll show you hers,' recommended Catriona.

Philomena opened her knees and shifting his position, Willie shining the torch ahead, peered under her nightdress.

'It's like a light shining in a tent,' observed Catriona.

'What d'you think?' asked Philomena anxiously. 'Is it all right?'

'It's more or less the same,' said Willie.

'We're sisters,' pointed out Catriona. 'Now let's see yours.'

'Your willie, Willie,' giggled Philomena. He handed the torch to Catriona.

'You'll probably not need that,' he said. He made to undo the zip at the front of his shorts but Catriona moved forward and handing the torch to her sister forcibly undid it for him. He pulled the shorts away.

'Oh, that's it,' said Philomena switching on the torch. 'It's ever so white, isn't it?'

'It's not been in the sun,' pointed out Willie.

'It's nice,' said Catriona. 'I think it's pretty.'

Conversation lapsed. Willie made to put his member away but Catriona reached out and tapped it with her finger as though for attention. 'We said we were going to do it,' she said firmly. She looked for confirmation to her sister. 'Didn't we Phil?'

'We promised ourselves,' said Philomena. 'Have you brought the condoms?'

Willie frowned. He put his hand in the back pocket of his shorts. 'I've got one,' he said doubtfully. 'I thought there was only going to be one of you.'

'I suppose it would be all right for both,' offered Catriona unsurely. 'Do they work twice?'

'I don't fancy that,' said Philomena. 'Imagine only bringing one.'

'How did I know?' said Willie grumpily. He dropped the condom into the sand.

'Oh, now look what you've done!' exploded Catriona. 'Talk about incompetence. I'm not doing it with all that grit on it.'

Philomena picked up the condom in two fingers and said: 'I'll wash it off in the sea.' She went down to the waterline holding it at arm's length.

Catriona at once began to pull her nightdress over her head.

Her dumpy breasts with their unused nipples were displayed for him. He reached up and pressed his fingers, then his hands against them. 'Take those shorts off,' she said quickly, 'before she gets back.'

Willie pulled his shorts away and flung them with bravado over his head to a rock. 'Good shot,' she said. Looking around he saw them hanging there. Philomena returned. 'It's all off,' she said holding out the rubber. She saw they were naked. 'Oh, you haven't started, have you. Spoilsports.'

'We'll do it first and you can watch,' said Catriona. 'As we arranged.'

Philomena grunted and pulled the nightdress over her head. Her body was whiter and slighter than her sister's. Her pubic hair was like a shadow and her breasts were scarcely more than nipples. 'There,' she said. 'You can start now.'

Willie was not sure how to begin. Catriona lay back on the Lilo and he moved towards her on his hands and knees. 'You're supposed to kiss and stuff beforehand,' pointed out the seated Philomena.

'Foreplay,' said Catriona sitting up. 'She's right.'

'Why didn't you think of it before,' grumbled Willie.

'We could do it afterwards, I suppose,' suggested Catriona. 'I mean there's no hard and fast rules.'

Willie was about to start shuffling towards her again when a cooing voice sounded directly above them. 'Girls. Girls. Are you there? Catriona, Philomena!'

Harriet's squeak was not urgent, only an enquiry. Catriona rolled her eyes sideways at Willie. She handed him the condom. He crawled away and hid behind an outcrop of rock. 'Here we are, Auntie,' called Catriona. 'We came down for a swim.'

'Ah . . . oh good. So there you are.' Wearing a dressing gown Harriet clambered down onto the beach. 'Skinny-dipping I see,' she said.

'That's right, Auntie,' confirmed Catriona. 'But we haven't been in yet.'

'Right. I think it's a beautiful idea. So free. Off you go then

337

and have your swim. I'll wait for you. Don't be long. Do you have towels?'

'We didn't bring any,' said Philomena. 'We'll soon get dry.'

She watched them affectionately, with a frown of doubt but not dismay, as they ran down to the shore and into the flat sea. When they returned she took off her dressing gown and let them use it to dry themselves. As they were leaving the beach, climbing the short grass slope, Harriet spotted Willie's shorts hanging over the rock. 'Ah, these are probably Willie's. He must have left them today,' she said. She took them. 'Boys are so forgetful.'

She carried the garment from the beach. The woman and the two girls, all in their nightdresses, went like moonlit ghosts back to the house. Catriona went in front with the torch. Willie waited several minutes behind his rock and then emerged and ran and crept naked back to his bed.

They had breakfast among the plants on the cool terrace. Deborah and Willie had gone almost at daybreak on a boat to an island.

Beyond the terrace the sun was already hot, the shadows of the olive trees deeply decorating the red ground in front of the house. 'Shall we take a walk on the beach?' Sarah suggested, a little to his surprise. She rose from the table. 'There won't be many more opportunities.'

He held out his hand and, after a moment, she took it. They strolled down the ragged path and through the broken boundary wall. Now Sarah ran before him lightly, almost girlishly, clambering up the rising ground before the beach. He climbed after her. They stood surveying the long emptiness of the shore, clear waves rolling in regularly and soberly on to the shingle. There was nobody else in sight.

They wandered towards the distant port, the white buildings just visible above the sand-dunes and grass. 'I have apologised to Deborah,' she said suddenly her eyes on the pebbles as they walked. 'I shouldn't have gone for her like that. Not while she's on holiday. She's going to live in London and I suppose I'm very nervous about that. But I shouldn't have quarrelled with her. We're friends now.'

'I'm glad,' he said. 'She takes everything from you very seriously.'

'I just don't want her to make too many mistakes,' she said.

'There's plenty available,' he agreed. 'So many things can go wrong.'

She left him and walked to where the sea was foaming against the beach. She took off her shoes. 'Come on,' she said. 'Come and get your feet wet.'

He grinned. The sun was filling her hair. Her arms shone in the light. She went to the shoreline, he took off his canvas shoes and began to yelp at the sharpness of the pebbles on the soles of his feet. 'Come in a bit,' she encouraged. 'This is the sandy stretch.'

Gratefully he detected the base. They waded together. Sarah lifted her denim skirt to keep it clear. 'I thought I'd tell you that I've read *Lost in France*,' she said suddenly, keeping her eyes on the water rushing around her legs. They continued to splash through the water. 'I brought one of your proof copies with me.'

'You did? You kept very quiet about it,' he said. 'I didn't see you with it.'

'I've been sneakily reading it when you haven't been around. In the afternoons when you've been snoozing.'

'And . . . ?'

She stopped and still not looking at him directly said: 'It's very good, Nick. Very good indeed.' They were close together in the water. She looked up. 'It sounds like a back-handed compliment but I could hardly believe you'd written it,' she said, her voice so quiet it was almost drowned by the easy waves. 'It's remarkable, wonderful!'

He grinned at her. 'Thanks,' he said uncertainly. He moved forward and they casually held each other and kissed. 'I couldn't have been more wrong,' she sighed. 'It's so different from *Lying in Your Arms*. I just didn't realise you had it in you to write like that.' He continued to hold her. 'I was almost afraid to read on.'

'Why was that?' he asked.

'I was . . . well, I was so envious of that woman.'

'Cécile,' he smiled.

'Yes, Cécile. And oddly envious of your Robert too. What a wonderful affair they had.'

'Only on paper,' he said.

'But we're real.'

'We are.' His heart was full. So was hers.

They returned quietly to the house. A cloud of red dust announced the approach of a vehicle. A bouncing van materialised.

'Gianni,' said Nick.

'It will be his last delivery,' observed Sarah. 'Next week it will be the Boxley supermarket.'

Gianni's van pulled up as they reached the house. It was difficult to tell the rust from the dust. Gianni, dusty himself, unloaded the groceries and handed a bunch of letters to Nicholas who returned to the breakfast table and poured himself an orange juice. 'Anything interesting?' Sarah asked. Gianni restarted the van's engine and clattered away. Soon he was a puff of red dust against the blue of the sea.

'One from Paul,' he said. 'It's about the launch for the book in October. They're bringing in an outside publicist, Holly Grant. They say she's the best. And the American publishers want me to go over to do some publicity for *Lying in Your Arms*. Early October. But it almost clashes with the publication of *Lost in France* at home, so it will have to be short, three or four days in New York and then back.' She took the breakfast plates into the house.

He called after her. 'You could come to New York if you like. They could arrange that.'

'Thanks,' she called from the kitchen. 'I won't come. I think I've been away long enough.'

They were almost ready to leave for Naples airport when Rico, the Italian youth they had seen working around Grenville's house, came running over the track. For the first time Nicholas realised he was the same boy who had danced with Deborah. '*Signore*,' he said pointing. 'You come now!'

'What's the trouble?' They were standing among suitcases.

'Willie,' said the youth urgently.

'What?' demanded Sarah starting forward.

'Willie on roof.'

'Christ,' exclaimed Nicholas. 'On the roof?' He pointed towards their own tiles.

'*Si*,' said Rico. 'On roof.'

They ran behind him through the red dust of the track. It was eleven in the morning and the sun was climbing. The young man was well ahead when they reached the house. Grenville and Harriet, with Catriona, Philomena and Deborah, were grouped in front of the house looking up at the roof. Willie was sitting next to the leaning chimney pot, holding it as if to keep it from falling. Deborah was near to tears. 'He won't come down,' she said.

'Willie, come down!' shouted his father. 'What are you doing?'

'This minute!' demanded Sarah. 'Are you mad?'

'I think he's mad,' said Deborah defeatedly.

'He's been aloft for a good hour,' Harriet informed them blithely. 'It was twenty minutes before anyone noticed. He appears to be quite desperate.'

'Come down, there's a good chap,' called Grenville Thurston throatily. He half-turned as though struggling for something positive. 'Good head for heights,' he said to the others.

Nicholas stepped forward. 'Willie, in half an hour we have *got* to leave for the airport.'

'Not me. I'm not coming,' said Willie. 'I love Catriona.'

'What about me?' howled Philomena starting forward. She waved her fists in the air. 'You promised me . . .'

'Oh hell,' muttered Grenville. 'They've been mixing.'

'It appears so,' agreed his wife.

Sarah's eyes were blazing. 'Come down at once,' she ordered. 'I'll smack your face, young man.'

'In that case I'm not coming down.' Both Catriona and Philomena were crying. Deborah was wiping her eyes.

'Willie, you can see the girls back home,' his sister pleaded. 'They'll be coming back to England in a couple of weeks.'

'Oh, all right,' said Willie surprising them all. 'I've made my statement. I'm scared up here anyway.'

Rico, who had summoned Nicholas and Sarah, called to him: 'No yet' and held up a cautioning hand. Willie was fearfully preparing to climb down the clay tiles. He paused precariously. 'If he falls he'll break his neck,' said Nicholas. He moved forward.

'It will teach him a lesson,' blustered Sarah. 'This boy is getting out of hand.'

The Italian youth reappeared with a ladder. He put it against the wall and agilely scaled it and then crawled up the tiles towards Willie who was now, suddenly, stranded and frightened. 'I love you, Willie!' called Catriona.

'So do I!' howled Philomena. 'With my whole body!'

Catriona glared at her sister. 'And me. With every bit of my body!' she called.

'Christ,' muttered Nicholas.

'Careful Rico, don't fall, please,' pleaded Deborah. Sarah's eyebrows went up.

The youth called back. 'It is okay. All okay.' He put out his arms to Willie and held on to him. The boy, now quaking at the drop in front of him, edged forward.

'How did he make the ascent in the first place?' enquired Harriet conversationally.

'From the rear of the house,' her husband calmly guessed.

'Why can't he return that way?'

'It's easier up than down, I imagine.'

'He enjoys the drama,' put in Sarah bitterly. 'I'll give him drama.'

Rico and Willie were edging down the tiles. 'Careful, careful,' pleaded Deborah.

'He's going to make it,' breathed Catriona. 'Oh, Willie.'

'He's so great,' sighed Philomena. She began to sing a sickly pop song.

342

The pair had reached the eaves now and Rico manoeuvred himself on to the ladder. His strong backside in his jeans was above them. Deborah could not take her eyes away. The youth hauled Willie over the last tiles and eased him with both hands on to the ladder. The three girls began to cheer. Down they came, a step at a time.

It was Rico who reached the ground first. Deborah rushed to him and threw her arms about him, kissing him passionately. 'Oh Rico, you're wonderful!' she cried.

'Oh God,' muttered Sarah.

Sixteen

They were seated around a transparent table on transparent chairs in a glass room that appeared to float above the London roofs with no visible means of attachment to the building in Kensington occupied by Mallinder and Co. From his chair Nicholas could look over his shoulder on to roofs, some, although not many, still with chimney-pots. A coatless man, probably a caretaker, legs spread contentedly, occupied a chair on one flat roof drinking a cup of tea, a cat squatting beside him. There were plants and even trees up there above the traffic. Other windows, on the same level as the Mallinder boardroom, were occupied by people at desks, curled over screens, or themselves engaged in meetings.

There were four others around the table in the Mallinder's room; Henry Newby, the chief editorial executive, flanked by his pond-eyed secretary who took notes, Paul Garrett and Holly Grant, the publicist. Nicholas could see her plump knees through the table.

'The first thing I would like to do,' said Newby, 'is to show Nicholas his book.' He motioned to his secretary who reached for a padded envelope and handed it to him. From it he took the first bound copy of *Lost in France*. 'Your new baby,' he said handing it across to Nicholas.

Nicholas stood and involuntarily held out both hands. The people around the table craned forward to look. With a smile he held it up. It was a handsome book, the cover deep blue with golden letters for his name above and in larger type than the title. 'It's beautiful,' he said. 'Thanks very much.'

'Thank you,' said Newby seriously. 'You gave it to us.' He

smiled. 'Eventually.' His secretary nodded in agreement. He remained standing. 'We think so much of the prospects for *Lost in France*,' he said, 'that we have brought in Holly Grant.' He extended his hand towards the broad blonde. She wore a green dress.

'We decided to bring in Holly because we are convinced that this novel will lend itself to a really incisive publicity campaign. We want to make it a book that doesn't just interest people and give them enjoyment – it gets under their skin. It's an evocative story and we want it talked about, discussed, argued by husbands and wives . . . and bought by a lot of people.'

Holly Grant said: 'I'd like to add to that list. I'd like to *puzzle* people.' She had tough blue eyes. To Nicholas she did not appear as a romantic woman. 'It's the romance we have to push,' she said, as if she had read his mind. She looked directly at Nicholas. 'And, of course, the mystery.' She reached for the book and turned it over in her manicured fingers and then studied him again. 'What got me,' she said touching her breast, 'was that Cécile felt very alive.' Newby's secretary was leaning forward, mouth open. Holly blinked carefully at Nicholas. 'Is she?'

Nicholas glanced towards Paul. 'I'd prefer the author to tell me,' said Holly quietly and strongly. Her eyes came up to him again.

'She is based,' replied Nicholas picking the words, 'on someone I met . . . once . . . briefly.'

'Was there a love affair?'

Nicholas swallowed. They all watched him. The secretary almost fell from her chair. Paul Garrett said: 'This is in confidence, of course.'

'Of course,' murmured Holly.

Nicholas said: 'It was not a love affair. Let's call it an adventure.'

'When was this? And where?'

'I'm not prepared to say.'

She did not appear to be put out but said: 'Right, I understand.' She turned her attention to Paul and then to

Newby. Newby's secretary had her mouth open. Holly said: 'There's a great opportunity to promote *Lost in France* on the premise that the mysterious and beautiful Frenchwoman, Cécile, might possibly be real, someone with whom the author has fallen in love and then lost.' Her blue eyes rose and fell again.

'I can see trouble ahead,' said Nicholas. 'I *am* married.'

'Nicholas,' she persisted. 'All you have to do is to deny it. Deny it and keep on denying it. To your wife and everyone else, and especially to the press. I'll put the hint, the rumour, about, but you will have to insist that Cécile is fiction, fantasy. Threaten to sue anybody who prints otherwise.' A thought struck her. 'Are they likely to find her? If they try?'

'I doubt it. She is a long way away.'

Holly looked around the table. 'Are we agreed on that?' She shifted her knees below the transparent table. The men nodded, so did Newby's secretary.

'Excellent,' said Holly. 'It gives me a basis on which I can go to work.' Her smile became all-encompassing. 'We can put it at the top of the bestseller list.' She looked at the schedule among her papers. 'Before publication on October 18th you have to go to New York?'

Paul Garrett answered. 'It's for the Brent Burbach publication of *Lying in Your Arms*. It will only be for a few days. I've told them they can't have him any longer. He has to be back in London.'

Holly smiled, more easily now, at Nicholas. 'Don't exhaust yourself over there. Keep your energy – and your snappy answers – for us.' She became concerned. 'And keep your mentions of *Lost in France* to a minimum, just general terms. Don't give the game away in New York or we'll have nothing to sell.'

Newby said: 'What about the launch?' His secretary looked towards Holly almost framing the question again.

'I see it as a champagne reception,' Holly told him. 'And then a dinner for twenty-five or so who are going to be most useful, reviewers and gossip columnists and so forth.' The secretary nodded and Newby confirmed the nod.

The publicist again turned to Nicholas. 'All you have to do is to brazen it out,' she said. 'The more you deny a love affair with Cécile, or even that she exists, the better it will be.

'What about Sarah, my wife?' asked Nicholas.

'Deny it,' said Holly carefully. 'Even more.'

'That Concorde is some aeroplane for time,' enthused Harry Rubicon who met him at Kennedy. He was a squat, rubber-faced man, perspiring in a camel overcoat. 'You're here before you're out of London.' Hopefully he surveyed the Arrivals Hall. 'I fixed to have one or two press. Not too many. There's nothing worse then saturation coverage.' Again he scanned the concourse. 'But nobody got here.'

They climbed into the car. 'It's going to be just fine,' continued the rotund publicity agent like a man reassuring himself. 'We've got some interviews in New York. It's just a shame that you can't get on the road, Chicago, Washington, LA, Sioux Falls. They'd love *Lying in Your Arms*. It's a great title.'

Nicholas asked: 'What's the significance of Sioux Falls?'

'Every significance,' said the American. 'I was born there. I can get you on *two* radio stations and on the midnight television show and spread right over two newspapers. My mother, she likes me to take authors there. She tells people how important I am.'

Nicholas smiled. 'I have to be back home for the publication of the new book.'

'The hardcover, right? That's a good arrangement. Softback in New York, hardcover in London, then softback London, hardcover New York. You could get rich like that. I'm crazy about the title, *both* titles to tell you the truth. *Lying in Your Arms* I love. You saw our cover? And *Lost in France*, oh boy. It says: "Come, buy me, read me, ask for more." '

The car joined the traffic streaming towards the Midtown Tunnel. Rubicon said: 'So you have a classy publication party and big promotion in London. Here we've got a chance of the *Ed Edwards Show*.'

'That's important is it?'

'Important! Big! It's more important than that. If we . . . if I . . . can get you on that they won't be able to print your book fast enough. Prime time, nationwide. It can't get better, please believe me.' He tapped Nicholas. 'In three years Brent Burbach have only had one author on this show.'

'With good results?'

'*Results* and results,' enthused Rubicon. 'Hundreds of thousands of results. Half a million sales.' His manner subsided. 'But we're not there yet. I need to take you along so that they can check you look nice and they'll ask you questions.'

'They sift people?'

'You bet they do. Sift them and sift them. There was some guy wrote this book about a brave dog. They had to see the dog, ask it questions.'

'Did it get on the show?'

'No. I guess it gave the wrong answers.'

He rang Sarah from the Waldorf. 'I don't know how many books the Midnight Hour on some Bronx radio station sells, or an interview in the *New Literature Monthly*,' he said. 'But I'm doing them dutifully. I did a television afternoon show out of town in New Jersey where I was supposed to sing with a school choir.'

'Did you?' asked Sarah.

'Sort of.'

'Did they talk about the book?'

'About the title,' he corrected. 'Here, nobody on TV has time to read the book. This afternoon I have to go for the vetting, to see if I'm smart enough for the *Ed Edwards Show*. According to Rubicon, the publicity man, they'll sell so many books they'll have to start chopping down more trees for paper.'

'Could you ring and tell me how it went?'

'Oh all right.'

When they had finished he shaved and had a bath. He cleaned his teeth and bared them in the mirror. Then he put on his English suit and his English tie and rehearsed being an English author. The telephone rang. Rubicon was downstairs.

Nicholas went down to the lobby. Rubicon, swamped in his massive camel overcoat although it was a warm October day, ran his eye over him. 'You look great,' he said. 'The genuine English author. In the tradition of William Shakespeare. It's going to be no problem. Get through the next couple of hours, sir and we're winners.' He glanced at the busy desk clerks a few yards away and then at other people in the vicinity. 'Remember Shakespeare,' he said quietly. 'Give them plenty of shit.'

When they were in the cab he began issuing warnings. 'You'll see one of two people. There's a good-looking woman who is rumoured to be Ed's screwing partner and then there's this guy Carl Gaylaw. I think he made up his name. The broad is called Ellen Peabody, but there's no way she's a peabody. The first thing they'll do is to throw some ridiculous question at you, maybe an insulting question, something to faze you. At least *try* to faze you. How you react is what they want.'

The cab dropped them at a tall carved building on the East Side. Rubicon gazed up at its glass precipice. 'Someone in there is going to love you,' he said.

They went to the forty-third floor. The frosted glass doors had a clear oval at the centre. Rubicon peered through, his head projecting from the voluminous overcoat. 'I wore this to impress,' he whispered to Nicholas. 'It's hot but impressive. Right?'

'Expensive?'

'No. Eccentric. These people have got to remember *me* coming through the door. It's okay for *you* to look like you do, conventional, like British, but *me* they have to remember. I need to come here again.'

They pressed a security button and eventually a tall black girl opened the door. She led them to a reception desk where the blonde with upswept hair pretended that she had no record of their appointment and asked them to sit down. 'They just do this to make you feel uncomfortable,' Rubicon whispered when they were occupying two of the cushioned tubular chairs. 'They don't want anybody feeling welcome.'

They waited fifteen minutes. On the glass table in front of them were some scattered magazines. Idly Nicholas picked up one and turning two pages found himself looking at a photograph of Thérèse Oiseau.

He was so astounded that he was scarcely aware of the opening of the inner door and a woman's voice saying: 'I'm Alice. You're in.' Rubicon stood quickly and nudged him. Nicholas slowly half-rose, trying to read the magazine page. She had been in New York; her vivid paintings, in a new style inspired by the French Caribbean, had attracted attention; she might still be in New York. He looked up to see the middle-aged, butterfly-spectacled, black-suited Alice and Rubicon both facing him. 'We're on,' said Rubicon nervously.

'Everybody's tight on time,' said Alice throwing looks over the wings of her glasses.

'Oh, yes, sorry,' mumbled Nicholas still with the magazine open at the page. He looked as if he were trying to remember where he was. Rubicon nudged him again. 'Yes, of course,' said Nicholas. He folded the magazine and put it firmly below his arm. The blonde left the desk and fussily tidied the other journals on the glass table. Alice led them through the door. They found themselves in another waiting area. She went away muttering: 'Let's see if they're still free.'

Nicholas was about to take the magazine from under his armpit to show it to Rubicon but the publicist almost snarled: 'Not *now*. Whatever it is. Not *now*. Think about what we're trying to achieve for Chrissake.'

Nicholas apologised and rolled the journal tightly. Rubicon handed him a copy of *Lying in Your Arms*.

'Remember, *lie* if you have to,' he said below his breath. 'These people love lies. They live one big lie, so they understand. Give them plenty of shit.'

Her eyes probing through the butterfly glasses, Alice returned. 'You're *so* lucky,' she told them. 'Follow me.' She frowned at Nicholas and then shot a look at the magazine. 'Maybe I had better take that,' she said holding out her hand.

'No, I'll hang on to it, thank you all the same,' smiled Nicholas grittily. Was Thérèse still in New York? He had to find her. Rubicon was almost pummelling him forward. They went into a surprisingly small, bare and square room, glass-walled, where two people, a beautiful frowning woman, and a man in a mauve shirt and gold glasses, were seated. 'Both of you!' exclaimed Rubicon. 'That's really something.'

'They're fumigating my interview cubicle,' said the woman. 'I just had a wrestler in there.' Rubicon laughed nervously. 'Hadn't he showered?'

'He smoked,' said the woman. 'Now, okay, let's do some names.'

The man in the mauve shirt stood up. 'I'm Carl Gaylaw,' he said.

'I'm Ellen Peabody,' said the woman.

'This is Nicholas Boulting,' said Rubicon. 'English author *extraordinaire*.'

'Tell me *your* name again,' suggested Ellen to Rubicon. 'We get so many people in here.'

'Harry Rubicon,' said the publicist with embarrassment. 'I talked to ... .' He pointed a sagging finger at her partner.

'Sure, sure,' sighed Gaylaw. 'I remember. Why don't we all sit down.' They did, Nicholas with the magazine on his lap, cover showing.

'*Art and Artists*,' said Gaylaw shifting to read the front. 'You're interested in art?'

'In an artist,' replied Nicholas deliberately. He opened the journal at the page and after looking at it again for a measured time, showed them the photograph of Thérèse. Rubicon was stretching over to look and he showed it to him. The publicist had the expression of a man who sees things slipping away. 'Hmmm, nice,' said Ellen. 'She's French. You don't even need to see her name. Chic.'

'Just beautiful,' yawned Gaylaw handing the magazine over.

'I didn't know she was in New York,' said Nicholas. 'I'm afraid it threw me. I only saw it in your waiting room.'

'Do you know Queen Elizabeth?' asked Ellen Peabody leaning towards Nicholas.

'Well . . . yes,' said Nicholas. Rubicon nodded happily.

'Does she know you?' asked Gaylaw.

'We have a cottage on the Sandringham Estate in Norfolk,' lied Nicholas. 'It is, of course, a royal estate and when Her Majesty is there we have the occasional chat.' He smiled at them expansively. 'You could say we're neighbours.'

Rubicon whistled in his ear. 'A neighbour of the Queen of England.'

'Do you have any unpublished anecdotes about the Royals?' enquired Ellen.

'Anecdotes? Well, let me see. There's so much really.' They were watching him like an inquisition. Rubicon was straining sideways, his eyes burning encouragement. Nicholas continued. 'There was the time when I accidentally dropped a glass of sherry on Her Majesty's feet. It was a reception, a charity occasion in London.'

'You did?' said Gaylaw. 'On the Royal feet?' He glanced at Ellen Peabody who asked: 'What happened? Did they put you in the Tower of London?'

'The feet of the Queen of England,' breathed Rubicon.

Nicholas said: 'No, in fact she was very gracious about it. Her Majesty merely smiled and said something about how easily glasses broke these days.'

Rubicon whispered: 'I love it.'

Ellen Peabody leaned forward: 'How about Di?' she said to Nicholas.

'You mean Her Royal Highness the Princess of Wales?'

Again Gaylaw glanced at Ellen. 'Naturally,' he said to Nicholas. 'Her Royal Highness.'

'I've met her on various occasions,' lied Nicholas airily. 'I have sat next to her once or twice.'

'Twice, I bet it was twice,' muttered Rubicon.

'Once I had a split in my trousers. It happened as I sat down. She was pretty amused at that.'

'Split your pants!' Rubicon almost yelped. He beamed at the other two. 'It's so good.'

'You said,' mentioned Ellen carefully, 'that you have a cottage on the Royal Estate. You said: "We have". That's with your wife?'

Nicholas appeared surprised. 'Yes, of course.'

'Where does the French artist lady fit in?' asked Gaylaw. He looked towards his partner. 'If she's still in town maybe we could get her on the show too.'

Nicholas knew he had gone pale. Rubicon muttered: 'Great idea.'

Nicholas said: 'She is only a friend. Even if she is still in New York – and this magazine is a week old – I doubt if she would appear. She is married to a Frenchman.'

'Wow,' said Ellen laughing. 'We could begin your divorce, two divorces in fact, right here on the *Ed Edwards Show*.'

'Thanks but don't bother,' said Nicholas getting up. 'There are no grounds for divorce.'

Rubicon could hardly believe he was leaving. Nicholas shook hands with each of his interrogators. He could feel Ellen Peabody's rings. 'We haven't talked about the book,' pleaded Rubicon.

Ellen and Gaylaw said nothing. Nobody had ever walked out of that room early. 'We could talk about the book on the show,' muttered Gaylaw.

'If we think the subject is right,' warned Ellen. 'What's it called again?' Rubicon tugged the copy from Nicholas and handed it to her. She looked at the cover and said: '*Lying in Your Arms*. Well, well.'

Red-faced Rubicon led Nicholas out. Alice ushered them towards the outer door. She reverted her attention to the magazine. 'Can I take that from you now?' she suggested pointedly.

'Of course,' said Nicholas. He opened it to the place where Thérèse's picture smiled and tore out the page. He gave the remainder to the sag-jawed Alice. As though seeking a witness the woman whirled around. Ellen Peabody and Carl Gaylaw were standing in the door of the cubicle. 'Did you see that?' snorted the secretary. 'Did you see what he just did!'

'This is *Art and Artists*. Hello.'

'Oh good. I was afraid it was too late to catch you.'

'It *is* too late. It's six o'clock and nobody else is here. I'm only here cleaning before I go to school. I'm studying the history of wood carving.'

'Perhaps you can help me anyway. I have a copy of your magazine, the current issue, with an article by Thomas B. Benjamin about a French artist, Thérèse Oiseau. Do you know whether Miss Oiseau is still in New York?'

'I have no idea.'

'Well, do you know where I can contact Mr Benjamin?'

'I have no idea. You see I only come here to clean the place before I go off to my class. You'll have to call back tomorrow.'

'Do you have a phone number for the editor?'

'Which editor would that be?'

'Of *Art and Artists*.'

'I don't even know who the editor is. I only clean before going to my class.'

Nicholas put the phone down. He tried the gallery. Renoir and Co., Sixth Avenue. There was no reply.

He pulled the slab of the Manhattan telephone book from its drawer. 'Benjamin, Benjamin . . .' He went through the pages. There were hundreds but no Thomas B. He tried Information. They had never heard of him either. He rang two of the listed Benjamins.

'Martha, do we have a Thomas B. in the family?' he heard the man say. 'Nobody called that? A writer?'

The voice returned to the phone. 'We don't have any writers called Thomas B. Benjamin, sir. We are mainly chicken people.'

'Benjamin, Thomas B.,' muttered the next Benjamin he rang. 'He's no relation of ours. Is it family? I think you'll find they're mostly white folks.'

He sat on the bed attempting to think logically. Abruptly he stood, put on his jacket and went down to the hotel lobby. Hurrying out into the New York evening he got a cab and went to Renoir and Co., Sixth Avenue.

The gallery was closed and barred but there was a dim glow inside and the shape of someone moving. Nicholas frantically rang a bell on the side of the door. The shape enlarged until it became the dark mass of a security guard. He stood within the door and looked out at Nicholas. Nicholas made signs. The man walked away. Nicholas jabbed the bell again. The shape returned standing again within the barred door. Carefully he held up a clearly, amost childishly, printed notice. 'This building is closed,' it announced. 'I am a security guard and I cannot open this door. Please call tomorrow.'

Nicholas walked emptily away, passing the second window of the gallery. He stopped. There was a painting on an easel. It was vivid with sunshine and colour and yet it had a look, a style. And there, in the right-hand corner, was her small bird. He stood staring until the security man loomed behind it. Again he held up his notice.

Nicholas returned to the Waldorf. He knew he should have telephoned Sarah but it was too late now. The telephone rang. It was a jubilant Rubicon. 'Nick, Nicholas, great news! They loved you! They want you on the *Ed Edwards Show*. Tomorrow. How about that!'

'Wonderful,' said Nicholas putting his mind to it. 'Well done you.'

'Me, I did nothing. It was *you*. And d'you know what clinched it? Can you guess?'

'The fact I live next door to the Queen?'

'No way. They know shit when they hear it. No, it was the way you tore the page from that magazine. Just before we went, remember. You just tore it out and that old broad with the glasses wanted to scream. That's what they liked.'

'They want me to tear up magazines?' said Nicholas. 'On the show? Or maybe the Manhattan telephone directory.'

'Don't, don't. You're killing me. They just want you to be on the *Ed Edwards Show* and do *something*. Nobody knows what. But you'll do something. Be outrageous.'

'What about the book?'

'Oh, they'll mention the book,' said Rubicon. 'They might even get the title right. But it's up to you to stick it up their noses. Make sure the cover gets in the show. Never mind the story.'

'This programme is recorded, I take it.'

'Forget it. It's live, that's the whole attraction of it. They skate on ice sometimes, Nick, believe me. They just have a time lag, a minute, so that they can cut any shit or if you drop your pants or something.'

'I'm not likely to do that. I'm trying to sell a book, remember.'

'Will I ever forget.' Nicholas felt Rubicon's enthusiasm surge over the phone. 'Is this going to be terrific, man,' he said. 'This book will be in places where they never read books.'

'And Sioux Falls,' smiled Nicholas.

'Especially Sioux Falls. Now listen. I'll come to the Waldorf to pick you up at four. Tomorrow afternoon. Okay, the show goes out live at six thirty. We need to be at the studio by four thirty. They like you to be there two hours before. It gives you time to worry.'

'Is that Mr Boulting? It is? This is the hotel travel desk. You were asking about the flights from New York to the French island of Guadeloupe. Right. We've checked them out, Mr Boulting, and there are no direct flights from Kennedy to Guadeloupe but American Airlines fly via San Juan, Puerto Rico, every day, and there are other flights via Saint Martin and Antigua. Did you want us to make you reservations?'

'Not at the present. Thank you for checking.'

He went down to the coffee shop that evening and read the article once more. 'Before I went to Guadeloupe,' she was quoted, 'I painted in soft, washy, European colours. But in the Caribbean nothing looks like that. My work has become more vivid, and I am pleased that it is now so popular in New York. This is a wonderful thing for me.'

The article described her exhibition at the Renoir and Co. Gallery, and her life in Guadeloupe with an adventurous man who ran a charter yacht company. She was very happy. Some time she might want to return to Europe. 'There are some places I would like to paint again. There is a place in England, on the sea, which I have tried to show but I do not think the work was very good. Perhaps one day I can try to paint that place again.'

He went to his room, poured himself a scotch and picked up the Manhattan phone book again. He went to the final entry under Benjamin. 'Sure I know Thomas B.,' responded a genial voice. 'He's my cousin. He lives up in New England. I'll get you his number.'

He returned with the number. 'You liked that article, eh? He's a good writer. He won't mind you calling. He stays up late. Writers do.'

Thomas B. Benjamin lived in Montpelier, Vermont. He was reading in his study when the telephone rang. 'Ah, of course. Thérèse Oiseau,' he answered. 'She's a beautiful woman. Very talented also. But I'm afraid I have no idea where you would find her. I think she may have even left New York by now, gone home to Guadeloupe.'

'Is there anyone . . . anyone you can think of . . . in New York who may know?' asked Nicholas. 'I'd be really grateful.'

'This sounds a touch urgent.'

'It is. Well, it is to me. I'd like to see her if she's still here. I'm an old friend.'

'I don't know where she stays. I can only think of one thing, Mr Boulting, at this hour. If it's urgent, she has an agent in New York. His name is Stanley . . . what is it? Hubert, that's it. Stanley Hubert. He'll be in the Manhattan phone book.'

It was almost midnight. Nicholas carried the huge directory to the bed and ran his finger down the Huberts. New York was a big telephone city. There it was: Stanley Hubert and Rappaport Agency. Forty-sixth East. His eyes went up the list again, Hubert, S., Central Park East. Glancing guiltily at the time he took his hand from the telephone. Then, quickly, he picked it up and dialled the number. A female voice, drowsy and elderly, responded.

'I'm sorry to call at this late hour,' Nicholas said. 'But is that the home of Mr Stanley Hubert?'

'It is,' said the woman rousing herself a little. 'Have you found him?'

'Well . . . er . . . no actually. I didn't even know he was . . . lost.'

'Lost,' she echoed. 'Absent, missing, absconded. Whatever you like to call it, sir. All I can tell you is that he's not here and he ought to be because I'm his wife.'

'Oh I apologise.'

'*He* should apologise,' she said tiredly. 'After all these years.'

'Yes, of course. I'm sorry. Goodbye.'

'If you find him,' she said practically, and he heard a brief sob, 'tell him he can still come home.'

He replaced the telephone. It was a city of dramas. He felt weary. He had another scotch and climbed into the big, solitary bed.

He was woken in the morning by Sarah. 'What time is it there?'

Why did people telephone to ask for the time? 'It's early,' he said. 'It's five minutes past six.'

'In the morning? Sorry, I mix up the hours. I thought you'd ring again last night.'

'I meant to,' he said remaining on the pillow, his eyes closed. 'By the time I had the chance it would have been too late. I'd have woken you.'

'Now I've woken you.'

'It's all right. Nobody can help the way the world turns.'

'Thanks. How is everything going?'

'Big triumph. I'm on the famous *Ed Edwards* television chat show tonight. Rubicon, the publicist, is turning cartwheels. We're going to sell millions so he says.'

'You don't sound as though you're turning cartwheels yourself.'

'That's probably because it's just after six in the morning.'

'We're not going to fight across the Atlantic are we, Nick. It was just that you said you'd ring.'

'I'm sorry. What's happening there? How are the kids?'

'Willie went missing.'

He sat up in bed. 'Where is he?'

'In the police station. Not the local one. At Harrow. He went in and said he'd come to give himself up after weeks of vandalism in the area.'

'Willie! But he couldn't . . . have . . .'

'He didn't,' she sighed. 'He hasn't been near the place. It was one of his mad things.'

'Getting attention,' muttered Nicholas.

'It wasn't what the police called it. They took hours to work out that he hadn't done anything. He could be charged with wasting police time.'

'Acting again,' grunted Nicholas. 'He'll *have* to go to acting school. He can have all the fantasies he likes there.'

He heard Sarah sniff over the ocean. 'He had such a good time, according to him, in the police cells that he's decided to become a policeman. He's perfectly all right today. Just as if nothing had happened.'

'Is Deborah all right?'

'She rang yesterday. She wants to interview you for her journalism course.'

He laughed drily. 'She'd be better off interviewing Willie. He has more hidden depths.'

'I wouldn't say that.'

They said dulled goodbyes and he lay back wearily. From outside came the first muffled honkings of a New York day. He went to the window. In the dead light cars and buses were moving along the grey avenue. The heights of the city were garlanded with mist, lights were insipid. Early aeroplanes were in the sky. He wondered where Stanley Hubert had gone.

Getting back into the bed he surprised himself by sleeping again. It was nine thirty when he awoke. At once he picked up the telephone and dialled.

'Stanley Hubert and Rappaport.'

'Could I speak to Mr Hubert please.'

'Mr Hubert is not in town.'

'Mr Rappaport then.'

'Prunella Rappaport,' corrected the girl. 'Who is calling, may I ask?'

'My name is Nicholas Boulting. I'm from England.'

'I can tell. Can I say what it's about? She usually asks.'

'Yes . . . It's concerning Thérèse Oiseau, the artist. I believe you represent her.'

'I believe we do. She was right here in the office yesterday.'

'Oh . . . she was?'

'Yes, I saw her. I'll tell Prunella you're calling.'

She was only moments. 'I'm putting you through.'

'Prunella Rappaport speaking.' The voice was deep, almost manly. 'How may I help you, Mr Boulting?'

'I was calling for Mr Hubert actually. About Thérèse Oiseau.'

'He's taken off,' she said bluntly. 'Heaven knows where he is. He's is love.'

Nicholas almost choked. 'Not . . . not with Miss Oiseau . . . ?'

The woman laughed deeply. 'Hardly his taste. He's gone off with a guy from the YMCA.'

'Oh I see. My mistake.'

'His too, I think. You wanted to ask about Thérèse?'

'Yes. I'm a writer from England. She's a friend. I didn't realise she was in New York until yesterday. Do you know where I can find her, which hotel she is at?'

'Stanley maybe does, but I don't,' said Prunella. 'She's his client. I have an idea she was leaving very soon. Maybe she left yesterday after she came here to the office. Before he took off with Merlin.'

'Merlin?'

'Merlin.'

'Oh, yes, I see. So unless I find him I won't know where she is.'

'That seems about right. If you find him ask him to call the office.'

'You have no idea?'

'Maybe they went to Fire Island. Maybe they're tucked up at the YMCA. I have no idea.'

He got a taxi to Renoir and Co. They had taken her painting from the window. A fussy young man was not helpful. 'I have no idea where Mademoiselle Oiseau would be,' he said spreading his hands. 'It could be she has left for home in the Caribbean.' He became more sympathetic. 'Stanley Hubert is her agent, you know. He should have some idea of her whereabouts.'

'Nobody knows Stanley Hubert's whereabouts,' said Nicholas.

The young man became interested. 'He's not about?' he said.

'He went off with somebody called Merlin,' Nicholas told him grumpily.

The gallery man smiled a touch wistfully and said: 'Ah, that Merlin.'

Nicholas had a final attempt. 'Would you, by any chance, know which hotel Thérèse was at?'

'I do,' provided the man at once. 'She was at the Waldorf.'

He saw the disbelief in the Englishman's face. 'The Waldorf,' he repeated. 'That . . . that's where *I'm* staying,' moaned Nicholas.

'It's a big hotel,' said the man.

'Can I use your telephone,' said Nicholas. 'Please.'

'Sure. Go right ahead.'

He called the Waldorf. 'Yes, Thérèse Oiseau. O-I-S-E-A-U. That's it.' He waited. The other man, drawn into the drama, was standing close and expectantly. Nicholas put his hand to his face.

'Oh . . . y . . . you're sure?' Nicholas found himself stammering. 'Y . . . y . . . yes. You're quite sure? Right. Thanks, yes.'

He stood with the telephone held in his hand. The gallery man moved forward smoothly and took it from him, replacing it on its cradle. Nicholas said: 'She checked out. Half an hour ago.'

'That's too bad.'

'I can't credit it.'

'My name's André, by the way,' said the young man suddenly eager to become involved with an interesting situation. Dazed, Nicholas shook hands with him. Now André wanted to help. 'She's on her way to the airport now,' he decided looking at his watch. 'You could catch her there maybe.'

'You're right!' responded Nicholas with such emphasis that the young man jumped. 'I'll get out there.'

He made to rush from the gallery but André restrained him. 'Take it easy,' he advised. 'We have security and they may think it's a getaway. You could be gunned down.'

Nicholas went out at a purposeful walk and hailed a yellow cab. 'Kennedy Airport,' he said. 'As quick as you can.'

The driver delivered a monologue as to why New York City was doomed within a year but got him to the airport in forty-five minutes. Nicholas made for American Airlines, his eyes searching for her on the concourse. 'Our connecting flight is not until late afternoon,' said the woman at Information. 'San Juan, Puerto Rico, connecting for Pointe-à-Pitre, Guadeloupe. But we have four flights a day to San Juan and your party could be on any of them.' She leaned forward. 'There are other airlines,' she said privily. 'Have you tried Newark? She could fly from Newark. Maybe even La Guardia. You can miss her in at least three places.'

He decided to stay. He asked if Thérèse Oiseau had checked in but they could not give information on passengers. The man by the scales was friendly. 'I haven't seen a single attractive Frenchwoman this morning,' he said.

Nicholas positioned himself where he could see the rank of check-in desks. He remainded watching for an hour and a half. Thérèse did not appear. The man at the desk told him the flight had closed. He wandered out to get a taxi and sat hunched all the way back to the city.

It was two thirty when he reached the Waldorf. He went to the bar and had a disconsolate drink. He felt wrung out. There was nothing for it now but to go to his room and get ready for Rubicon's arrival at four. He must forget Thérèse Oiseau and how close she had been; he must think of the *Ed Edwards Show*. He groaned.

Waiting at the elevator he heard his name being paged. 'That's me,' he said to the man standing next to him. 'Lucky you,' the man told him. 'Somebody wants you, *needs* you.'

The reception clerk was holding the telephone. He handed it over as Nicholas approached. 'Hello, Nicholas Boulting here.' It might be Rubicon merely making sure he was getting ready. But it was Prunella Rappaport. 'Mr Boulting,' she said. 'I'm glad I caught you. I've just heard that Thérèse Oiseau is at a lunch at the Lincoln Center. Something connected with the Manhattan Arts Foundation.'

Checking his watch and thanking Prunella at the same time, he turned and made a dash towards the front of the hotel. The doorman blinked. 'Lincoln Center,' he told the taxi-driver. It was the same man who had brought him from the airport and had stayed on the hotel rank. 'It's a hurry, hurry day,' he said.

Outside the Lincoln Center, as he was almost blindly paying the driver, Nicholas saw a crowd, people shaking hands and waving. Then, with a leap of his heart, he saw *her*. Thérèse, wearing a lilac suit and a beautiful hat, was getting into a taxi. He ran along the pavement but people got in his way and when he reached the spot the cab was moving off. Shouting and waving he ran after it. The guests coming from the lunch halted. A New York policeman appeared. 'You have a problem, sir?' he enquired solidly pushing his arm out like a barrier and stopping Nicholas. Defeated, he regarded the cop. 'Yes, I have,' he agreed. 'But I don't think you can help.'

Some of the spectators had remained. 'I'm a friend of Thérèse Oiseau,' he pleaded with them generally. 'She's just gone off in that cab. Does anyone know where she is going?'

A smart couple stepped forward and the policeman stepped back. 'Thérèse?' said the man. 'You're a friend of hers?'

'I am. Nicholas Boulting from England. I've been trying desperately to contact her. Can you tell me where she's gone?'

'Kennedy Airport,' said the woman firmly. 'She's flying home to Guadeloupe this afternoon.'

'Thanks so much,' breathed Nicholas. He turned and ran back to the taxi he had just left. The driver blinked. 'Kennedy,' gasped Nicholas. 'Airport.'

'Is this a movie or somethin'?'

'Hold it. Just slow a moment will you.'

Abreast of the group on the pavement Nicholas leaned out and called: 'Do you know which airline?'

The couple looked bewildered. In the background the policeman was scratching his head with his cap.

'Oh yes, Thérèse,' the man called back. He looked quickly at his wife. 'American Airlines,' she said.

Nicholas waved. 'Thank you. Thanks a lot.' He urged the driver on. The man whistled and asked: 'Is there a prize?'

'There is,' said Nicholas. 'If we get there in time.'

Suddenly he realised he had forgotten about Rubicon. He had forgotten about the *Ed Edwards Show*. He looked at his watch. It was ten past three. 'Oh God,' he said. The driver's eyes went nervously over his shoulder. 'You got a problem?' he asked. 'I mean another problem?'

'I'm supposed to be on television,' muttered Nicholas. 'On the *Ed Edwards Show*.'

Staring in his mirror the man said: 'Sure.'

They reached Kennedy at a quarter to four. He paid the driver, who was relieved to see him go, and rushed, jacket-flying, into the American Airlines section. She was just walking away from the check-in desk. He went joyfully, his arms opening. 'Thérèse!'

She turned and saw him, her face widening with astonishment. She dropped her handbag. He picked it up. Thérèse was speechless, then began to laugh. 'Oh, you're so crazy,' she said.

She held out her arms and they embraced, their bodies together, her soft cheek against his face. They kissed. She was still laughing. 'You . . . appear,' she said still with her arms about him. '*Pouf!* Like some magic! In England, in Paris, now New York. And I am just leaving.'

364

'Thérèse,' he pleaded. 'Do you have to leave? Right now?'

Still she could not believe it. 'Let us sit and talk a little,' she said as though trying to make some sense of the situation. She took him by the hand and led him across the front of the Departures area. They sat on two seats next to a curled and bearded Orthodox Jew who began to take an interest in their conversation.

'Nicholas,' she said. 'I must be on my plane. I am going home. It is not possible to stay here.'

'You have a new husband,' he said bleakly.

'He is not my husband yet,' she said. Her eyes widened. 'You have been investigating, checking up. . . .'

'I've been following you, trying to catch up with you,' he said. He could not take his eyes from her face. 'I've been desperately trying to find you. And we've been in the same hotel, for God's sake, the Waldorf.'

She nodded slowly trying not to smile. 'You also?' she said. 'The Waldorf?'

'I didn't know until you checked out.'

'I still have my key,' she remembered. 'Always I forget to give the hotel key.' She took the key from her handbag. He stared at it. 'I don't believe anything any longer,' he confessed. 'Four hundred and ninety-eight.'

'That was my room,' she said. Realisation dawned. 'Nicholas . . . you were not . . .'

'Four hundred and ninety-six,' he moaned. '*You were in the next room.*' He put his face in his hands. 'I'm bloody fated.'

She was laughing again. 'I cannot help this,' she said helplessly. 'I must laugh, it is so terrible.'

He nodded and began to laugh too. 'It's incredible,' he giggled. 'As you always say, crazy.'

'Always I say that for you,' she replied tenderly. 'Crazy.' They held hands. 'But you must go?' he asked her again.

Thérèse nodded, her eyes becoming misted. 'It is so romantic,' she said. 'It makes me cry and laugh also.'

'You're still not married?'

'No. He is married already, Nicholas. But it is okay. I am

content.' She grimaced. 'I am sorry to tell you. He sails his yachts with his clients and I sail too with him sometimes. Also I paint.'

'I know. You have become famous.'

'Almost as famous as you. I saw your picture in a French newspaper and it talked about you being interviewed for television . . .'

'Rubicon' he whispered.

'What is Rubicon?'

'He's a man.' She began looking about her. He corrected her. 'He's at the Waldorf now. I'm supposed to be on a television programme *now*! The *Ed Edwards Show*.'

'But you are here. Will you be in time?'

'No,' he sighed. 'But there it is. I'll have to telephone Rubicon when you have gone. If you *are* going.'

She smiled and held her hand out to him once more. He took it gently. 'I am going,' she repeated glancing at her watch. 'And very soon.' She paused. 'You and your wife?'

'We're still together,' he said.

'Your agreement, your truce, is until the end of November,' she smiled.

'You remember?'

'Of course. You told me.'

'It is now October,' he said.

Thérèse touched him softly and rose from the seat. The Orthodox Jew looked disappointed they were going.

They walked towards the Departures exit. They embraced and kissed again with warmth. She held her face against his cheek. 'For us, Nicholas,' she whispered, 'it must always be October.'

'Where are you?' enquired Rubicon when they had paged him at the hotel. He sounded flat, finished.

'At Kennedy Airport.'

'God help me. Are you quitting? Going home?'

'No. I'm coming back to the city.'

'It's too late. Too late for the show.'

'It's four forty-five. I can make it, still. I'll see you at the studio.'

'But unless you got a jet engine up your ass there's no way.'

'I'm sorry. I had to see her.'

'You saw her? Well, that's something. I'm glad. I guess in the end you made the right choice. Is the big love story now on?'

'No. She went home.'

'In that case it wasn't the right choice. Okay, Nick, get to the studio. You have the address. I'll go over and see if I can stall them. But I don't think sweet-talking will do anything. They'll slip somebody else in, a recorded interview, or show a cut of a film or something. They're not going to be happy people.'

He arrived at the studio on Broadway ten minutes before the *Ed Edwards Show* was going on the air. Rubicon in his overcoat was hunched in the reception area like a crumpled camel. 'Too late, too late,' he said waving a limp hand as Nicholas ran through the doors.

'But I'm here! I'm ready to go on.'

'Ed Edwards won't *have* you on,' he said. 'Don't go through there or they may stab you. I thought they were going to kill *me*.'

Nicholas sat down heavily. The receptionists across the floor were pointing him out to each other. 'Nobody's ever screwed up on this show,' said Rubicon. 'Before today.'

'I'm sorry,' breathed Nicholas. He frowned. 'I hope you don't get fired over this.'

'Fired? I can't get fired. I'm a one-man band. I can only fire myself.'

'I mean the publishers drop you. I'll talk to them. I'll tell them it was my fault.'

Rubicon shrugged. 'I think they were going to drop me anyway,' he said. 'This might have saved me, getting you on the show, but not for long. I expected to go. Only now it will be sooner.'

'I don't know what to say.'

'You said it. You said you're sorry. Well maybe you didn't

367

miss much. That asshole would try to crucify you anyway, and the book I bet.'

'You think so?'

'Sure I think so. And think of the rain forest we're saving.'

'You're a good guy.'

'I'm independent,' sniffed Rubicon working his rubbery lips. 'You've never seen anybody so independent as me.'

'Let's go and I'll buy you a drink.'

'You owe me more than one.' Rubicon stood and wrapped the overcoat around himself. 'There's a crap bar around the block. It should suit my mood. You can tell me about your big love story and I can tell you about mine. All of them.'

Seventeen

Sarah looked down on the Park Lane traffic from the lofty window of the hotel suite. Thoughtfully she viewed the October patterns of London. She stood for more than a minute before turning and surveying the room with its pale blue sofas, its tinted prints, its dark wood, heavy carpet and long drapes. She stepped into the bedroom. It was luxurious; the bed too good to sleep in. The bathroom was gleaming, the towels thick.

A bottle of champagne stood in an ice bucket on a squat glass table with a message wishing Nicholas success that evening. It was assured anyway; the reviews of *Lost in France* in the previous day's Sunday newspapers had been serious and favourable. Paul Garrett had telephoned Sarah that morning at Boxley after Nicholas had left for a day of interviews. He exclaimed: 'He's done it! We're on our way!'

So, they were on their way. To where? To what? Her apprehension was growing. She twisted the champagne bottle in the bucket and listened to the ice slushing. The *Evening Standard* lay folded on the same table. She picked it up and opened it. There it was again; she put her hand to her mouth. It was not even a review this time but an article over a whole page with the headline: 'COULD YOU FACE A MYSTERY LOVER?'

Nervously she read the preamble: 'Nicholas Boulting's new novel poses a challenge for literary marriages. Can a writer be so obsessed with a fictional lover that the lover becomes real?' There followed the views of four authors with their photographs. At the top was a grinning picture of Nicholas. She meant to drop the newspaper back on to the table but, as though it had taken umbrage, it slipped and slid on to the carpet. She almost picked it up but changed her mind and left it there. As she returned to the window she trod on it.

Looking out from the high place she traced the paths of the planes descending to Heathrow in the west. Directly below her was Hyde Park, the traffic streaming through, splitting, turning away, syphoning in different directions. In her mood she thought how it was like life itself; as many lives as there were cars. She calculated the direction in which Boxley lay and she narrowed her eyes to the horizon that way but her gaze came to an end at the mist of London's edge.

It was only three o'clock but there were autumn lights in the buildings at the fringe of the park. She did not expect Nicholas from his round of interviews for at least another hour. She took her dress for the evening out of its cover and hung it in the wardrobe and then unpacked her case. The telephone rang. It was Nicholas.

'I just wanted to make sure you had arrived,' he said. He sounded breathless. 'I'm at the Television Centre and I've got one more interview after this. Its terrific, isn't it. There's a huge piece in the *Standard*.'

'I saw it; it's outrageous,' she said.

'Sarah, don't be upset. It's just the newspapers.'

Deflated, she said: 'What time do you think you'll be here?'

'By five at the outside. We have to be at the Garbo Club by seven.'

'I'll be ready.'

'Willie didn't come with you?'

'You knew he wouldn't. He wanted *us* to go and see *him*.'

'His début,' sighed Nicholas. 'What is the group called again?'

'Bliss,' she told him without emphasis. 'According to Willie it's a sell-out at the Hop Pole, Wembley.'

'Another time we'll go,' he promised. 'It might even make another angle,' he added thoughtfully. 'Author's son has big night of his own, absent from Dad's party, sort of thing.'

'He believes it's *his* big night,' said Sarah patiently. 'Your book launch is secondary.'

Nicholas laughed. 'He didn't even tell us he could sing, or was singing with a band anyway, until last week. All this was fixed by then.'

'I know, but he wouldn't realise that.'

'The car picked you up all right?'

'Yes, everything went to schedule. I'm here in this enormous suite. Top floor. You're certainly going up in the world.'

'Sarah,' he said. '*We* are.'

'All right. *We* are.'

His voice dropped. 'And try to be a little more enthusiastic.'

'I am enthusiastic, but worried.'

'Be enthusiastic. Don't worry.'

'Nicholas,' she responded biting her lip. 'I'm very glad for you.'

When she replaced the telephone she sat motionless, expressionless. She had plenty of time; she could go for a walk, perhaps indoors, around the unfamiliar hotel. She then considered ordering tea from room service, or of combining the two and going down to the lounge for tea. In the end she opened the refrigerator and made herself a large gin and tonic. She carried it to the window, turning her nose up in a sniff at the golden neck of the champagne projecting from its bucket, and stood scanning the diminishing outline of London. It was afternoon dusk and the cars in the park already had their lights on. She finished the drink standing and watching, then turned, opened the fridge, and made another.

Going into the bathroom she turned the gold bath taps. There was a telephone: she had never called anyone from her bath and the prospect engaged her. But who? For a moment she was tempted. She looked at the time. But instead she went back to the bedroom, undressed and put on her silk robe. Her drink, to her surprise, was low in the glass and she went into the sitting room and replenished it with tonic. On an afterthought she topped it up with a measure of gin.

Walking towards the bathroom she picked up the *Evening Standard* from the floor and took it with her. She stood the gin and tonic on it while she took off the robe. She examined her

371

reflection in the mirror, hoping that the careful lighting would be flattering, but she looked much the same. She poked her tongue out at herself and climbed into the bath. Sipping the gin and reading the page in the newspaper, she lay back among the suds. 'Who,' asked one of the women in the article, 'can this woman be? I would be uncomfortable to have to live with her, knowing how my husband felt about her.'

' 'Oooo can this woman be?' repeated Sarah among the suds. ' 'Ow can I save my darling 'usband from 'er wiles and 'er charms?' She dropped the paper over the side of the bath and said: 'Eet es fucking rubbish.'

The glass was almost empty again. She stood, slightly unsteadily, in the bath, the suds on her body rolling down her stomach and hips. She turned towards the mirror and raised the gin. '*Chérie*,' she said in her thickest accent. 'You 'ave come 'ere to ruin my life.' Her tone returned to normal. 'Go on, ruin it.' She raised the glass in a toast. 'See if I care.'

To her surprise she had some difficulty in getting out of the bath. She used the luxurious towels and then cleaned her teeth briskly, telling herself it would make her feel steadier. It did not. Gingerly she left the bathroom and went towards the bed. She tipped stiffly forward on to her face on the quilt. '*Au revoir, chéri*,' she muttered. She fell to sleep.

When Nicholas arrived hurriedly an hour later she was still sprawled on the bed. Almost before he was through the outer door of the suite he called: 'Darling, it's really zooming!' He went into the lavatory from the sitting room. 'They're reprinting,' he shouted. 'And all the London bookshops have reordered.' He zipped up and pushed the flush. 'Paul is sure it will be in the bestseller list this . . .' Turning the corner he saw her flat on the bed in her silk robe, her legs spread inelegantly, a gentle snore blowing her hair. 'Sarah . . . ,' he said urgently moving towards her. Her gin glass was on the bedside table. 'Sarah. . . .' He nudged her and woke her. 'Wassermarra?' she mumbled.

'It's *you*,' he said. 'That's what's the matter.' They surveyed each other, her staring, him glaring. 'Are you all right?' he said.

'Of course I'm all right.' She pushed her hair away, blinked and sat up. 'I was just having a nap. What time is it?'

'Five thirty,' he said brusquely. He went into the vestibule of the suite where the porter had left his suitcase. 'Some of us had better get a move on.' The three small empty gin bottles on top of the refrigerator caught his glance. 'We've got an hour,' he called.

'That's plenty,' she said appearing unsteadily at the bedroom door, stretching and yawning. 'I won't be late for your night of triumph, don't you worry yourself.'

'You'd better have a bath,' he suggested. 'It will wake you up.'

Sarah blinked. 'I've *had* a bath,' she said. She advanced swaying a little, her arms stretched out. 'Smell me, I smell lovely.'

He picked up the telephone and dialled. 'Bring me a pot of coffee, please.'

'You think I'm the worse for wear,' she said pointing an accusing and quivering finger. 'Look, I haven't even touched your champagne.' She smiled idiotically. 'Let's have a few glasses now.'

'No,' he told her sharply. His voice moderated. 'No, please. I don't think we ought to open it now.'

'I've only had a couple of lousy gins and tonics,' she said sitting without grace. 'I won't let you down, I promise. I *will* have a bath. I'll have another one.'

He watched her with a sinking heart as she went crookedly towards the bathroom. The water started to run and Sarah began singing loudly and tunelessly. He crept to the refrigerator and, looking over his shoulder, poured himself a whisky. There was another empty gin miniature on the shelf inside. Sarah was still singing truculently in the bathroom. He telephoned Paul Garrett. 'Listen, Paul,' he said in a low voice. 'Sarah's pissed.'

'Is that her singing?' asked Garrett calmly.

'You can hear her?'

'I can hear someone. It's not very good is it.'

'Her singing?'

'No. The situation. You'll have to get her to the party. Otherwise all the press people will want to know where she is. They'll put their usual two and two together. But she can't turn up smashed. That would be even worse. I'd better warn Newby and Holly Grant.'

The buzzer on the outside door sounded. 'I've just got some coffee,' Nicholas told him. 'I'll get her there somehow.'

'Not somehow,' said Garrett. 'Sober.'

Nicholas put the telephone down and went to the door. The coffee was in a silver pot. When the waiter had gone he poured a cup and, without adding milk, took it into the bathroom. Sarah was half-submerged, her breasts projecting from the water. 'Ah, coffee,' she said amiably. 'Put it on there will you, my man.' She pointed to the breast floating nearest him.

'Oh, come on, darling,' he encouraged desperately. 'Don't mess about. We're going to be short of time.'

'Sorry, spoilsport,' she commented. Her sigh heaved her breasts clear of the water. 'All right, you hold it while I drink it. If you want to make sure I get it down my throat.'

Nicholas tightened his lips. 'I'll hold it,' he agreed sternly. 'You drink it.'

She took the coffee, a sip at a time, silently and apparently chastened. 'Would you mind leaving while I get out of the bath,' she requested primly when she had drained the cup. He left her and went into the bedroom, taking off his clothes and putting on the hotel dressing gown. She came in, pink-faced. 'You look like a boxer,' she said nodding at the towelling robe. 'A beaten champ.'

'Sarah,' he said. 'Sit down, please.' He patted the bed. She sat down. 'I'm sorry,' she said sadly. 'I had a few gins. I shouldn't have done it.'

'You'll be fine,' he said. 'But remember who is coming tonight.'

'All the press,' she sulked. 'The rotten, bloody press.'

'And our daughter. Deborah is coming, remember.'

'Yes, I know. I won't show anybody up. I promise.'

She asked him to pour her another cup of coffee and she drank it black. He went into the bathroom. When he emerged she was sitting in front of the dressing table brushing her hair. He was relieved. 'It should be a good party,' he encouraged. 'And it *is* important.'

'For us,' she said. It was a statement. 'You've been busy all day.'

'I've been everywhere. God knows how many interviews I've done.'

'I heard you on the radio,' she said. 'In the car coming down. The man turned up the sound for me. What a pity they can't think of anything else to ask you except about that woman.'

'It's not important. It's just press talk.'

'It's important to me,' she said watching him in the mirror. She mimicked: ' "Is she real?" "How did you think of her?" "You sound as though you're in love with her." All that claptrap.'

He shrugged apologetically. 'It sounded a great idea at the time,' he admitted. 'Holly Grant thought it was an angle and the publicity people went for it. Unfortunately, but fortunately for the book, it took off. She's very good at that. That's why they pay her. And once the press get hold of a good man-and-woman idea they'll never let it go. They follow it like a pack of hounds.'

'And tonight we'll be thrown to the hounds,' she said.

He regarded her reflection seriously. 'If you don't want to come, Sarah,' he said, 'you don't have to. I'll say you were taken ill.'

'No, no,' she said. 'I'll come. And I'll do you proud, Nicholas. And Paul Garrett, and what's-his-name Newby and Holly Grant. We're all in this together. We're going to make a fortune. We'll be rich.' She paused and arranged her hair. 'And remember the date.'

'It's October 18th,' he said.

'Exactly. Next month our year is up. You remember *our* year, *our* bargain. I don't want you running away from me again, not now that everything is looking so rich and so rosy. That would never do.'

*

At the Garbo Club Sir Handley Mallinder presented him with an expensive, red leather-bound copy of *Lost in France*, the title and his name tooled in gold. There were a hundred people in the room and they grouped around the dais to hear what he had to say. Nicholas found himself confronted by strangers looking up in admiration and expectation. Some had note-books held in the hand that did not hold a champagne glass. Holly Grant, in a green dress, was standing apparently casually to one side, but her eyes were flicking carefully about the room. He caught a reassuring glimpse of Sol, at his side a flaxen-haired girl with a baffled face. Sol winked towards him. Sarah was next to Paul and Yvonne with Henry Newby and the group from Mallinder's. Deborah was there, a little self-conscious but her eyes soft as she watched her father; she held a notebook and a tilted pen.

He thanked Sir Handley for the book. 'The books, I should say, I suppose.' He held up the presentation copy. 'This splendid copy which I will treasure and also for the book at large, so to speak. My publishers have supported me through-out the writing of *Lost in France* in the same way as my agent, Paul Garrett, has supported me, bullied me, cajoled me, and threatened me.' They laughed conventionally. 'And, of course, I must thank my wife, Sarah, for her understanding and forbearance.' There was a noticeable stir, as though they had been waiting for this. 'Both she and I have been asked a lot of questions about the possible identity of the French lady, Cécile, in my novel. She exists, very much so – in the imagina-tion of the author . . .'

Sarah was going to do something. He sensed it and then he saw that she was trying to climb on the dais. It was too high and her skirt was too tight. Someone jocularly gave her a lift and she arrived, inelegantly, at his side. He fixed a smile. 'Will the real Mrs Boulting please stand up,' she said uncertainly. She gathered herself and smoothed her skirt. 'If she can.'

Paul, standing among the crowd, seized the initiative and began to clap. Holly Grant tried to rally some applause. Yvonne did also. A few others joined in loyally. Sarah stood surprised. Nervously Nicholas reached out and took her hand. She was trembling. She seemed to collapse inwardly, her resolve, her anger, or whatever it was that had made her mount the platform, drained. 'Thank you very much,' she mumbled and left him standing there. She got down awkwardly. Two or three people clapped.

The reception lasted two hours and was to be followed by a dinner for twenty-five. Paul waited until Nicholas had finished talking to yet another gossip columnist and then approached sharply. 'Sarah's having a hard time,' he said quietly. Nicholas looked towards the stairs where his wife was sitting, drink hung in her hand, with a well-dressed, worn-looking woman. 'That's Nancy Hitch,' he said. 'You know, Hitch the Bitch. She'll crucify both of you if you're not careful. She's doing a job on Sarah. I think I'd better move in. I'll bring her over to you. She'll swap Sarah for you. Otherwise I'll never be able to detach her.'

Nicholas watched the journalist, her head pecking like a bird as she put her careful questions. Asking then asking again, persuading, pushing, pointing. In her hand she held a tape recorder the size of her thumb. When Paul interrupted the conversation she did not appear put out. Sarah looked up with a dozy gratitude. God knows what she had been saying. Paul adroitly took her away and led her across the room to Deborah and Yvonne. Nancy Hitch lit a cigarette and strolled across to Nicholas.

'I'd finished anyway,' she said. 'I've got all I want from Sarah.'

'Good,' said Nicholas. He regarded her coolly. 'Now you can have a go at me. I wrote it.'

Glass in one hand, cigarette smouldering and tape recorder purring in the other, Nancy Hitch said: 'Right, Nicholas, I might as well come straight to the point, and you know what that is.'

'What would that be?'

'Listen, it's got to be good publicity for you. The book will take off. I want to know about this woman, Cécile.'

'She's a character in a novel,' responded Nicholas doggedly. He lifted his glass: 'Cheers.'

'Your publishers have said she is based on a real lover.'

He laughed. It was louder than he intended, like a bark. She stepped back, her eyes tightening. He apologised. Then he said: 'It was the publicity people. You know what they're like. You ought to. It was Holly Grant drumming up interest.'

'Did you know she was putting this story about?'

He shrugged. 'It was suggested as a media angle,' he admitted. 'But frankly I didn't realise it would gather pace like this, you people actually swallowing it. It got out of hand that's all. It was too successful.'

The tape recorder was still turning. 'So this mysterious French woman does not exist?' she put to him.

'Only in my fevered imagination.'

She knew something. He could tell she knew something. 'Your wife does not seem so sure,' she said. 'She thinks there is a distinct possibility that the lady could be real.'

'Sarah would not say that,' he argued, trying to sound sure. 'She is not accustomed to being interrogated by journalists, that's all. She's a wife and a mother.'

'She's a nice woman. Not so exotic as a French painter perhaps.'

'Oh, for God's sake . . . ,' he began angrily. She put her champagne glass to his lips to silence him. 'Nicholas,' she said very quietly. 'One of our New York stringers came up with a story this week that you had missed an appearance on the *Ed Edwards* television show. According to him you were at Kennedy, trying to catch up with a French lady, an artist called . . .' Horrified he watched as she took a folded fax page from her handbag. It was the article with the picture of Thérèse from *Art and Artists*.

'You seem to know what I'm talking about,' she smiled gratefully.

'I don't,' he muttered. 'I don't for a moment. You're just out for some of the shit for which you are famous, lady.'

'Justly famous,' she responded. 'The two researchers on the show told our stringer about it.' She examined the fax: '. . . Carl Gaylaw and Ellen Peabody.' She looked up. 'Remember them?'

'They . . . they know nothing,' he managed to say. 'They are trying to get revenge because I didn't go on their crappy television programme.'

'Right. Because you were at Kennedy chasing a French lady . . .' She checked the fax again. '. . . Thérèse Oiseau.' She drained her champagne. 'Do you have any comment on that?'

'I have nothing to say except it is a fabrication. I'll sue.'

'I bet you will,' she smiled grimly. She walked away. At the door she turned and gave him a slow, brazen wave. He stood dumbly. The party, *his* party, continued around him. He searched the room for Sarah. Paul appeared. 'You don't look like a happy novelist,' he said.

'That Hitch woman knows everything. All about Thérèse,' grunted Nicholas. Paul, for once, looked astonished. 'Who told her?'

'They picked it up from New York. I missed that bloody television show because I was trying to catch Thérèse at the airport. . . .' He took in Garrett's expression. 'I didn't tell you.'

'No,' the agent said carefully. 'I seem to have missed that one. It sounds like another novel.'

'I'm sick of *this* one,' snapped Nicholas. He thought about it. 'The fact is, Paul, I have never, *never* believe me, had any sexual relations with Thérèse Oiseau.' He pursed his lips. 'She *wouldn't*. So let that bloody newspaper or any of the other rags say so and I'll sue.'

Garrett tutted. 'I doubt if they'll *say* it. They'll insinuate it.' He smiled wryly. 'They'll probably think that it's a better story – that after all the chasing you've never done more than shake a friendly hand.'

'God, what can I do? What about Sarah?'

'What about Sarah, indeed?' said Garrett swivelling his eyes. 'Did she put *that* much away before she came here tonight?'

'A few gins,' Nicholas told him. 'Is she bad?'

'She's getting towards bad. We can go up to dinner soon. I'll get her wedged in with me and Holly Grant. You've got to be at another table with Sir Handley and it's probably just as well to keep you at a distance.' He regarded Nicholas seriously. 'Does she get violent?' he asked.

'She can,' admitted Nicholas dolefully. 'Do you want me to take her back to the hotel?'

'No. It's your party. It's to get publicity. It's odd how many things can go wrong,' said Garrett glancing towards Holly whose eyes were swivelling. 'You dragging Sarah away would make a better story than ever.'

'Paul, what can I do?'

'Pray,' suggested Garrett. 'Deeply.'

As he turned Deborah came through the people. 'Dad,' she said diffidently. 'I want to interview you now. Can we sit down somewhere?'

He kissed her on the cheek. 'Why not? I'll give you an exclusive.'

'It's only for college,' she said with a touch of embarrassment. They went to a table and sat down. She surveyed the room. 'I'm not sure I want to do this journalism,' she said at once. 'Some of these reporters have been giving Mum a hard time. Especially the women. All about the French lady in your book.' She turned her eyes directly to him. 'They're making out she's real.'

'Cécile is a character in a novel,' he said carefully. 'It was a publicity move that seems to have backfired.' He spoke carefully so that he was not lying to her. She opened her unused notebook. A waiter went by carrying a tray of empty glasses. Nicholas asked him to bring two glasses of champagne for them but Deborah said: 'Not me, thanks. Not when I'm working.'

Deborah smoothed the page. 'I know all about your age and everything,' she said awkwardly. Nicholas smiled and touched her hair. 'So I don't need to go into all that.' She glanced up from the notebook. 'This is the first interview I've ever done,' she said.

'Well, make sure you ask something interesting,' he advised gently. 'Then you'll get an interesting answer.'

'All right,' she said. She took a deep breath. 'Mr Boulting, what sort of effect, do you think, being famous all of a sudden has had on your family?'

*

The tables in the restaurant were set around the walls below pictures and ornate mirrors. Sarah appeared to find the stairs a happy difficulty and Nicholas watched her anxiously as she laughed her way up, helped by a bemused Sir Handley Mallinder and Henry Newby. Paul, close in attendance, shook his head, indicating that Nicholas was not to worry. The invited columnists, reviewers and other guests were to sit at named places. 'Is there anyone especially spiteful on Sarah's table?' Nicholas whispered to Paul. 'I think she's had enough.'

'Enough questions?' Paul was to sit on her right, Holly on her left.

'Enough of everything. Keep the bottle at a distance if you can.'

Nicholas sat himself with an amiable group who appeared to have done with their interrogations and were preparing to concentrate on the food and wine. Deborah sat gravely next to him. 'My daughter,' he said to the table in general. 'Wants to become a journalist. She is doing a course at college. Any advice will be welcome.'

'Do something else,' muttered a weary-eyed man. 'Anything.' He was hushed down by a motherly woman columnist who began to converse earnestly with Deborah. Sir Handley sat on the other side of Nicholas who directed successive glances towards Sarah's table. Once she looked towards him but did not appear to spot him. At intervals Paul's head would project around Sarah's and he would nod. Nicholas had never seen him nervous before.

The man with the spent face, sitting opposite Nicholas, emptied his glass and mouth in almost the same movement and said: 'If for a moment, Nicholas, we can get away from the subject of the dark lady of France in your novel . . .'

'And I would be grateful,' smiled Nicholas.

'It's been overdone,' muttered the motherly woman.

'Can't understand how it came up,' put in Sir Handley. 'Fiction is fiction, surely.'

The journalist said: 'The *quest* is something which invariably

381

fascinates, the tracing of someone, something, by a tentative thread. From Sherlock Holmes onwards people have always had an interest with clues, with finding out, with adding two and two, with picking up the smallest fragment.' He became theatrically animate. '*There it is* . . . they cry. . . .'

'THAT'S IT!' The bellow came from Sarah. Every face went towards her. Sir Handley tipped his wine over his suit. Deborah's eyes filled with concern, her hand went to her mouth. Nicholas, alarms sounding, half-rose. . . .

Sarah levered herself into a standing pose at the head of the table. Holly was trying to hold her down but failed. 'I've had ENOUGH!' Sarah shouted. Her face was deep, blotched pink, her eyes were glittering, her fists clenched. 'ENOUGH! Do you hear?' The guests at her table leaned away anxiously. 'Enough of all you dirt-diggers.' Majestically she swung towards the silently gesticulating Nicholas. 'Enough of *you* as well, Mr Clever Author!'

The weary-eyed man started to smile gently at his plate as if he had known it would happen. The motherly woman was trying to fumble her notebook from her handbag. Deborah was whispering: 'No, no . . . Mum . . . ,' and beginning to cry. Nicholas said loudly: 'Sarah, please stop it.'

His wife turned and blew a wet raspberry at him. She rounded again on the astounded guests at her own table. 'Parasites,' she sneered, bending forward. Paul and Holly were powerless. Sir Handley called: 'Hear, hear!' Continuing the movement Sarah grasped her end of the table and to howls of dismay and protest, heaved it on end, tipping food, wine, cutlery, crockery, knocking the occupants from their chairs. Standing at her side Paul Garrett remained immobile. 'Now you've done it,' he observed quietly. 'I'll say,' added Holly Grant. There was a look of suppressed delight on her face.

'I'VE DONE IT!' echoed Sarah. 'And I'm bloody glad I've done it!'

Four journalists were pinned below the table, peering out from its perimeter with consternation and astonishment. One woman began to panic like a trapped horse, a man was seized with a fit of wheezing, another thought his leg was broken.

Nicholas moved. 'It's time we went,' he said marching smartly towards his wife.

'I'M GOING!' she howled in his face. 'Don't worry! Hypocrites!' She gave him a hefty push which sent him stumbling over the guests still immobilised under the table. The staff were advancing, arms held out ineffectually. The manager said the police had been called.

Picking up her handbag Sarah strode in a surprisingly straight line to the door. She revolved and with an extravagant gesture to the occupants of the room, vanished from sight. Deborah was crying bitterly at the table. 'She didn't mean it,' she sobbed to the motherly journalist who wrote it down.

Attempting to look dignified Nicholas picked himself up. 'Yvonne,' he said to Paul's wife. 'Look after Deborah will you.' Ashen-faced Yvonne nodded and looked towards the girl sitting with her hands to her face. Paul said to Nicholas: 'I'll sort things out here.' He surveyed the mayhem. Two waiters were lifting the table and the people were shuffling on their backs from below it. 'I'll try anyway.' Holly Grant, white-faced but hardly able to believe her luck, made some attempt at restoring calm.

Nicholas stumbled down the stairs for some reason still holding his presentation book. He sensed the reporters following him. There was a small congregation of staff at the door, their eyes on the street. 'She escaped in a taxi,' said one helpfully.

Half in the gutter Nicholas ran searching for a taxi light. He saw one and waved.

Pale-faced and exhausted he leaned back in the cab. There were reporters on the pavement; a camera flashed. He closed his eyes. What did it matter now?

He reached the hotel and fumbling for his key went up to the suite. As he reached the door it was violently opened revealing his wife, her eyes like knives, her face creased. She was going out with her suitcase. 'Just a minute, lady,' he said. She saw his expression and backed away into the room. He shut the door. 'Where are you going?' he said. 'I'm running. Like you did,' she answered stoutly. 'Don't try to stop me.'

'I won't, believe me. But first I think you owe me an apology.'

'Apology? Apology? Don't be a ninny all your life, Nicholas. Why should I owe *you* an apology? I'm sick of you and your bloody book.' She pointed at the presentation volume he had put on the table. 'I can't run away quickly enough.'

'You're jealous,' he said ramming his finger at her. 'That's what it is. You're jealous of me.'

'You! Jealous of you, you prat! I'd never sink as low as that.'

'You behaved tonight like some moronic teenager.'

She burst into tears, but wiped her hand across her face and glared at him again. 'I can do without you,' she said simply.

He stepped towards the window, his eyes wet and angry. He heard the door open slowly and close sharply. When he turned around she had vanished.

'Good riddance,' he said. There came a howl from the corridor outside. He swore and hurried towards the door. Outside he saw her at the distant end of the passage. 'Goodbye, you ninny!' she called, giving him the finger. She opened a door and vanished through it. He shouted something at her. One of the room doors opened as far as the security chain would allow. 'What's going on?' demanded a man's voice.

Repeating: 'Sorry, sorry,' as he went Nicholas hurried the length of the corridor. The door through which she had gone was marked: 'Fire Exit to Roof.'

No. No. She would never do that. Not Sarah. He flung open the door revealing a flight of stone stairs illuminated by a single bulb. As he began to go up the door at the top opened and Sarah stood outlined in the frame. She looked wild, the night wind blowing her clothes, her hair flying. 'I'm going to do it!' she shouted manically. 'You just see if I don't!'

'Sarah!' he howled. 'Sarah, stop being so bloody stupid. Sarah!'

He pounded up the sounding steps. She had closed the door

on him and he prayed there was no lock on the other side. There could not be. It was a fire escape. He threw the door open. His wife was standing on the roof, by the parapet, outlined by the late glimmer of the city. She was calm and resolute. 'Want to see me?' she challenged.

He halted, the cold of the night on his face. 'Sarah,' he pleaded. 'Don't. Think of Deborah, think of Willie.'

She hooted. 'You really are a prat, Nicholas. If you think *I'm* going to jump, then I'm *not*. But *this is*!' To his horror he saw that she had his book in her hand, his leather-bound presentation copy of *Lost in France*. Given to him by Sir Handley Mallinder.

'You cow,' he choked.

'Moo!' she replied. She brought her arm back like a grenadier pitching a hand bomb and projected the book far out into the London night sky. He saw it fly and drop and vanish. 'There,' she said turning and smiling and rubbing her hands together. '*Au revoir, mon* fucking *chéri.*'

'Hello, Nicholas, you're there. What happened? Are you all right?'

He groaned. 'Absolutely fine for a man who's spent half the bloody night on the roof.'

'On the roof?'

'Of this hotel. God, Paul, she went berserk. She threw my book, my leather one, off the top and then she locked me out there. I was up there for an hour in the cold. I only got down by slinging a piece of rope over the side and banging it against a window. I could be up there now, frozen solid.'

'I take it that Sarah is not there,' Paul said gingerly.

'You can take it she isn't. God knows where she has gone. She's probably at home. Or at a police station. She rang the hotel in the early hours to inform them that I was out on the roof but by that time I was down. Somehow I don't think they'll welcome us here again.'

'You haven't seen the papers?'

'Tell me the bad news.'

'Nancy Hitch has made hay with your French lady. The headline says *Lost in France* – which can't be bad for the sales of the book – then underneath: "The real woman who is an author's dream." Then there's a whole screed about how they traced Thérèse Oiseau. It looks as if they even got as far as Guadeloupe but the trail ran dry. For this edition anyway.'

Nicholas groaned: 'It's terrible. It gets worse.'

Garrett said: 'Mallinder's are doing cartwheels, I might as well tell you. It's in every morning paper. The book is flying out of the shops as if it had wings.'

'I'm glad of that,' Nicholas said hollowly. 'I'll tell Sarah. She'll be pleased.'

'Do you think you and she have come to the end of the road?' asked Paul seriously. 'I have to say it looked a tiny bit like it.'

'I don't know,' Nicholas sighed. 'I'd better go home and see if she's there.'

'You'll have the press on your tail again today,' warned the agent. 'They're probably doorstepping outside your house now. And watch for loitering reporters in the hotel lobby.'

Nicholas called the duty manager. The man said: 'There are two journalists in the foyer. They've just arrived. Do you wish to avoid them?'

'Can you get me out of the back door?' said Nicholas.

'We have several back doors, Mr Boulting, I'm sure we can use one of them.'

'In the meantime can you monitor any calls coming through here. I don't want any press interference. Just ask who it is.'

'I am so glad you were able to get down from the roof,' mentioned the duty manager. 'The people you woke with your . . . er . . . rope trick live in New York. They did not seem to find it an unusual occurrence.'

'I was grateful, believe me. It was not nice out there. You could have found me coated with frost. I'll be ready to leave in half an hour.'

'I'll make sure the back door is open, sir.'

There were two men standing outside his gate as he drove up to the house. One produced a camera from below his coat and took a picture of him. The other, a man with an untidy moustache, orange at the fringe, and a face full of broken veins, asked him rapid questions. 'It's all going to be in the *Evening Standard*, anyway,' the man said like an assurance.

'No comment,' muttered Nicholas. He had sometimes wondered how it felt to say that. 'Nothing,' he added sharply and unnecessarily. He went into the house and slammed the door then spied through the window at them. The moustached man was writing in a notebook. The cameraman was taking a picture of his car. A woman cleaner emerged from the house next door and the reporter began busily to interview her. She kept pointing to Nicholas's house. Then the photographer asked to take her picture and she gave her hair a push and posed.

Sarah was not there. From the evidence of the bedroom it was apparent that she had packed and gone. On the lavatory cover he found a letter in a long envelope curiously addressed to: 'Nicholas Boulting, Esq.' He picked it up, sat on the cover and opened it.

Dear Nicholas,
Now it is me who is running away. Last night was the last straw. I know it's not all your fault but I can't see any point in trying to hang on any longer. We are not happy together and we both know that. Whether either of us has anyone else has nothing to do with it. If we had nobody else in our minds at all it would still be the same. I don't want to be married to you and, if you are honest with yourself, you must know that you feel the same about me.

By the time you read this I will be on my way to Chicago. I am taking Willie with me but Deborah is remaining in London because of college. My parents will be bringing Jenkins back some time today for you to look after. I knew a dog would never save us.

The signature was: 'Sincerely, Sarah.'

He was still scowling at it when the chimes rang. The first thing he would do would be to get rid of that bell; that sickly sound of domestic peace and well-being. He put the letter on the table and went to the door. The journalists had gone. Standing outside with Jenkins cagily behind them were his in-laws. The dog shuffled into view and regarded him with hopeful, wet eyes, unsurely wagging its hind quarters.

'We've brought your animal back,' announced Doreen.

'Your dog,' said Herbert.

'Oh good. I missed him.'

He stood aside and they walked in. Doreen's eyes went around like those of an ace investigator. Her nostrils worked. The dog, released by Nicholas from its lead, rushed into the kitchen and tried to hide in its basket.

'Can you smell something?' Nicholas asked Doreen. 'Perfume perhaps.'

She coloured. 'I didn't say anything' she said.

'She always has sniffed,' put in Herbert. 'Ever since I've known her.'

Nicholas picked up the letter. 'I've only just got home,' he said.

'You've seen the newspapers?' Doreen sniffed again.

'I haven't read them yet.'

'You ought to,' said Herbert practically. 'You might be able to sue them.'

Tapping the envelope on the table Nicholas said: 'I've just read Sarah's letter. I take it she telephoned you.'

'Naturally she did,' said Doreen. 'She would.'

'At five o'clock this morning,' added Herbert. He walked into the kitchen with the dog's lead. The dog cowered.

'Poor Sarah,' said Doreen scowling towards him. 'She's had enough.'

'She had undoubtedly had enough last night,' agreed Nicholas mildly. 'Anyway she is now on her way to Chicago. And she has taken Willie with her. I think she is going to visit a Mr David Fawkes who used to be my friend, golfing partner and solicitor.'

Doreen's face broadened with pleasure. 'Ah, I thought it might be him.' She called towards the kitchen. 'It's that David Fawkes, Herbert,' she said. 'Remember how nice he was.'

Her husband came from the kitchen and faced Nicholas apologetically. 'I think we'd better be off,' he said. 'It'll just be about time for long walkies.' He nodded towards the kitchen.

Nicholas took them to the door he let them out. 'Lovely day,' said Doreen sniffing the air. She smiled to herself. 'A solicitor.'

'Make sure you take Doreen for a long walkies,' Nicholas said to Herbert. He closed the door and he went to the living room window and watched them cleaning their car before they drove away. Doreen's hand came into view around the yew and she pointed towards the house. He knew she was saying: 'Fancy living in a vicarage.' Nicholas went to the kitchen. Jenkins looked at him stupidly and seemed overwhelmingly relieved when Nicholas gave him a pat. 'You're a poor bugger,' said Nicholas.

He stood up. 'I'm a poor bugger too.'

He bent and ran his fingers through the dog's indifferent coat. 'In fact we're a couple of poor buggers together.'

He telephoned Paul Garrett. 'The situation is that Sarah has cleared off to Chicago, to pay a courtesy call on David Fawkes – you remember, my solicitor – taking Willie with her and I'm at home with Jenkins the dog. End of story.'

'Have you had any press people there? There's a big piece in the *Evening Standard* about Sarah demolishing the table. There's a nice picture of you.'

'I suppose you have to expect something when it was the press who were actually *trapped* under the table. There was a reporter and a photographer outside the house when I got here this morning but they don't appear to be over-enthusiastic.' He surveyed the front of the house from the window. 'They've gone now. Probably to the pub. I might go down and get drunk with them. Tell them my side of the story.'

Garrett said: 'I wouldn't do that. I've already had two offers from newspapers for your true-life love story, the *Daily Mail* and *News of the World*. How you have followed this entrancing French woman all over the world, how she's become an obsession with you. And how you will now go to her and together you'll walk off into the sunset.'

'They've already written the story.'

'That's the story they want. It could be a nice little earner.'

'You *wouldn't*.'

'It's not *my* story they want. It's yours. Mallinder's would love it. Holly Grant's a big success. They've been glugging champagne all day on your behalf anyway. You've got a big seller.'

'I'm not telling my *all* in any newspaper, and that's flat. Christ, Paul, I feel worn out. I feel like I'm coming apart at the seams.'

'What are you going to do?'

'Take Jenkins for a walk. Then I'm going to go to sleep.'

'Jenkins? Oh, the dog. I wish you hadn't called it Jenkins, Nick, it sounds like a butler.'

'I'll change it by deed poll when I get a minute.'

'You're going to stay in the house?'

'Do you have any better ideas? I've got to look after the dog.'

'Won't the dog go in a kennels?'

Nicholas grimaced at the phone. 'It's not his fault the marriage failed. The poor bloody animal has just been stuck with Sarah's parents. If I send him to a kennels he'll top himself.'

'A suicidal dog,' murmured Garrett. 'I must suggest that to Sol.' He paused. 'You could go and stay in Sol's place. He's going back to the States until after Christmas. You could move in there.'

'It might be a good idea. I can walk Jenkins along the canal.'

'Your love for this dog is touching.'

'I've got to love something. I'll ring Sol and ask. I don't know what I'll do in this house.'

There was another interval. 'You could write the screenplay of *Lying in Your Arms*,' Garrett suggested. 'Mr Zaltpepper's office want a contract now. They've offered a hundred thousand dollars for the script.'

Raising his glass Sol said: 'Welcome home.'

Nicholas thanked him. 'I seem to treat this place as a refuge,' he said.

Sol grinned. 'Would I mind?' he said. He examined Jenkins who examined him. 'Nice dog,' he decided, 'but kind of sad.'

'So would you be if you'd failed like Jenkins has,' Nicholas pointed out. He accepted another scotch. 'He was supposed to keep a marriage together.'

'Yeah, I guess he screwed up. But what I saw last night I think it would have taken a whole pack of hounds not one lonely dog.'

Nicholas patted Sol on the shoulder. 'It's good of you to let me hole up here,' he said. 'I can lie low, I hope. Keep out of the way of the press, for one thing. I'll get on with this script. At least now I don't have a marriage to worry about.'

Sol eyed him. 'Loretta won't bug you. She's coming to the States with me. I may even show her my family, if I can find them.' He shook his head. 'She's writing too. I guess she thinks that anything I can do, she can.'

'What's she writing?'

'It's at an early stage. She has a talent for titles. Like me, remember before I had to write a whole book. She has some good titles. *God and Constipation* was one and *Nobody Fucks Like a Fat Girl*. Could be she'll be up there with you in the bestseller list.'

They went out to the Italian restaurant where they had gone on the first night Nicholas had lived in the apartment. 'It's like a sentimental journey,' reminisced Sol. 'They still have the same drapes at the windows. Same squares as the cloths on the table. The same spaghetti, same sauce.' He looked across his plate. 'Are you going after the French lady?'

Nicholas was surprised. 'Going after her? Thérèse?' His face clouded. 'For what? She's just my imagination, Sol. She's just as much fiction as the girl in the book. She'll never be mine. She has a man with a yacht in the Caribbean. That's what she wants. I can only thank God that the press didn't find her.'

'So they looked? I thought maybe they would.'

'To them it's a big romantic story. They couldn't find her in Guadeloupe. She must be off sailing somewhere. I don't know.'

'She's put Guadeloupe on the map,' philosophised Sol. 'People who never heard of it will go there.' They walked home. Nicholas took Jenkins on his lead along the side of the canal. The dog looked as if he believed it was all a dream. Every time Nicholas spoke to him he looked up nervously. Nicholas told him not to worry.

'You and I, mate, are in this together,' he told the dog moodily. He surveyed the wintry water. 'Up the creek.'

Eighteen

With Sol gone, the flat by the canal became a hermitage. He went out only at night to walk Jenkins by the dim water or to buy drink and late groceries at an Indian shop in Edgware Road. Every day he worked single-mindedly on the script. He slept late and sat up late watching television. His conversation was mostly directed at the dog or to his own reflection for he was reluctant to answer the telephone. He switched it to the answering device. The seclusion fitted his injured mood. He was there to hide and to lick his wounds.

The newspapers had lost interest in him within a few days, after both he and Sarah had vanished. Paul Garrett had advised: 'When threatened with the press, run away.' Little Venice was not far to run but he remained undetected even if the newspapers had not moved on to other sensations. The sales of *Lost in France* were sustained. Garrett rang him from the office once a day, at five thirty before going home to Yvonne.

'Are you having your mail from Boxley forwarded?' he asked conversationally.

'No. I meant to but with one thing and another I didn't do it.'

'And you haven't been back to your house.'

'No.'

'So the post is piling up on the doormat.'

'Yes.'

'What's keeping you from going up there?'

'Nothing, not really. I've been busy on this script. It doesn't come easily.'

'I know. But you can take a couple of hours off, surely.'

'Yes, I could,' Nicholas was embarrassed. 'To be honest I've been putting it off. Going there.'

'The haunted vicarage, eh?'

'You could say that. I'm not looking forward to it, that's all.'

'Even so, you should do it. There may be some nice surprises on the doormat. Perhaps a letter from Sarah saying she is coming back. Money, invitations.'

'Thanks for the jokes. I'll go up there tomorrow.'

'Do you want me to come with you?'

'No. No thanks. I'll go by myself. It's only a house.'

His car was standing neglected in the street, coated with dust and leaves. Someone had written: 'Clean me you swine,' across the windscreen. He wiped the advice off and cleaned the windscreen at the same time. He lifted Jenkins into the car and together they went through the car wash. The dog did not seem to be afraid as long as he was there. Jenkins trusted him.

They drove to Boxley. As they neared the animal craned its neck in the rear seat apparently recognising landmarks. He began making disgruntled grunts. He had become enclosed, safe and content with the recent routine and for him Boxley evoked memories of a large and uncertain world. 'Stop fretting,' Nicholas assured him over his shoulder. 'I don't want to hang around for long either.'

It was a ragged, wintry day, clouds blowing across the cold sky, wind blowing up the street. Cautiously he turned the car into the old road to the vicarage. He stared at the materialising house like a gunner looking through the armoured slit of a tank. No one was about. Jenkins was groaning. 'Shut up,' ordered Nicholas brusquely. 'You don't have to go in there. I do.'

The dog seemed to take comfort and lay down in the back seat, with one eye cocked. Nicholas drove the car between the yews and, looking left and right as he did so, got out. There were dead leaves and litter on the path. A copy of the *Daily Mirror*, aged and yellow, and a crisp packet, both doubtless left by a journalist, were wedged against the doorstep. He picked the paper up and grimaced at his own picture on the page: 'AUTHOR VANISHES.'

Kicking cracked leaves from the step he put the key in the lock, turned and pushed. It needed a hard thrust because of the buttress of letters behind the door. He had to use his back against it. The concerned face of Jenkins watched him from the car window.

He eased himself into the hall. The afternoon was dark and he turned on the light. Letters, junk mail and newspapers were piled two feet high. He should have cancelled the newspapers. He waded through them. Leaning back he pushed the door closed and gently surveyed the place.

An indifference had fallen over it. The furniture, the ornaments, the pictures, the rugs and carpets were without life or warmth. He turned on the table lamps in the sitting room but their illumination was sullen. The cleaning woman had been in. Her letter of resignation and a bill for her final week's labours were on the draining board in the kitchen. 'I am not working here any more,' the note announced. She was right. In her pique she had not washed up two cups in the sink. The dishwasher was full of foul-smelling crockery. He took out a plate and tried to recall the last meal from the pattern of food stains. He put some powder in the machine and, after some fiddling, turned it on. Its hum gave a small touch of life to the house.

Moodily Nicholas walked from room to room. Their bed had not been made. He made it, then continued his tour. Deborah's room had been little occupied since she had been in London. She had left the teddy bear and it sat with its arms forever hopeful of an embrace. In Willie's room on the hurriedly opened bed were some sheets of paper with words written in block letters, his songs for his début with Bliss. Nicholas picked up the top sheet:

> I won't walk this way again,
> I won't walk with you.

If I come this way again,
I'll be with someone new.

How had his début been at the Hop Pole, Wembley? Now he would probably never have the chance to ask. All their activities, their familiar lives, had come to an abrupt and full stop.

The house smelled musty and he went to the rear bathroom and opened the fanlight an inch.

There seemed nothing more to do. Nothing needed doing. It was just an empty house. He walked around once more. In the back garden the grass was discoloured and seemed to have grown even though it was winter. Nothing else was amiss. He lifted a dustbin-liner bag from the lower cupboard in the kitchen and returning to the hall, piled in handfuls of mail. The dishwasher was still humming. He did not know how long it took. He decided to wait and have a cup of coffee. He would have to drink it black. The kettle was frowsty but he washed it out and its sound added itself to the industry of the dishwasher. Sitting on a kitchen stool he drank the coffee and studied the wall calendar. It was November now. He got up and tore October off. He saw that November 30th was marked with a tiny cross in pencil. They had never reached it.

The dishwasher appeared to be making hard work for itself. When he had finished the coffee he rinsed the mug and up-ended it on the draining board. Going into the sitting room he looked about him again, then into the hall and up the stairs. He thought of the night when he had thrown a bucket of water from there and wondered how much the house would fetch.

Outside Jenkins, fearing the house, was barking and Nicholas opened the door to tell the dog he was coming. As he did so he saw that wedged behind the door was a yellow post office form. There was a registered letter that they had not been able to deliver. It was available at the Boxley post office.

He returned to the kitchen. The dishwasher had finished. He switched it off. He closed the front door and locked it, giving it a consoling pat; it looked shabby, unused. He drove to the Boxley post office.

There was a parking place only yards away but he crept along the pavement like a robber. He claimed the registered packet and sidled back to the car. The label said: 'Harrogate.' Rina's name and address were on the outside of the package. He drove a mile until he was out of the suburb then pulled into a lay-by and opened the envelope. Inside, within a plastic sheath, was a stiff wad of clean banknotes. There was an inexpertly typed letter:

Dear Nicholas

It's almost one year since your dad died. I thought it was time to send you this money – one thousand pounds (£1,000). It rightfully belongs to you. Your father gave it to me but I never spent it. All of us here have seen the news in the papers about you. I have even bought your book, the first book I have ever bought new, and I loved reading it. I could see you in it. The patients who are still here from last year all recognised your picture in the papers (or said they did – you know what they're like!) and there's even one old boy, Mr Marshall, who has only been in a few months, reckons that he knew you during the war! He tells everybody that you were in Italy. I asked him specially and he said a place called Anzio. I didn't bother to tell him that you weren't even born then.

Me, I go on much the same as before. I'm the longest-serving one here now except for Matron who says she'll stay until she can be a patient herself! Even Dr da Souza has gone. He said it was making him old. I know how he feels. I expect you'll be asking yourself why I sent you this money. Well here goes, I will tell you.

Your father gave it to me for sleeping with him. You'll probably be shocked and I don't blame you, but one evening he asked me to come back later when everything was quiet and sleep in his bed with him. He said he would pay me a thousand pounds. Well, you

can imagine! I mean, it was cash! He seemed ever so sad
and lonely and anyway I did. I went back in my
nightdress and got into his bed. He had actually stayed
awake, which was not easy for him. We didn't actually *do*
very much needless to say. I think I was more out of
practice than he was. But I cuddled up to him and he told
me all about the lovers he remembered. Quite a lot of
them. It took a long time. We cuddled, like I say, but it did
not go much beyond that. He just wanted company in
bed. I know how he felt. I had a fancy that when you
brought me back here from the Happy Land restaurant
last Boxing Day that we might end up in bed too. That
would have been something, wouldn't it, going to bed
with father and son?

Anyway I never touched the money. He had it all
counted out and he told me to go off on holiday with it. But
I couldn't. It's just been in my drawer all the time and
here it is.

I was sorry to read in the papers about all the trouble
with your wife. I can understand her. I wouldn't like that
sort of thing either. When I read the book the French lady
seemed real to me as well and I was just as jealous as
Sarah.

I'll sign off now. Please don't try to send the money
back. I could never spend it. Just send me a card this
Christmas with your love. I will look forward to that.

*

He was waiting for Deborah as she arrived from college,
cradling her books, getting off an evening bus in Wandsworth.
She regarded him thoughtfully. 'I'm glad you've come, Dad,'
she said.

He saw how tight her face had become. She looked as though
she were going to cry. There was a public house opposite and
he suggested they went in there. He sat her in the corner of the
empty bar. 'What will you have?' he asked.

'An orange squash,' she said firmly.

He had a half pint of beer. 'Not much of an order,' he said to the woman behind the bar. She looked at the money in her hand. 'Only just opened,' she said. 'It's a start.'

'I don't drink,' said Deborah. 'Not much anyway.'

'What you saw at the launch party was probably enough to put you off for life,' he sighed.

'I really can't understand you two, you and Mum. What were you sticking together for in the first place?'

'You,' he said simply. 'And Willie. And for ourselves. We thought we could make it work. We gave ourselves a year.'

'And?'

'We never made it.'

'Well, she's gone now. She rang me at six in the morning when I'd been awake all night and told me she was going to Chicago. To live with that man.'

Illogically Nicholas said to her: 'Drink up.'

She did so. 'Drink up, drink up, it will be all right,' she pantomimed sourly.

'Look,' he told her firmly. 'I'm sorry, Deborah. But at least the decks are clear now.'

'You can go to your French lady,' she said.

'Don't you start. My so-called French lady is on the other side of the world. There has never been anything between us. There isn't now.'

'Do you love her?'

'How can I tell?'

'It looks like it from the book.' For the first time she smiled. 'It's a good book, Dad. Because it's true. When you were writing it I used to sneak into the attic and read bits.'

'You did? You crafty thing. . . .'

'In the middle of the night sometimes when you and Mum were asleep. When I read about the French lady I could tell that she wasn't just written on the page.' She regarded him softly. 'You should go and find her again.'

He sighed: 'I've told you, that's not possible. She doesn't want me.'

'You ought to have gone when you had the chance.'

'There *was* no chance. There never has been. She was

someone I met and that was as far as it got.' He patted her books. 'How's the course going?'

'All right. I think I learned more about journalism at your launch party than I could learn from ten years in college.' She shook her head and began to laugh. 'It was so grotesque. All those people trapped under the table. Mum was magnificent. The way she chucked the whole thing up.'

Nicholas said: 'She didn't quit then either. She threw my book, the leather one I was so proud of, from the top of the hotel and then locked me out on the roof in the freezing cold.'

She laughed and then began to cry, bending and putting her face to his coat. She wiped her eyes with the lapel. 'You two,' she said. 'What a mess.'

'What did Willie think?'

'The same. Except he shows it in a different way. That day you didn't turn up for his race in the sports . . . well I . . . can't tell you what he was like then; in a way the more you and Mum tried to mend your marriage, the worse it was for us. At least now I know where I am. God knows what will happen to Willie. He'll end up in jail if he's not careful.' She kissed Nicholas on the cheek. 'And what about you? Are you at home by yourself?'

'I'm not at home. After all the press hoo-ha I thought it would be wise to lie low for a while. And I'm not alone because I've got Jenkins with me.'

She put her hands to her mouth. 'Oh, Jenkins, I'd forgotten about Jenkins.'

'We got Jenkins as an extra bit of cement for the marriage,' he said almost shamefacedly. 'But it didn't work.'

'Nobody took any notice of him,' she said. 'Poor dumb dog.'

'Anyway he's very happy with his new situation. Sol went to America this morning and I'm living in the flat with Jenkins. I took him for a walk by the canal last night. He seemed to enjoy it. But then he never expects much.'

'And our house is empty,' she said.

'We'll sell it eventually when it comes to a settlement,' he told her. 'But now it's empty.'

'At least it's peaceful at last,' she said.

They went out and walked along the street. It was a chill evening but the lights of the shops, the windows above them, the passing buses and cars, made 'it cheerful enough. 'Everybody going home,' she said. 'You never think of other people having troubles do you? Yet they've probably all got some.'

She lived on the upper floor of a bay-windowed house with the door directly on the street. 'I feel rotten not asking you to come up,' she said. 'The others will be home now, or coming home.'

'And they've all read the newspapers,' he smiled. 'I understand.'

'No, it's not like that.' She smiled lightly. 'You're a celebrity and the girls would be thrilled to meet you. They keep asking me about you.' She paused. 'No. It's just that this is where I *live* now. We'll keep in touch, Dad, because I know you love me and I love you. But this is my home and I want to start again, just me.' She looked at him. 'Does that seem cruel or unreasonable?' she whispered. She kissed him and he kissed her.

'Not at all,' he said. 'It's your life now. Don't mess it up.'

They said goodbye and as he walked away the lights of the cars and the buses and the shops fused into one in his wet eyes. He heard her call from the doorstep: 'Dad.' He turned. 'I suppose you think it's me who's running away now.'

He could not answer. He merely shook his head and turned away again. He was going to his home where doubtless Jenkins would be waiting to welcome him.

'Hello, Mr Boulting? This is Doug Berry of the Neighbourhood Watch, Boxley here. I've had to trace you through your publishers and your agent. Did you leave a light on in your house?'

'Not as far as I know, Mr Berry. I was at the house last week but I'm sure I put the lights out.'

'Well, one of our patrols spotted this light, upstairs in your front bedroom last night. It's been very difficult getting your number.'

Nicholas apologised. 'I should have let you know. It's kind of you to bother.'

'It's my duty. That is what Neighbourhood Watch is all about.'

'Exactly. I had better come over and check.'

'I would have informed the police but they get a bit niggly with us. Giving them work I suppose.'

Nicholas looked at his watch and said: 'I'll come over now, before the rush hour.'

'It may be a false alarm. We do have a lot of false alarms.' There was a pause. 'I would like to come with you.'

'Oh, don't put yourself out. I'm sure it's all right.'

The voice became persuasive. 'I'd like to, if you don't mind. It goes on our report, you see.'

Nicholas left immediately driving through the mid-afternoon traffic, and he was at Boxley within the hour. Berry met him at the corner. 'Rendezvous timed exactly,' he said with satisfaction. His watch, thick-strap and heavy metal, looked huge for his wrist. He saw Nicholas notice it. 'It can be transformed into a knuckleduster in a trice,' he boasted. 'See.' He slipped the buckle and slid the strap down over his fist before tightening it. 'A handy little tool, don't you think.' He smiled gravely. 'We know a few tricks.'

They drove through the lane to the house. 'There,' breathed Berry. 'Look. It's still on.'

'If it's a burglar he's taking a long time about it,' observed Nicholas. He stopped the car fifty yards short of the drive. Berry suddenly said wistfully: 'It's a nice house. It's a house that wants guarding.'

'It will be for sale soon.'

'So I understand. The word gets around. I'm afraid it will be beyond me.'

Carefully Nicholas opened the car door. Berry got out the other side. Narrow-eyed, he slipped the watch into the knuckleduster position. They advanced cautiously. Nicholas could see that the light was not directly in the room. It was in the bathroom or perhaps on the landing outside.

'I should have left a light on anyway,' he said to Berry. 'To deter burglars.'

'They know that old trick,' said the watchman shaking his head. 'They observe and wait. Then strike.' He stopped on the pavement. 'It's a war, Mr Boulting,' he breathed. 'A war.'

Nicholas took out his key and gingerly opened the door. From the hall he could see the glimmer of the light from the landing. Berry was close behind him. 'I'm with you,' he said unnecessarily. 'I've never seen a burglar.'

The paused at the bottom of the stairs. Then, a careful tread at a time, they went up. He could hear Berry's thin breathing behind him. They reached the top. Berry raised his knuckle-dustered fist. The light was in the bathroom adjoining the main bedroom, its glow issuing out on to the landing. They heard a movement, a groan. Nicholas stiffened. The Neighbourhood Watch man backed away. 'I'll call the police,' he whispered.

Nicholas signalled for him to wait. Quickly he stepped along the corridor and into the bedroom. The floor was strewn with clothes, and food and litter. A drained whisky bottle was on its side and flat on the bed, face down, was Willie.

He wearily raised his head and then his eyelids. 'Where have you been?' he asked.

Willie was in the front of the car, his head against the seat back, his eyes red-rimmed and shut, his face white, pimpled, his mouth tight. 'She knows I'm here,' he said without altering his attitude. 'She told me to clear off.'

'She's had enough of you.'

'I'd had enough of her more like it. And that nerd she's with.'

'I'll have to tell her you've got here,' said Nicholas.

Willie opened his weak eyes. 'I already did,' he said. 'I rang her from home. Just after I'd got in. I told her I'd arrived and you weren't there, you'd gone to the shops. She doesn't care.' He snorted. 'She thinks she's in love.'

'Did you ring Deborah?'

Willie shifted his head in surprise. 'No, I don't know her number.'

'She might have been interested that you were back. And she would have been able to tell you where I was.'

'Deborah's all right,' sniffed her brother. 'We sorted it out a long time ago. As soon as we could we were going to get out anyway, leave you two. Run away. Blow you out.'

'That's nice to know.'

'We could never work out why you didn't pack it in long ago.'

Nicholas drove solidly. It was raining and the traffic going towards London was clogged. 'We stayed together because we thought we could make it work,' he said eventually. 'And for you and Deborah.'

Willie emitted his scornful snort again. 'Well you needn't have bothered about us.'

Nicholas sighed. 'Anyway, you rang your mother.'

'I rang her.'

'Did she give you the fare?'

'He did. The dork.'

'And what do you intend to do now?'

'Live with you.'

'Then you'll have to get a job. I'm not having you hanging around doing nothing. You'll go straight downhill in London.'

'I'm looking forward to London,' said Willie with a faint smile. 'When can I start at acting school?'

'Acting school!'

'That's what you said. You promised.'

'But . . . you never said another word about it.'

'I might have if somebody had asked.'

'Right. All right. You can go to drama school, if it's possible, if you're going to treat it seriously. Tomorrow we'll start working on it. You won't be able to start until next term now, after the New Year.'

Willie leaned over and patted his arm on the steering wheel. 'Thanks Dad,' he said. 'I'm glad I'm home.'

They drove down Finchley Road. There were Christmas lights hanging in the rain and decorated trees flashing out messages. 'We can have Christmas together,' said Willie.

404

'We can. But meantime you can get a job. Work in a shop or deliver mail or something. There's plenty of seasonal work.'

'Oh, all right. I'll do that. I might get some more gigs with Bliss.'

'What's gigs with . . . oh, I see. The pop group.'

'The band,' corrected Willie. He began to sing melodiously:

> I won't walk this way again,
> I won't walk with you.
> When I walk this way again,
> I'll be with someone new.

As they were driving by the canal Willie said: 'This is where Sol lived?'

'That's right. I thought you realised. I'm staying in the flat. He's in America.'

'He's a cool guy, Sol. I like him.' As Nicholas pulled the car into a vacant kerb space Willie asked: 'So there'll just be you and me.'

'And Jenkins.'

'Oh . . . good. You've still got Jenkins. When I was on the plane I was wondering what had happened to Jenkins. I thought you might have had him gassed.'

Willie slept until the following afternoon, twenty hours. Nicholas did a fry-up and they ate together as he and Sol had often done. 'So you've been hiding here,' said Willie looking around. 'After all the fuss.'

'I've gone to ground,' agreed his father. 'After the stuff in the newspapers I wanted to get out of the way.'

Willie seemed only mildly interested. 'I thought Mum was going off her rocker,' he said without lifting his head from the plate. He balanced baked beans on his fork. 'That night she came home and grabbed me out of bed and said we were off to Chicago. I'd only just got back from my gig at the Hop Pole in Wembley. You ought to have been at that.'

'Yes,' said Nicholas feelingly. 'It might have been better if I had been.'

'She called a taxi at that time of the night and we went straight to the airport. We had to wait for hours and she got the papers and saw all about herself and you. And this French bit of stuff you've got.' He lifted his eyes. 'Where is she by the way?'

'She's not in this country and she's not my "bit of stuff" as you put it.'

'Pity. She sounded cool. Not to Mum though. When she read all that stuff that woman had written about the French piece she went ape. She threw the paper down on the ground and cried and jumped on it. It was a good job the place was almost empty. Then she got the other papers and saw it all in there. I thought it was funny but I couldn't tell her. She'd have hit me.'

'What was the matter with Chicago?' asked his father.

'Oh it was a drag. He didn't live anywhere near the middle. Miles out, just like Boxley. It was freezing all the time and I didn't know anybody.'

'What made her agree for you to come back?'

I got a bit drunk. Some bloke came off his motor bike swerving round me in the street. Stupid sod. I would have got out of the way easily. He went on about suing and all that and I had a row with Fawkesy, who's a prat if ever I saw one. I can't think what Mum sees in him. He goes around with a posh English accent, not like he used to speak, just ordinary, and he's got Mum to speak like it too. She sounds ridiculous.'

'And all that sparked off you coming back.'

'Fawkesy gave me the fare. He couldn't wait to get rid of me. He's never liked me. So back I came. I got in through the bathroom window at home. I rang Mum as soon as I got in the house. She said she had rung a few times but there was no answer. She didn't know you'd cleared out. Anyway I told her that everything was all right. That you were at home but you'd just gone out for some food. I asked her if she wanted you to ring her and she said not to bother. As long as I'd arrived. And here I am.'

Nicholas said: 'You've got to get your life together. Otherwise you'll just drift.'

'It runs in the family,' sniffed Willie.

They finished the meal. 'Tomorrow,' said Nicholas, 'we'll start making enquiries about a drama school. I don't know anything about them. And then we'll see about getting you a job over Christmas.' He faced his son seriously. 'I mean it Willie. I'm not having you lounging around here.'

'I know, I know. I'll find out what's happening with Bliss and see if I can get some gigs. That's sort of acting, isn't it.'

'I suppose you could say that.'

'I'll take Jenkins for a walk,' decided Willie. 'I think he'll get used to me again. He *is* my dog.'

When Deborah rang twenty minutes later she was in tears. 'Dad . . . oh, Dad. Have you seen the evening paper?'

'No. What's wrong?'

'It's Willie. He's gone missing in America.'

Nicholas could hardly speak. 'Willie . . . he's here,' he said. 'He's here with me.'

'But. . . . how . . . ? He's *there*? With you? He really is. Thank God for that.'

'He's out with the dog. I tried to call you last night but I couldn't get any reply. Nor this morning.'

'But . . . when did he get back? The *Standard* says he's been reported missing to the Chicago police. After all the fuss about you and Mum it's in headlines. For God's sake what goes on with this family? . . . It's crazy. They say that Mum is going frantic . . . how does all this happen, Dad?'

'It happens,' said Nicholas slowly, 'because Willie has a great talent for telling lies. The bigger the lie the better he is at it. According to him his mother sent him back here after a row. . . .'

'How did he find out where you were?'

'He didn't. I found him. I went up to Boxley because a light was seen in the house. And there he was, flat out with a whisky bottle on the floor.'

'He just doesn't care.'

'Well, he's here now. I've had a long chat with him. I've agreed that he can go to drama school, if we can get him in anywhere. And he's going to do some more singing with that band, he hopes, and he's promised to get a job over Christmas. I need your help, Deborah. Perhaps we can straighten him out.'

'Before it's too late,' she said full of doubt. 'You'd better telephone Mum.'

Nicholas decided: 'I'll call her when he gets back. Then he can speak to her as well. She may not believe me.'

He waited for Willie to reappear with Jenkins. An hour went past and then another.

Several times he went to the door and scanned the street with its doleful pools of light. The main road traffic moved at the end but by the canal there were no walkers, no youths, no dogs. He sat and attempted to read through his week's work completing the script. At last it was finished. He poured himself a drink but did not drink it.

He had just returned from his fourth visit to the street, and was frowning towards the telephone wondering whether to risk ringing Sarah without Willie there, when the doorbell rang briskly. Almost leaping from the chair, he pulled himself up on the way to answer it, composed himself, walked slowly and opened the door carefully. Willie was standing there with Jenkins. 'Where have you been?' he said.

'We had a long walk, that's all. He's a slow walker.' He stepped sideways in a curiously quick but sly fashion and then mounted the step beside his father. 'Look at that!' he exclaimed pointing into the darkness. Nicholas looked, so did Jenkins. A man holding a camera stepped from the shadows and in a flash had taken their picture.

'Smile please,' encouraged the man. 'Let's have a happy one.' Nicholas felt Willie's hand on his shoulder and scarcely realising what was taking place he put his on Willie's. The shadowy man took another picture and then another and then kept taking them.

'What is going on?' demanded Nicholas eventually

recovering. He addressed the question to the photographer, but then realising, turned to his son. 'What's all this about?'

'The *Mail*,' said Willie as though that explained everything. 'Cheers.' He waved to the retreating photographer. Nicholas found himself waving a bemused goodbye.

'It's all right, Dad,' assured his son leading the way into the flat. 'It'll be good publicity for both of us. Missing son and missing father. Get it? It'll be good for your book and good for my career.'

Stiffly Nicholas shut the door. From outside came a bark and he opened the door again and let Jenkins in. Willie was searching in the fridge. He took out a can of beer. Nicholas caught him by the shoulder. 'Sit down,' he snapped. Like the boy he once was Willie sat down. 'All right,' sighed Nicholas. 'So you went out and telephoned the *Mail*.'

'And sold them the picture,' said Willie proudly and as if surprised at his father's tone. 'Five hundred quid. You won't have to keep me.'

'Can't you do anything straightforward?' asked Nicholas angrily. 'I came here because I wanted to have some privacy.'

'But, Dad, you don't need that now. All that was over a month ago.' He leaned forward eagerly. 'Don't you realise what a cool idea this was? I got a *Standard* when I went out. The bloke wasn't looking so I nicked it. And there, what do I see but that *I'm missing in America*. Me, Willie Boulting, I'm famous!' Attempting to look shamefaced he said: 'I didn't tell you all the truth about getting out of Chicago.'

'You didn't tell me the truth about anything,' protested Nicholas. 'Deborah rang me. She'd seen it in the evening paper. I'll have to telephone your mother but you'll have to explain yourself to her.' He put his face in his hands. 'I don't understand you. How could you just walk out of here and ring the press?'

'Easy,' said Willie without insolence. 'They were dead keen. I reckon I could have got more than five hundred, don't you. The publicity will be great.'

'Why do you want publicity?'

Willie looked astonished. 'For my career,' he said patiently. 'As an actor and a band singer. And – you'll be pleased with this – I've got a job there at the *Mail* – just helping out over Christmas.'

'That's something I suppose. They've said that?'

'I've got it in writing. That's why I was away so long. I took Jenkins to the *Mail* office in Kensington.'

'I don't need all this hassle,' moaned Nicholas.

'There's no hiding place,' replied Willie dramatically. 'No man is an island.'

Nicholas sighed. 'Come on, we had better ring your mother. Tell her you're safe, if that's the word.'

The newspaper was spread on Paul Garrett's desk. 'One for the family album,' he smiled.

'Don't. I've had enough,' muttered Nicholas. He put the script on the desk. 'That's it,' he said. 'Finished. Let them tear that to pieces.'

'I expect they will,' said Paul. He returned to the photograph. 'Looks like the really big drama has been literally on your doorstep.'

'Willie's unbelievable,' said Nicholas. 'He stole the money to get back from America. I phoned his mother. She calls him a liar and a cheat, among other things.' He regarded Garrett bleakly. 'They went away for a weekend and he was supposed to go somewhere else, to Boston with friends, but he never got there. Instead he turned up at Boxley.'

'He managed to keep out the nasty bits.' Garrett tapped the paper. 'He's quoted as saying that he came back because he missed England.'

'It makes you cry doesn't it. I've never met anyone so full of bullshit.'

'It will sell the book again,' hummed Garrett. 'Just coming up to Christmas.'

'At what cost? I don't know what to do with him, Paul. When I left he was being interviewed by the *Evening Standard*. Telling them absolute crap.'

'You should let him handle the press,' suggested the agent. 'He sounds as though he makes up more than they do.'

'He's got a job on the *Mail*,' said Nicholas. 'Over Christmas. It was part of the deal he did with them. They paid him five hundred quid and some sort of general job in the newsroom, work experience, for God's sake. He got that out of them. The experience may be theirs. But at least it will keep him busy until Christmas. I was telling him he'd have to deliver the post or work in Selfridges. Imagine, and there's Deborah trying to get into journalism through college.'

Paul laughed. 'He seems to be ahead of everybody in the game. I shall watch the *Mail* with interest.'

'He could destroy it,' said Nicholas.

He thought it would be impossible for Willie to spring any further surprises. His son's days at the newspaper seemed to occupy him with sufficient fantasy. Sometimes he came home and sometimes not. 'Half the time they don't know what they're doing,' he announced leaning against the bar in the pub that Nicholas and Sol had frequented. The man who had said he was as lonely as a toby jug was still there. So was the toby jug. That day there had been an office Christmas party in the bar, a crowd of loud, unaccustomed drinkers and vulnerable seasonal females. Some of the people were still drunkenly there when Willie arrived. 'Look at this lot,' he said scornfully. 'Bloody clerks. Half a pint of cider is their limit. They just get the typists in here, get them pissed, and feel them up. That's their Christmas bonus.'

'That sounds like a newspaper article,' said Nicholas.

'They won't let me do it,' grumbled Willie. 'They haven't got a clue. I'm just the office boy as far as they're concerned. Call it work experience? I want to go out and talk to mass murderers.'

'It's better than Selfridges,' suggested his father.

'A bit. But I've been there ten days and . . . nothing.'

'You can't be editor yet.'

'I could. Easily,' said Willie. He saw a girl come in the door

411

and, as though he had been waiting, he moved quickly in her direction. Nicholas turned but his view was obscured by his son's back. Willie brought her to the bar. Nicholas saw her with disbelief. 'You . . . ,' he said. 'I know you. . . .'

'I'll say you do,' she smiled seriously. She was young, dark with a long, intense face and deep eyes. 'We've even shared a bed.' Willie watched smirking: 'Don't you remember it Dad?'

Nicholas pointed towards her. 'You're . . . the girl. Bonnie's daughter. When we were in Torremolinos. Your family . . . the twins . . .'

'That's right,' she nodded. 'You let us sleep in your bed.'

'But . . . how . . . ?' he shook his head. He turned to his son. It had to be something to do with Willie. 'Want a drink?' Willie asked the girl. Hiding her face from the barman she said she would have a vodka.

'How?' repeated Nicholas still disbelieving. 'Go on, tell me how you're here.'

'Willie found me,' she shrugged.

'Outside the flat,' added Willie. 'Last Saturday night.'

'You're Penny,' remembered Nicholas. 'But how amazing . . .'

'There's nothing amazing about it,' said Willie giving the girl the vodka. 'She was hanging around there waiting for one of us to come out.'

Penny said quietly: 'I saw all the stuff in the newspapers. First about the row about your book, and your wife doing a runner and that. Then there was the picture of you and Willie and it said your address so I came up on the underground to see you. I was just trying to find out which flat it was when Willie turned up. . . .'

'She's my lover,' said Willie.

'. . . And here I am,' finished the girl.

Nicholas sensed the gathering of more dark clouds. He spoke very carefully. 'And how . . . is your mother, and the twins and your sister?'

'Still the same,' Penny shrugged. 'Mum still struggles, Tupper still craps and my sister grizzles. Dad's inside. Three years, at least, thank God. We're all on the social.'

412

*

On Christmas Eve Deborah called him from Zürich. 'I got here Dad.'

'Good. I've been thinking about you. Is there any snow?'

'Not here but it's on the mountains. It looked magic from the plane. Is Willie with you?'

'He's gone out but he promised he'd be back in time to hang his stocking up.'

'Dad, you *are* a fool you know.'

'I know.'

'You didn't mind me coming here with the girls did you? I feel rotten leaving you at Christmas but I knew Willie would be there. Are you going to have a turkey?'

'A small one. Enough for two plus one dog.'

'Jenkins will like that. Give him a kiss for me.'

'I'll try.'

Her voice hesitated, then she said: 'Last Christmas your father died. You don't have a very good time, do you. You should have gone and stayed with friends.'

Nicholas smiled to himself. 'Friends are a bit limited, I'm afraid. That's the sign of a lazy man. Paul and Yvonne have gone to Los Angeles and Sol is in America too. Anyway, where would I go where I could take Willie?'

He heard her giggle. 'Is he behaving?'

'I don't know. I hardly see him.'

'But he *will* be there tomorrow?'

'He said so. There's going to be a lot of turkey for Jenkins if he isn't.'

'Dad, I feel guilty leaving you.'

'Don't worry about it. Have you spoken to your mother?'

She was slow to answer. 'Yes. She seems fine,' she said eventually. 'She asked if I had been in touch with you.'

'You'll be the family listening post from now,' he told her. 'Someone always has to be. A point of contact.'

'I suppose so. Anyway I must go. Have a happy Christmas. I'll call you at New Year.' Sadly she said: 'I love you.'

Thoughtfully he replaced the telephone. He looked around

the room and wondered when Willie would be back. 'Come on Jenkins,' he called towards the kitchen. 'Let's go and have a pint. . . . Jenkins. . . . Jenkins. . . . Where are you?' He felt a shaft of cold air. The front door was opened. 'Jenkins. . . . Jenkins. . . .' He hurried into the street. It was windy and empty. He went as far as the main road but there was no sign of Jenkins. God, now even his dog had run away.

Willie did not come back that night either. He felt slightly ridiculous reporting a missing dog to the police on Christmas Day when his son had vanished too. Except that Willie was always likely to vanish.

Every hour he went searching for the dog, through the damp and vacant streets, along Edgware Road, empty as a canyon, lights in upstairs windows over empty shops. Morbidly he surveyed the grim water of the canal. He cooked Christmas dinner and as he was sitting down alone to eat it the thought recurred that Willie and Jenkins had perhaps gone off together. Willie had left, full of promises, at seven the previous evening. Nicholas tried to remember the last time he had seen the dog. He dismissed the notion. Wherever he had gone his son would not take on the encumbrance of an animal. He would think about himself.

It was a pessimistic meal. He watched the Queen making her speech and, on a thought, went into the bedroom and telephoned Rina. 'I knew it would be you,' she said when they brought her to the phone. 'It's exactly a year, isn't it. Almost to the minute. Thanks for the Christmas card.'

'Thank you for the letter,' he said solemnly. 'And the money. You should have kept it.'

'I just couldn't. Like I said I felt I didn't have any right to it.'

'You had every right. Not many people made the old man happy. You can change your mind, Rina. Would you like me to return it?'

She sounded almost shocked. 'Oh no, don't do that. It wouldn't be right.'

'If you do think again let me know. It's here in a drawer just as you sent it.'

He was sitting on the bed and as he said it opened the drawer as though to illustrate the point. The envelope had gone. 'Willie . . . .'

'What was that?' asked Rina. 'I didn't quite hear, Nicholas.'

'Oh . . . ,' he said still shocked. He was frantically searching the drawer. '. . . Oh, nothing. It's just Willie.'

'Your son.'

'Yes he is,' said Nicholas grimly.

She missed the intonation.

'It's nice you've got someone there for Christmas,' she said. 'Has he given you a surprise present?'

'Yes,' said Nicholas. 'He's done that all right.'

In the early evening there were three telephone calls; first Paul and Yvonne from Los Angeles and then Sol from La Jolla, Southern California.

'You having a great time?' enquired Sol uncertainly.

'Great, but quiet.'

'That's how Christmas should be. I'd like to believe in it.'

'How is Loretta?'

'Crazy. Maybe I could send her back to you like a present, wrapped in holly paper. I need a break. Since she's been a writer it's gotten worse.'

'What's she writing now?'

'Titles mostly. She gets these titles. She's writing *Understanding Necrophilia* right now. It's a novel.'

The third call was Deborah from Zürich. 'Just to wish you Happy Christmas again. I had to ring,' she said almost shyly. 'Is everything all right?'

'Fine.'

'Is Willie behaving?'

'We've had our Christmas dinner,' lied her father. 'Jenkins had his too. We've been watching television. Nothing exciting.'

'Can I speak to Willie?'

'Well . . . no. Nor Jenkins for that matter. One has taken the other out for a walk.'

'I can't call back. We're going out. Everyone is waiting for me.'

'Don't worry. I'll tell them.'

'Happy Christmas, Dad,' she said sadly.

'And you, darling. Have a good time.'

After a final search for Jenkins at ten o'clock Nicholas returned and went miserably to bed. He took a tumbler of scotch with him. He took out all the contents of the bedside drawer and put them on the bed. The envelope with the notes in it was not there. Then he remembered Rina's letter that went with them. He groaned and sat back against the headboard. There was not a sound from the street outside. He lifted the whisky and forlornly wished himself a happier New Year. The telephone rang.

'Hello, Mr Boulting. It's Doug Berry here, Boxley Neighbourhood Watch.'

'Yes, Mr Berry. A Happy Christmas if it's not too late.'

'Thank you. Thank you. Mr Boulting I have to tell you that there has been a noisy party at your house. It looks like youngsters.'

'Oh,' breathed Nicholas. 'That's where he is.'

'Who is?'

'My son. He must be there. I'll get up there right away. I'm sorry about this, I hope it hasn't ruined your day.'

'Not ours, Mr Boulting. We live some distance away as you know. But our patrol has reported the noise. The police should be called.'

Nicholas drew a deep breath. 'Right. I'm on my way. I'll be there in forty minutes.'

Angrily he got from the bed. The tumbler of whisky was still on the bedside table. He picked it up and then slowly put it down again. Cursing he got dressed. The phone rang again. 'Mr Boulting, more bad news I'm afraid. The fire engines have just gone up there.'

'To my house!'

'Yes. There's a glow in the sky, Mr Boulting. We can see it from here.'

His car was parked half a mile away and he ran madly. He speeded up Edgware Road and was in Boxley in half an hour.

He swerved into the road leading to the house. There was a crowd gathered around three fire engines. Lights twirled through hazy smoke, there was a cackle of radios, men in heavy wet waders stumped about. Horrified he left the car on the pavement and pushed through the spectators. Someone called: 'There's Mr Boulting. Hard luck, Mr Boulting.'

He arrived at his gate. Hoses were draped across the yews. A policeman was standing staunchly. 'There's nobody inside is there?' Nicholas panted.

'No sir. It's all clear.'

The house was a charred shell. The firemen were pouring water through what had been the windows. There was a gaping hole in the roof.

'Roof fell in about twenty minutes ago,' the policeman told him. 'That was some sight, I can tell you.'

'There's definitely no one in there is there?' he said slowly to the policeman.

'All out, sir. Got out before it actually went up. The fire blokes have had a good search. Little devils. What they get up to these days.' He took a few measured paces up the garden path and bent below the yew trees. He returned displaying a scattering of white tablets on the palm of his hand. 'See them. Ecstasy they call them. They have all sorts, these kids.' He looked intensely at the tablets. 'I might try a few myself,' he said sombrely. 'I could do with a bit of ecstasy.'

When he returned to London, shredded, despondent, defeated, he found Jenkins sitting on the doorstep. 'At least *you're* back,' he said gratefully. 'I suppose it's no good asking you where you've been.' The dog wagged its tail. It seemed fresh and fit. It could not have been very far.

He went inside and cut a few slices off the turkey. He put

some on a plate with a tomato and some pickle and then filled the dog's bowl. Jenkins merely sniffed at it and turned away, clambering into his basket and closing his eyes. 'Wherever you've been,' muttered Nicholas, 'you've had a better time than me.'

He poured himself a long scotch, drank it moodily and rolled into bed. After hours of dreams and nightmares he woke as a washy light was creeping around the curtains. His eyes were sticky; he lay trying to think of what to do. He had a shrewd idea where Willie was at that moment. As though to confirm the thought the telephone rang.

'This is Penny,' said the voice. 'Penny Ware, remember.'

'Yes, of course, Penny. Bonnie's daughter.'

'Mum says Happy Christmas.'

'That's kind. Is that why you rang?'

'Well, no. I promised Willie I would. He said to tell you not to expect him home.'

'Where is he?'

'On his way to America. He went straight from the party. He had his passport and plenty of money. I saw it.'

'You were at the party at my house?'

'That's right.'

'You know the house burned down.'

'Did it?' She appeared unsurprised. 'It was all right when we left. I went down to the airport with him but because it was Christmas there were no planes until today. So we stayed at one of those posh hotels there. He's just gone off this morning.'

Nicholas said: 'Thank you Penny. Thanks for letting me know.'

'You're welcome.' She paused. 'Willie is all right you know. He just needs understanding.'

'So do I,' sighed Nicholas.

He drove back to Boxley taking Jenkins with him. The dog was seized with his customary apprehension which increased as he sniffed the odour of the fire. Nicholas left him in the car. People were standing outside the house looking at the hole in the roof. There was a blackened mountain of debris in the front garden. A policeman was conversing with a man in a heavy macintosh and bowler hat.

'Don't worry,' said the man approaching him. 'I'm not press. They've all gone. Not keen on working on Boxing Day. I don't mind. I'm an insurance assessor. Fred Dankley. My card.' He handed it to Nicholas. 'Would you like me to act for you in your claim?' He surveyed the house with professional grimness. 'Looks like a near write-off.'

'Right,' said Nicholas taking the card. 'I'd be glad to give somebody else the responsibility. I've had enough.'

Curiously the man raised his bowler. 'Good. We'll start right away.' He nodded at the wreckage. 'Do you want to have a look inside? I understand it's quite safe.'

Nicholas sighed. 'I suppose I'll have to.'

They walked to the front door. It had been battered open by the firemen. Out of curiosity Nicholas pressed the chimes and they sounded cosily. They did not know when they were beaten. Followed by Dankley he stepped inside. Everywhere was charred and wet giving off a damp and acrid smell. He turned to the assessor. 'Do you mind if I just go around by myself for a few minutes?'

'Not at all. It's your home.'

'At one time,' corrected Nicholas.

'You must have sentimental feelings,' said the man. 'I'll come back when you've done.'

He went out of the front door, stopping by the blackened pile of wreckage in the garden and sniffing at it. He wrote something in a notebook.

Nicholas went from room to room. Each one was a shambles. A deep sadness came over him. There were odd creaks and the insistent dripping of water. It was like being inside a dead body. It was cold, a wet, grim cold; colder than the day outside. Windows were broken and doors hanging from hinges or lying prostrate on the soggy carpets. The fire had started in the kitchen which was just a blackened hole. The wall to the garden had fallen down and he could look out on the strewn lawn to the single apple tree. What appeared to be a piece of modern sculpture was, he realised, a fusing of saucepans. The kettle was burned flat, the refrigerator door was open and a tongue of charred contents hung from the aperture.

There was a chill in his heart that matched the feeling of the house. He almost crept into the dining room. Someone had tidily piled all their chairs on the top of the table facing forward, orderly as the seats on the top deck of a bus. He picked up a cushion from the floor and dropped it again. It fell like a loaded sponge.

Upstairs Deborah's room at the end of the house was almost intact, although the bedclothes were bundled. He picked up the soggy teddy bear, ever awaiting an embrace, and tucked it under his arm. There were wine bottles on the floor of Willie's room, the glass twisted by the heat.

He went into the main bedroom after hesitating at the door. It was here that the sky stared blatantly in. Every wall was charred, the bedclothes reduced to brown fragments. Now, all at once, he felt the whole sense of defeat. He sat on the corner of the bed and it collapsed. He did not get up but remained there with his head in his hands. What a waste.

He went out and finally up to his study. He opened the door straight out on to the sky. There was nothing left of the room, just a charred hole. The Boxing Day breeze moved through the empty branches of the trees and the angles of the housetops.

Sad and angry he went out, unnecessarily closing the door carefully on the void which had been his own private place. He went down the stairs. There was nothing he wanted to take away except the teddy bear. He opened the front door and tried the mocking chimes for the last time. They still sounded. In the front garden, by the pile of unrecognisable rubble, the assessor was standing diffidently. 'I'll get a tarpaulin put over the roof, Mr Boulting,' he said looking at the bear. 'It should have been done already but it's Boxing Day.'

'Fine,' said Nicholas. 'You carry on. It's all yours.'

'Hello, Sarah. It's Nicholas.'

'He's here,' she said before he could say any more. 'He

rang us from O'Hare, David had to go and fetch him. What's he been up to?'

'He and his friends have burned the house down.'

'Oh God. Boxley? That's ridiculous. Are you sure?'

'Very. I've seen it.'

'Good God. Well, it was insured.'

'Yes, there's nothing to worry about there.'

'How did they do that?'

'You'd better ask him. By the time the fire started everyone had cleared out, including Willie. I've been living at Sol's place. While you're asking him questions you might enquire how he got the money to fly to America.'

'He's already told us. We asked him. He says you gave it to him. It was a thousand pounds that his grandfather left for him and you'd kept it until he needed it.'

'He should write the books.'

'I've always said that. Anyway he's here now. God knows what we're going to do with him. David is naturally not very keen.'

'It's like pass the parcel,' said Nicholas.

'With the loser left holding it,' she agreed. 'He says that he hated it in England and he's going to stay here, and settle and work and all the rest of it. I've always told you, Nicholas, that he'd be trouble.'

'He's the sort of kid who gives divorce a bad name,' said Nicholas.

'Very clever, I'm sure. But *you* don't want him, do you?'

He sighed. 'No I don't. He just does what he feels like doing next.'

'Well, here he is. We'll have to have another try I suppose. Is Deborah all right? She called me from Zürich.'

'Yes, she telephoned at Christmas. I think she's fine. I rescued her teddy bear from the house. It was all there was to salvage.'

'I didn't want anything from there,' she said.

'Neither did I.'

Nineteen

On New Year's Eve he packed a case and with the dog went out into the still and comfortless day. He was carrying Jenkins across the road to his car when a whiskered man leaned over the stern of one of the moored barges and called: 'Hello, Pudding.'

Both Nicholas and the dog looked up. The animal's rump began to vibrate. 'Pudding?' Nicholas enquired.

'He's your dog is he?' said the man. He sauntered down a painted gangway. He was large and middle-aged with a multi-striped pullover over which his beard hung like a warm scarf. 'We had him all Christmas Day.'

'I was looking for him,' said Nicholas. He had reached the pavement. 'Everywhere.'

'You should have looked over here on the barge,' responded the man amiably. 'He was with us, eating turkey and Christmas pudding. That's why we called him Pudding.'

'His real name is Jenkins,' corrected Nicholas. 'I spent half of Christmas searching for him.'

'Sorry, but we weren't to know. We intended to report him found on Boxing Day to the police, we didn't want to bother them before, but then he vanished, quick as he appeared. If ever you want someone to look after him we'll have him. He took quite a fancy to us too.' The man had been paying much attention to the dog, ruffling its ears and scratching its ribs, but now he recognised Nicholas.

'Ah, of course,' he said. 'It's *you*. We read about you in all the papers. And you had your picture taken outside your door, across there with your son. That was a nice picture. You're the writer chap.'

The man shook his hand enthusiastically. 'And to think we had your dog,' he mused. 'Wait until I tell my Annie. She's having a lie-in this morning.' Nicholas said he had to be on his journey. 'Taking Pudding with you?' asked the man suggestively. Nicholas said he was. 'I'd never leave him behind,' he said. 'Not willingly.'

The man offered his hand a second time and Nicholas shook it. He unlocked the car door. 'You must come and have a look at our narrow boat some time,' the man invited. 'Have a cup of tea.' Nicholas said he would. The man mounted the coloured gangway. 'My name's Len King. I wish I'd have been a success,' he said without complaint. He smiled. 'I never had the ability.'

Nicholas drove the route out through the eastern suburbs and into the flat country. There were still the journeying trucks making for the ports, but other traffic was light and the day became more cheerful.

He did not know why he was going there, except that there was nowhere else he wanted to go.

He reached Littlehaven by lunchtime. There was yet another new landlord at the Hope. 'They moved,' the man told him. 'To Fingringhoe. Back to civilisation. There's not many can stand it out here for long.'

There were no other staying guests. He had a snack in the bar hung and pinned with Christmas cards and then took Jenkins on a walk along the sea path. The dog sniffed the air and ducked nervously under the diving gulls but soon began to enjoy it. Jenkins was adaptable. Nicholas snorted quietly. Pudding indeed. The dog was loping along, sniffing the shingle. 'Pudding!' he called against the bright wind. The dog lifted its nose, wagged its tail and climbed back obediently.

The coast was again empty, the sea deserted; it remained, as it always would to him, like one of her water-colours, almost ghostly. But no matter how much he tried to imagine her, she was not there. The sea rolled in irresolutely, orange-streaked by the afternoon sun, the grass and reeds blew in the stiffening breeze, the landscape was diminishing by the minute. He looked out to the place where he had first seen her, picturing her in her bright red coat against the monochrome land, coming towards the sea path. He saw her once more on the path walking towards him and saw again her face for the first time. He stopped at the place where they had conversed while the geese had honked overhead. For a while he stood there. Then he sadly called the dog by its proper name and went back towards the Hope.

The landlord said his name was Mr Blakerod. 'We'll have a quiet New Year,' he forecast. 'Like we had a quiet Christmas. It's always quiet around here.'

'Quiet and wet,' put in his wife.

'This is Mrs Blakerod,' said the man.

She recognised Nicholas. 'You're trying to keep out of the way for a while,' she guessed. 'I don't blame you if you are. It must be terrible being in the papers. Well, we won't tell anybody you're here.'

'I've been here before,' he told them. 'A couple of times. Only briefly. You used to have a black girl, a waitress.'

'Enid,' said Mrs Blakerod. 'She's still here. She's off-duty but she might be in tonight. We'll have a few in.'

He had dinner in the empty dining room, the fire shifting in the grate, the walls and alcoves cosseting shadows. In the lobby were the usual notices. A whist drive was promised for mid-January and a sports quiz for the twenty-eighth. Larry Evercreech was still wanting to take people fishing. The winter timetable for the Harwich–Hook of Holland ferry was displayed.

A few people came into the bar at about nine o'clock and then a few others and a dozen or more after ten. 'Mrs Blakerod rang us and told us there was a resident celebrity,' a woman confided in him. 'I've never heard of you but she's had a good ring-around by the look of it. Most of these would have stayed at home tonight. New Year's Eve doesn't mean a lot around here. We generally see it in sitting by the television.'

By eleven thirty the bar was jolly. Nicholas had drunk five

pints of beer and was conversing with Larry Evercreech. 'Surprising thing,' said the fishing man. 'Though this place is nothing to look at, Littlehaven, people who get to like it never seem to forget it. They always come back. If they don't they try to keep in touch. I've had Christmas cards from people from years back, customers I've taken out in the boat.' He waved his hand. 'And look at these cards. They're from all over the place.'

That was the moment Nicholas saw it. He stopped with his tankard suspended in front of his chin. He craned forward. Yes, it must be. His eyes narrowed. 'That card,' he said almost to himself. 'That one in the corner.' The landlady was serving at the far end of the bar. 'Mrs Blakerod,' he called. She looked around. 'Won't be a moment.'

Her husband came over. 'Something you wanted?'

'That card, over in the corner. Can I see it please?' His mouth had dried. He took a hurried drink.

'This one? It's a sort of postcard.' The landlord went over and unpinned it.

'Somebody sent it to Enid,' said his wife, still serving. 'It's like a painting.'

Mrs Blakerod brought the card over and handed it to Nicholas. He thought his hand shook. It was her. Thérèse. There was the bird in the corner. The landlady observed him oddly. It was a scene in vivid colours – her new style – of the coastal path with a metallic sky and the roofs of the village low in the background. 'It's Littlehaven,' said the landlord. 'Some foreign lady painted it. Enid knows all about it.'

'Where *is* Enid?' asked Nicholas turning around, attempting to subdue his eagerness. 'When will she be in?'

'They've got a party,' said the youth along the bar. 'But they said they're coming over.'

They all watched with curiosity as Nicholas turned the card over. In her flowing hand it said: '*Joyeux Noël* to my friends at Littlehaven.' It was signed: 'Thérèse Oiseau.' He held it carefully looking at her name. There was no sender's address, the message occupied the whole of the back of the card. It must have been sent in an envelope.

425

'Was she here, I wonder,' murmured Nicholas to himself. 'Or did she paint it from memory?'

'You know this lady?' asked Larry Evercreech.

'Yes, yes I do.'

Mr Blakerod was regarding him with curiosity. Nicholas asked him: 'Do you remember her being here recently? Her name is Thérèse Oiseau,' he asked.

'Can't say I do. But we've only just moved in. It could have been . . .'

'The register,' said Nicholas realising. 'She'll be in the register.'

'I'll get it,' said the landlord catching the importance. 'More drinks, gents?'

Larry bought two beers. 'You've gone pale,' he observed. 'Is she that important?'

'Yes,' said Nicholas. 'I can't believe it.'

Mr Blakerod appeared with the bulky book. 'Can't pick out her name,' he said. He put it on the counter and opened it. The guests for the past two months hardly occupied a page. She was not there. Nicholas said slowly: 'She must have painted it from memory. I should have realised.'

He felt a nudge at his elbow. ' 'Ello, Mr Boulting. Back again.' It was Enid.

'Enid,' he said eagerly. 'Thérèse sent this card.' He held it out to her.

'That's right. She came back 'ere about a month ago.'

He caught his breath. 'Was she alone?'

'That's right. She stayed for three nights. All by herself.'

'She's not in the register,' said the landlord.

'Probably nobody asked her,' shrugged Enid. 'That was the change-over time. Just before you came.' She turned grinning to Nicholas. 'You're still after her then, Mr Boulting?'

He smiled in return. 'I still am, Enid.'

'She was sort of mooning about here, doing her painting. She weren't a happy lady. She didn't talk much to anybody. Only to me when I was on dinner. I got the feeling she'd split from somebody.' She laughed. 'I even thought it might be you.'

'The card came in an envelope?' said Nicholas carefully.

They were all leaning and listening now. 'It's not still around is it?'

Enid shook her head. 'No way,' she said at once. 'It would have been thrown away. . . .' She hesitated. 'No, wait a bit. It had a foreign stamp on it. I gave it to Marge because her Ronny saves stamps.'

'Where's Marge?' asked Nicholas.

'At 'ome in bed,' said Enid with certainty. Everyone nodded. 'She's the miserable one I work with. You remember.'

'Can we go and see her?'

They all look astonished. 'Now?' asked Enid. 'This time of night?'

'It's New Year's Eve. She may be up.'

'Not Marge. She don't believe in New Year's Eve.' She brightened. 'We could have a go though. She only lives in the village. If there's a light on we could knock her up.'

'It'll be the first time Marge has been knocked up in years,' observed Larry.

'You'll have to buy me a drink,' said Enid to Nicholas.

'Of course. What will you have?'

'When we come back,' she smiled. 'Come on Mr Boulting, we might as well go. It's only a walk. It's not worth taking a car.'

He went with her and they hurried along the pavements to the centre of the village. 'This is ever so exciting,' panted Enid. 'You're in love wiv her, ain't you?'

'I'm afraid so, Enid.'

'What about your wife? You brought her in for lunch.'

'We're not together any longer,' he puffed.

'I'm not surprised. She had it in for you.' She stopped for a moment. 'The lights are out,' she said. She considered him in the darkness then said: 'Come on. Let's get her up. It's New Year.'

The cottage was across the damp, empty street. Wind blew cold from the sea. Enid knocked on the door. Nothing happened. She knocked more fiercely. A reluctant light appeared in the window above. The window grated open. Marge was holding a candle. 'Who is it this time of night?'

'Marge, it's me, Enid. I've got Mr Boulting here. You know Mr Boulting, the writer bloke. Remember he gave us a tenner tip. . . .'

'I know, I know who he is,' responded Marge irritably. She glowered down. 'But it's nearly midnight.'

'Happy New Year,' called up Nicholas tentatively.

'What do you want?' demanded Marge. 'I'm not coming out. I'm in my bed.'

'Marge, this is important. You know the letter, the card we got from the French lady, you know the artist, Osso. You know.'

'What about it?'

'You gave the envelope to your Ronny, didn't you. It had a foreign stamp from somewhere.'

'What about it?' Marge repeated.

Enid became cautious. 'Can we 'ave a look at it?'

'Now! This time of night?'

'Yes, Marge. Come on, be a sport. It's important.'

'How is it important?'

Enid said: 'It's a love story, Marge. Come on. Be a sport.'

The face backed inside and the window closed. The candlelight diminished. 'She might have gone back to bed,' sighed Enid. 'She's a misery sometimes. Most of the time.'

But the light grew in the panes over the front door. Then an electric bulb went on. There was a rattling of chains, the drawing of a bolt and then the door was opened. Marge, her hair in a bag of curlers, stood truculently in a ponderous dressing gown. Her feet were bare. 'Fine time of night this is,' she grumbled.

'Marge, you're an angel,' enthused Enid. 'You know Mr Boulting?'

'Yes, I do,' said Marge flatly. She had put the candle on a hallstand. 'We only have the electric downstairs,' she added.

'Fine, fine,' said Nicholas. 'It's so good of you, Marge. I really appreciate it.'

Inside the cottage they stood together in the low front room. Nicholas felt his head against the ceiling. 'Now what was it?' she asked. 'The envelope?'

'That's right,' Enid told her. 'The one you gave to Ronny.'

'He might not still have it. He might have swapped it for something. They're always doing that. I'll have to wake him. Mum and Dad are out for New Year. Dancing. Just hang on here, will you.'

She climbed the dim stairs again. They heard her rousing Ronny and his sleepy voice complaining. Eventually she returned down the stairs with a skinny boy in too-small pyjamas. 'You'd better tell him,' sniffed Marge.

Enid said: 'Hello, Ronny. Sorry to get you up. This is Mr Boulting. You know that envelope with the foreign stamp Marge gave you just before Christmas, have you still got it?'

'In my box,' said the boy. Rubbing his eyes he went to a small cabinet in one corner and brought out a cardboard file. 'In here,' he said. He put the box on the table and opened it. 'There is it,' he said. 'Right on top.'

Slowly Nicholas picked up the envelope. It was not from Guadeloupe. The stamp was Greek, the postmark stamped in Greek letters with the upper half obliterated. Enid leaned over his shoulder. Marge and her brother stood puzzled and watching. 'Where's it come from?' asked Enid.

'Greece,' said the boy. 'It's a Greek stamp.'

'Where in Greece I can't tell,' said Nicholas. 'The postmark is in Greek, the bit that's visible. But that shouldn't be too difficult to find out.' He looked at Ronny. 'Can I buy this from you, Ronny?'

'Is it valuable?' asked Ronny shrewdly.

'I don't want the stamp, just the postmark,' said Nicholas. 'I could copy it, I suppose.'

'No,' said Ronny. 'You can buy it from me.'

'Would ten pounds be enough?'

Ronny paled in the lamplight. Marge put in firmly: 'Ten pounds would be plenty.' She looked at Ronny. 'It can go towards those shoes,' she said.

'All right,' said Ronny. 'Ten pounds.' He held out his hand and Nicholas put the note in it saying: 'Thank you. I'm so sorry to have disturbed you.'

'It's all right,' said Ronny. 'I've got some other stamps if you'd like to have a look.'

Nicholas smiled. 'Not tonight.'

He and Enid made to leave. Ronny went up the stairs. Marge said a grumpy goodnight and they wished her a Happy New Year. She closed the door heavily on them and turned out the light. She picked up her candle and went upstairs to her lone room.

'Love,' she mumbled to herself. 'Ruddy love.'

'Our late dog fell into the canal and drowned,' said Mr King.

'He was drunk, mind,' put in his wife. 'He'd drunk all that port wine when the bottle spilled.'

'He was swimming all right.'

'Zigzagging,' said Mrs King. She remembered: 'Although he did get as far as the zoo.'

Nicholas left Jenkins, now Pudding, with them. They still had the basket belonging to the late dog and the new one fitted it perfectly. He sat puffed with satisfaction in their warm cabin on the barge, not seeming to mind for a moment that Nicholas was going away, running away, from him.

Nicholas drove at once to Heathrow taking one piece of cabin baggage. At the Olympic Airways desk he produced the envelope which Thérèse had sent to Littlehaven and asked the man if he could read the postmark.

'It says "Scythos",' said the man regarding him with curiosity. 'This is an island in the Aegean.'

'I'd like to go there.'

'Today?'

'Today. As soon as possible.'

'You cannot fly to this place,' the desk man tapped the postmark. 'You must go on our flight to Athens and then it is by a ferry boat.' He called to one of his colleagues in Greek. The man made a doubtful face and a rocking motion with his hands. 'It is about eight hours,' the first man told Nicholas. 'It is a small island, and not a tourist place, so the ferry maybe does not go every day. You must ask in Athens.'

They had a flight in two hours. It was late evening when he arrived in Athens. At the airport information desk they examined the ferry timetables for him. There was a service the following day at noon from Piræus. The weather was so rough the journey might take perhaps ten hours.

'It is not a good time to visit,' shrugged the Greek girl. 'You should go in the summertime.'

'I can't wait,' said Nicholas.

He was at Piræus at eleven on a lambent Greek morning. The ferry sailed at twelve and headed for the islands through a sea reflecting the January blue of the sky. They called at several islands on the route and it was not until the evening that the clouds gathered, pushed by a cold, wild wind from Turkey.

The old boat ploughed on, turning and dipping in the folding sea. It began to rain torrentially. There were only fifty or so passengers and as far as he could see none of them were tourists. People, some wearing several coats, got on and got off at the island ports, carrying bags and cases ashore, being met by emotional relatives. He wondered how it would be for him.

She might not even be there. Perhaps she had only visited the island and was now back in Guadeloupe with her yachtsman. But he kept hearing Enid saying: 'She weren't a happy lady.' Perhaps she would be there.

He had paid for a cabin, an oil-smelling box, and when the weather became rough in the evening he went there and lay hanging on to the rough mattress of the bunk as the ferry plunged on. He even went to sleep and awoke with the motion of the vessel lessened and shouts coming from the deck. Washing his face in the solitary spurt of water that he coaxed from the tap overhanging the corner basin and wiping it on his sleeve, he went out into the rainy night. There were watery lights; they were approaching a shore. The sea was wallowing and the wind had dropped. It continued to rain.

'Scythos?' he said to a man standing with a bundle on the deck.

The man began to cry and nodded wordlessly. Nicholas

431

wanted to ask him why he wept but he knew he would not be able to make himself understood. The man kept wiping his face with his flat hands and picking up his bundle and putting it down again. A grunt, like a sound of relief, came from the funnel of the ferry as it manoeuvred into the indistinct harbour. Passengers had gathered on the deck, under shelter from the rain, the women bundled up with coats and headscarves, the men in thick clothes and hats, every face towards the shore. As they neared the jetty figures could be seen moving under the weak lights. There were shouts from land to ship and back again. Nicholas, crammed with doubts, stood alone, peering at the dark shore.

The vessel scraped alongside the jetty and ropes were thrown. People on board began to call and gesticulate to shadows grouped under umbrellas ashore. The gangplank was put in place and the passengers began to troop on to the quay. Nicholas was almost the last. In Athens he had sought a map of the Aegean islands but Scythos was hardly to be seen, an irregular shape in the middle of many others. It showed no towns, no roads. He stepped ashore. The Greek passengers and those who had embraced them were piling into old cars and taxis. They drove away through the streaming rain leaving him on the jetty. 'Taxi?' he called to no one in particular. 'Is there a taxi?'

The man who had been weeping on the ferry was still doing so. He was climbing into the back of a mule-drawn cart, hugging a fat woman who was sobbing also. The man wiped his face with his hands and beckoned to Nicholas. He spoke in Greek, patting the woman to comfort her, and pointing to one of the seats in the open conveyance. Nicholas climbed up with them.

'Thank you, thank you,' he said. He was soaked. The rain was running down his face and his back and inside his trousers. He could not tell if the couple were still crying because of the rain on their faces. Nor did he know where he wanted to go. In the end he said: '*Taverna?*'

'*Taverna,*' repeated the man. The woman had taken the reins of the mule and he tapped her on the shoulder. She sobbed and nodded.

The mule whined as though it had sadnesses of it own and began to stumble forward through the rain. After the jetty and the few buildings there were no more lights. The lamps on the cart guttered and it groaned on. The man put his face in his hands and his back heaved. Nicholas awkwardly patted him on the shoulder and the man patted him in thanks for the comfort. Some lights appeared beyond a stony hill up which the mule was straining. '*Taverna*,' the woman called over her shoulder. The man pointed.

Down the other side of the slope the cart trundled and arrived alongside a hill-fringed harbour with low houses set around it. A few spaced lamps glimmered through the wet darkness. At the centre of the harbour was a place with three lights showing. '*Taverna*,' pointed the woman. '*Taverna*,' confirmed the man.

They stopped the cart and he shook hands with both and thanked them again. They looked curiously at his single small case. They had stopped crying now but it was still raining. The cart creaked away.

Nicholas stood on the cobbles outside the *taverna*. He could get no wetter. Slowly, as though afraid of what he might discover, he walked steadily forward, the water running from his clothes. There was a half-open door. He went in. Inside was dimly lit. There was a bar and some tables. Half a dozen men were sitting at the bar playing dominoes. They stopped when he entered. He turned on a smile and tried to wipe the rain from his hair. The barman handed him a newspaper and indicated that he should use it as a towel. He did so and the men grinned. One said something to the barman and a glass of brandy was put in front of him. Then he took out the page from New York *Art and Artists* and showed them her photograph. 'Thérèse Oiseau,' he said carefully. 'Is she on Scythos?'

With joy he saw that they knew her. The barman came from behind his counter and ushered Nicholas to the door as he was drinking his brandy. He pointed through the rain to a single damp light on the other side of the harbour. 'This is,' he said. He tapped the magazine page.

Nicholas paid for a round of drinks. They all came to the door with him to make sure he was going the right way and did not fall into the harbour. It was still pouring. He walked around the water's edge with its rocking boats. The single light got nearer and nearer. He was almost there. He crossed the cobbled street and stood in front of the door. There was no bell nor any knocker. He tapped with his knuckles. There was a movement inside. He was hardly able to breathe. Soaking wet, holding his single bag, he waited.

Thérèse opened the door. There she was. She saw him and began to cry and then to laugh and in the end pulled him into the house, where they embraced and kissed and held each other. Water ran from him on to the floor. 'Oh, you're crazy!' she cried.

Long into the stormy night they talked, her eyes glowing in the darkness. At last she was close to him, her face inches from his. He described how he had followed and found her; from Littlehaven to this small, far island. She laughed gently when he told how he and Enid had run through Littlehaven to get Marge from her bed on New Year's Eve.

Then Thérèse told him quietly how she had returned to Guadeloupe and made a voyage with Henri. 'Then I found what they were really doing,' she sighed. 'It was smuggling of drugs. He told me to leave the boat at Anguilla. He left me there. He said that he did not want me any longer. Three days after that he was arrested and he was with another woman, a woman from Martinique. She was also his lover. I did not know, but he had many. It is easy for someone who sails in boats.'

She was silent. He kissed her nose as they lay in the dim room. 'The police they came to me and searched everything. When they had finished they said I could go. They knew I had no connection with what Henri was doing. His lover, the one on the boat, was in the matter also. They can be together when they come from prison. I went to Paris.'

434

'And from Paris you returned to Littlehaven,' said Nicholas. He touched her naked shoulder.

'Why, I do not know. Or perhaps I would not tell myself. I needed somebody and perhaps I thought that you would be there, in that place where we met.' She laughed softly once more. 'I went there again on the ferry to Harwich.'

'From 'Ook of 'Olland,' he smiled.

'From 'Ook of 'Olland,' she agreed. 'For a few days I stayed. I was very sad. I could not paint. It was still raining.'

'It still is,' he said listening to the weather on the window.

'Not for me now,' she whispered.

'Nor for me,' he said.

They lived together in her house by the harbour on Scythos for six months, the best and happiest time of both their lives so far. Thérèse painted and Nicholas began working again on his abandoned novel *Falling from Grace*. As the days became warm they swam in the sea, ate and drank in the *taverna*, and lay together in the powerful, peaceful darkness of her bed. Sometimes she would read to him from Babar the Elephant. 'C'est le coq qui crie de toutes ses forces. "Avis aux habitants et visiteurs de l'île! . . . On hisse les éléphants sur les grands arbres. Ce sont les places d'honneur." '

Nicholas wrote to Deborah telling her where he was, also to Paul and Sol, asking each to keep secret the place where he had gone. He had never known days fly so swiftly.

At the beginning of July they were on the jetty, sitting drinking wine, and watching the distant approach of the ferry. The day was hot and blue. At the end of the pier, a few paces from the café where they sat, was a telescope on a stand. Islanders sometimes paid a coin to see the ferry far off and shouted to each other when they recognised the passengers.

On this clear July morning Nicholas idly walked to the telescope and dropped in a coin. He focused the lens on the white smudge of the approaching vessel. He stiffened. Thérèse heard him cry out and hurried to him. 'I've just seen Willie,' he breathed. 'He's on the deck.' He spied again. 'And he's got that

435

Penny with him, the girl of the family. . . . Oh my God, Thérèse, *her family are all there!*' His voice shook. 'The mother, Bonnie, the other girl who's bawling her head off, and oh God no, the twins! They're all sitting on a van of some sort.' He turned white-faced to her. 'We've got to get out of here.'

Thérèse looked through the telescope. 'Also there is a dog,' she said calmly.

Nicholas looked again. 'Jenkins,' he breathed. He turned, his face distraught. 'Honestly, we *must* get out *quickly*. I cannot tell you what this will be like.'

She allowed him to tug her by the hand. They mounted their motor scooter and he drove madly over the bumpy road towards the other harbour and their house.

'Quick, quick,' he urged. 'Get everything you need. Valuables, documents, money. . . . We've got twenty minutes.'

She held his arm. 'Nicholas,' she said. 'Where are we going?'

'We'll take the dinghy and get over to Thetos,' he said. 'It's only a couple of miles. Then we'll wait over there for the ferry and stay on it to Athens.' He saw her face.

'Are you sure this is necessary?' she asked.

'Necessary! I'll say it is,' he urged. 'It will be bedlam here. One of those twins keeps crapping. The whole family are unruly, mad. She's hopeless. And Willie will ruin our lives. Thérèse, it is more than I could stand.'

'All right,' she said unhappily. 'I will get my paintings and my passport. I must stay with you.'

'Please, please,' he pleaded. They kissed hurriedly and began to gather their goods. In ten minutes they were crossing the street to the small harbour. Nicholas hid the motor scooter in a boat shed, putting the keys in his pocket. They clambered into their dinghy, sorted out their belongings swiftly, and Nicholas started the motor. His face was set. She regarded him with alarm.

'Let's get out of here,' he muttered. He turned the small boat towards the harbour entrance. They cleared it and headed for the heavy blue of the open sea. As they rounded the headland

436

they could see that the ferry had just docked. 'In the nick of time,' breathed Nicholas. He saw her sad, set expression. 'I cannot describe what it would be like,' he said.

She remained silent, watching the diminishing island as he pointed the bow to Thetos, rising across the strait. 'Where will we go?' she called against the wind.

'I don't know, Paris, New York, the North Pole. Anywhere.'

'I will take it,' she said nodding to the tiller. 'You come to the forward.'

He said: 'All right,' without thought. His mind was still full of what he had seen. Willie was disaster enough but the mad Ware family as well. My God. . . .

She swung the tiller. 'We are going back!' she exclaimed.

The dinghy curved in the sea. 'No!' he pleaded. 'We can't. You have no idea what . . .'

'I don't care! We're going!' she shouted at him. Her eyes were firm. 'We must. Nicholas, this time you must *stop* running away!'

His shoulders dropped. He sat down heavily. The small boat curved its way back towards the island.

The End

The End